LAST MAN STANDING

THE COMPLETE SERIES

•▼•

KEITH TAYLOR

BOOK ONE

•▼•

HUNGER

THE FOLLOWING IS a rough draft of an article of mine that appeared in the October 2017 issue of Time Magazine, recovered from an old USB stick I found stuck to a chewed piece of gum in the lining of my jacket.

This was the last thing I was ever paid to write, and my first article in an international magazine. The final printed version – with the cursing removed and a couple of paragraphs switched around – is still out there somewhere, but it's probably not worth sifting through the ruins of America to find it.

LAST MAN STANDING
Thomas Freeman

"THERE'S ANOTHER THING they don't show in the movies," Paul chuckles bitterly, playing with the moist, half peeled label on his sweating bottle of Singha. "The bathroom arrangements. I spent three weeks stuck in that damned apartment, and by the end I was about ready to throw myself off the balcony just to escape the smell."

I wrinkle my nose and nod sympathetically. Even now you can't go anywhere in Thailand without experiencing the intensely *human* odor of five million refugees and not nearly enough bathrooms. The air is infused with the hot, cloying stink of excrement, and in the camps the gutters run blue with the residue of countless leaking chemical toilets.

"Reminded me of the time we spent a month dog-sitting for Zaya in Ulaanbaatar. You remember that?" he asks. "What was it, January 2013? Minus forty degrees outside, and as soon as the dog took a shit on the balcony it froze solid." The carefully peeled label tears in half between his fingers and he rips it angrily from the bottle, his face locked in a violent scowl.

Paul's pent up frustration is palpable, quite intimidating and entirely out of character. Those who know him (full disclosure: I've known Mr. McQueen socially for a little more than five years) would invariably describe him as a gentle giant, his actions always measured and his voice unusually soft for such a large man, as if to compensate for the implicit threat of his hulking frame. The man in front of me looks as if he's struggling to resist the urge to punch someone. This is not the Paul McQueen I used to know.

"Couldn't get rid of it with a paint scraper, it was so frozen." He tears the paper to scraps as he speaks, in a way that makes me wonder if he's even conscious he's doing it. I look down at his fingers and notice the nails are bitten down to the quick, with traces of blood at the edges where he's nervously gnawed at them.

"When that first warm morning arrived a month's worth of shit defrosted like a bowl of ice cream. The smell was so bad Ogi had to move in with her sister for a week."

I nod again, urging him on. "And you had the heat, of course. Must have been even worse." I pull a sour face, almost gagging at the thought.

"*Jesus*, the heat. April in Bangkok. Hottest month of the year, and no AC once the power went out. It probably wouldn't have been so bad if I'd been living in one of the big new tower blocks with a little breeze, but our place was..." He shakes his head. "Well, you remember our old place at Sutti Mansion, right? $250 a month, and nothing in front of the balcony but the wall of the building next door. Back before the outbreak we used to have to run the fan 24/7 just to keep it below 100 degrees. I guess it wasn't the smartest thing to do, shitting in the only place with a hint of fresh air. Still, you live and learn..." Paul sighs and stares at his bottle for a moment.

"Well, some of us do."

He drains his beer and waves the empty bottle in the direction of the waitress. He either doesn't notice or doesn't care that it catches the lip of the glass bowl of bar snacks, sending nuts and glittering shards crashing to the tile floor. The pretty bar girl quickly scurries along with dustpan and brush, and Paul stares covetously at my drink as she sweeps unnoticed beneath his feet.

"Mind if I...?" He picks up my bottle before waiting for an answer, draining the lukewarm beer in one pull.

"Please, go on. Tell me how it started." I shoot an apologetic glance at the waitress but she doesn't look up from the broken glass. I get the impression she's become accustomed to Paul's drunken behavior over the past month.

"Well, I'm sure you know what the Thais tell you, about the Iranians smuggling in some sort of chemical weapons? I take it you haven't come all this way to hear the fairy tale, right? All this shit came a couple of months after some inept Iranian fuckers accidentally blew themselves to pieces up in Ekamai, so the Arabs made good scapegoats when it all went to shit. No, that bullshit story may play back in the States, but I was there. I saw how it started, and since I'm the only one who saw it start and made out alive I'm... well, I'm uniquely qualified. I'm done lying about it."

"You mean it wasn't a chemical attack?" I'm on the edge of my seat. Paul was cagey and evasive in the emails we exchanged over the last few weeks, usually sent late at night after he'd returned home from the bar. He implied that there was something amiss with the popular narrative, but this is the first time he's gone on record with a claim that the Iranians may not have been responsible.

"No, I'm not saying it wasn't chemical," he continues, shaking his head. "I'm just saying it didn't happen like they said. There sure as shit wasn't a fleet of trucks spraying down the streets with toxins and blasting readings of the Koran like a fucking ice cream van tune. I was there when the first of them turned, and I know it started in one place: Sala fucking Daeng. All the outbreaks later up on Sukhumvit came from the trains."

I look down at my notes, but can't find the right page. Paul's claims would later seem accurate, according to Twitter and Facebook archives reconstructed in the days after the outbreak and reported by Al Jazeera and the BBC. The first social media reports came from the Silom area at Sala Daeng, a station on the BTS line in Bangkok's central business district, at 14:32. Seventeen minutes later tweets began to flood in from around the stations further to the north and south. They radiated out along the BTS and MRT lines (the overhead and underground train lines that served central Bangkok) for a little more than twenty minutes before the cell networks became overloaded with traffic and the 4G signal dropped out.

*Songkran is too crazy for me this year. Lots of fights on Silom Road. Heading home.**

*Text translated from the original Thai. The tweet was accompanied by a blurred photo that appears to have been taken through the window of the McDonalds at the south end of the road, around fifty feet from the bulk of the crowd. The photo clearly shows a teen boy biting a middle aged woman on the thigh.

"I didn't even want to be there, to be honest. I was too old for water fights two decades ago, and the idea of getting doused with dirty water by a few thousand drunk kids didn't sound like my idea of a fun Saturday. You ever spend time in Bangkok during Songkran?"

I shake my head. I'd left Thailand two weeks before the outbreak to work on a story on illegal logging up in Vientiane, Laos.

"It's a bloody disgrace. It used to be traditional to wash your shrines and images of Buddha with fragrant water during Thai new year, but over the years that nice little tradition somehow turned into a drunken week long water fight. Every year hundreds die in drink driving accidents, and already there'd been a few murders in the city. Just drunk fights getting out of hand. It gets worse every year." He shakes his head with disgust.

"Now Sala Daeng, that's Songkran ground central in Bangkok. They shut down a section of Silom Road, everyone loads up on cheap booze and for days the whole street becomes a huge party. Thousands of people chuck buckets of water at each other, spray each other with water guns and throw around a ton of minty chalk shit. Not sure what it is, but *that* was what started it."

I frown, confused. "How do you mean?"

"It was the powder they throw at each other. It's like... what do you call it, talcum powder, but it smells like mint. They love to soak you with water then cake you with the stuff. Nasty shit at the best of times, but this stuff was different. This was bright yellow, like turmeric. Nobody else was throwing yellow shit, and from where I was standing up on the flyover I could see exactly what was happening. There was this weird little group of people in the middle of the action, white folks dressed like they'd just come from church, with heads shaved clean like Buddhist monks. They were the ones throwing the yellow stuff, and everywhere they threw it people started acting like they'd been hit with tear gas, trying to blink it out of their eyes. It was like the stuff was burning their skin. A few people fell to the ground, and the rest tried to pour water in their eyes to clear them. Too late, of course. It all went to shit pretty quickly after that. Thank you, my dear."

These last words are to the waitress, who sets down two fresh bottles wrapped in foam coolers (*beer condoms*, as Paul describes them). He hands over a wad of cash, tipping the waitress heavily, and lifts his bottle unsteadily. He'd been drinking for hours before I arrived, and after taking a long pull on the ice cold beer he excuses himself, pushes back his chair and stumbles unsteadily towards the men's room.

At 1,000 baht (around $35) a bottle, Paul is one of the few who can still enjoy the dwindling supply of Thai beer here in the interim capital of Hua Hin. He's done the rounds on the morning shows, popping up via satellite on news broadcasts around the world to support the official story of the Thai government, a job for which he's been paid extremely well. Not a day has gone by in the last two months without this handsome, square jawed Australian appearing on our screens to rail against the Iranians, telling the same story of a massive terrorist attack; of white vans roaming the streets, spraying down the sidewalks with a fine mist. He spoke of masked 'Arabs' (his word, not mine) throwing what he described as tear gas canisters into crowds of civilians.

The new military junta has used Paul as a tool, hailing him as a hero for his escape from the dead city. He fought bravely through a million-strong crowd of the walking dead to bring word of the Islamic terrorists to the wider world, and his story has served to bolster support for the new government both at home and abroad, allowing it to award itself ever more emergency powers in the name of national security. The junta now has complete control of Thailand from this coastal stronghold, and few knowledgeable commenters really believe the promises of a return to democratic elections by next summer.

For our part the western media is captivated by the spectacle. Of the nine million Thais who lived in the capital city almost half were wiped from the face of the earth in the space of just a few hours. Of those not a single man, woman or child made it out alive from the Silom area, the origin of the outbreak, apart from this man who could, conveniently, be played by Hugh Jackman in the movie. When it's inevitably made it will save Hollywood the effort of convincing western audiences that Jackie Chan came from Bangkok.

Paul wobbles back to the table, and as I see him approach I steady our bottles to make sure he won't upset them as he sits. At these prices I can't afford to spill a drop.

"I've only gone and broke the seal," he says, landing heavily in his chair. "Five hours without a piss, and now I'll be up and down every ten minutes."

"Paul, why don't you walk me through what really happened?" My tone is a little impatient. I've been waiting for two hours now while he rambles aimlessly, dropping hints here and there that the story he'd peddled on TV had been as scripted as any soap opera. He'd been the one to reach out to me, not the other way around, and I'm quickly running out of money while he struggles with his conscience.

Paul visibly sobers in front of me. He sighs, reaching for his bound bundle of acrid, hand rolled Indian beedis – the only thing, he says, that blocks out the smell of the undead. He lights one with my fake Zippo and offers the bundle to me. I shake my head and reach for one of my own Marlboro Lights from what must surely be one of the last packs in Thailand.

"OK, here's the truth. It started near the containers of yellow powder. A few of the kids rubbing their eyes, they just went crazy. One cop was helping pour water into the eyes of a little boy, a tiny kid no higher than your waist, and I was staring right at them when the little one launched into him with his fists. The cop slapped him hard and he went down, but by then a few more around him were turning. Poor fucker never stood a chance."

I glance at my notes. "And you were on the flyover at the time, above the street? What about Ogi?"

Paul visibly flinches at the mention of his wife of four years.

"Yeah, I was well out of it. I was up on the pedestrian walkway above the street, armed with nothing but a fucking camera. Ogi wanted to get in amongst them and get wet, but I was recovering from a broken rib so I didn't want to get jostled. I lost track of her the moment she got down to street level." He stares intently at his beer, once again peeling the label. "Only spotted her once after that."

I wait patiently for Paul to continue, sensing he won't respond well to further prodding.

"Anyway... Once the first couple of guys turned the people around them started to notice. They were right on the edge, near the blockade at Soi Convent, and for a moment even the guys closest to them didn't know what to make of it. They just watched as a group of people launched themselves at the cop. I think they were more surprised than anything else. In Thailand, even drunks don't dare attack cops. That's the quickest way to earn yourself a trip to the hospital." He takes a swig from his beer and lets out a soft, bitter chuckle.

"You want to know why people took a few seconds to get the picture? There was no biting, not at first. We've seen too many zombie movies. We think these things are just teeth on legs, groaning and biting chunks of flesh out of anything with a heartbeat. Zombies – yeah, I know I shouldn't be calling them that – they only bite when they're hungry. That's why most of Bangkok ended up dead rather than infected. Zombies will sooner beat you to death than eat you for lunch."

He falls silent for a moment, pulling angrily on his cigarette. "I tell you, George Romero should be shot. People were taken by surprise, acting like they were up against movie monsters. I saw a lot of people try to stand their ground with improvised weapons, expecting to give these fuckers a quick crack on the head when they lumbered in. They must have had the fright of their lives when the undead came sprinting, throwing their fists just as hard as real people."

"How did they attack?" I know the answer already. I've seen the snatches of shaky, low-res video a few people around the city managed to upload before the signal dropped out.

"The truth is they're not so different from us. The only real difference is that regular humans have a little switch in their head that tells them to stop punching when the other guy goes down. The infected don't. It's like their anger is turned up to eleven. These bastards attacked like they were on PCP, fucking vicious, like a beaten wife who's had enough after years of taking the belt. They used everything they had. Fists. Feet. Fingernails. By the time they were finished with the cop there wasn't much left. Even his eyes were gouged out. Nobody was eating him, though. I guess they weren't peckish."

"Had people started panicking?"

"No, not at first. It only started to go crazy when the group backed away from the cop. That's when people saw it wasn't a regular fight. No way you could make that mistake, not after seeing the body." He stops for a moment as a young family walks by the table, then leans in and continues with a low voice. "You ever seen a riot? A real one, I mean. Not just a protest, but a full on riot? You wouldn't believe it until you saw one. You just can't imagine how much power there is in a crowd. You'd think you could just slip out and get to the edge, but it doesn't work like that. As soon as those things turned towards the crowd, that's when people started to panic. There were enough of the things to block the street, so there was only one way to run: back into the crowd. As soon as that happened, everyone was doomed."

I think I understand what he means. I remember watching footage of the Hillsborough disaster as a child. 96 people died and almost 800 were injured when crowds at a British soccer stadium crushed forward against crowd control barriers during a cup semi-final. The people at the back of the crowd had no idea they were killing people. There was no way they could have known.

"The problem with Sala Daeng is that you've got a few thousand people packed into a tight space. There's music, laughter, yelling. No way anyone could hear the screaming over the noise. People started to push and shove desperately into the crowd, but what else is new? The crowd just pushed right back and threw their water. It wasn't until someone knocked over the big speakers at the side of the street that the music cut out, and suddenly everyone could hear the screams."

For a moment Paul seems to drift away. His eyes lose their focus, and when he continues it's with an odd tone, as if he's reading from a script.

"A scream is... it's a strange noise. You've been hearing them all your life in the movies, but real screams don't sound like that. Actors can't do 'em justice. It's like the difference between a fake laugh and a real one, you know? You can't mistake it. What I heard that day I pray never to hear again. People were screaming so much their voices gave out, but it still wasn't loud enough to drown out the pleading. People were begging for mercy even as their bones broke." He shivers despite the close heat.

"One girl, some skinny blonde tourist with a long ponytail, panicked and tried to run through the pack to get back to Soi Convent. One of them grabbed her hair, easy as you like, and just tugged it right off her head. I wouldn't have believed it if I hadn't seen it. Fucker just pulled and pulled until her whole scalp just slipped off. Someone must have bit her in the crowd, because she was back on her feet a minute later and joining in the fight for the other side, that ponytail still hanging by a strip of skin halfway down her neck."

I cringe with disgust at the image. I've seen a few walkers with horrific injuries, thankfully on TV rather than up close, and it's all I can do not to wonder how they'd come by them. I thank God I'd never had to watch as someone was turned, or killed.

"Everyone else, of course, pushed right into the crowd. Once the music was gone and people started to hear the screams they all started to shove, but when you've got a few thousand people crowding down half a mile of narrow street it's impossible to get everyone moving as one. Hundreds were trampled. The unlucky ones at the back... well, they were torn to shreds pretty quickly. The really lucky ones, those at the other end of the street, some of them must have managed to get away, but it was the people in the middle who lasted the longest. They were squeezed in by the crowds. Some of them managed to stay on their feet. Maybe some even managed to slip away into the shops along the street. That's what I hoped Ogi had done."

"You said you saw her again? In the crowd?"

Paul falls silent for a moment. He stubs out his beedi on the surface of the wooden table, ignoring the ashtray by his bottle.

"Yeah, I... I think so. Seems stupid to say this, but I can't be sure. You know how people say all Asians look alike? Well, it's bullshit. Ogi was Mongolian, looked more Korean than anything else. She definitely didn't look Thai. In that crowd, though, I couldn't have picked her out if she'd been wearing a big sign. Almost everyone had black hair, and I was looking down from above. Everyone was moving too much, squeezing, pushing, pulling. The whole crowd moved like the ocean, waves of movement pulling people this way and that. Some people tried to scramble over the top of the scrum, only to fall down and get trampled beneath thousands of feet.

"I think I saw her dress. She was wearing this long, flowing blue floral thing I'd bought for her a couple of weeks earlier in Cambodia. She loved that dress. Said it made her feel like a Parisian, whatever that means. I think I saw it. I saw a figure clambering up on a big ceramic planter at the side of the street, and I saw that flash of floral blue for just a second or two. Whether she fell, jumped or was pulled I have no idea. I just know she vanished backwards behind the plants, and that was the last I saw."

"Did you try to call her phone?" I ask.

Paul shoots me a withering look. "Of *course* I tried to fucking call," he snaps. "I called, I sent texts. I called her sister. I called all of our friends. The network was busy every time. Of course that was later, after I got out of Silom. When it all started I had my own problems to deal with. There's another thing I'd like to speak to Romero about. These things are quick as hell. As long as they haven't injured their legs they're just as fast as you and me. It's only later that they slow down, when their joints dry out.

When it all kicked off, though... *shit*, they could move."

"You were chased?"

Paul nods. "I was chased. I made the same stupid 'movie zombie' mistake as everyone else. I assumed I was safe up on the walkway above the street. It never occurred to me that these things could climb stairs. I didn't think they could *think*. I wasn't all that worried about my own safety until I heard a scream to my right, and I turned just in time to see a young Thai woman tip over the railings as she ran to escape a small group that had managed to climb the stairs. She landed down on the street with her legs straight, feet first, just behind the pack. I probably imagined it, but I'd swear I heard her bones snap. I don't know. All I know is that she was still alive and awake as they began to close in on her. I didn't have time to watch what happened next, even if I'd wanted to." Paul plays with his bundle of beedis for a moment, but doesn't light one.

"One of the group that made it up the stairs locked eyes with me. Just stared me down from fifty feet away. For a moment – and I know this is stupid – I wondered if I could just slowly back away, no sudden movements, as if I was dealing with one of those crazy soi dogs that run around the city. No chance. The second I twitched he started sprinting at me. You know, people who've seen the movies will tell you there's nothing more terrifying than a zombie shambling towards you, groaning all the way like Frankenstein's monster. Film critics say there's something about the slow, unrelenting pace that taps into our primal fear, but if you're ever unlucky enough to meet a freshly turned fucker you'll know it's bullshit. I'll see your groaning zombie and raise you a pair of my damp trousers that there's nothing more terrifying than one of them silently sprinting at you full pelt. Fortunately mine hadn't been too quick on his feet when he was alive. He was a little heavy, and he seemed to have trouble running in his sandals. I kicked mine off my feet and shot off down the walkway, towards the MRT station at the end of Silom Road."

I glance down at the hastily sketched map in my pad. "Isn't that where the rest of the infected were heading, too?"

"Yeah, but I had the advantage that I wasn't stopping along the way to tear thousands of people to pieces. The walkway was almost empty, and I soon passed over the crowd. Before long the one chasing me peeled off, too. I risked a look behind me and saw him throw himself over the railing back down to the street, where he landed right in the middle of a group of kids trying to escape. That's one thing that came in handy. They'll always go for the easiest target. If you can run them in the direction of a limping granny you'll probably get away safe."

Paul notices my expression.

"What, you think you wouldn't? Fuck you, Tom. Trust me, if you ever saw how they kill up close you'd soon change your mind. It's easy to be a hero in theory. In real life... well, you find out pretty quick just how brave you really are."

He pauses for a moment, lifts his drink for a swig then reconsiders. "I got back down to street level on the corner of Silom Road and Rama IV. The underground station was right there, but there was no way I'd head down beneath the streets. Unless there was a train waiting for me on the platform... well, I don't want to think would have happened if I'd been trapped down there between the platform barriers. Thousands tried to escape that way, and they're still clearing out the bodies today."

"I ran across the street towards Lumphini Park, the only real green space in the city. Behind me I could hear the traffic go crazy as people were pulled from their cars. As I reached the park gate I turned to see what was happening, and I really I wish I hadn't. It's strange how irrational people become when they're afraid. I saw people jump into cabs that were snarled up in traffic, yelling at the drivers even as the dead came in through the windows. If only they'd kept running they might have gotten away."

"Why do you think they did that? Got in the cabs, I mean," I ask, realizing the pointlessness of the question. Paul looks at me like I'm simple.

"How the fuck should I know? Maybe they thought these things couldn't open doors. They'd be right, for the most part, but a few dozen of them pounding on a window is just as good. A tuk tuk almost managed to get away, jumping onto the sidewalk and cutting through the crowds, living and dead. If only it hadn't hit a hydrant it may have made it, too, but it clipped the steel and bounced off into a shop window. The whole thing went up in flames – those things are death traps at the best of times – and I started running again as the shop began to burn. I can't be sure, but I think that was the start of the fire that tore through all of Silom. I'm damned certain nobody came back to fight it."

"How did you make it to safety? Wasn't your apartment in Thonglor?"

"Yep. It was at least five kilometers as the crow flies, and longer through the streets. I ran all the way once I was in the park. Didn't stop to take a breath. Made a few wrong turns, too.

Luckily for me, between Lumphini and Thonglor there weren't any train lines. It wasn't until I reached my apartment block that I realized they'd used the trains to overtake me. Some of the wounded from Silom must have made it up to the platform at Sala Daeng. Some may have even made it all the way to Ratchadamri. I know they didn't turn until they reached the interchange at Siam, 'cause some of them had switched to the Sukhumvit line before it hit them."

"God knows what the other passengers must have thought. Most of the wounded, I'm guessing, would have just had broken bones. It was only the ones who were bitten that would have turned. Imagine making it through that hell, escaping onto the train only for your friend to turn in the seat beside you. I don't like to think about it. All I know for sure is that the trains were running on auto. They kept making their stops even after all the passengers were dead. All along Sukhumvit those fuckers poured out at each station. That's why Bangkok got out of control so quickly. The bloody trains. Over the streets and underground those bastards outflanked us all, right out into the suburbs. We never had a chance."

"So why didn't they stop the trains once word got out?"

"Well that's the problem. I don't think word ever really got out. The first most people knew about the outbreak was when it came down their street, through their front door, and the trains just kept running, ferrying the blood-thirsty buggers efficiently around the city. That's how they were waiting for me when I got back to Thonglor. An hour of sprinting through back streets, two more hours of creeping around, and when I got back to safety I found they'd beat me to it."

Paul excuses himself once again, waving for a fresh drink as he walks to the toilet. I light up a Marlboro, take a deep drag and frown at my notes. So far his story bears little resemblance to what had been heard on the news. Paul's official story – the one he'd been spouting on the talk shows every day – was that he'd watched from the flyover as vans sprayed some kind of toxin onto the people on the street below. He'd run down to the street and bravely tried to save as many as he could, killing a terrorist in the process. The body had been recovered by the army, and an investigation of his apartment had found that it had been converted into a lab. The junta had announced that many more such labs had been found across the city, all linked to renters from the Middle East. They'd cited these facts whenever they made a fresh arrest; whenever they confiscated property, deported a foreigner or executed an 'accomplice'.

When Paul returns I ask him why his story had changed.

"Fuck, what does it matter?" he sighs, lighting another foul smelling cigarette. "I liked the idea of being a hero. When I finally made it out of the city and collapsed at the blockade out at Bang Pakong I was too tired to argue. They told me, you see. They told me I had a choice. Either tell the story they wanted me to tell and live like a king, or try to tell the truth and... and they'd send me back in to the city."

"So why are you telling me this now? Why did you reach out to me?"

When Paul looks at me it's with eyes much older than his thirty eight years. His voice sounds like it's coming from the bottom of a deep pit far underground, and it cracks a little as he speaks. More than anything, he just sounds tired.

"It doesn't make a difference. They could drop me right back into Silom, and I wouldn't care. Someone should know the truth, before... Anyway, you want to know the worst part? I didn't kill a single zombie. Didn't have it in me. You like to think you'd go all Rambo in that situation. You'd pick up a gun and make a few head shots, at least take a few of them with you before they get you. I just couldn't do it. The moment I got through the security door in my block I cut the power to the keycard reader and pushed a desk in front of the door to wedge it closed. I could hear people banging on it, trying to get in behind me. They were still alive, I know that from the screaming. I just went up to my apartment on the fourth floor, locked the door and waited until the streets were quiet. Three weeks. All I heard were screams. I didn't try to find my wife. I called until my battery died, but the calls would never connect. Maybe she survived. Maybe she was one of the folks screaming at the ground floor, trying to get through the door to safety."

Paul drains his beer in a long gulp, slips another cigarette from his pack and lights it up.

"You always think you'll be a hero, you know?"

He suddenly rises from his chair, throws a handful of cash on the table and walks out of the bar without another word. I wait for half an hour, but he doesn't return.

Paul McQueen was found hanged in his apartment several days after this interview was recorded. He left no suicide note.

•⁊•

YOU HAVE BEEN tried by God, and found wanting. He gave you free will, and He weeps to see how His children have chosen to abuse the precious gift He bestowed upon us. We have strayed from the path the Lord laid out. Men lay beside men. Wives no longer serve their husbands. Children no longer respect their parents. Men no longer respect even themselves. They choose to degrade themselves with pornography, and indulge in sinful pleasures that do nothing but destroy the purity the Lord gave them. God is sickened and disgusted by the path we have chosen.

Bangkok was a warning. An ultimatum. A promise. That sinful fleshpot was nothing but a modern day Sodom. The world is purer now its unrighteous denizens have been sent to face the judgment of the Lord, but it was far from unique. Every inch of this planet drowns in sin, and we must now prostrate ourselves before the Lord or be cleansed from this earth.

We offer this message as our final warning. This is your last chance. The human race has one year from today to embrace the Lord God as its sole savior. If you fail to repent you will face the final judgment.

We are his divine messengers.

The Sons of the Father

•▾•

:::1:::

THAT WAS HOW it started. A simple message mailed to media outlets and governments around the world. Everyone from the White House to Fox News to the BBC to Buzzfeed got a copy in their mailbox, and the response from most of them was *"Huh, this crackpot has nice handwriting. How come we don't teach kids cursive anymore?"*

Of *course* nobody took it seriously. Why would they? They must get hundreds of letters every day from bored pranksters and unmedicated psychopaths, each of them claiming that the world will end next Tuesday, or that 9/11 was a false flag operation orchestrated by Walmart, or that the dog next door had started to speak, and it was craving baby blood and fish tacos. Most of the time those letters go straight in the trash, and most of the time that's exactly where they belong.

It was the same story when the President was fired on in Savannah last summer. When the Secret Service admitted they'd received a threat from the shooter days earlier the media went insane, accusing them of failing at their most important task. The mania only died down when the President herself came out and released records of the sheer volume of threats she received every day. Thousands of unbalanced assholes scrawl warnings on the back of a napkin. Hundreds of them still have a tight enough grip on reality to figure out how to buy a postage stamp and use a mailbox, and it's up to the Secret Service to trawl through them all and determine whether any present a credible threat. It's not an easy job, and sometimes they call it wrong.

In the case of this particular letter... well, absolutely *nobody* thought it was worth a second look. Smart people with years of experience in threat assessment concluded that no terrorist with the capacity to develop sophisticated weapons of chemical warfare would make a threat that looked liked it was written with a quill. They also wouldn't make such a vague, ill defined demand. How could the entire world agree to accept God as its savior? What would happen if everyone got on board but the Swiss? How would you get the OK from every last Masai tribesman? Every herder working high in the Tajik Pamirs? And even if you *could* somehow get everyone to agree, which God are we talking about? The Christian God with the long white beard? Allah? Vishnu? Bill Murray?

No, none of this fit the profile of a legitimate threat. It was just a bad, weird joke from some addled crackpot who didn't understand the meaning of 'too soon', and it was filed away with the rest of them.

The letter was reported, of course, simply because it went everywhere. Thousands of them were mailed out, each one exquisitely handwritten, and that was enough to make a few reporters sit up and take notice. They didn't believe the warning but they thought it was interesting that someone had clearly gone to a lot of effort to scare the shit out of people. Interesting enough to report it in the *And finally...* segment of the nightly news, anyway.

And then it was forgotten almost as soon as it was mentioned. The President was gearing up for a tough re-election campaign. The Saudis were threatening to flood the market and push oil below $15 a barrel again. There was a mass shooting at Disney World. We all had bigger things to worry about than some random crackpot with excellent penmanship. Hell, even the fall of Bangkok was quickly pushed aside by more urgent news. Sure, millions of people had died, but it happened on the other side of the world and it happened to people who weren't Americans. Bangkok might as well be on Mars for all it mattered to folks from Tulsa.

Even *I* let it slip to the back of my mind, and it meant more to me than most. In the months following my interview with Paul McQueen I couldn't sleep through the night without waking in a sheen of cold sweat, my twisted sheets stuck to my skin and the image of Paul's sunken, haunted eyes burned into my mind like the afterglow from a bright light. I imagined I could smell the acrid smoke of his disgusting Indian cigarettes as I woke, their odor masking the stench of decaying flesh. The nightmares followed me all the way back home where I took a room in a Brooklyn apartment owned by Jim Bryson, an old high school buddy who'd made it big in apps.

This shit *scared* me. I became convinced that Paul hadn't been crazy. The story he told me was entirely true, I was sure of it. The western world was certain that the culprits were Islamic jihadists – a comfortable narrative that fit our preconceptions and helped justify our disastrous ground campaign in Syria – but I knew better.

Paul had described the terrorists as western with shaved heads, and one of the few things anyone had been able to learn about the Sons of the Father was that – before they suddenly vanished from the face of the earth a decade ago – they'd been a small, ultra-radical offshoot of the Baptists, more extreme in their beliefs than the crazy bastards at the Westboro Church. The Sons also held a strange belief that it was immodest for body hair to be exposed. They shaved every last strand down to the skin.

For months I tried to get people interested in the story. I ran a failed Kickstarter campaign to raise money for a documentary on Bangkok and the threat of the Sons. I self published a book that moved fewer than a hundred free copies. I spent endless hours on conspiracy forums, trying to get someone – *anyone* – to pay attention to the idea that the warning might be legit, but even the tinfoil hat brigade couldn't be distracted from the latest GMO scandal long enough to give me more than a dismissive *'cool story, bro.'* It was frustrating, to say the least.

And then... then I met a woman, a cute barista who worked at my local coffee place. She had dimples in her cheeks. She stole good coffee beans from work for me. She warmed her feet by squeezing them between my thighs as we sat curled up on the couch watching Daredevil on Netflix. I don't want to say I fell head over heels – there have been too many women over the years to kid myself that this one might be *the one* – but it was *nice*. It was comfortable and safe, and that's exactly what I needed.

Suddenly it seemed a little pointless to obsess about my theory. It seemed crazy to sit at my laptop until 3AM, raving on forums while Kate was waiting for me to keep her warm in bed. I managed to convince myself that I'd just gone a little crazy. Meeting Paul just days before he took his own life had sent me off the deep end, and Kate was helping pull me back to dry land.

Gradually, day by day, week by week, I spent less time trying to convince people that the world was going to end and more time enjoying the world I had now. Kate made me forget it all. She made me forget my plan to leave the city for a shack out in the woods. She made me set aside my plan to learn how to shoot, trap game, filter water and dress a wound with my eyes closed. She made me forget everything but those cute little dimples that appeared whenever she smiled.

Looking back, this was a pretty fucking huge mistake.

Dimples aren't worth shit at the end of the world.

•▼•

:::2:::
April 7th, 2019

IT'S THE RAIN that wakes me. Thick, heavy drops, bouncing like ball bearings against the window above the bed. It sounds like it's gusting outside, pushing the rain in sheets so it falls unevenly on the glass... *tap, tap, tap, tap, taptaptaptap, tap, tap, tap, tap,* like a sudden flurry of applause.

I crack open one eye and crane my neck to the old fashioned alarm clock on the bedside table, a black cast iron beast with a scrap of sponge squeezed beneath the bell to muffle the alarm. It's just after eleven in the morning. I roll on my back and stretch, grinning to myself as I remember it's Saturday. Nothing to do today but watch TV in my underwear until Kate gets home from work. Maybe I'll cook. Nah. Maybe I'll just order pizza. It feels like a pizza day.

Taptaptaptaptaptap.

I feel something wet and cold splash against my cheek, and I look up at the window to find it's cracked open a few inches. With each gust a little spray finds its way through the gap to my bed. It's kinda nice. Brooklyn has been unseasonably warm these past few days, and we don't have any AC in this old place. It's nice to be woken by a cool shower and that strangely pleasant smell of city rain. Musty and damp, but oddly refreshing.

I reach out to hunt for the remote buried somewhere in the sheets on Kate's side of the bed. I know it's in here somewhere. Kate always watches dumb cartoons late into the night, and she usually falls asleep clutching the remote like a security blanket. I fish around blindly for a minute before finding it hidden beneath her pillow, then point it in the direction of the TV and mash at random buttons until the screen flickers to life.

"– new information at this time, but we'll stay on the air and keep you updated as long as we can. We're hearing... We're... Hold on, please, I have my producer in my ear..."

I squint at the TV, confused. The little orange network logo in the corner of the screen tells me I'm tuned to Nickelodeon, but there's a news anchor on screen, some middle aged silver haired guy. I want to say Anderson Cooper, but

I'm not sure. Skinny dude, looks like a prematurely gray college senior.

"... OK... Uh huh..." He presses his ear as he speaks, listening to someone through an earpiece. He looks flustered, his face shiny and flushed. "OK, I'm being told that the President is preparing to address the nation. We'll take you live to the White House just as soon as– " The image switches to the presidential seal without warning, cutting the anchor off mid-sentence.

I sit bolt upright, suddenly fully awake. *What the fuck is going on?* The seal stays on screen for ten seconds. Twenty. I start to wonder if there's been some sort of technical problem, or maybe my signal has frozen. I quickly flip through the channels to see what else is on, but each channel shows the exact same seal, as if every frequency has been hijacked.

Tap, tap, TAP, taptaptaptap.

The seal finally vanishes, replaced by a color pattern, and a few seconds later the image flickers to what looks like the Oval Office. The ornately carved Resolute desk fills much of the screen, but there's nobody in the seat behind it.

A few moments of silence, and then an irritated voice calls out off camera. "No makeup, Karl. Look, just... *oh, for the love of God, just give it to me.*"

An urgent voice whispers, "We're live, ma'am."

The room falls silent for a moment, then comes the rustling sound of a mic being attached to clothing, and a few seconds later the President appears on screen and lowers herself behind the desk. She looks awful, like she's aged ten years overnight. Behind the desk she looks much smaller than the larger than life ballbuster we elected three years ago. She looks... well, she looks like a little old lady. It's hard to imagine that this is a woman about to embark on a year long high energy re-election campaign. She looks like she should have been buried yesterday.

"My fellow Americans," she begins, her voice hoarse and rasping, "it pains me deeply to break this news, but I must report that our great nation is under attack. A little more than five hours ago law enforcement in New York City and here in Washington D.C. began to report acts of unexplained large scale rioting and civil disobedience. Local authorities were quickly overwhelmed, and following the advice of the Pentagon, the Secretary of Defense and my Joint Chiefs of Staff I dispatched units of the National Guard to assist in operations to secure these cities. The current status of these units is unknown."

She looks as if her attention is distracted by someone off-camera. I hear the sound of a door creak open, and quiet but insistent voices in the background. The President scowls and shakes her head. She turns back to the camera.

"We don't yet know if these events are related to last year's attack on Bangkok. I cannot currently give you the exact details of the situation, or of any ongoing operations undertaken by our military and civilian forces, but you can rest assured that the brave men and women of our armed forces, police force and fire department are working tirelessly to bring this situation under control and restore peace."

She keeps her eyes trained on the camera, but raises a warning hand to someone off screen.

"As of this moment I am declaring a national state of emergency. All air, rail and sea transport has been grounded until further notice. Our national borders have been closed, and stock market trading has been suspended. I urge citizens to follow any and all directions given by the authorities, and I implore you all to keep– what? *No! I'm not finished!*"

These last words are angry and directed off-camera. Moments later the view is blocked by a posse of black-suited Secret Service agents who hustle the President to her feet, loudly protesting, and whisk her quickly from the room. I can barely make out anything in the confusion, but I think I hear one of the agents say something like "They've breached the perimeter." There's an edge of panic in his voice.

Taptaptaptaptaptap, tap, tap, tap.

In the confusion someone must have knocked the camera. The image wheels away from the desk, blurring until it suddenly comes to rest pointing at a desk leg and the plush blue carpet. For a few seconds the camera struggles to find focus, alternating between the desk and a random point on the floor while sounds of movement come from off-screen. The final words I hear are "Eagle moving" before the image suddenly cuts back to the anchor, who looks like he wasn't expecting the camera to be on him. He's staring off-screen at a monitor, and it takes a few seconds for him to realize he's live. He hurriedly drops something he's holding to the ground, but from the curl of smoke hanging in the air it's clear he was smoking in the newsroom.

"Umm... We'll... Yeah, OK, we'll try to get the White House back as soon as possible. In the meantime I'd like to repeat our earlier message. If your area is affected, please remain in your home. Do not attempt to leave. If you are at your place of work, do not attempt to return home. Do not attempt to..." He looks off screen.

"Jack, I'm not fucking telling people to..." He sighs, exasperated. "OK, OK. Do not attempt to reach loved ones. Lock all doors and windows, and move to the most secure room in your building. Gather any food you have and fill as many containers as you can find with water, and prepare as best you can for possible power outages.

"If your area is *not* currently affected you should tune your set to local broadcasts for details of evacuation plans. Jack, do we have the frequency? The... umm, the emergency... OK, I'm being told that the emergency alert system will soon be broadcasting local information across all radio frequencies, including digital bands. We understand that authorities are currently establishing safe zones on the outskirts of several cities with sufficient food, power and fresh water to support all those who wish to – "

The signal suddenly drops out, leaving the room cast in the blue glow of the screen, and eerily silent but for the rain drumming against the window.

Tap, tap, tap, tap, tap.

My mind is running a mile a minute. I have no way of knowing for sure, but I can only assume that my worst nightmare has come true. The deadline given by the Sons of the Father was a little more than a week ago. That day came and went like any other, and it was so far from my mind that I barely registered my relief when the sun set without incident. Now it seems like I was right all along. The shit just hit the fan a little later than scheduled.

Taptaptaptap.

I pull myself to my feet, almost in a trance. None of this seems real. *Did the President say New York? Jesus. Am I safe? Is Kate safe? Is this really* – I almost laugh out loud at the insane thought – *is this really a fucking zombie out-break?*

I suddenly feel like I'm suffocating. I've never had a panic attack, but this sure feels like one. I feel like the walls are closing in, and the air feels like it's been drained of its oxygen. I stagger over to the window and yank it fully open, stick my head out and inhale a lungful of fresh, cool air.

Tap, tap, taptaptap.

The street outside my window is empty of traffic, but that's not out of the ordinary since this is a dead end road. It's usually pretty quiet out there. Something is niggling at me, though, tickling at the back of my mind. There's some-thing obvious that I really should have already noticed, but my mind doesn't seem to want to connect the dots. *What are you missing, Tom? Think!*

I stare out at the street and try to imagine what's going on in the city. I wonder where Kate might be. Her coffee shop is just a few streets over. Surely she'd try to come back here when she heard the–

My mind suddenly clears, and I realize what my subconscious is yelling at me to notice.

Tap, tap, taptaptaptap, tap, tap.

The sound of raindrops, still bouncing off the window like ball bearings.

Only it's not rain. The rain has stopped.

Tap, tap... tap.

That's the sound of gunfire.

And it's close.

•⸙•

:::3:::

"BRYSON! JIM, ARE you home?"

My voice echoes through the halls, but it's not met with an answer. I didn't really expect one. Bryson usually spends his Friday nights with an interchangeable cast of the many women of Manhattan who are more than happy to push their soft toys to the floor for a good looking guy with a wallet bursting at the seams. Right now he's probably sleeping off a champagne hangover in some NYU student dorm.

I stalk down the hallway aimlessly, still struggling to get my head around the enormity of what's going on. I lean back against the wall and take a deep breath, trying to focus and center myself, then I slap my forehead in disbelief that I haven't thought to check my damned phone yet.

I run back to my room, dive on the bed and fish my iPhone from beneath the duvet. 17% battery. Three bars.

Jesus, a dozen missed calls, and almost as many texts. I had the damned thing set to silent.

"*Oh fuck oh fuck oh fuck* please be OK, Kate. Please God, let her be OK."

I tap the screen and bring up the log. Most of the calls are from Kate, along with a couple from unknown numbers. I tap on the texts and my blood runs cold as I read them.

Heading to work babe. Korean BBQ tonight?
****

Cn u call me? Hearing weird stuff from customers.
****

Babe, pick up.
****

DUCKING PICK UP!
****

Jesus, turn on the news! Have you seen what's happening on the bridge? I'm coming home. Stay there!
****

PLEASE let me know you're safe. In the antique place. People trying to get in. Scared.
****

Hefl us were flicking stuck
****

Tom I need to turn off my phone they can. Hear me. Don't call just get out I love you so much.
****

The phone slips from my fingers onto the bed, and I feel the crushing weight of guilt squeeze at my chest. I was sleeping soundly while Kate was going through all of this, terrified. The first text was sent three hours ago, at 8AM when she was arriving at work. I scroll to the final message, and my heart leaps into my throat when I see it was sent twenty minutes ago, just minutes before I woke up.

OK, what the fuck do you do now, Tom? Think! Take a breath and just fucking THINK!

"OK," I say out loud, trying to calm myself with my own voice. "She's three blocks from here. Let's say five minutes on foot. Move slowly. Look around the corners. Keep to cover. OK, weapon. Weapon, weapon, weapon."

As I tug on my clothes I scan the room for something suitable, thinking back to what Paul McQueen had said when he described the Bangkok attack. He said people tried to fight as if they were up against slow, lumbering movie monsters. They thought they could be taken out with a quick blow to the head, but the things moved too fast for the survivors to properly defend themselves.

At least I have the benefit of a minute or two to catch my breath and think. Those poor bastards in Bangkok had only seconds to react, and they were limited to whatever they had to hand. Plastic water guns and buckets, mostly. I'm sure I can find something a little more suitable.

My eyes settle on the aluminum baseball bat poking out from beneath my bed. I'd give my right arm for a gun and a box of ammo, but beggars can't be choosers. I tug it out and swing it a few times, accustoming myself to the weight and balance.

I know it's not an ideal weapon. It feels much too light to take down an adult, but it might just do the job until I can get my hands on a gun. I figure I'll do my best to stay away from anything moving, and if I'm forced into a confrontation I'll go in at a dead sprint and just swing away at anyone coming at me. I won't go for a head shot, but I'll just try to get them the fuck out of my way and tear ass out of there.

I'm about to walk out of the room when an image flashes into my mind, of Brad Pitt in that zombie movie. He taped magazines to his arms as makeshift gauntlets, protecting them against bites. I don't have any tape in the house – I shake my head in disgust at my lack of even the most basic preparation – but I might be able to give myself similar protection. I drop to my knees and reach blindly under the bed, probing with my fingers until I find what I'm searching for.

It's my old high school baseball mitt. Thick, stiff, biteproof leather. This thing has been sitting under the bed so long it's dried out and turned brittle, but there's no way in hell anyone could bite through it. On the off chance an attacker decides he's hungry I want to be able to hold him off with something other than a handful of tasty, chewable fingers.

I tug the mitt down over my left hand, tap the bat against my leg and scan the room, looking for anything else that might be useful. Once again I curse myself for neglecting to prepare for this shit. I can't believe I allowed myself to become so fucking complacent. I don't even have a basic bug out bag. No real weapons. No water filter. Not even a bag of trail mix to keep me going. What the hell was I thinking? I had such big plans. I was going to become a *real* man, one of those guys who takes the apocalypse in his stride. I wanted to be Daryl from The Walking Dead, a badass tracker with a crossbow slung across his back. Right now I wouldn't even make it to the end of the first episode.

OK, time to go, Tom. Get out of your damned head. Be careful. Pay attention. Don't do anything dumb.

I leave the room and walk down the hall, trailing the bat behind me across the wooden floor. I reach the front door of the apartment, grip the doorknob, take a deep breath and...

"*Jesus*, Tom," I sigh, slapping my mitt against my forehead in disbelief at my own stupidity. "Put on some fucking shoes, you moron."

•ፕ•

:::4:::

DISTANT GUNFIRE ECHOES through the otherwise silent streets. It sounds like it's coming from all directions, shifting with the wind. Most of it sounds like it's way off, but every dozen steps I flinch as a shot rings out dangerously close.

I pause at the end of the street, peering timidly around the corner to the main road. Empty. Silent. About half a block away a Prius sits in the middle of the road facing in my direction, blocking the street between both banks of parked cars. The front driver's door hangs open, but there's nobody to be seen.

I lean back against the wall and take a mental inventory to calm myself. I look down at my feet, starting from the ground up. A pair of thick, scuffed Alden boots, a hangover from the days I liked to pretend I was Indiana Jones while

I tooled around the Mongolian countryside. Heavyweight jeans, the thickest I own. I've no idea if they'll help if some infected bastard tries to take a bite out of me, but it won't make me an easy meal.

I move further up. Two plain gray t-shirts, layered one over the other in case I need spare cotton for... I don't know, bandages? Might come in handy. Onto my coat, a vintage Belstaff Trialmaster motorcycle jacket. I'm pleased with this one. The thick waxed cotton might offer my some bite protection, but the really useful thing is the detachable belt. Could come in handy as a tourniquet, if it comes to it.

I pat my pockets. Cigarettes, because fuck it. If the world is about to end at least I don't have to worry about cancer any more. Two disposable lighters, and a freshly filled Zippo that still stinks of lighter fluid.

In my right jeans pockets I feel the outline of my house key, looped to a tiny little three inch Victorinox pen knife with a blade so blunt it'd struggle to cut through fresh air, and in my left my iPhone, complete with documentary evidence that I'm just the shittiest of shitty boyfriends, sleeping off too many Friday night beers while my girlfriend pleaded for help.

I've been thinking about that final message since I saw it, and even now at the worst possible time I hear it repeating over and over in my head. *I love you so much.* Beneath the fear and dread twisting my hungover stomach I feel the unpleasant grip of... guilt, I guess? Shame? I don't know what it is, exactly, but a pretty big part of me wants to turn around and run in the opposite direction.

I don't love Kate. I don't know how else to put it. I just don't love her, and I never said I did. I *like* her a whole bunch. I love *spending time* with her – that old dodge – but I'm not *in* love with her. It was a bad idea to ask her to move in with me, but it just felt right at the time. It felt like the adult thing to do, and a good way to rescue myself from the pit I'd fallen down.

And now I'm walking through Brooklyn with a flimsy aluminum baseball bat trying to rescue her, because once again that's the grown up thing to do. It's the thing Paul McQueen *didn't* do, and even with my world collapsing around me I don't want anyone to judge me the way I judged him. I don't want people to think I'm a coward who'd abandon his girlfriend. I'm putting myself in harm's way *because I don't want people to think less of me.*

Jesus, I'm fucked up.

I push the thought from my head, take a deep breath, heft the baseball bat so I can grip it in the middle, and turn into the street. I stick close to the walls on the south side of the road, the red brick still wet from the rain. The sound of my jacket scraping against the rough surface sounds deafening in the eerie silence. I take a step away, terrified that a thousand killers might hear me and come flooding around the corner.

Nothing comes.

Where is everybody?

The Prius is just a few dozen feet away now, and I stop behind the cover of a parked Lincoln to cautiously check it out. It's not crashed. It just looks abandoned, like the driver had to get out of there in a hurry, and I wonder if he might have left the key in the ignition. The roads look clear enough, and I figure the quiet electric motor might make it a perfect stealthy getaway vehicle once I find Kate.

I decide to risk stepping out into the open. The gunfire sounds like it's all far away now. Whoever was shooting nearby a minute ago seems to have stopped. I step out from behind the Lincoln and slowly, carefully make my way towards the Prius, creeping from car to car, my head low.

It's just a few feet from me now. I cross the street stealthily, and slowly lower myself to the ground to check out the space beneath the car. All clear. I stand up and walk to the door, but the moment I reach out and touch the frame I hear a sound that makes my blood freeze in my veins.

Breathing. Slow, wet, rasping breath, like the sucking sound made by the gross little spit vacuum at the dentist.

And it's coming from inside the car.

She comes out of nowhere, launching herself from the back seat towards the dashboard. It all happens too fast to take anything in, but I fall back onto my ass and kick out reflexively, randomly, like a toddler who doesn't want his diaper changed. I don't even realize my foot has connected with the door until I see it slam shut in her face just as she throws herself towards me. Her head bounces against the window with a sickening *thunk* as the door slams shut.

My ears are ringing and spots flash in front of my eyes, and it takes a few seconds before I realize the crazed, gulping sobs I hear are coming from me. I swallow hard and force myself to take a slow, shuddering breath. *Control yourself, Tom. Stop fucking panicking.*

I sit there for a moment, my foot pressed against the door just long enough to be sure that the latch has caught, then push myself from the ground and look in the car.

She's just a kid. Can't be more than ten years old. A cute, chubby little blonde thing, her long hair plaited like the princess from Frozen. She doesn't look like there's anything wrong with her. I can't see any visible wounds from here, apart from the bright red trickle of blood rolling down her forehead from the wound that opened up when she hit the window. She doesn't even have that glazed, milky contact lens look these things always have in the movies. She just looks like a little girl. Snarling and crazed, but a little girl all the same. If I didn't know better I'd assume she was just a normal kid throwing a violent tantrum.

I can't help but feel sorry for her as I watch her watching me. Now the door is closed and I lock eyes with her she holds still, meeting my gaze like a dog asserting its dominance. She looks like she's gone into low power mode, like she's waiting for the next stimulus to trigger an attack.

Not for the first time I wish the Thais hadn't been so fucking stubborn and pigheaded in the wake of their attack. The junta burned most of the bodies, and nobody knows what happened to the few walkers still on their feet after the military firebombed the remains of Bangkok. The Thais refused to share much of what they'd learned about these things. They insisted it was an internal matter, and as General Kantawat descended deeper into paranoid madness the government stopped even talking with the wider world.

God, the things we could have learned if they'd just shared with us. We might have been able to stop this. We might have found a vaccine. We might even have found a way to cure it. This cute, chubby little girl might have been saved with a simple injection, but instead she's staring into my eyes through the glass, a glob of bloody pink spit drooling down her chin as she snarls. She's done. Gone. If her parents are still alive they'll never see their daughter again.

I'm not sure they'd even *want* to see her. Not like this. I don't know her, and even *I* can hardly bear to look into those eyes and see nothing I recognize as human looking back at me. She's just an animal now. This sweet little kid probably woke up early this morning to catch some cartoons while she munched on Cheerios, and now she's nothing but a vehicle for violence. I know she'd try to kill me if I gave her an inch. She'd sink her teeth into my flesh and tear away a chunk if I opened the door right now.

I feel hot tears stream down my cheeks. I know the smart thing to do would be to get the fuck out of here before this little monster breaks through the window or figures out the door handle. If she manages to get out of her prison I'd better be far away.

A small part of me, though, whispers that I should free her from this hell. I should crack open the door just enough to slide my bat through the gap and give her a few sharp jabs in the face with the handle until her brain switches off. After all, what kind of a life does this pathetic little thing have to look forward to? Her best case scenario is that she escapes the car and goes on to kill and eat a bunch of people. It's not like she can look forward to college. She'll never have an awkward first date. She'll never make out with some kid from the football team in the back row of a theater. She's lost. Whatever made her human has been torn out of her and replaced with something else. The kind thing to do would be to end her suffering.

Common sense kicks in before I let myself reach out for the door handle. I have no clue how strong these things are. My only experience of them is a second hand story from an old friend who, to be fair, wasn't of sound mind when I last spoke to him. I don't know what this girl is capable of. Maybe she could spit the infection at me. Hell, maybe it's airborne. Maybe just opening the door again would be enough for it to work its way into my system and turn me into one of these mindless monsters. It may be too late already, for all I know. It might already be in my blood. The countdown may have already begun.

In any case, I have no idea if I could even bring myself to kill her. They make it look easy in the movies. A quick swing of the bat and the thing goes down, threat neutralized, but a nasty little thought in the back of my mind tells me that the reality wouldn't be quite so PG13. I'm guessing the reality is much, much messier, and the kind of thing that would lead to years of therapy. I'd pound away with the heel of the bat until this sweet little kid's face caved in. She'd probably keep snarling as I turned her face into jelly, and she wouldn't stop until I finally drove enough shards of shattered skull into her brain to turn the fucking thing off. I don't know if I have the will to do that. Or the strength, for that matter. I haven't so much as thrown a punch in ten years, and who knows how much force it would take to kill her?

I turn away from the car before I can dwell on it any longer, and jump with shock as the little girl begins to pound her head hard against the glass. My movement set her off again, and now she's once again crazed. With each dull thump against the window the wound in her forehead spreads open wider, and the glass quickly smears with so much blood it looks like she's looking at me through a stained glass window.

I can't watch any longer. It doesn't look like she has the strength to break through, but I can't bear to see her destroy herself.

I hurry away from the car, moving on in the direction of the antique store where I hope – where I *need* – to find Kate, and as I walk I can't help but wonder what it's like to be one of those things. Is that little girl still in there somewhere, trapped in the back of a mind now controlled by a monster? Is she watching what's happening to her through eyes she can't control, watching her own limbs move against her will, like a puppet?

Can she feel pain? Does she miss her parents? Is she afraid?

I shake my head to evict such thoughts, and remind myself that the more I dwell on questions like this the more likely it is that I'll get to learn the answers first hand. I need to be vigilant. I can't walk around in a daze, asking myself pointless questions while the world goes to shit. Survival is all that matters right now. Philosophy can take a number.

I reach another intersection, the last before the commercial block with Kate's coffee shop at its center. After reading her texts I expect the antique store across the street from her place to be swarming with the infected, and I feel my heart thump madly in my chest as I creep towards the corner.

I crouch down low and hold my breath before I poke my head around the wall, as if the things could hear my breathing at fifty paces. I hardly dare look. I know that what I see around the corner will tell me if she's alive or dead, and... well, I really don't want to know. I don't want to replace the terrifying hope of *maybe* with the crushing, leaden finality of *no*.

I force myself to look. With the handle of the bat gripped tight in my fist I creep forward to the corner of the intersection and slowly poke my head out, peering down the road.

Nothing. No one.

The street looks like it would on any other quiet Saturday morning. No bodies. The road is free of traffic. A couple of cars are parked illegally in the no stopping zone like always, a calculated risk while the drivers run in to grab a coffee to go. My eyes scan the street looking for signs of movement but it's quiet as the grave. The front door of the old used bookstore is wide open, as is the door of the Whole Foods next door. Kate's coffee shop still has tables sat outside, with paper cups resting there as if the customers have all stepped inside to take a piss.

I walk out into the street, a little more confident now, and hurry along the row of parked cars until I reach the antique store directly opposite the coffee shop. As I approach it my pace slows, and I come to a halt out front with a sinking feeling in my heart.

The big bay window has been shattered from the outside. In the dim, dusty interior I can see shards of glass sprayed across the ground. I try the door, but it only opens a couple of inches before hitting up against some sort of heavy object.

Slowly, carefully I climb into the store through the broken window, watching out for the glittering shards still clinging to the frame, and I immediately see what happened. A heavy armoire has been pushed up against the door to form a blockade. It looks like it worked, but there was nothing to stop those things coming in through the window.

I feel a lump rise in my throat as I imagine hordes of snarling, wailing creatures flooding in through the shattered window like water, filling every inch of the space inside and overwhelming anyone hiding within. It must have been terrifying.

I choke down a desperate sob and lean against the armoire, fishing my phone from my jacket pocket. I guess there's no harm in trying to call now. Whatever was looking for Kate surely found her, but I don't want to give up that last scrap of hope that she might answer and tell me that she's fine. That she's sitting pretty in a chopper that arrived at the last minute to carry her to safety, and she's on her way to a safe zone outside the city. That I don't have to feel this *guilt*.

I scroll to Kate's name, hover over it for a moment with my thumb, then bite the bullet and press the screen. I don't really expect the call to connect. I have two bars, but I don't know what that really means. I've no idea if the cell network is even still working. I've got to–

Wait. I hear a sound. Faint, right on the edge of my hearing.

It sounds like a phone.

"Tom?" A tinny voice calls out, too loud, and I press the phone to my ear to take it out of speaker mode. "Tom, is that you?"

"Kate!" I cry, too shocked and ecstatic to keep my voice down. "Oh my God, I thought you were dead!"

"Tom, can you hear me? I can't hear you."

In the background I can hear a male voice whisper. "It sounds like it's going away. We have to move *now.*"

"Kate, can you hear me?" I hear the desperation in my own voice. "Please, tell me where you – "

She speaks over me. "I don't know if you're there, but I'm stuck in the antique store across the street from work. One of them was trying to get through the door, but we think it just left. We're gonna make a break for it, OK? I'm gonna try to get home." I hear her voice waver with emotion. "Oh, please tell me you can hear me, Tom... I love you."

"I love you," I whisper, but the call has already cut out. I don't know why I said it. It just seemed like the right thing to do. *Jesus*, I'm an idiot.

I slip the phone back in my pocket, then I freeze as my brain finally catches up with what the call means. Kate is here somewhere, still in the store. Still alive.

And one of *them* is in here with us. Not trapped behind a door. Out. Free. *Roaming*.

I hear a loud thump from somewhere in the back of the store and I feel my grip tighten on the bat.

Another thump. Whatever it is, it's coming closer.

Another, even closer this time, as if a drunk guy is stumbling his way towards me. The bat suddenly feels far too light and flimsy.

It occurs to me that it was my own voice that drew the thing away from Kate. It heard me, and now it's come to hunt me down. The hairs on the back of my neck stand on end, and the grip of the bat feels slippery in my sweaty hands.

The thing finally appears, limping slowly through the door to the back room. I pull back against the wall into the shadow of a large grandfather clock, trying to blend into the shadows as best I can. Trying to make myself small.

It's an old man, maybe late sixties. Neat, short gray hair and a fussy little silver beard that looks like it received loving attention each morning. As he emerges from the behind the counter I see why he's limping. He has an enormous shard of glass embedded in his bony thigh, jutting forward about six inches and buried so deep that it barely wobbles as he walks.

He doesn't seem to notice the pain even as he bumps against a low table and presses the shard deeper into his thigh. His cream trousers are soaked crimson down one leg. His knuckles are bruised and bloody.

I hold my breath as he slowly approaches, wishing the grandfather clock was just a little bigger. In the silence all I can hear is the slow drag of feet and soft, rasping breath from the creature. He seems to be moving away towards the window, and I pray he'll climb through.

He reaches the glass and pauses, as if his slow, broken mind is processing the best way to negotiate the window frame. I can almost see his mind tick over like an idling engine, and once again I wonder what's going on in there.

He seems to reach a decision. Slowly – far too slowly for my bursting lungs – he lifts his bad leg clumsily over the lip of the window. He moves to set his foot down in the street, and–

– And the minute hand of the grandfather clock beside me ticks over, breaking the cloying silence with a loud, dull *tock*.

The creature whips his head towards me and locks eyes with mine. I freeze in place, shocked by the cold, mindless hatred in those eyes, and stifle a cry as he pulls back into the store and suddenly runs – *sprints* – towards me with terrifying speed.

I know I don't have the space to swing the bat. I don't have the time to think straight, but I instinctively know I'll still be on the back swing by the time he's on me. There's only one thing I can do. As he barrels towards me I thrust out the heel of my left hand, still clad in the heavy leather mitt, and drive it forward and up into the man's chin, my arm locked at the elbow. I watch in slow motion as he opens his mouth to bite, and I cringe as my blow forces his mouth shut, catching his tongue between his teeth and cleanly severing the tip. I imagine I can feel the tiny chunk of wet flesh spit against the palm of my hand as the man falls backwards, stunned.

Now I'm working on autopilot. No conscious thought passes through my mind as I lift the bat and step forward to take my first heavy swing. I swing like I'm chopping wood, bringing the aluminum rod over my head and down hard onto the man's forehead. He seems to react with anger rather than pain, snapping at me and trying to lift himself back to his feet, but I move too quickly for him. I swing again, sending him back to the ground with a fresh gash in his cheek, and again. Again. Repeating, over and over, his face caving in deeper with each blow until he isn't recognizable as a man any more. Now he's just a mass of swollen flesh, as misshapen as a Picasso portrait, one cheek sunken and caved, the other exposed, raised bone.

I keep swinging long after he's stopped struggling to stand. Long after he's stopped moaning. I swing until I can't tell the difference between head and floor. Until he's just a body cut off at the wrinkled, sinewy neck, ending in a glistening pink and white jellied mass of flesh and bone.

"Tom!" A voice cries out to my left.

I swing the bat toward the sound instinctively, my arms barely connected to my mind, and the aluminum crashes against the dark wood of the grandfather clock.

"Tom, *stop*!"

The voice finally breaks though. The red mist starts to fade, and I feel myself regaining control. I blink a few times and try to make sense of what I'm seeing.

It's Kate, her face just inches from the end of the dented, bloody bat. She looks down at the mess twitching at my feet then back up at me, and slowly, carefully reaches out to pluck the bloodied bat from my hand.

"I think you got him, babe."

•⸙•

:::5:::

I STARE AT my reflection in the curved, mir-
rored surface of the cappuccino machine, and I
barely recognize the face looking back at me.

It's the same face I was wearing when I visited
the coffee shop yesterday and the same face I
woke with this morning, but now a thin crust of
brown blood dries quickly on my cheeks. My
hair is matted, clumped together and stuck to
my forehead. I reach up and run my fingers
through it then stare dumbly at my stained
hand.

The hand I just used to murder a fellow human.

I flinch when I feel Kate's hand on my shoulder, then look down and see that my clothes
didn't escape the blood spray. I look like I've
spent my morning painting a room red with a
hose, and as my sleeve comes into focus I notice

a small shard of gray white... something caught in a crease in the fabric.

It's a fragment of skull.

"Don't touch me!" I yell, pulling away from Kate's hand.

She steps back in surprise. "What? Why?"

I tug my jacket off and drop it to the ground. "Look at me, I'm covered in this shit. Here, give me your hands." I pull her to the basin by the register and twist open the faucet with my elbow. "We have to keep ourselves clean. Who knows how this thing spreads? Maybe a single drop of blood in your eyes or mouth is enough to fuck you up. We can't take any risks until we know what's going on, OK?"

I wait for Kate to clean herself off, then dunk my head under the tap with my eyes closed and my lips pressed shut. After a minute I risk cracking open one eye, and I see the water swirling down the drain is running clear.

Next comes my jacket. I grab a towel from the stack by the basin, soak it wet then wipe down the waxed cotton until the worst of the blood seems to be gone. Death by contaminated jacket would be a really dumb way to check out.

Kate watches me as I dry myself off. She reaches her hand to her mouth and moves to chew her thumbnail, a nervous habit, but catches herself in time and forces her hand to her side. "Shit, this is really happening, isn't it?" she says, with fear in her voice. "All that stuff you used to say about Bangkok. This is it, right? Sons of the whatever, zombie plague, end of the world shit. It was all true?"

I nod solemnly.

"Well... *damn.*" She lowers herself to a stool by the counter. "I always just assumed you were a little weird when you talked about that stuff. You know, like someone who thinks they faked the moon landings. It never occurred to me that you might actually be right."

I manage a hollow laugh. "Well thanks, honey. It's nice to know I can always count on you for support."

"Oh, you know what I mean. It's just... Jesus, I mean this is really *it*. No more coffee shop. No more McDonalds breakfast. No more... oh shit, no more *Game of Thrones.*"

She sees my expression.

"Come on, don't look at me like that. I just mean... you know, it's *over*. All that day to day shit we took for granted, it's *done.*"

"Yeah, pretty much," I reply, shrugging my jacket back over my shoulders. "I just wish I'd done more to prepare for it. I don't have a plan. I have no clue where we go from here, Kate. Shit, I don't even have a gun. How am I gonna protect us?"

Kate smiles for the first time. "Oh, I don't know. You were pretty good with that bat."

I look down at the bloodied aluminum bat resting on the counter. "I guess. It won't last long, though. It's already dented to shit. Couple more skulls and it'll be worthless. That reminds me." I grab the bat and start to run it under the tap, letting the blood circle around the drain.

We both jump at the sound of the coffee shop's security shutter lifting from the ground, and I cringe at the loud rattle as it rolls up. That noise will carry all the way down the street.

"Quiet!" hisses Kate as a figure ducks under the half open shutter. It's Arnold, the retired firefighter who holed up with Kate in the antique store. This is hardly the time to bring it up, but if I saw him in the street on a regular day I'd probably ask for his autograph. He's the spitting image of Danny Glover. It's just uncanny. I swear, if he tells me he's too old for this shit I'll start looking for the hidden cameras.

"Sorry 'bout that," Arnold replies meekly, rolling it back down behind him much more carefully. When it reaches the ground he turns to us and grins. "Got my gun."

Kate smiles, relieved. "And the radio?"

"Police scanner," he corrects, shaking his head. "It's wired up to the car. Couldn't bring it along without lugging the battery with me, but I managed to pick up a little chatter before the signal dropped. It's just like I said, alright. They took down the bridge. Smart motherfuckers."

I look from Kate to Arnold, confused. "What are you talking about?"

Arnold walks to the open chiller cabinet, grabs a Coke and cracks it open with a hiss. "Brooklyn Bridge, son. They took it down, right in the center. That's why it's so quiet hereabouts." He shakes his head in wonder. "I swear I never thought they'd go through with it."

I feel like I'm missing something, like I'm only hearing one side of a conversation. I turn to Kate with a questioning look.

"Tom wasn't here earlier, Arnold, remember? Why don't you catch him up?" Kate speaks to him like she'd speak to a senile grandpa, and I wonder if Arnold is quite all there. He looks at me blankly for a moment, as if he's forgotten who I am, then the brightness returns to his eyes.

"Oh, right, right. Sorry, senior moment." He lowers himself to a stool and sets his Coke on the counter. "You remember Bangkok, right?"

I nod. "Of course I remember. Millions of people died."

"Sure, sure. OK, well, after Bangkok the government started planning contingencies in case of an attack. You know, crazy blue sky shit they never thought they'd really need, like what to do if aliens invade and whatnot. That was how they came up with... Oh, what's it called? That old fairy tale with the guy who lured all those rats and kids away with his... what, like a magic flute or some shit?" He creases his brow for a moment, deep in thought. "Pied piper!"

I shoot a worried glance to Kate, but she shakes her head almost imperceptibly. *Don't worry, he's cool.*

Arnold continues, growing more agitated and jittery with each word. "Operation Pied Piper, they called it. See, they figured these things, you know, they're probably pretty dumb, right? Not too much going on in the old brain box, so they'd probably be easy to trick. They figured they'd probably be attracted to sound, so they came up with this plan to clear the city after an attack." He runs a hand across his stubble. "God damn genius, whoever came up with it."

"What? What was the plan?" I ask, impatiently.

Arnold grins. "Blow the bridges. Wash the fuckers down the river like flushing a gutter. You get it?"

I shake my head. Am I just being dumb, or is this old guy making no sense at all?

Arnold swells his chest proudly. "I was a firefighter. Marine Company One. Twen'y eight years on the *John D. McKean*, and six more on *Three Forty Three*. We were part of all sorts of crazy plans, but Pied Piper jumped out at me more than most. See, in the event of an attack it was the job of *Three Forty Three* to drop anchor right between the Brooklyn and Manhattan bridges after they were blown. *Firefighter II* would go to Williamsburg, and *Bravest* would head up to Queensboro." He notices my blank expression. "Those are the names of our fireboats, son."

"We had these, you know, these huge speakers, like you get at a music festival. Big, bulky things. Good and loud, so the sound carries. We were supposed to rig them up and play all sorts of shit to lure those things out to the edge of the bridge and get 'em to jump in the river. Didn't really matter what, so long as it was loud. Looks like they went with the fireworks track."

It takes me a minute to figure it out. "You mean that noise about an hour ago? That was the boat? I thought it was gunfire."

Arnold shakes his head. "Nope, that was a recording of July 4th. 2011, if I remember right. Personally I would have gone with Springsteen, but I guess it doesn't matter, so long as it worked."

He sits back and takes a smug sip of his Coke, as if he came up with the plan himself.

"So you see now, right? That was the plan. Blow the bridges, then draw those bastards into the water with the noise, right off the edge into the middle of the East river. Hey presto, you got an empty street outside instead of a million homicidal bastards trying to break in through that shutter."

I frown. "But what about everyone downstream? What happens to them when thousands of those things float ashore?"

Arnold chuckles. "A net, son. A really big goddamn net. Last year, just before I called it a day, we helped set up one of those huge things they use on fishing trawlers. You know the ones, those big factory ships that drag them back for miles and just hoover up every fucking thing? We got one of those bad boys running right across the Narrows a couple of miles downriver. You just winch that up to the surface and you got yourself a nice little marine barrier."

I can't help but be impressed. "That's... OK, that's really damned clever. So, do you know what comes next? Is there a second part of the plan, or did they stop at the big net?"

Arnold gives me a toothy grin. "I'll tell you if you hand me one of those cigarettes." He juts his chin towards the pack of Marlboros resting on the counter. I chuckle, slip one from the pack for myself then slide it over to him. "Help yourself."

He lights up, and closes his eyes as he takes a long, blissful pull. "God *damn*, I miss that."

He holds the cigarette up and looks lovingly at the smoldering tip. "Marcy – that's my wife, Marcy – she made me quit when I retired. Told me she wanted to keep me around until I'd finished repainting the kitchen. I don't suppose it makes much difference now, right? Chances are none of us will be around long enough for a little smoke to hurt us."

He takes another long drag, coughs and winces. "Looks like I'm out of practice." He sets the cigarette down on the lip of the counter and takes a sip of his Coke. "Prospect Park. That's what's next." He turns his eyes up to the ceiling, trying to summon his memory. "Prospect, Lincoln and James J Braddock. Oh, and the Bronx Zoo. That's where they'll set up rally points for the city. They've all got fresh water, and they'll bring in generators, food, tents and what not. Gotta keep the city empty until the army can sweep it clean, so I guess we'll all be sleeping on camp beds for a while." He shrugs his sleeve up and takes a look at his watch. "That's where Marcy will be waiting, God willing. We live a few blocks from Prospect, and she knows to head there when everything goes to shit." He stubs out his cigarette on the table. "On that note, kids, I think it's high time we mosey."

I turn to Kate. "You good to go?"

She nods and grabs her jacket, but I sense some hesitation.

"What's up?" I ask.

"It's nothing," Kate replies, lowering her voice. "Just... let's talk just the two of us when we get out, OK? There's something you should know."

I nod, and I'm about to reply when Arnold grabs his gun, tucks it into his jacket pocket and lifts himself from his stool with a sharp gasp. "You OK, Arnold?"

"Yeah, yeah," he replies, waving away my concern. "Nothing to worry yourself about."

Kate shoots me a wide eyed look, as if to draw my attention to something. She nods towards Arnold, but I don't get it.

"OK, let's move, kids. Time's wasting."

That's when I see it, as Arnold turns from us towards the shutter.

He's bleeding.

The back of his right thigh is stained red where he put his weight on the stool. The blood has seeped through his gray trousers, and the sodden material clings to his leg. He doesn't have a limp, but from the look of the blood his injury is more than just a little cut.

Kate takes my arm as Arnold raises the shutter, and she silently mouths the words to me.

He got bit.

•¶•

:::6:::

WE DRIVE SLOWLY south on Flatbush, Arnold feathering the gas just enough to keep us rolling without building up the revs. Even driving carefully the engine sounds worryingly loud in the otherwise silent streets.

"Where are all the people?" I ask, peering down the empty roads at each intersection. "How come we're not seeing many bodies? I've only seen a couple in the last five blocks."

Kate shrugs. "Saturday morning. I guess most of them were still in bed when it started. I know the coffee shop was pretty dead. And it was raining pretty bad this morning. Maybe they waited for the crowd to pass then headed for the park?"

"Maybe," I agree. "Maybe a lot of them got out of town before it all went bad. What time did it come on the news?"

Kate shrugs. "I don't know. We don't have a TV in the shop. First I heard of it was a couple of customers talking about a riot going on in Manhattan, then it all went to shit pretty quickly."

Arnold slows the car to maneuver around a mail van blocking our side of the road, and I turn to the townhouses at the sidewalk. "Wait a minute," I mumble. "You seeing this, guys?"

I point out the window to the houses. Almost every second door is wide open, and as we slowly coast by I can see the carnage within. Behind each door a long hallway stretches towards the back of the house, and in almost every one bodies lie, twisted and broken, like chocolates revealed from behind the windows of a macabre advent calendar.

"Jesus, they were all caught at home," mutters Kate, crossing herself as she spots the beaten body of a small boy in SpongeBob pajamas He's lying halfway across the threshold, as if he was trying to escape when he died. He'd look like he was sleeping if it wasn't for the fact that his left leg is broken and twisted forward at the knee, like an ostrich.

I shiver despite the warmth of the car. I can imagine it all too well. Waking up to the sound of a crowd running outside. Rushing down to the front door to check out the commotion, only discovering what was going on when it was too late. When they were already through the door. Already beating, tearing and biting. Who knows how many died in their nightgowns? How many were killed before they even awoke?

Thank fuck I live on a dead end street.

This must be why I didn't see anything on the way to the coffee shop. Our place is in an old, sketchy industrial neighborhood that used to be home to a few small factories and warehouses. It's in the process of being gentrified, but right now the buildings are mostly boarded up and gutted. If the infected are attracted to sound, or light, or... I don't know, the *smell* of humans there wasn't much to draw them to my little cul-de-sac. They must have flowed right by as I slept, drawn by the sound of the fireworks from the boats on the river.

"Heads up, kids." Arnold tears me back from my imagination. "We got action here." He points ahead, a little further down arrow straight Flatbush to the intersection with 7th Avenue. A truck trailer has been pulled most of the way across the road, its rear shunted up against the front window of a Duane Reade, leaving a gap just large enough for a car to pass between the truck and the stores on the other side of the street. On top of the trailer a couple of soldiers – or, at least, guys who look like soldiers to my untrained eye – stand and watch us. One peers through a set of binoculars for a long moment then turns and speaks to his partner, who lifts a hand and waves us closer.

Arnold pulls the car forward at a little more than walking pace until we're just a few car lengths from the trailer, and one of the soldiers holds up a hand then waves it in a circle. *Roll down your window.*

"Do you have any injured?" he calls out.

Arnold pokes his head out the window and calls back. "What was that? Speak up, son."

The soldier leans forward and yells. "Any injured? Anyone bitten or scratched? No injured allowed."

Arnold turns to Kate with a questioning look. She looks at me for approval, then gives him a nod. "It's OK, we won't tell." Fuck that. I'm sure they're hurting for medical supplies in there, but I'm not about to leave Arnold to fend for himself after he kept Kate safe. If he's infected we'll deal with it later, after he's had the chance to say goodbye to his wife. He doesn't deserve to die out here, all alone.

"Uh uh," he calls back. "Nobody here but us chickens. You got survivors in the park? I'm looking for my wife."

The soldier doesn't answer. He lifts a radio and speaks into it for a moment before turning back to us. "Turn right on 7th," he yells, his voice echoing across the street. "Then continue forward to 9th Street and add your car to the roadblock."

At that he waves us through with his gun. Arnold doesn't wait for anything else. He shifts the car into gear and drives quickly through the gap, his face glistening with sweat and his breathing heavy.

"Thank you," he says in a quiet, shaky voice. "I know you should have turned me in." He shifts in his seat and winces at the pain. The cream leather beneath him squeaks as he moves, and I see it's stained red. "Don't worry, Marcy'll know to have brought a first aid kit. No need to waste supplies patching up an old timer like me."

We slowly drive down 7th Avenue, and for the first time since the moment I flicked on the TV this morning I almost feel safe. At each intersection the street is blocked by cars and trucks, some of them piled on top of one another. They must have some kind of heavy plant nearby to shift the vehicles, I figure, or they've recruited the Hulk to help them build their roadblocks.

This continues all the way down to 9th Street, where a yellow JCB with an enormous scoop slowly levers an old cab up onto its hood until it finally falls, upside down, on top of a beautiful silver Porsche 911 ragtop. I can't help but wince as I watch the windshield cave in under the weight of the cab. It feels like such a waste. The street is thronged with old beaters. Couldn't they have spared the nice cars?

A young soldier flags us down, and Kate rolls down her window.

"OK, guys, you can just pull it into that gap right there." He points to a break in the cars by the Porsche. "Wedge it as best you can, understand?"

Arnold leans over Kate and berates the soldier. "Son, I've been driving this car fifteen years. She's like a *child* to me. Why don't you just use one of these other cars and leave her be?"

The soldier shoulders his rifle and leans in the window. He looks like a twelve year old preshaver, but he does his best to stick out his chin and act like a tough guy. "Because, *sir*, we don't have the keys to these cars. It takes ten minutes for this fucking earthmover to push each one onto the pile, and I need to get this street secured by sundown. Now shut up and wedge the damned car."

Arnold turns away from the soldier and puts the car in gear. "Sorry, Bessie," he sighs, pulling it slowly into the gap. "I guess this is where we part ways." He coasts it gently up to the Porsche and stops a couple of feet from the front bumper. "You were a good girl." He pats the wheel and cuts off the engine with a sigh.

The young soldier turns back from his work directing the JCB and calls out. "Pull it in closer, old timer. I want it wedged right up against that Porsche. No gaps."

Arnold reluctantly restarts the engine, shifts into gear and slowly, gently pulls the car a few more inches closer before putting it back into park. There's still a solid six inches of space between the vehicles.

"Jesus!" yells the kid. "We're making a roadblock here. Stop being so fucking precious about it. Pull. It. *Closer.*"

Arnold shuts off the engine and calls out. "You know what, fuck you, kid. This is my damned car."

"Easy now, Arnold," I warn, resting my hand on his shoulder. "We don't want any trouble, OK? We have bigger things to worry about than a car."

My words have no effect. Arnold seems to have slipped into that recalcitrant state shared by crotchety old people and little kids who flat out refuse to eat their vegetables. I'm sure he knows deep down that he's acting irrationally. He knows it's crazy to try to protect a car when the world is collapsing around him, but he's been pushed too far by an uppity kid holding a gun, and now he won't move another inch. He crosses his arms and stares down the soldier.

"Oh, for the love of God," the kid sighs. He pulls his rifle down from his shoulder and holds it menacingly, pointed at the asphalt in front of the car. "I'll do it myself. Get out of the car, sir." Arnold stares straight ahead and tightens his arms. "Get out of the car *now*."

With the final word he lifts the muzzle of the gun and points it directly through the window at Arnold. Kate flinches in the front passenger seat and lets out a panicked cry. She grabs Arnold by the arm and shakes him. "Do what he says, for God's sake! Arnold, this is crazy!"

Kate's voice seems to get through to the old guy more effectively than the gun pointed at his head. He looks at her and sighs, slowly uncrossing his arms, and mumbles. "It's just..." I can't see his eyes from the back seat, but I can hear tears in his quivering voice. "Bessie belonged to my son." He places both hands on the wheel and holds it tight, like he's holding the hands that used to rest there. "He didn't leave much when he went to Iraq, but I promised him I'd take care of her until..." his breath catches in his throat, "until he came home to us. And I always did. Washed her every Sunday, rain or shine.

Kept her running smooth." He looks up at Kate with tears in his eyes. "It's what James would have wanted, you know?"

Shit.

The young soldier moves closer, the stock of his gun pressed up against his shoulder. He taps the barrel against the window. "Get out *now*," he orders. I can see the barrel shaking a little. This kid has probably never fired a shot in anger. There's fear in his voice. Panic. His finger twitches over the trigger. He's liable to do something stupid.

I slowly, carefully push open the back door, making sure not to startle the kid, but he still wheels around on me, the gun pointed right at my face. "*Woah, woah, unarmed!* Steady now, there's no problem. I'm stepping out of the car, OK? Please don't fire." I hold my hands palms forward above the door and slowly climb out, taking care not to make any sudden movements. When I'm finally on my feet I gently push the door closed and take two long steps back towards the trunk of the car, just to make sure the kid doesn't think I'll make a lunge for him.

"Please, sir, can you just give him a minute to say goodbye?" I plead. I realize how stupid this sounds, but I guess there's no other option. "Look, this was his son's car, and the kid died in the Gulf. He's not trying to be an asshole, it's just his last connection with his kid. You're a soldier, you must understand what it's like for the parents. Can you give him a break? Please?"

The kid's eyes dart from me to Arnold and back again. His finger is still on the trigger and the barrel is still shaking like crazy. I'm terrified that the the slightest breeze might make him twitch. I've never had a gun pointed in my face before. My adrenaline is spiking, and I can feel my heart thump in my chest. It takes all my strength to avoid ducking behind the car, but I know the slightest move might set him off.

Time passes. Who knows how long? Every second feels like an hour with that barrel pointing at my nose, but eventually I see the kid's trigger finger relax a little. The hyper, agitated look fades from his eyes, and he slowly lowers the gun. I can *feel* it running down my body as the barrel moves, tracing a line from my head to my feet. I don't dare take a breath until it's finally pointed at the ground.

"OK," the kid sighs, nodding. "I'll give him one minute."

I duck my head down and look into the car. Kate's comforting Arnold. His shoulders are shaking, and his head is pressed against the steering wheel.

"Thank you," I sigh, taking a long, shuddering breath. "I really appreciate it. I'm Tom." I hold out my hand, but pull it back when I see the kid take a tighter grip on his gun. "Umm... Can I offer you a cigarette?" I point to my pocket, and with slow, exaggerated movements reach in and pull out the pack.

"Karl," the soldier replies, still a little nervous. "I don't smoke."

"OK, well I do, and if I don't have one now I might have a coronary. You sure know how to make a guy shit himself." I let out a little chuckle, and start to relax when I see a shy, embarrassed smile appear on the kid's face.

"Sorry about that," he says, speaking like a human for the first time. "Rough day, you know? Between you and me I'm scared out of my mind."

I nod in agreement. "You and me both. I'm still hoping I'll wake up soon. This has to be some kind of fucking nightmare, right?" I light my cigarette and point to his fatigues. "So what are you? Army? Navy?" There are a couple of patches on his shoulders, but nothing I recognize as a branch or rank.

Karl looks down at his uniform, seemingly embarrassed. "Umm..." he mumbles, "JROTC."

I shake my head. "Sorry, I'm pretty clueless about the military. What's that?"

His cheeks burn red. "Junior Reserve Officers' Training Corps," he mumbles quietly, suddenly looking like even more of a scared kid. All of his bluster has evaporated. "I'm in high school. I'm just a cadet." He shakes his rifle. "I've never even used one of these. We train with old M1 Garands, and I never even used live ammo before..." His voice trails off. His lower lip starts to quiver for a moment, but he manages to pull himself together. "And now they've put me in charge of building this roadblock. Just me and Gary." He points to the guy in the cab of the JCB, carefully maneuvering his scoop beneath another car. "I just wanna go home. I don't wanna do this any more."

I don't really know what to say to that. "There's nobody else who could help?"

The kid laughs bitterly and shakes his head. "Last I heard there was a unit from Fort Dix coming to relieve us, but that was three hours ago. Who the fuck knows what happened to them between there and here?"

"So who's in charge?"

Karl snorts. "Some Lieutenant Colonel. I don't know his name. *In charge* might be the wrong term, though. There are only a couple of dozen soldiers. *Real* soldiers, I mean, from the 69th. Most of the battalion was deployed months ago. There's only a couple hundred reservists left behind, and they're spread pretty thin across the city. Most of the guys here are either retired veterans or cadets, like me." He looks down at his oversized fatigues. "We got plenty of uniforms, but no soldiers to fill them."

"Jesus," I gasp, suddenly acutely aware of just how exposed we are here in the street. "I thought this was some kind of huge military operation. You know, battleships off the coast, jets flying overhead, that sort of thing. You're telling me it's just a few guys and an earthmover?"

Karl leans back against the hood of a wrecked car and rests his rifle against the tire. "Yeah, pretty much. I'm only here because I live down the street in Bensonhurst. Guy on the news said FEMA was setting up a camp in the park, but when me and my dad got here there was only the colonel and a few guys. No sign of FEMA anywhere. It's FUBAR. We're blocking up the streets as best we can, but who knows what comes next? We don't have any tents. No cots. No medical supplies. The only food we got is whatever we can find in the stores behind the roadblocks, and who knows how long that'll last?"

I get the feeling Karl is only holding onto his cool by a slender thread, and I can't blame him. I can't imagine what it must feel like for someone his age to be handed a gun and told to defend a bunch of helpless civilians. He looks like he could burst into tears at any moment. I don't want to push him, but I need to understand the situation. "How many people came to the park?"

The kid shrugs. "Too many to count. Hundreds. Maybe a few thousand. The man on the news said... you know, we just thought it'd all be OK if we came down. He said it'd be safe for us here." He turns away from me, embarrassed, and wipes a tear from his cheek. "And now all I can think is how safe can we be if kids like me are in charge of building the roadblocks, you know? The situation's gotta be pretty desperate, right?"

I drop my cigarette and crush it beneath my boot. "Well, you look to be doing a damned good job to me, Karl. I'm sure you'll make a fine officer. Your dad will be proud." I feel dumb saying those words. I don't have a clue if he's doing a good job, but he seems to straighten his back a little at the compliment. He rubs his moist eyes and smiles awkwardly.

"Thanks," he mumbles, embarrassed. He stands and points to the car. "OK, we better get this thing moved. You think he's had enough time?"

I nod. "Yeah, that should be enough. Thanks, Karl."

I walk to the driver's door of the car and tap on the window. Arnold's head is still resting against the steering wheel, but he seems to have stopped crying.

No response. I tap again, but still he doesn't move. I pull open the door.

"Come on, Arnold. It's time." I place my hand on his shoulder, but I can tell right away that something isn't quite right. Something... I can't put my finger on it, but the hairs suddenly stand up on the back of my neck. There's something I'm missing. Something my conscious mind hasn't noticed.

"Arnold? Hey, buddy, can you..." My voice trails off as it finally clicks. I can feel Arnold's muscles moving beneath my hand. They're... rippling. Tensing. Bunching together as if he's preparing himself to get up. But he's not breathing. His chest isn't moving. Hasn't moved since I opened the door.

"Kate," I whisper quietly, barely loud enough to drown out the sudden thumping of my heart. "Get out of the car, honey. Quickly."

Kate looks up at me with a a puzzled expression. "What– "

"*Now*, Kate," I hiss. "Get out *now*."

She doesn't see what's going on, but the urgency in my voice makes her move quickly. She turns and fumbles for the door handle, but beneath my hand I can feel Arnold's muscles twitch and quiver like there's a light current passing through his body. I tighten my grip, pressing his shoulder down as best I can.

"Kate, *get out!*" I yell.

She finally pushes open the door and tumbles out into the street as Arnold lifts his head from the steering wheel, moving as if I wasn't even holding him down. Kate kicks her door closed and the old man's head snaps around to chase the sound, giving me the chance to back away and slam the driver's door.

Now he turns back to me, and my fears are confirmed. This isn't Arnold any more. The twinkle has gone from his eyes. They're just blank now; dark, unfocused orbs surrounded by ashy skin, hunting for the next target.

I back away from the car slowly, remembering the little girl I saw in the Prius. I figure I can keep him from attacking if I just move slowly enough, but he proves me wrong. The moment I move a muscle he launches himself at the window, his muffled bellow drowned out by the sound of the JCB engine droning by the roadblock.

"Karl!" I yell, stumbling back away from the car. "Shoot him!"

The kid grabs up his rifle, but doesn't point it at the car. "I can't!" he cries.

I turn to him, grab his shoulders and roughly shake him. "Karl, fucking shoot him!"

The terrified kid lifts his gun up to me and flips it over. "*I can't!*" he yells again. "It's loaded with fucking blanks!" He points to the magazine. "It's a training rifle. We don't have enough ammo to go around!"

"Oh *Jesus*. Some fucking safe zone." Arnold continues to throw himself against the door, and I just know it won't hold out long. A crack has already appeared in the window and it's spreading with every blow.

I look around for my bat, and swear under my breath as I realize I left it on the back seat of the car. Far too risky to try to get it back now. The kid's rifle might make a half decent club, but something tells me Arnold will take more killing than the guy back in the antique store. He's an old man but he has a good few inches on me, a barrel chest and thick arms. I can only imagine what would happen if he got the chance to launch himself at me.

I cast my eyes around the street and panic for a moment when I realize Kate has vanished from beside the car. It's not until I hear her yell that I realize what's going on.

"Get out of the way!" I look up and see Kate clinging onto the cab door of the earthmover, waving me aside. The driver turns the wheel and powers forward towards the car, and as the enormous tires bump against it he pushes a lever and sends the heavy scoop pressing down.

I run towards the earthmover and yell out for the driver to stop, but the sound of the hydraulics drowns out my voice. I can see right away that his plan to crush Arnold won't work. The scoop isn't nearly large enough. It only reaches halfway across the car, and as it pushes down, bending the steel frame with a tortured squeal, the weakened driver's side window bursts outwards.

Arnold squirms his way out through the window, falling to the ground as the bench seat of the car folds and cracks behind him. His foot is caught for a moment in the twisted door frame and I imagine I can hear the ankle snap as the crushed frame pins it, but he pulls his foot clear with a yank, tearing off a shoe and leaving a bloody smear down the side of the door.

I watch, helpless, as he pulls himself to his feet and breaks into a limping run, closing the dozen feet between him and the frozen, petrified kid in the space of a single breath. Karl holds up his gun like a shield, but it does nothing to stop Arnold. The old man takes the kid down like a bowling pin. They both vanish behind a car, and as the engine of the earthmover cuts out I hear Karl's frantic, petrified screams, broken by dull thumps that sound like a meat tenderizer slapping against a steak. The screams gurgle and fade until the thumps are all that's left. Steady. Regular. The sound of Arnold's fists pounding against Karl's lifeless body.

"We have to get out of here, *now*," I whisper, holding my hand up to Kate. She takes it and climbs quickly down from the JCB. "You too," I say, nodding at the guy in the cab. "Get out of there."

The guy clings to the steering wheel and shakes his head frantically. He's too scared to speak.

"Get down *now*," I hiss, pointing at the ground. *What the fuck is with this guy?*

The driver leans over and grabs the edge of the door. "Fuck that," he says, shaking his head frantically. Before I can stop him he pulls the door closed, shutting himself, in, and the clapping sound of steel on steel rings out across the street. The thing that used to be Arnold stands from behind the car and swings his head towards us.

I don't wait to see what happens next. I hop down from the cab, grab Kate by the hand and set off east at a dead run, the JCB blocking us from Arnold's sight. Behind me I hear him wail, and as we sprint I have just enough sense to feel ashamed that my first thought is to hope he'll pick the driver as a target before us.

We've cleared around ten car lengths by the time I hear the JCB engine sputter back to life. I risk a quick look behind me, and I'm horrified enough by the sight to come to a halt. The vehicle plows forward towards the roadblock as Arnold climbs clumsily up the side. I don't hear the driver's scream above the sound of the engine, but I can imagine it clearly enough as Arnold forces his way through the open window and into the cab. His legs vanish inside as the JCB hits the roadblock, pushing the cars aside with ease, opening up the road to anyone – any-*thing* – that might try to come through.

Kate grabs my hand and pulls. "Come *on!*" she cries. "There's nothing we can do for him."

I start sprinting again, struggling to keep pace with Kate as she tears away towards the park. My throat burns with each breath. My legs ache but I keep going, following Kate until we reach Prospect Park West, pass through the gate and burst through into the park. We sprint by a parking lot to our left, through a row of thorny bushes and out onto a broad tree lined jogging trail. Still we run, following the path through the silent, empty park. We pass the baseball diamonds where I play with a team from my local bar every Sunday. We turn left at the calm, peaceful lily pond where I walked with Kate after our first date, then through a copse of thick, dense trees until we burst out onto the broad field where families picnic every warm day through the summer.

We slow. I almost stumble and trip over my feet as I break out of the sprint into a jog, then a walk. Finally I stop, gaping in awe at the sight ahead of us.

The field is full. Bursting with people, with barely a blade of grass to be seen among the thronged crowd. Old people. Little kids. Husbands. Wives. Families. Thousands of them stretching as far as the eye can see, just sitting there as if this is a regular Saturday afternoon. As if they're here for a picnic, and they're about to fire up the barbecue and toss a football.

And barely a soldier in sight. Just a few guys in fatigues overwhelmed by countless civilians. Not a single APC. No Humvees. No tanks. Not even an old Willy's Jeep.

These people are sitting ducks.

They're all going to die.

•᷉•

:::7:::

FOOD?

ARNOLD ROLLS himself from the body of the driver and lands awkwardly in the gap between the seat and the door. His body doesn't seem to be responding to his commands quite as well as it did just a little while ago. Everything feels a little... creaky, like old, rusted hinges. There's no pain, though. His body just feels numb.

His head is foggy, too, like everything has gone a little soft and fuzzy around the edges. Everything apart from the hunger, that is. And the rage. Both are painfully sharp, like needles digging into his brain.

He rests his back against the door and watches the body for a moment, like a cat watching a dead mouse, waiting – hoping – for it to start moving again. His fists open and close, ready to launch into it once again at the first twitch.

His heart isn't really in it now, though. The body had seemed so attractive just a few moments ago, with its yelling and squirming, back when it had been... different. It had been irresistible. The noises it made sent Arnold's brain fizzing. The way it tried to scramble out one window as Arnold climbed in the other both excited and enraged him. The sound and movement were like catnip. He just couldn't resist reaching out and grabbing it, catching it by the belt of its pants and pulling it back into the cab. He couldn't resist pounding until it stopped struggling. It was... satisfying.

Now, though? Not so much. It just lays there like a rag doll. Still. Grey. Dull. Arnold reaches out and touches it, hoping against hope the movement will start again. If it starts again maybe he can take a bite this time. It seemed so enticing just a moment ago, but now the body holds little interest.

Still it refuses to move.

And still.

Still nothing. This is getting boring now.

Moldy bread.

The random synaptic misfires that pass for thought in what's left of Arnold's mind dredge up a dusty old memory, back from... back from before, the other time. The memory plays out in his head like a foreign movie without the subtitles. He doesn't really understand the nuance, but he can just about grasp the general drift.

He's standing in a dark room, carefully, quietly reaching for things. Bags. Jars. Knives. He's putting something together in the darkness by feel, remembering where everything is kept. He moves slowly, trying not to make too much noise. Two slices of bread with something between them. Tasty. He's been looking forward to this for hours.

He lifts the thing to his mouth and takes a big bite. Chews. Chews again, then stops. Something tastes wrong. He reaches out to the wall and pushes something, and suddenly the room is painfully bright. He squints his eyes for a moment until they adjust to the light. He looks down at the thing in his hands, and suddenly he understands the problem. The bread is covered in gray and green patches of mold

Mold is wrong. Doesn't belong there. Shouldn't eat.

It's in his mouth, wet and mashed up and sticky and disgusting, pressed into the gaps between his teeth. Stuck in the crevice where a molar cracked and rotted to the root years ago. Deep in there, where his probing tongue can never reach. Where only a toothpick can free it. He gags, bends over the counter and spits the wet, mashed glob onto the white surface, but he can still taste it. He can still feel the texture of the mold, sticking to him like a sheet of rice paper pressed against the roof of his mouth.

He gags again, but this time he feels the vomit rise up his throat, hot and stinging. It splashes on the counter and the liquid brings with it thick, wet chunks that stick in his throat on the way up. Something goes the wrong way and lodges somewhere deep in his sinuses. He can smell it. He tastes it in his throat. He can *feel* it there, coating his tongue. He presses a finger against a nostril and snorts, trying to dislodge the chunk stuck deep in his nose, but it only makes him retch even harder.

He tries to make it to the basin before the next wave arrives, but he doesn't move quickly enough. Another retch, and the fresh puke joins the rest with a sickening splash on the countertop. Above his gasps he hears the dull, wet spatter of liquid dripping from the counter to the linoleum below. Thick, acrid bile burns his throat as his vision swims through tearful eyes, and a bubble of spit and puke bursts on his lips as he gasps.

The movie stops playing, and now Arnold understands. The thing next to him is like moldy bread. He thought it was good, but it's not good. Not now. Now it's gross. Gone bad. Don't eat. Only eat the fresh ones. Only eat the ones that move.

He lashes out and pushes the body further away, suddenly disgusted with it. It slumps against the door of the cab and the head dangles out the open window on its broken neck, like a baseball glued to a Slinky.

It's still too close for comfort. Arnold doesn't want to be trapped in here with it a moment longer. He's... *scared* isn't quite the right word, but it's close enough to describe the confused stew of instinct, impulse and childlike emotion running through a brain that's operating on little more than the stem. He twists his body to the right and sees the door he entered through. There's some sort of catch on it, a black steel stick jutting out from the shiny yellow door. Some dim half-memory tells him he could use it to make the door swing open, but he seems to have forgotten exactly how that would work. No matter. The window is open. He can still think clearly enough to know he can squirm through the gap to escape, just as he squirmed through it to enter.

It seems a little more difficult this time. He moves more slowly now he isn't so excited, and his clothes keep catching on things. It takes a long while, but eventually he gets enough of his weight over the edge of the window to tumble out and fall back to the street. He lands on his shoulder and hears something snap, but still there's no pain. He's just numb.

Arnold stands slowly, using the side of the earthmover for support. He can't really turn his head to the right now. When he tries he feels like there's something blocking him. There's something wrong with his right foot, too. He looks down and sees pink and white bone just above his ankle, jutting out from the side like a sharp blade. The foot is bent inwards, and his weight rests on its side. He can still walk, though. After just a few clumsy steps the bone has torn through enough skin that he can rest his weight on the pointed tip. It crumbles a little, but soon enough it seems to smooth to a decent stump. The foot drags uselessly behind it like a sad, deflated balloon.

Up ahead he sees another body slumped against a car. Small. Dressed in oversized fatigues, the chest and face caved in, and the light brown desert camo scheme of his jacket darkened with blood. Arnold curls his lip in disgust and makes sure to stay well away from it. Moldy bread. Bad. What a waste. He's hungry now. Famished.

He bumps up against something hard and turns quickly, ready to fight. It's a car, the roof crushed down almost flat. Another memory tries to break through, but this one doesn't come with a movie. It's just a vague hint of a thought, like a dream that seemed so vivid just a moment ago but now slips just out of reach. Something about this car was important, but it doesn't look like there's anything of interest there now. Just a little smear of blood down the side of the door. It doesn't look appetizing.

There were more here. More... what's the word? People. They were in the car. He dips his head beneath the bent door frame and peers into the wreckage curiously, but the broken seats are empty. They were here. He knows they were here, but now they're not here. His mind no longer has a firm grasp on the concept of time, but the randomly firing mass of flesh still works well enough to tell him that the people must have gone somewhere since he last saw them.

But where?

His head jerks up at a distant sound carried on the breeze. Some kind of high pitched feedback squeal, somewhere far away. He turns his head this way and that, trying to home in on the noise. It seems to be coming from everywhere, bouncing through the streets and echoing off the walls. There's no way to tell–

No, wait. There it is. It's coming from somewhere ahead. Through the broken line of cars and down the long, straight road. Whatever it is it's coming from that direction. That's where he has to go. He can feel that fizzing sensation return.

His head spins around at another sound behind him, but he quickly sees that it's nothing to get excited about. It's just another one of *them,* like him. Hungry. Angry. Excited. Can't eat it, though. The smell isn't right. Another one appears from behind a car, and then another off in the distance from around a corner, far behind. They all heard the sound, and they're all moving in the same direction. Some can move faster than him. Some aren't so broken. Some don't have to drag a useless foot behind them. It makes him angry to see them walking faster. Jealous. The other ones might get there before him, and all the food will be gone.

He sets off as quickly as he can move, dragging himself towards the distant sound. It's stopped now but he remembers the direction it came from. All he can hear now is the slow, steady click and grind of his bone against the asphalt, and the low, curious groans of the others quickly catching up to him.

He's excited now, but he doesn't know how to show it. His mouth doesn't seem to work like it used to. He wants to speak, but all he can do is groan.

No matter. He'll get to eat soon.

•۷•

:::8:::

I CAN'T HELP but think of 9/11.

I remember I'd turned eleven years old a few days earlier, and my party had marked the end of a long, glorious, lazy summer. The school year had officially begun the previous day, September 10th, but my first day back been postponed for a week thanks to some emergency with the plumbing in the cafeteria.

I didn't really give a damn about the reason, I was just over the moon to get a bonus vacation week. It felt like magical extra time had been conjured up out of thin air, just like when as an adult you wake up thinking it's time for work, then feel that soft, warm little thrill when you look at the clock and realize you still have two more hours to sleep. It was fucking fantastic. One more precious week of waking up late and watching cartoons in my pajamas

Unfortunately my mother had other plans. She had to go to work, and since couldn't find a sitter on short notice I was packed off to my great uncle's deli on Fulton Street, a weird little place that stank to high heaven of pickled beets and, forever creeping from the little cubby behind the stock room, stale cigar smoke. Mom said a week of honest work would be character building, much more valuable than anything I'd learn at school, and she was right. By the start of my second day I'd already learned an important life lesson: the smell of pickled beets and old cigar smoke makes me gag.

I was sneaking in a quick nap on the toilet when Flight 11 hit the north tower, really stretching out that first crap of the day as long as I could, hoping my uncle wouldn't knock on the door and make me help out in the store. I'd been in there for twenty minutes when I heard a dull rumble and felt the room shake a little. I remember the mirror trembled on the wall, and my reflection blurred for a moment. I had no clue what was going on, of course. No one did, not when it started.

At first I thought a transformer might have blown somewhere nearby. That was usually the answer to any mysterious explosive sound, much to my disappointment. Whenever I heard something potentially exciting I'd always rush as quickly as I could out to the street, hoping I might be lucky enough to find myself faced with a gory car crash or a cool fire, but it was always another damned transformer, overtaxed by the summer heat.

This time was different. By the time I reached the street there was already a confused crowd gathered around. The traffic had stopped, and people were out of their cars and looking up at the sky to the west where a thick, dark shroud had already started to draw over the city like the ash cloud from an erupting volcano. This *never* happened, not in New York. Even if one of those city-sized spacecraft from Independence Day really did hover over the city people would barely break their stride. New Yorkers don't stop unless they're on fire, and even then it'd have to be a big one.

I started to run without thinking. I didn't know what the hell was going on, but I knew this was exciting. Finally something interesting was going down, and I was there to see it. By the time I reached the Hilton on the corner of Fulton and Church I knew this was big, and when the north tower finally hove into view my sprint slowed to a jog, then a walk. Then I just stood there and gawped, like everyone else.

You'd have to have been there to really get how it felt. It was just... confusing. The streets were packed with hundreds of people who'd been attracted by the noise. Thousands. Some stood there and watched. Others tried to get as close as possible. A few ran as fast as their legs could carry them in the opposite direction. People kinda laughed and shook our heads at those guys, because... well, if you run away you're not a real New Yorker, y'know? Nobody wants to be thought a tourist. Certainly not me, Brooklyn born and bred, always eager to make it clear that I was a true city boy.

At first it was all a little lighthearted, believe it or not. A couple of people were making dark jokes about... I don't know, something about the Merrill Lynch annual company barbecue. I don't want to make these people sound awful, but you have to understand they didn't have a clue what was going on. Of course they wouldn't have cracked wise if they'd understood what was happening. And again, these were New Yorkers. You don't last long in the city without developing a strong grasp of gallows humor

The jokes stopped when the south tower was hit.

I couldn't see much from where I was standing. The Hilton blocked my view of the south tower, but everyone on the street heard the impact even if they couldn't see it. We suddenly knew that this wasn't a regular fire. This wasn't just some *how was your day, honey?* story people would be telling over the dinner table. This was serious.

Whispers started to pass back through the crowd. Some people nearby said they'd seen a plane through a gap in the buildings, and a couple of minutes later a cab driver said the radio was reporting that a light aircraft had hit the north tower. Those around him corrected him at first, telling him he must be confused. The guys on the ground were saying they'd *just now* seen a plane, right before the south tower erupted in smoke and flame, but the radio seemed to be talking about the first explosion. There can't have been two planes, right? *Right?*

That's the way it went for the next hour or so. It was just a huge game of Telephone, rumors passing through the crowd as we all watched the towers burn. After a half hour of confusion and fear news of the Pentagon attack rippled down the street. That one came straight from the radio and the TVs playing in the cafes and delis along Fulton, so we assumed it was legit, but other rumors couldn't be so quickly confirmed. There were whispers of an explosion outside the White House, and another at Sears Tower. Someone mentioned something about an attack in London, or maybe Paris. A woman beside me managed to get through to her sister on the phone, and she said there were more planes in the air headed for the city. It was just endless. Rumor upon rumor, rippling through the crowd and carrying waves of fear and confusion along with them.

That's just how I'm feeling now, almost two decades later, standing in the middle of a crowd of thousands in Prospect Park, clutching Kate's hand for dear life. Nobody has any solid information, but in a situation like this rumors flood in to fill the vacuum.

A guy in a torn suit in front of me waves his phone in the air. "I've got no bars, is anyone getting any bars?" A few around him shake their heads, frowning with concern at their useless phones as if the lack of signal is a greater tragedy than the hordes of murderous creatures roaming the city.

"My sister said the army's taken back Manhattan up to Central Park," a woman claims, waving her phone in the air as if it amounted to proof. "I just got through to her before the signal died."

"Bullshit," grumbles a wiry old man, pointing his cane at the woman. "My son was on the payphone, and he says the news said there's nobody left alive in the city."

The guy in the torn suit takes a knee in front of the old man. "When was this, sir?"

"Just now!" he proclaims. "Ask him yourself, he's right there. Hey, Ron! *Ron!* Come over here and tell 'em what you told me."

The old man's overweight son looks up from a conversation with a young woman and turns in our direction, then slowly makes his way over to us, red faced, overexerted by the short walk.

"Umm," he says, catching his breath. "Yeah, so Fox says they lost contact with D.C. about a half hour ago. They don't know where the President is."

"No, you idiot," the guy's dad scolds, "tell them what's goin' on here."

"Oh right, right," he replies, ignoring the insult. "New York is *gone.*" He waves a hand in a slicing motion. "Just... gone, all the way up to, like, Yankee Stadium or something. They sent a traffic chopper over the city and it's just overrun. Corpse city." He lets out a nervous laugh and a woman beside him gasps, reaches out and claps her hands over her kid's ears.

"Jesus," she sobs tearfully. "My husband's in Manhattan. Can you show some damned respect?"

"Umm, sorry ma'am," the guy replies, cowed.

The first woman waves her phone again. "That's not true. My sister just said the army's at Central Park, pushing north."

"What, your sister told you?" the fat guy snorts. "Who are you gonna believe, your sister or Fox News?"

"*Duh*. My sister. Those assholes at Fox are probably just trying to get a bump in the ratings. They'd *love* it if New York was ruined. I bet– " Her voice is drowned out by a painfully loud high pitched squeal as someone switches on the PA system. The sound continues for a solid five seconds before someone pulls the plug and the agonizing feedback cuts out.

I pull Kate away from the group by the hand and lower my voice as we pass through the muttering, gossiping crowd. "OK, we need to get the fuck out of here right now. Let's go."

She tugs back on my hand, drawing to a halt. "What? Why? We're safe here, right? Why the hell would we go back out there?"

I shake my head and lean in closer. "Look... OK, you can't react to what I'm about to say, OK? I don't want to panic people." I drop my voice to a whisper. "That kid back there, the soldier? His gun was loaded with blanks. He said they don't have enough ammo to go around. These people can't protect us."

Kate shakes her head in disbelief. "What are you talking about? Who told you that?"

"He did. Karl, the kid. He said there's supposed to be an army unit coming up from Fort Dix to secure the safe zone, but they never showed. All they've got is a few reservists and a couple of cadets. This isn't a safe zone. It's all just..." I wave my hand around, searching for the right word. "Theater. It's a fucking *buffet*. Just a few old guys and kids playing soldiers, trying to keep people calm. They can't keep us safe." I look across the field at the thronged crowd. "And look at these people. Look how unprepared they are."

Kate looks around and shrugs her shoulders. "What do you mean?"

"I mean look at these guys." I point to a young family sitting in the shade of a tree nearby. They have a suitcase open before them, their hastily grabbed belongings piled inside. "Look at their stuff. There must be a dozen pairs of heels in that bag. And what's that, an Xbox? Seriously? No food. No water. No weapons. No warm clothes. Just... stuff. Random crap they don't want to get looted. They think they're going straight home once this all blows over, but they're *not*. Those things are coming, *soon*, and even if they don't find us this bunch of morons will tear itself to pieces when they realize there's nothing to *eat*. If FEMA doesn't arrive with water purifiers there'll be nothing to drink, either. They're not prepared for this. Hell, neither are we, but at least we understand how deep in the shit we are."

I nod my head towards a skinny, tearful hipster kid sitting cross legged on his own, clutching a cotton Whole Foods grocery bag to his chest. Peeking from the top I can see dozens of vinyl sleeves.

"Jesus, look at this asshole. Does he thinks he's gonna fight off a bunch of infected with his limited edition Smiths album? Where are all the fucking guns?"

Kate stays silent. We've often argued about the need for stricter gun control – her for, me against. I agreed with her that it was pretty pointless to keep one for home protection, but even though I'm one of those knock-kneed lefty wimps the NRA people laugh at I always insisted they were necessary for just this kind of situation, when the shit hits the fan and law enforcement collapses.

Kate thought that was a crazy idea. Her late father had been a cop, and she couldn't wrap her head around the concept of a world in which he and his kind wouldn't be there to protect us, or might even work against us. A cop had tucked her in every night as a kid, and the idea that the uniform meant anything other than absolute safety just didn't fit with her world view. I could never figure out a way to convince her that the society we knew might not last forever.

It didn't help matters that her dad had been shot and killed in the line of duty when she was twelve. A bodega robbery gone bad. Wrong place at the wrong time. Her opinion on guns was fixed for life on that day.

Just a few months ago, a couple of weeks after she moved into my apartment, I told her we should buy a handgun just in case. Just as last ditch insurance, to be kept locked securely in a glass case marked *break only in the event of the apocalypse*. I told her we could keep the ammo right on the other side of the house. Hell, we could keep the gun in pieces, scattered around the apartment like a damned jigsaw puzzle so it was impossible it could ever be used by accident. She gave me an ultimatum: I could live with her or I could live with a gun, but not both.

I chose her, like an idiot.

I get the feeling now wouldn't be a great time to say I told her so.

"OK, so where do you wanna go?" Kate finally asks. "I'll follow your lead, but I don't want to go back out there without a plan, OK?"

"Agreed," I reply, resisting the urge to rub her nose in it. The last thing I want is to have to face the apocalypse with a girlfriend in a bad mood. "We need information. *Real* information, not this rumor mill crap. Karl told me there was some colonel running the show."

"Babe?"

"If we can find out where he is maybe we can pin him down and get some intel."

"Babe."

"OK, so keep your eye out for one of the soldiers. They must know where to look."

"*Tom!*"

I finally realize she's tugging on my sleeve. "What is it?"

"Follow my finger, genius," she replies, exasperated. "Doesn't that look like somewhere a colonel might hang out?"

I look over in the direction she's pointing, out at the edge of the field. It's the park administration office, a squat gray concrete building with a cell tower climbing from its roof. The front door is wide open, and beside it a soldier stands guard, his M16 slung over his shoulder.

"OK, yeah, that looks like a good place to start," I grudgingly concede, and start walking towards the building. I know it's dumb but my injured pride forces me to open my mouth again. "You were still wrong about gun control, though."

Kate slaps me lightly on the back of my head. "Whatever, babe. Keep walkin'."

•⸙•

:::9:::

"*WHOA WHOA WHOA*, hold it, guys. The building is off limits." The soldier sidesteps to block the door as we approach, and reaches behind him to pull it closed.

I take a couple of steps back. I'm in no mood to have an M16 pointed at me again today, even if there's a good chance it might be loaded with blanks. "Is the lieutenant colonel inside? We just need to get some information."

"That's affirmative," replies the soldier, hiking his gun up against his chest and staring straight ahead. "And he's far too busy to deal with civilians. What do you need, kid?"

I bristle a little at the word 'kid.' This guy may not be a young cadet like Karl, but he's not all that much older than I am. Maybe mid-thirties, well built with a close cropped head of salt and pepper hair. I check the insignia on his chest and dig through my memory for his rank. "We need to know which direction is safe to get the fuck out of here, Sergeant. We want to get out of the city."

The sergeant shakes his head. "Negative. Orders are to keep civilians within the safe zone perimeter until reinforcements arrive. We need to sweep the whole area before we release anyone. Can't have folks running around the streets while we work. Just relax, OK? You're perfectly safe."

I feel my hands ball into fists at the thought of being detained. "*Safe?* You know this area isn't secure, right? We just came from the roadblock at 9th Street, and I can tell you it's been compromised. At least one of those things is on this side of the barrier. It killed one of your guys. Karl. You know him, Sergeant? He was sent out there with fucking blanks in his gun."

The sergeant's stern expression softens a little, and his shoulders slump from attention. "Karl? Jesus. He was a good kid." He tugs his radio up to his mouth. "Kilo Six, this is Alpha Niner. I have critical intel, copy? Over."

A tinny voice comes back a few seconds later. "Alpha Niner, copy. Send it."

"We have a potential breach at– " He turns to me. "You said 9th Street?" Back to the radio.

"9th Street roadblock. Possible man down, possible hostiles within perimeter. Over."

"Roger that, Alpha. I'm aware of the situation. I have two friendlies down, and multiple hostiles have been taken out. Roadblock was breached, but has now been secured. Over."

"Kilo, acknowledged. Alpha out." The sergeant lowers the radio. "See? Nothing to worry about, guys. We got this. Now, I'm going to have to ask you to– "

"*Negative*, Command! We have multiple civilians on site. Confirm your last!" An angry male voice booms through the wooden door, and the sergeant falls silent and turns his head to listen.

"Request recall on those bombers, Command. I got more'n three thousand healthy, uninfected civilians here waiting for an evac route. You have to give them at least *some* chance."

"What's going on?" I ask.

The sergeant holds up his hand to silence me. "Shhh. Hang on." He turns and pushes open the door a couple of inches with his foot, careful not to make any sound, and tilts his head to hear more clearly.

"Sergeant, what's going *on*?" I insist.

He waves me away and hisses impatiently. "Will you shut the fuck up for a minute?"

When I hear the voice through the door again it's much quieter. The anger seems to have vanished, replaced with a dejected acceptance. "Understood, Command," the man sighs. I hear the faint, tinny response, too quiet to make out the words. "No, I'll *do my duty.*" Those last words are spat out, a hint of the anger returning. "May God have mercy on you all. Out."

"Fuck." The sergeant pulls his foot back and lets the door swing closed, and when he turns back to us his face has lost all color He grabs his radio and raises it to his mouth, but seems to reconsider before he holds down the button.

"What is it?" Kate demands. "What's going on?"

The sergeant ignores her, takes a deep breath and finally clicks the send button.

"Kilo Six," he mumbles. "Operation Clean Sweep is a go. Repeat: Operation Clean Sweep is a go." He closes his eyes tight and presses the radio against his forehead for a moment before continuing. "Sal, I'm bugging out. You're with me, right?"

The sergeant keeps his eyes tightly closed, as if he's silently praying until the response comes a few seconds later. "That's affirm, Alpha Niner. Will rendezvous at 5th and Prospect. Maintain radio silence. Out." He sighs with relief.

"Sergeant," I insist, "what the fuck is going on?"

The sergeant swings his rifle up to his shoulder, takes a brief look behind him at the closed door and starts to jog towards the trees, calling back over his shoulder. "If you want to live, follow me."

"What are you talking about?" I continue. "Hey, *stop*!"

The soldier doesn't break stride. "Come or stay, guys, it's all the same to me. I'm getting the hell out of here."

I turn to Kate and shrug my shoulders. "What the fuck? What do you wanna do?"

Kate chews her thumbnail for a moment, deep in thought. "I don't know," she finally replies, "but I think it might be a good idea to follow the guy with the gun."

I nod in agreement. Something about this sergeant rubs me the wrong way. I don't trust him as far as I can throw him, but the ashen look on his face makes me think that sticking around here to wait for help might be a bad career move.

"OK, sergeant, we're with you." We run to catch up with him as he vanishes into the trees, and both of us struggle to keep pace with his stride. "Now what the hell's going on?"

"What's going on, son," he says darkly, keeping up his steady pace, "is that an hour from now New York is going to have a sudden heatwave. Now keep up. There's a damned good reason I'm moving quickly."

·⸙·

:::10:::

ARNOLD SEES THE trees ahead of him. He's lost the trail. The sound stopped a while ago and he can't track down the source, but the gentle movement of the trees draws him in. Behind him the streets are silent and still. Up ahead the branches sway and rustle in the breeze, and that's enough to urge him forward. Movement means life. Life means food.

He stumbles across a low chain blocking the entrance to the park, almost losing his footing, but he manages to plant his broken stump down on the other side and stay on his feet. He looks around. The others are still behind him. They don't seem quite as smart as he is. They move with less purpose, and they don't seem as driven. Maybe it's because Arnold has already taken lives. Maybe he's got more of a taste for it.

Maybe he's just a little more hungry than the others. He doesn't know. Doesn't care.

He drags his ruined leg across the silent car park and out onto a patch of grass. Ahead of him he sees trees and bushes, but none of that interests him. His senses are tuned to something else, and something tells him he's not too far now. Soon he'll get to eat.

As he stumbles through the bushes and emerges onto a broad field of baseball diamonds a dim memory sparks in the slurry that used to be his mind. He remembers... something right on the edge of his memory, fighting its way through. Something about noise. Cheering. People. Right here. Something about this place means people. Maybe there are some still here, hiding somewhere.

He stumbles towards a row of white wooden bleachers. This is the place. This is where the people come, but there's nobody here. It doesn't make sense. This is where the people come, so why aren't they here?

The others behind him grunt impatiently. They want food, just like him. Where's the food? Where's the–

His head spins around at a sound carried on the shifting breeze. It's faint, but unmistakable. Voices.

The others pinpoint the source of the noise before he does, and they're already moving before Arnold sets off in a new direction. They all move north, more quickly now, towards a thick copse of trees.

People are somewhere on the other side. He's just sure of it.

He's excited.

•▼•

:::11:::

"OPERATION CLEAN SWEEP, that's what they call it." The sergeant shrugs his rifle to his shoulder and quickly vaults the low stone wall separating the park from Prospect Park West. I help Kate across and we jog to catch up with him. "Clean Sweep means we're royally fucked. It means we've lost control of the situation, kid."

"It's Tom," I say, scowling at him. "And this is Kate."

"Well, I'm Sergeant Laurence," he replies, his voice dripping with sarcasm, "and I'm positively *thrilled* to meet you. Now do you wanna stop and have a little tea party, or do you wanna shut the fuck up and let me explain?"

My fists ball up, but I manage to hold down my anger. "Fine. Go on."

"That's what I thought. OK, so we've got a pretty slim playbook for this kind of end of the world shit. We're not geared up for homeland defense on this scale, so we don't have many great options for a city like New York. Our first and best hope was to blow the bridges, and use our– "

"Operation Pied Piper," Kate interrupts. "Yeah, we already heard about that." Laurence gives her a surprised look. "We came in with a firefighter who was involved in the planning," she explains. "He... he didn't make it."

"Right. OK, then you know Pied Piper was designed to cut off Manhattan and clear the city of hostiles. Maybe not completely, but enough to clear the way for ground forces and Operation Dragnet."

"Dragnet?" I ask. I haven't heard of that one.

"Sweep and clear. That was supposed to come next, once Pied Piper had taken out the bulk of the hostiles. Heavy ground forces would move south from the Bronx to secure and sanitize Manhattan one block at a time. Nothing fancy. Just slow, methodical work with well equipped and well armored infantry. Would have taken weeks for them to reach Battery Park, but it would have left the city intact and ready for reoccupation." He stops beside a parked Escalade on the corner where 5th Street meets the park, looks around and nods, satisfied there are no hostiles nearby. "OK, we wait here," he says, climbing up onto the hood for a better view of the street. "Sal will be along in five, then we get the fuck out of here."

"So, Dragnet," I say. "Sounds like a good plan to me."

Laurence snorts. "Yeah, it *was* a good plan, and it might have worked if luck had gone our way." He shakes his head and spits. "Whoever started this shit, they knew exactly how dumb we can be. See, all the scenarios we gamed out to retake the city, they were all based on the idea that the shit would start in one place. We thought they'd pick a crowded, central spot and infect hundreds of people at the same time. Thousands, maybe. Get a good swarm going."

"They didn't?" I ask, trying to hurry the story along.

"Uh uh. Now, I'm not far enough up the chain of command to know all the ins and outs, but I know a couple of guys in army intel who know the score. They said the NSA keeps constant surveillance on multiple key targets across the city. You know, Times Square, Central Park, most of the subway stations, that kind of thing. Since Bangkok they've been snooping on everything from police chatter to webcams to Instagram, watching out for anything that looks like an attack at those sites. They thought they could identify an outbreak within a few minutes and set things in motion before it had time to spread. They ran drills for this shit."

I pull my cigarettes from my pocket and offer them around. Kate shakes her head, and Laurence pulls one from the pack without thanking me. He plucks my Zippo from my hand and cups it against the breeze, taking a long pull before continuing, the cigarette bobbing up and down between his lips as he speaks. "I've no idea if the fuckers who did this knew we were watching for it, but they decided to kick it all off where we didn't have eyes. The first reports that came in were from places like, I don't know, Hoboken. Red Hook. Astoria." He blows out a cloud of smoke. "We were expecting it to start with a huge riot in Times Square, you know? Not with a couple of guys attacking a cab driver in Harlem at six on a Saturday morning. I don't know Harlem well, but I'm guessing that's not all that uncommon."

I light my cigarette and take a drag. "So you mean we were taken by surprise?"

"Surprise? Shit, there's an understatement. Forget five minutes, they didn't figure out what was going on for fucking hours. By the time they managed to get Pied Piper in place the infection had already spread. It was in Manhattan, Brooklyn, fucking Jersey City. Everywhere, man. Game over. All Pied Piper did was save *our* asses.

It cleared out most of Brooklyn, so we get to sit here on this nice quiet street and enjoy a smoke, but shit... these things are everywhere else, and they're spreading further by the minute."

I can feel an icy shard in my chest. It's been there since I first heard the colonel on the radio, but now it's grown so large it feels like it's hard to breathe. I don't want to ask the obvious question. I don't really want to know the answer, but I know I have to.

"So... Operation Clean Sweep? That's what I think it is, right? They're gonna destroy Manhattan?"

Laurence nods. "Bingo, kid. Clean Sweep is the nuclear option." He sees my shocked expression. "Not *actual* nuclear. We're not dumb enough to nuke ourselves, it's just an expression. Right now six B-2 bombers are on the way from Whiteman AFB in Missouri, loaded with a fuckton of the latest in thermobaric ordnance. Those are fuel-air bombs, kid. Nasty fuckers. 500 yard blast radius, massive damage. An hour from now they'll raze the city to the ground and rip out the lungs of everyone from Yonkers to Newark. Trust me, we *don't* want to be around when those bombers arrive."

"Jesus," I mutter. I've read about fuel-air bombs, and I know there are few worse ways to – "Wait, *what?* Newark to Yonkers?"

Laurence nods. "Of course. We have to stop these fuckers spreading, and they're not just in Manhattan. We have to make sure we get every last one. I figure they'll try to cover a ten mile radius, so long as they have enough firepower."

"But what about everyone back in the park? We're just gonna let them die?" I look over at Kate and see tears pricking her eyes. "There were *kids* back there, man."

"Hey, get off my back!" Laurence snaps. "I'm not dropping the damned bombs, am I? I didn't sign up for this shit. What do you want me to do, stick around and die with them out of solidarity? Sit in a nice little prayer circle and hope we fly right up to Heaven? Fuck that."

"We could at least warn them. Jesus, at least we could give them a fighting chance to get out before the bombs hit. How can we just leave them?"

Laurence sneers. "You really don't get it, do you? This is about survival of the *species,* boys and girls. This is it. If a few thousand uninfected have to die to make sure we hold that line it's a small price to pay. Hey look, our chariot awaits."

I follow Laurence's pointed finger south, where an enormous armored vehicle decked out in desert camouflage turns from a side street onto Prospect Park West. It's so wide it clips the wing mirrors of the parked cars, and I wince at the painful screech as its armored flank scrapes along the side of a panel truck sticking out too far into the road. The thing looks like a tank, apart from its eight huge wheels. As it draws closer I notice some kind of machine gun mounted to the roof.

"What the hell is *that*?" Kate asks, mouth agape.

Laurence slides down from the hood of the car. "That, my lady, is a Stryker Interim Armored Vehicle." He turns to us with a broad grin on his face. "She's beautiful, isn't she?"

The Stryker pulls up alongside us, and Laurence pats its side as he steps to the back. "Hop in, kids," he says, tugging open the rear hatch and climbing into the compartment. "For your safety please note the location of the emergency exits, which can be found here, here and here. We'll be cruising at an altitude of around six feet, and our flight time today will be however the fuck long it takes to clear the blast radius of several dozen face melting thermobaric explosives. You stewardess will circulate the cabin shortly with a variety of refreshments, and the in-flight movie will be the laugh a minute Bill Murray classic Groundhog Day."

Kate gratefully takes his hand and climbs into the rear compartment of the Stryker. I'm about to follow, but when I reach the door I freeze.

"This thing is... *Jesus*, Laurence, you could fit twenty people back here. And twenty more on the roof."

Laurence sighs angrily. "What's your point, kid?"

I step back from the vehicle and throw up my hands. "My point is that you could save three dozen of those poor bastards in the park. You don't even have to warn them all. Just grab a handful from the edge of the field and sneak them out. We have to go back!"

Laurence pinches the bridge of his nose as if he's coming down with a headache, and he squats down in the rear compartment to my head height. "Look, kid, I've done my two tours. See this leg?" He tugs up his right pant leg, and I'm shocked to see there's nothing there but a carbotanium shaft surrounded by black, calf-shaped muscular mesh. "This country has already taken its pound of flesh, with fucking interest. I've given five years and a leg to the service, and now it's time for Sergeant Laurence to get his dues, understand? I got my buddy, I got my Stryker, and I got my gun."

I feel the hairs stand up on my arms as he looks down at his rifle. A grin spreads across his face, and when he looks back at me his eyes are ice cold. "See, I was gonna be a nice guy about this. I thought you two seemed like nice enough kids, and I decided to do one last good deed before the world goes completely to shit, but you just had to get on my last nerve, didn't ya? You had to peck away and make old Sergeant Laurence feel like a bad guy just for looking out for himself." He levels his M16 at my face. "Well, you just lost your ticket to the fun bus, son. Now why don't you go ahead and take a few steps back?" I shuffle back, my eyes fixed on the barrel of the rifle pointing right at my eyes. "That's right, a little further. There's a good boy."

My throat feels like it's closed up with fear, but I manage to croak out a few words. "Kate, climb down."

Kate starts to move behind Laurence, but he holds out a hand to stop her. "*Ah ah ah*, stay right there, missy. Sal, you got her?" he calls out, keeping his eyes fixed on me.

"Uh huh, I got her," comes a voice from the front of the vehicle. I look behind Laurence and see a young Hispanic guy in fatigues, leaning back from the driver's seat with a pistol pointed towards Kate.

"Please, just let me go, OK?" Kate begs quietly, her voice quavering. "Just let me get out and you guys can leave. We won't make any trouble."

Laurence chuckles and shakes his head. "No, I think you'll be better off with us," he laughs. "I'm sure we can find some use for you."

My hands bunch into fists, and my heart pounds deafeningly in my ears. I've never felt this kind of pure, cold hatred towards another human being before. I want to beat him in the face with the butt of his own gun until I feel it hit the back of his skull. I want to pin him down under the wheels of his Stryker and drive slowly forward, waiting for the weight to squeeze his guts from his mouth like toothpaste from a tube. I want to watch him *burn*.

"Let her go, Laurence," I growl, my voice hoarse. "If you take her I'll hunt you down, and my face will be the last you ever see." Even I know how ridiculous my threat sounds, directed at a trained soldier pointing an M16 at my head from the back of his armored car. I've never felt more hatred, but I've also never felt weaker. I've never felt like such a worthless, powerless pussy, unable to so much as keep my girlfriend safe from harm. I feel like a little kid trying to stand up to a bully twice my size, jutting out my chin and puffing up my chest, knowing that the re-sult will be a fist in the face and more humilia-tion.

Laurence bursts out laughing "Oh, you should see your face, kid," he chuckles, reaching out for the door handle. "Red as a fucking beetroot." He shakes his head and sighs happily. "Well, we gotta go, Liam Neeson. Enjoy the fireworks, y'hear?"

With that he starts to slam the door in my face, but through the gap I see Kate launch herself at the sergeant with murder in her eyes. The door swings back open as her head reaches the guy at stomach level, and the sergeant doubles over in pain as she winds him. I grab the door and climb up as the driver yells out, his pistol waving wildly. Kate scrambles up from the floor and kicks out at Laurence as I grab her and pull her back towards the hatch.

I don't register the shot. I know it's deafeningly loud in the enclosed space, but my ears just don't pick up the sound. All I see is a quick muzzle flash that lights up the dim cab for a moment, then I feel myself pushed backwards as Laurence kicks out at Kate's belly.

The two of us tumble out of the Stryker. I land first, cushioning Kate, and roll her off me onto the asphalt. The first thing I see is blood. Hers? Mine? I can't tell. It all happened too quickly.

"Kate? Kate, get up!" I lift myself to my feet and try to pull her from the ground, but she's limp in my hands. I tug again and her jacket falls open, exposing the white shirt beneath. A red patch spreads across her chest like a terrible Rorschach test. Her eyes are wide open, staring blankly at the sky. I stare at her lifeless body as a pool of blood gathers in the hollow of her throat and overflows, running in twin lines down both sides of her neck.

She's gone.

I barely notice the engine of the Stryker roaring back to life, and before I can react the vehicle suddenly reverses at speed straight towards me. I barely have time to blink before the protruding running board hits me in the stomach, forcing me to double over in pain, bringing my head down just in time to connect with a dull thump against a Jerry can mounted to the back.

The lights go out. I don't feel anything as my body is thrown back onto the road. I don't feel my back as it scrapes along the ground, and I don't feel my head thump against the asphalt. I feel nothing. I hear nothing. I see nothing. I don't see the tires run over Kate's lifeless body.

I don't even hear the screams as they draw ever closer.

•⁊•

:::12:::

FOR A MOMENT my world is nothing but a high pitched tone and a distant point of light.

Slowly, bit by bit, my glazed, unfocused eyes open on the gray sky above, the dark clouds pinpricked with flashes of colored light. My ears are ringing and I can hear each breath as a muffled roar in my head.

Suddenly the pain returns. Shocking. Sharp. I manage to turn my head before the vomit burns my throat, and I cough a spray across the black asphalt from the depths of my empty stomach.

The urge to sleep is overpowering. I'd like nothing more than to curl up on this asphalt bed and just take a moment to rest. Just a couple of minutes, I think, and then I'll be ready to move again. It's only the throbbing pain in the back of my head that keeps me from slipping away, an insistent jab of hot needles that forces my mind to wake. With a monumental effort I manage to raise myself onto my elbows, then force my body up into a seated position. I slump forward and puke again, this time between my legs. I cough again as it dribbles down my chin, spraying my pants and boots in vomit.

I reach gingerly to the back of my head, wincing at the sharp pain as I run my fingers through my hair. They come away bloody, but it's not quite as bad as I feared. I can't feel an open gash. Nothing that feels like it might need stitches. It just feels as if someone has taken a belt sander and gone to town on the back of my skull. The back of my head feels like a piece of tenderized meat, and my vision blurs as I stare at my bloodied fingers.

Apart from the pain in my head I feel... numb. Like I'm trapped in a dream. Everything about this just feels like it can't be real. I can't have woken up this morning to find the city overrun by insane, murderous creatures. I can't have beaten a man to death, and watched as another turned into one of those things. Most of all, I can't have just watched my girlfriend–

Oh. Kate.

I look over at the lifeless body ten feet ahead of me. There's no question she's gone. The vehicle crushed her. I don't even want to look closer. I don't want that to be my memory of her. Not as a crushed, broken rag doll splayed on the ground in the middle of the street. I turn away and blink tears from my eyes.

This can't be real. It's ridiculous. Any minute now I'll wake up in my bed with Kate beside me, just another lazy Saturday with nothing to do but chill out in front of the TV and call in a pizza. It has to be a dream. *Just relax, Tom. Maybe it's OK to lay back down and just take a break for a little while. None of this is real. Why not just rest?*

Moments later reality hits me like a hammer. A sound I've been hearing subconsciously since I hit the ground finally forces its way through to my waking mind, and it shocks me awake in an instant, like a torrent of ice cold water to the face.

Screaming.

Thousands of voices, all of them screaming.

•▼•

:::13:::

ARNOLD'S EXCITEMENT GROWS with each step. He can sense the mood in the group around him. They all sense it. They're all moving more quickly, and they know they're getting close to the food.

The first of the group finally crests a small rise, and Arnold know their search is over the moment he sees the first one break into a run. He's lightning fast. Much faster than Arnold, struggling on his frustrating crumbled bony stump. He's moving slowly now, the spur of bone digging deep into the soft soil with each step, giving him a pronounced limp as he moves eagerly forward.

The moment he hears the first scream his limp is forgotten. Arnold finds fresh reserves of energy and breaks into a clumsy run as the first of them bursts out of the trees and into the crowd. The people scatter, terrified, but they can't move quickly enough in the crowd to escape.

Arnold doesn't pick a target. He simply throws himself into the tumult, reaching out with his good arm for anyone within grasping distance. They keep frustrating him, darting just out of reach as they scatter like a bait ball of swift, nimble sardines evading hunting tuna fish. He can't seem to move quickly enough with his ruined leg and his shattered shoulder throwing him off balance. He fears he'll never get to eat.

And then it finally happens. A woman sprints blindly towards him, so focused on escaping the quicker creatures that she barrels right into him and takes them both to the ground. Arnold doesn't look a gift horse in the mouth. He sinks his teeth into her shoulder as they fall as one, and by the time they hit the grass he feels her blood gush down his throat and spray across his face. She screams frantically right in his ear, but the sound only excites him. It only makes him bite deeper.

Her delicious, exciting screams only last a few moments before they die away into bubbling, whimpering gasps. Arnold raises himself clumsily onto his hands and knees, twisting his head like a crocodile to tear a strip of warm, wet flesh from her neck. The woman convulses beneath him, and with a final breath she coughs hot blood in his face as he chews.

Beneath him he feels her body grow still. Her eyes, so full of terror, panic and pain just a brief moment ago, soften and lose focus, drifting from his face to stare glassily at the sky. He senses she's gone. Her meat is still attractive, but it's not perfect any more. Not quite as fresh and enticing as that of the people still fleeing. Why limit himself to just one body when there are so many to choose from?

He lifts himself slowly to his feet, still chewing his tasty treat as it begins to slide down his throat, and sets out towards the loudest screams. As he stumbles away on his broken peg leg he doesn't notice the woman begin to convulse once again.

He neither knows nor cares what will happen to her, but a few minutes from now she'll be back on her feet and hunting alongside him. She won't remember his face. She won't realize he has a thick strip of her neck coiled inside his belly. She won't know anything, apart from the rage and endless hunger.

She certainly won't care about her luggage, an open suitcase spilling over with a dozen pairs of expensive shoes, nor the broken bodies of her husband and son laying beside it.

•ᵥ•

:::14:::

THE NOISE IS deafening. Terrifying. It's like standing in the bleachers at Yankee Stadium, only the cheers have been replaced with blood-curdling screams.

But it isn't the volume that scares me. The screams pass over me like a wave, and a thousand are no more terrifying than a hundred. Quite the opposite. What scares me – what chills me to the bone – is that as the screams approach I can hear the cacophony grow steadily quieter. I can almost pick them out, one by one, as a voice falls silent, then another, and another. Maybe the people have simply lost the breath to scream. Maybe they've lost their throats. Neither thought is particularly comforting.

I hear the closest screams now, just on the other side of the park wall. Just beyond the trees, growing nearer by the second. I stand frozen, peering into the foliage, searching for movement, and it takes my concussed mind a moment to realize that the low park wall offers me no protection at all. I'm not a bystander here. I'm not passively observing the situation like I'm watching the news on TV. These screams will reach me at any moment. They'll surround me and pass me, and the things that caused them will follow soon after.

I snap out of it and finally wake up. The fog lifts from my mind in an instant, and I hear my own voice above the screams. "You have to get out of here, Tom," I hiss to myself. "Go. *Now.*"

I feel awful leaving Kate's body lying there like discarded trash but I know there's no other choice. My legs listen to my commands for the first time since the Stryker hit me and I launch myself into a clumsy, shambling run towards the intersection with 5th Street. My legs still feel like jelly. They send me careening straight into the side of a parked car on the other side of the street, but they at least propel me away from the screams and towards... it doesn't matter. *Away* is the only word that matters right now.

As I stumble onto 5th Street and start heading west I hear for the first time the groans and pants of the infected, loud enough to carry over the few screams that remain. The ungodly howls force my legs to move faster, launching me down the street at a speed I didn't know I was capable of attaining after almost three decades of junk food and sloth.

Behind me I can hear panting breaths, each one louder and closer than the last. Something is catching up fast, and I don't dare turn around to see if it's human or something else. I can't help but think of runners warning of the temptation to look back in the moments before crossing the finish line. Just a quick, momentary glance to see if there's anyone on their tail can be enough to make them fall behind; enough to cause them to break stride or stumble. For them the error could mean losing their lead by a nose, but for me it could mean death. I don't dare look back. I *can't*.

And yet... it keeps gaining, whatever it is. I won't allow myself the luxury of a panicked cry. I can't spare the breath. I scan the road ahead, searching desperately for some kind of escape route. I know my legs can't keep up this pace for much longer, and I can feel the bile rise in my throat again as my concussed, addled brain yells at me to stop and rest. It insists, firing warnings to my every muscle, forcing my vision down to a narrow tunnel and filling my ears with an insistent, sickening buzz.

My heart soars as I see the door of a townhouse swing open just a few car lengths ahead.

For a moment I wonder if it's an hallucination. The bright red door seems to glow at the top of its stoop, beckoning me in to safety. It can't possibly be real, can it? Surely it's just a cruel joke played on me by my broken mind, tempting me to slow enough for the creatures to catch me. Enough for them to tackle me to the ground, climb up my body and sink their teeth into me as as I waste my final breath on a futile scream.

I've just about convinced myself it's a mirage. I've convinced myself it would be safer to keep running and hope I can outdistance the things chasing me, when a man steps out from the door and waves frantically, beckoning me towards him. I can see his lips move as he yells, but I've no idea what he's saying. Can't hear a word above the ringing in my ears. All I know is that he's undeniably *real*. I don't think my mind is sophisticated enough to hallucinate this fat, bearded guy, his stained white painter's overalls half hiding a T-shirt with a picture of Kevin Bacon's face constructed from strips of bacon.

I reach the stoop at a dead run and launch myself up the steps two at a time. That final explosive effort leaves me running on fumes and feeling as if the air is as thick as water. My legs finally give out as I hit the top of the stoop. They buckle beneath me, but the man saves me before I can stumble, reaching out to grab a fistful of jacket in his meaty hands. He lifts me bodily through the door, throwing me into the hallway beyond like a sack of potatoes before spinning on his heels and kicking it closed behind him.

As soon as the door slams closed, before I can even take my first ragged breath, the wood shakes in its frame as someone – some *thing* – slams against it. I can only assume it's one of the infected. It must have been the thing I could hear breathing, chasing just a few steps behind, and I'm amazed and relieved in equal measure that I managed to reach the door just a moment ahead of it. It must have been almost within grasping distance. Almost close enough to grab me by the clothes and pull me back. I shiver at the thought.

Then I hear the voice. Frantic. Pleading. Gasping. Begging to be let in. Whoever's on the other side of the door is *alive*. He hammers his fists against the heavy wood as he pleads. The man who rescued me rushes back towards the door and grabs the handle, and he's about to twist it when he freezes. The banging stops, suddenly replaced with an ear bleeding scream.

"Oh Lord, I thought he was chasing you," the guy cries, dropping to his knees and lifting the letterbox. "I thought he was one of *them*." He peers through the slit in the door, then immediately falls back in horror. I can only imagine what it is he sees, but I have a fairly good idea when he turns his haunted eyes towards me and raises a shaking finger to his lips. *Quiet.* There's nobody left to save on the other side. Not any more.

I take in my new surroundings as the man moves back to the letterbox and crosses himself. I'm in a long hallway, roughly decorated in the sort of Bohemian, artistic style that cost either fifty bucks or tens of thousands of dollars. I lean back against the curved leg of a wooden table covered in peeling paint and gasp with pain as my head nudges the corner of the tabletop. I forgot all about my head, but now the pain comes rushing back with a vengeance as the adrenaline begins to wear off. I reach to the back of my skull and find a lump that feels about the size of half a baseball bulging under my hair. Shit.

"Do you have a first aid kit?" I whisper, looking around the hallway as if I'll find a video game style medkit lying around.

"Me? Naw," he whispers, with a relaxed Southern drawl that would have seemed oddly out of place in Brooklyn even before its residents started eating each other. He turns away from the door and slides down to rest with his back against it. "This ain't my place, though. I was just here to paint the bedroom. You might wanna check the bathroom or something." He leans in towards me with a hopeful look. "Hey, don't suppose you got any cigarettes?"

I nod and fumble through my pockets for my pack, and when I pull out the box of Marlboros the guy's face lights up. "Thank the good Lord." He catches the pack and the Zippo as I toss them over, and his hands shake as he gratefully slips one out. "I know this sounds shitty, but I pretty much only let you in to see if you had a smoke. Haven't had one all day, and I don't know about you but I really don't wanna go through the Rapture and the shakes on the same day." He takes a long pull and looks up at the ceiling as he exhales. "Ah, that's the stuff. You can call me Bishop, by the way."

"Tom. Freeman. Look, Bishop, we need to get out of here right now."

Bishop gives me a look like I just suggested we climb to the roof and fly away. "No, no, no, no, *fuck* no. Are you crazy? There's no way I'm going out there. I got everything I need right here. Enough food in the kitchen to last 'til Christmas, and I've filled both bathtubs with water. This place'd be perfect if we had more cigarettes. We should just ride it out here until the cavalry rides in and sorts this shit out, y'understand?"

I shake my head. "There's no riding it out. The whole city's going to be flattened by the Air Force in less than an hour. Unless this place has a bomb shelter we need to get the fuck out of here right now. Please tell me you have a vehicle."

"OK, so we can hide downstairs, right? There's a big old basement. Hell there's even a pool table down there."

"That's no good, Bishop." I look at his simple, vacant expression. I hate to make a snap judgment, but I'm not sure he'd be able to get his head around the idea that a basement would be no match for a fuel-air bomb exploding a couple of streets away. I barely understand the weapon myself, but I think talk of blast fronts and the fact that such a bomb could suck the oxygen right out of the building would just confuse him. Better to tell a simple white lie. "They're going to nuke the city. Now, do you have a car?"

"Jesus, it's that bad? Yeah, I got my truck right outside, but you don't wanna go out there. The street's full of those things. We wouldn't get two feet before they tore us up. Here, come take a look."

I pull myself to my feet and shuffle painfully across to the door. Every limb aches now, and I know I won't be able to push myself much further without medical attention and a fistful of painkillers. I crouch down and push open the flap of the letterbox, and my heart sinks when I see what's on the other side. Four infected fight over the remains of a body between the front door and the truck parked by the sidewalk, a beat up old red pickup with the words *F. Bishop Decorators* stenciled on the door.

"OK, we need to get them away from your truck. Do you have a gun?"

"Uh uh," his jowls swing back and forth as he shakes his head. "Couldn't get a carry permit from the city. I've got a bunch of paint brushes and a sandwich I brought from home. I didn't come tooled up for the end of the world, y'-know? You can bet they're dealing with it better in the south, that's for sure."

"Fuck." I wonder for a moment if I should go searching the house for some kind of weapon, but I'm painfully aware that we're running out of time before the bombs drop. We need to be on the road in the next few minutes if we want to clear the blast radius. "We need some kind of distraction. Something to draw them away."

Bishop scratches his beard, deep in thought. "Umm... I don't know, maybe one of us could run down the street and distract them while the other fetches the truck?"

Again I shake my head. "I'm pretty sure I'd pass out if I tried to run right now, and... look, I hate to be rude, but I'm pretty sure you're too heavy to outrun those things."

Bishop looks down at his hefty gut and nods glumly. "Oh wow. I never thought I'd get fat shamed during the apocalypse."

"Shit, sorry, I didn't mean to– "

"Nah, I'm just fucking with ya, man." He flashes a grin and takes a puff of his cigarette. "I think all that PC shit died when people started eating each other, right? You're right, though. A guy like me ain't worth shit in a foot race." He flinches as the burning tip of his cigarette drops into his lap. "Ow! Fuck!" he yelps, brushing the burning ash away.

A thought suddenly occurs to me as I watch the embers glow on his pants. "Wait a minute. You said you were a painter, right? You have all your gear inside?"

Bishop nods. "Yeah, it's all upstairs."

"You have chemicals? Paint thinner, stuff like that?"

"Yeah, some. Why?"

"Show me," I say, pulling myself painfully to my feet. "I think I have an idea."

•⁊•

:::15:::

I PEER THROUGH the curtains of the living room window, scanning the street to make sure the infected by the truck aren't about to be joined by more.

"You think this'll work?" Bishop looks down at the bottle in his hand, holding it at arm's length as if he's afraid it might explode if he so much as breathes.

"Of course it'll work." I carefully pour the clear liquid into another glass Coke bottle, then tear a strip from my spare T-shirt to stuff in the neck. "Look, this is arson 101. You have nothing to worry about. Just watch what I do, OK?"

I stuff the rag into the neck of the bottle, then tip it on end until the gray rag darkens with soaked up liquid. "See what I'm doing? Get the rag good and wet with the acetone, then light it a couple of seconds before you toss it. Piece of cake. Understand?"

"Got it," he nods. "Umm... it's just, well, are you sure this is safe?"

I fill the third and final bottle, and stuff in the rag. "Bishop, I think at this juncture safety is very much a relative concept, don't you think?"

He frowns. "Huh?"

"Yeah, it's safe," I sigh, "so long as you don't drop it at your own feet."

Bishop still looks unsure. "Look, I don't want to say you're dumb or nothin', but see this label?" He picks up the plastic acetone bottle and points at the warning sign. "That means this stuff is explosive." He looks at me, and takes my blank expression for misunderstanding. "That means it might, y'know, blow up. You don't mess with this shit, understand? Are you sure you wanna set it on fire?"

I take the bottle out of his hand. "Bishop, look out the window. Look at those things in the street. Now look at this warning label and tell me what you're more afraid of." I set the bottle down on the windowsill beside the three Molotov cocktails. "The time for warning labels is over, know what I'm saying? Now look, don't worry about this stuff. I'll toss it out. You go look out the letterbox, and as soon as they move away from the truck sneak out and get ready to drive, OK?"

Bishop smiles, relieved, as if he thinks he's been given the safer job. "OK, sure, I can do that. You gotta hurry though, OK? I don't want to wait around for you out there."

"I'll be right on your heels, trust me." I glance at my watch. "I think we have about a half hour to get clear. OK, go on now. Good luck, Bishop."

The lumbering giant takes a deep breath, then heads out to the hallway with a nervous look on his face. I turn back to the window, push it open as quietly as I can and pick up the first of the bottles. The acetone has already evaporated from the rag, so I tip the bottle again until it darkens once more.

The wheel of the Zippo lighter sounds far too loud as I strike it, and I freeze for a moment as one of the infected outside looks up from his meal and casts his eyes around the street. He looks like he heard me, but I have no time to worry about it now. I hold the flame to the rag and flinch as it catches with a soft *woomph* and a pall of greasy smoke, and I slowly, carefully lean out the window and toss the flaming bottle with a slow, swinging underarm throw as far as I can down the street.

It lands with a dull thump around twenty yards away, in a little gated patch of grass beside a stoop three doors down. I can barely see it from the window, but it looks like the flame went out before it landed. *Shit*. Maybe the acetone isn't flammable enough?

I grab the second bottle and tip it on end, holding it upside down even longer this time, soaking the rag until it starts to drip onto the floor. Again I light the rag, and this time the fire is much more excitable. I lean out the window and toss it high up into the air and right in the middle of the street. I pray as it sails in a graceful arc and thank God as the bottle shatters on the asphalt, the sound echoing between the houses. The mob of infected look up as one at the pool of fire spreading in the middle of the road.

Their excitement is immediately obvious. Three of the group sprint at full speed towards the flame, and when they reach it they circle, confused, unsure whether it's something to be attacked.

But there's a problem. The fourth creature is still hunched over the body by the truck, facing away from the flames and oblivious to the excitement, and now his cohort has gotten out of the way I see why. The side of his face I can see is almost completely gone, eaten away. Even from this distance I can see his exposed jaw move as he uselessly chews, the meat falling out of his mouth as soon as he scoops it in. Where his ear once was is now just a pink, pulpy mass of blood and matted hair. He must be half deaf, and couldn't hear the bottle shatter.

My mind races as I try to think of a solution. Maybe I could toss the bottle a little closer to him in the hope that his other ear is good, but that might only draw the others back towards the truck. Maybe if I–

I freeze at the sound of the front door creaking open. I lean out the window and almost call out when I see Bishop step outside. He walks as if he's trying to be stealthy, but for someone that large it would be impossible. Even from here at the window I can hear each footstep as he treads down the steps.

The three infected at the fire seem oblivious, still entranced by the dancing flames, but I know the fourth will launch himself at Bishop the moment he sees him. There's just no way the guy can get into the truck without being detected, and his hands are empty apart from the keys. He doesn't even have a stick to fend it off.

There's nothing for it. I know it's a terrible plan but I grab the final Molotov cocktail and tip it up, soaking the rag. I only have a few seconds before Bishop is fucked. I light it with a *woomph* then toss it as precisely as I can, aiming for a spot just in front of the truck, within the creature's eyeline but out of view of the others.

As the bottle sails through the air my heart sinks. The flame goes out almost as soon as it leaves my hand, and it's wildly off target. In the time it takes to complete its arc I picture what will come next in my head. The bottle will shatter on the street, and all four infected will look up and see the big, lumbering oaf Bishop standing there with nothing but his dick in his hand. They'll tear him apart before he can take so much as a slow, leaden step, and he'll go to the grave with the truck keys. All that will be left for me is to find out whether I'll die in a fiery explosion or get torn apart by those fuckers outside running in through the wide open front door.

My mind is running so fast I barely notice the speed with which Bishop moves. Everything seems to move in slow motion as he sees the bottle, reaches out and scoops it from the air moments before it hits the asphalt, gripping it by the neck with his meaty fist. I don't dare breathe as I watch, amazed, as he brings the base of the bottle down on the back of the creature's head like he's stamping a library book. It doesn't even shatter. It just sends the thing silently sprawling to the ground with a knockout blow.

Bishop turns slowly to the window, gives a cheery wave and flashes me the most shit-eating grin I've ever seen.

I don't waste any time. Already the fire down the street is dying, and I know as soon as Bishop starts the engine the three remaining infected will notice him. I limp as quickly as I can through the house, ignoring the pain radiating through my body, and reach the front door just in time to watch Bishop fire up the engine and fishtail out into the street with the squeal of spinning wheels.

"You *fuck!*" I yell after him, feeling the dull, impotent certainty that my last chance at survival is tearing away faster than I could ever hope to run. "You rotten fucking *cunt!*" I know there's no way to catch him, but I need to try anyway. I can't just stand here and wait for the end to come. If I die I'll die running, dreaming of what I'd do to that fat, cowardly prick if I ever caught up with him.

I almost fall down the steps in my rush to reach the street, swearing under my breath. The three infected have already begun to sprint towards me, and it's all I can do to force my legs to obey my commands. I break into a run knowing that every step is futile. I can't outpace them, and I sure as hell can't outdistance them. Even if

I could I'd never make it out in time before the –

I hear a squeal at the end of the street, the tortured revving of an engine, and I almost can't believe what I'm seeing as I emerge from between the parked cars and get a clear look down the street.

The pickup barrels back down the street towards me, frighteningly quick, and in the moment before it reaches me I see Bishop's grinning face as clear as day through the windscreen. He speeds past me so close that I feel my jacket shift in the turbulence and I spin around just in time to see the truck mow down the three infected, scattering two of them like bowling pins and sending the third beneath the wheels. The truck bounces over it, crushing it to a pulp and leaving the thing sprawled in the middle of the street, twitching its shattered limbs and silently moving its jaw as if trying to bite the memory of the tires.

The truck cruises to a halt, and I see Bishop turn in his seat and look through the rear window as he shifts it into reverse. He drives backwards at speed, aiming for the broken creature, and this time shatters its skull beneath the wheels before bouncing off it and pulling to a stop beside me.

"Woo, what a *rush!*" Bishop grins like an overexcited kid and leans over to push open the passenger door. "Well, you waiting for a red carpet, your majesty? Come on, get in."

I don't say a word as I climb in the car and buckle up. I don't speak as Bishop shifts back into drive and bounces over the pulped body of the creature a final time. I only manage to catch my breath long enough to direct him south to the Verrazano bridge. My heart pounds in my throat, and my vision narrows to a pinpoint as unconsciousness finally overtakes me.

Fucking Bishop.

•⫶•

:::16:::

I DREAM.

I dream the story told to me by Paul Mc-Queen, my old friend back in Bangkok. I'm standing above the street, watching the terrified crowd turn, searching for Kate in the chaos, hoping – *praying* – I'll find her in time to pull her away from the grasping hands trying to pull her down with them to hell.

There she is. I see her hiding from the violence by the side of the street, a solitary blonde head in amongst the dark haired crowd. I yell out to her at the top of my lungs, begging her to run, but my voice emerges as nothing more than a whisper. She can't hear me above the crowd. Doesn't even look my way. She's staring open mouthed at the horror around her. Teeth tearing into flesh. Fingers forcing their way into wounds, tearing them wide open as the victims scream. The street is awash with blood, flowing into every crack in the sidewalk. Filling the gutters until they overflow.

I try to run down to the street to pull her away to safety, but it feels as if I'm wading through molasses. I can't make any headway, and the crowd is only growing more frantic by the second.

Then I see him, standing between me and Kate, blocking the stairway down to the street. Sergeant Laurence. He towers over me, eight feet tall and grinning as he spots me. Blood drips from his smiling lips and runs down his chin and he chews a mouthful of flesh. My feet stick to the ground as if they're buried in cement. I can't move a muscle, even as Laurence charges towards me.

He tackles me by the waist and pushes me to the ground, pinning me down. I can't fight back. Can't even get in a punch as he begins to pummel me. I open my mouth to scream as he leans down over my prone body, but nothing emerges even as his hands reach into my mouth, one gripping each row of teeth, and he pulls my jaw wide open until the skin of my cheeks stretches so much it begins to tear.

Then... a bright light. Blinding. A sound like a freight train in my ears, overwhelming my senses until I can't even feel the pain any more. I close my eyes tight but the brightness doesn't diminish. I manage to raise my hands to my ears but the sound doesn't fade. It only grows louder, and louder still.

"Tom." I barely hear the voice above the roar.

"Tom." A little louder now, breaking through. I open my eyes just in time to see Kate standing above me, a silhouette against the blinding light.

"*Tom!*"

•⸙•

:::17:::

THE SKY FALLS away below me as I open my eyes. I see two suns set at once, one behind me, red, muted and hidden in haze, the other ahead, blindingly bright, impossibly large and close. Just a few feet away I see fire hanging down from above, the fierce flames swept towards me by the wind.

It takes my mind a moment to figure out what I'm looking at. I'm upside down, pinned to my seat by the belt that digs into my shoulder and cuts deeper into my skin with each breath.

I'm still not fully awake. I feel like I'm sitting safely in the back of my own head, watching my life roll by dispassionately on a screen. I look up, craning my neck to the ceiling, and see a shallow pool of blood gather in the creases of dented bare steel. Another drop splashes into the pool as I watch, and I smile at the hypnotic sight of the liquid rising from my head and levitating its way to the ceiling until it hits the pool and sends a ripple across the surface. For a moment I try to figure out the trick. How did they manage to make the blood weightless?

Oh yeah. Upside down. Huh.

It's the next explosion that finally tugs me back to the world. Through the cracked windshield I watch as a black plane drops something, then banks and gains altitude as the falling object sprouts a parachute. It's weird to watch it upside down. It looks like the plane is sailing across a cloud sea, firing its payload high into the sky.

The rumbling of the jet finally reaches me as the parachute nears the ground, but I can't see it any more. It's vanished from my narrow little window on the world, and the thing it dropped falls slowly, gracefully, its silence in counterpoint to the roar of the jet. From my point of view the parachute looks like it's rising slowly into the air, like a balloon that slipped from a child's hand.

The first silent burst makes me flinch in my seat and wince as the belt cuts deeper. It pops silently in a gray cloud, like a monochrome firework, and my mouth gapes open as the gray burst suddenly erupts, a fraction of a second later, in a blinding flash of light, darkening to a deep orange. It's... I've never seen anything quite

so beautiful. I can't tear my eyes away from the
–

The shockwave hits me like a punch to the gut, forcing the air from my lungs. Colored spots appear in my eyes as I struggle for breath, and just a second later the noise reaches me, deafeningly loud. Distant car alarms begin to sound, and somewhere far behind me dogs howl, startled by the noise of the blast.

My mind clears in an instant, and with it the pain returns with full force. I reach up to my side and fumble for a moment until I find the seatbelt release, and I press the button without thinking. I fall hard, landing headfirst in the pool of blood gathered above me, and I scramble quickly through the broken window, my palms digging into shards of shattered safety glass strewn like gravel across the ground.

"Bishop," I call, my voice hoarse and low. "*Bishop!*" I feel like I've swallowed a bag of sand, my throat hurts so much.

As my vision clears I lay on my hands and knees and stare, confused and bewildered, at the scene around me. On either side of the road great steel rods climb high into the air like the bars of a giant's prison cell. Out in front an enormous archway towers over me, the road leading beneath it and on towards the setting sun, away from the artificial sun burning bright in the opposite direction.

It's only after a few moments of confusion that I realize I'm on the Verrazano Bridge, a couple of hundred yards from the Staten Island shore. I haven't crossed the bridge in years – nobody goes to Staten Island without a damned good reason – but I've seen it in the distance often enough to recognize the shape.

Ahead of me the world looks perfectly normal, just as it did yesterday. The sun sets on another lazy spring Saturday in America. Tomorrow it will rise like always to light gardeners tending their yards, golfers perfecting their swing on pristine, overpriced courses, moms cooking and freezing next week's gluten free, low carb meals, bored kids firing racist slurs through their gaming headsets, and everything else people do with their Sundays.

Behind me...

Behind me life will never be the same again for those few who managed to get out. I turn back to look at the Long Island shore and see nothing but destruction. A thick pall of black smoke climbs high in the sky and spreads as far as the eye can see, hiding the bare, bleached bones of my city. Buildings are flattened right up to the shore parkway, and more collapse as I watch. The smell reaches me, carried on the breeze. It's indescribable. *Everything* burning, all at once. Wood. Tires. Trees. Gasoline. Plastic.

People.

My mind can't possibly grasp the extent of the destruction. It's just too big to fit in one head. I can stare at the ruins, but I can't make myself believe that somewhere hidden beneath that shroud of smoke my apartment has been blown apart by an unimaginable force, and everything in it scattered to the wind. My clothes. My ATM cards. My passport, laptop, cameras, the half finished memoir I've spent the last year of my life writing, and every photo I ever took. I can't believe that my parents' house in Queens is gone, following the path they themselves took years ago. Somewhere in the smoldering wreckage their bones are buried, six feet beneath the ground in a cemetery within a cemetery.

My old high school is gone, and the playground where I had my first kiss with Tammy DiMicco. The dank, smoky little bar on Doughty Street where I once got an awkward drunken handjob in the restroom from a middle aged woman who wore heavy jade rings on all her fingers. The humid little bodega where I buy my cigarettes, always filled with a strange, overpowering spicy smell I could never quite place. All gone.

And then there's Manhattan itself.

I can't even think about that right now. It's too much. Too big. Its destruction belongs in movie theaters and nightmares, not the real world.

I look north, and for a moment – just one brief, beautiful moment – I manage to forget the destruction. Far off in the distance, almost too small to see and hidden beneath the smoke, a familiar sight stands tall. Marooned in the middle of the upper bay, caught in the light of the setting sun, the Statue of Liberty rises high above the black water.

"At least you made it, girl," I whisper. I know it's dumb, but I feel comforted that some remnant of the city I've called home for almost thirty years still stands. Even if everything else has been wiped from the earth and ground into the dirt, at least she's still there to mark the grave on the map.

Here Lies New York City.

•T•

:::18:::

A HALF MILE away at the Long Island shore a high pitched hum pervades the air, just at the edge of hearing, if there was anyone left alive to hear. Above the crackle of fires and the creak of settling concrete the hum grows louder by the second. It's the sound of straining. Of tension.

If anyone was around to see they might hear the occasional tortured *twang*, like the snap of an immense guitar string. If they were paying close attention they may just notice, in the heavy concrete anchorage of the bridge's main suspension cables, hairline cracks appearing in the concrete, weakened by the force of the blasts.

•⫶•

:::19:::

"TOM?" THE WEAK voice carries above the breeze whistling through the cables. "Tom, are you there?"

My eyes dart around, searching for the source of the voice. "Bishop? Bishop, is that you?"

"Over here, buddy. Under the truck."

I turn back to the overturned pickup and fall to the ground, peering beneath the wreckage. I see him immediately, his pudgy face smiling weakly out from the narrow gap between the asphalt and the mangled bed of the truck.

"I see you, Bishop." I run over to the truck and crouch down to look through the gap. "Jesus, how did you get under there?"

"I don't rightly remember, buddy," he laughs, then loses his breath and descends into a coughing fit in the dusty air. "I guess I should have been wearing my seatbelt," he mumbles, his voice dry and scratchy. "I just looked around when I heard the first bombs, then it all kinda went to shit. I think I must have hit a barrier or something, 'cause next thing I know I'm out of the truck and all I can see is sky. I'm sorry, Tom, I fucked up. You OK?"

I nod and wave my hand. "Yeah, yeah, don't worry about me, I'm good. Just a few scratches."

Bishop twists his head so he can look out at me, and he winces when he sees my face. "That don't look like a scratch, Tom. You're redder'n a strawberry."

I reach up and touch my forehead, and my hand comes away sticky. "Don't worry about it," I assure him, "head wounds always look worse that they are. Now, we gotta get you out from under there. Can you move?"

Bishop wriggles a little beneath the truck, and nods. "Yeah, thank God. Don't seem to be caught under anything. Lucky escape, huh?"

"I think someone's looking out for you, Bishop," I laugh. "If you were anyone else you'd have already died three times today. Now, we need to lift this thing somehow. I don't think you can squeeze through this gap."

Bishop shakes his belly with his hands. "I knew I shoulda started that diet at New Year. Couple less pizzas and I might have been able to fit. Hang on, I think I can squeeze through if you can just lift it a few more inches."

I move around to the back of the truck and grip the tailgate, but as much as I strain to lift it the truck won't budge. I try again, pulling up until I feel bile rising in my throat and see spots in my eyes, but I can only manage to move it an inch or so before my strength runs out.

"No dice, Bishop," I gasp. "I need some kind of leverage to get this fucker off the ground. It's just too heavy for me."

Bishop bangs his head against the asphalt, frustrated. I crouch back down to see if I can figure out another approach, but it doesn't look good. His body fills most of the space beneath the overturned flat bed. The base of it is just an inch or two from his protruding belly, too low for him to use his arms or legs to offer any help. The only other thing under there is...

"Bishop?" I ask slowly, almost afraid to finish the thought. "What's that thing next to you?"

He turns his head to the squat red canister strapped into a housing in the bed of the truck. It's about the size of a gas bottle for a camp stove, and so dirty I can't quite be sure if it is what I think it is.

"That's the, umm, bottle jack," he says, as if I just asked him to identify a bird that just flew by.

"Bishop..."

He gives me a blank look. "Yeah?"

"You wanna pass me the damned jack so I can lift the car and get you the fuck out from under there?"

The light appears in Bishop's eyes as he finally understands. I wonder if he's always this slow, or if he's just suffering from some kind of shock from the events of the day. He twists awkwardly in place and stretches his arm out until he can just about scrabble at the strap, loosening it with his fingers.

The hum reaches me before the vibration. For a moment I think it's just the same ringing that's been in my ears all day. I think it's just a symptom of stress, or something to do with the fact that I haven't had a bite to eat or a sip to drink since last night, paired with a couple of nasty head wounds.

But then I feel the road shake.

It would be difficult to describe it to anyone who hasn't felt a good sized earthquake. It's not like the road is visibly bucking beneath me. It's just a tremble, easily ignored if I wasn't paying attention, but I can feel it all the way up my legs. Something's happening, and my Spidey sense starts tingling.

"Bishop," I say, trying to keep my voice calm, "maybe you should hurry up and get me that jack. Come on now, get it moving."

"I can't quite..." He bears his teeth and tries to stretch further, but he's at his limit. The thick strap is loosening, but only by a fraction of an inch with each tug. At this rate it'll take forever. I drop to my belly and shuffle as far as I can beneath the truck, and with a little effort manage to reach my hand out to loosen the thing with a quick tug.

I feel the vibration in my stomach as I slide the jack out from under the car. I can't be sure, but it seems to be growing stronger, quickly, and every few seconds I'm certain I can feel a slight jolt. I just pray it's in my head.

"OK, man, get ready to slide yourself out as soon as it starts to lift." I search for a decent jacking point at the bent lip of the flatbed. There's no spot I'd choose in a perfect world, but the nearside corner seems solid enough for the job at a pinch. I plant the bottle firmly on the asphalt beneath the steel, and with shaking hands insert the collapsible lever and start pumping. The piston creeps up painfully slowly, and by the time it finally connects with the steel the hum in the air has shifted to a distant, tortured squeal.

"Hear that noise, Bishop?" I try to keep the growing panic from my voice, without much success.

"You too, huh? I was hoping I was just going crazy." I hear the exact same scared tone echoed in his voice. "That... that's not a good sound, is it?"

I'm pumping frantically now, raising the truck achingly slowly, a fraction of an inch at a time. "No, that's not a good sound. I think the bridge might be coming down. You think you can start to move?"

"Just a couple more inches and I think I'll be able to– what the *fuck* is that?"

•⸱•

:::20:::

BACK AT THE shoreline the tortured cable finally gives way at the south anchorage point.

With the sound of a thousand gunshots the cable snaps loose from the concrete, whipping out across the roadway and tearing the vertical suspension cables from their moorings.

In just a few seconds the unsupported deck begins to tilt down like a swinging trapdoor, held in place only by the single remaining main cable. A wave ripples down the length of the bridge at breakneck speed as the entire section of deck before the first tower crumbles away and collapses into the water below.

•⊽•

:::21:::

BISHOP WRIGGLES FRANTICALLY out from beneath the truck, scraping his ass across the glass-strewn asphalt without a care for the pain. I look back towards Long Island and see the main cable catapult into the air. At this distance it appears as slender as gossamer, but I know I'm watching a couple hundred yards of three foot thick steel spring high into the sky like it's weightless. When the sound reaches me I immediately abandon the jack. There's no time to raise the truck higher. I run around to the side and grab Bishop by the scruff of his neck, leaning back and dragging with all my might to tug his weight clear. He twists and struggles in my grip, fighting to free himself, and the moment his feet clear the truck the road bucks and rolls wildly. The jack tips and the back of the truck collapses, closing on the asphalt like a bear trap.

"Come on!" I yell, pulling Bishop to his feet. "We gotta get the fuck out of here!"

He doesn't need any more encouragement. As we start to run we both hear the tortured snaps as each vertical cable in turn breaks under the load, unable to support the weight of the deck without the help of the broken cables before it. I'm running as fast as my legs will carry me, but if I could see how quickly the chain reaction was catching up with us my legs would be a blur.

•ᛉ•

:::22:::

THE TREMBLING DECK of the bridge collapses piece by piece, dropping a twenty yard section at a time into the frigid black water of the Narrows. The vertical support cables snap from their moorings like cut tendons, springing upwards with the release of tension. The deck beneath each broken section tilts, listing towards the south, straining on the opposite cables until they too collapse under the strain, sending the deck tumbling down into the churning waters below.

The collapse only accelerates as ever more cables fail. The first few sections fell slowly, holding the strain for several seconds before plummeting, but now they fall like a row of dominoes as each remaining section strains under the weight, not only of itself but of the thick, heavy cable sinking to the bottom of the Narrows.

•⸙•

:::23:::

THE NOISE IS deafening now. Each tumbling section adds yet more force to a rumble I can feel resonate through my body. It's barely even sound any more. It's so loud it's become almost a physical presence surrounding me. Beneath my feet the deck of the bridge shakes so much I feel like I'm trying to run across the surface of a bounce house. My knees buckle with every step, and beside me Bishop is doing no better.

"We're almost there!" he yells above the roar, pointing towards the tall gray archway on which the suspension cables rest. It's less than fifty yards ahead of us, and Bishop believes that's the finish line.

I know better. I wish I didn't.

A few years ago, stuck in a cramped aisle seat on a late night Aeroflot flight from Ulaanbaatar to Moscow, I found myself so bored that I spent an hour watching a Russian language documentary about marvels of engineering. I drifted in and out for most of it, but I remember paying close attention when a simulation of a bridge collapse showed up on screen. The image creeps back to the front of my mind now, bringing me little comfort as it dredges up half forgotten facts I'd set aside as useless as soon as I heard them, never imagining it would ever matter to know exactly how a suspension bridge works.

The fact is that reaching the tower won't ensure our safety. Nowhere near, in fact. Beyond the tower there's at least two hundred yards of bridge remaining before it ends in the cable anchorage, and that means there's at least two hundred yards of three foot thick, immensely heavy cable on that side of the tower. I look up, and wish I hadn't. I see four cables, two on each side, along with at least a couple of dozen vertical support cables holding up the bridge. Once the bridge collapses as far as the tower all those cables will go slack, sending the rest of the bridge to the bottom of the Narrows. The cables don't just hold up the center span of the bridge. They hold up the whole thing, all the way back to shore.

No, the only safe place here – and 'safe' is hardly the word – is the tower itself. The tower is the only part of the bridge that's properly grounded, and can stand without the support of the cables. Once this is over there's at least a slim chance it will still be standing.

Bishop tries to accelerate ahead of me, panicking at the sound of approaching collapse. I don't dare look behind to see how close it is, but I know running beyond the tower won't help. We need to find– ah, there it is.

"Bishop!" My voice barely carries over the noise, and he only hears me on the second attempt. "Follow me!" I turn towards the north edge of the deck, terrified that the next big shake will flip me over the edge, but I know there's no choice. The edge is where the only hope of salvation lies.

We finally reach the tower, and I vault clumsily over a railing onto a steel grated walkway probably built for service staff. Through the grating I can see the lower deck of the bridge, surrounded by the thick steel support structure that I'd swear could withstand an asteroid strike if I hadn't already seen it torn apart like wet tissue paper. I feel the grating rattle as Bishop lifts his bulk over and I grip the railing, suddenly afraid that his weight might be the straw that breaks the camel's back.

I don't even try to yell this time. The noise is just overwhelming, and I can see the collapse is only fifty yards from us. I grab Bishop by his collar and point to the steel stairwell running around the outside of the tower, heading down towards the lower deck. I don't wait to see if he understands. I just run.

The steel rattles wildly as the deck collapses around it. I grab hold of the railing for dear life, and my stomach flips over as I feel the stairway break away from the concrete wall. All around me the deck of the bridge tumbles away down to the water far below, and I just cling to the railing and squeeze my eyes closed, praying to be saved by a God I don't believe exists.

The torture goes on for another minute before the noise finally fades. The sound of shattering concrete and rending steel was so loud that its absence sounds even louder. As the last of the bridge hits the water the silence that returns sounds deafening. Alien. Bizarre.

I risk opening my eyes, and when I see where I am my knuckles whiten on the steel railing. The staircase is at least ten feet from the wall of the tower, disconnected at the top and hanging on at the bottom by just a few bolts driven into the concrete.

"Bishop?" My whisper sounds like a yell in the sudden quiet.

"Yep?" The voice comes back muffled, and I look over to find Bishop with his arms wrapped around a steel bar, his face buried in his chest to avoid having to look at the ground fifty yards below.

"You still alive?"

"I don't know." He finally looks up at me and wrinkles his nose. "Does heaven smell like people who've shit their pants?"

I manage a soft laugh. "I don't think so, buddy."

"In that case I'm probably alive. And I need a bath."

"Do you think you can work your way down to– " The staircase creaks ominously, and my heart skips a beat at the sound of a bolt pinging from the concrete. "Move, Bishop, *now*." I try not to sound panicked, but there's no concealing it. I can feel the staircase swing in the breeze, and I know it won't support our weight much longer.

Bishop reaches the foot of the staircase first, sliding across the steel on his belly like a snake, moving nervously from one section of railing to the next. I follow quickly behind, and when I catch up I find him frozen in place, unwilling to cross the yard wide gap between the foot of the stairs and the thick support girder still firmly fixed to the tower.

"Come on, man, you have to climb over there. This thing's gonna fall any second now, understand?"

He clings to the final railing and looks back at me, shaking his head with tears in his eyes. "I can't. I've got a thing about heights, Tom. I can't move."

"Bishop, you have no choice. If you don't get out of the way I can't get across. Either move now or we'll both die. *Move!*"

His mouth just opens and closes silently, and he shakes his head once more. I can see every tendon in his chubby hands picked out like taut violin strings as he clings onto the railing for dear life.

There's nothing for it. I reach forward, stick my hand between his legs and squeeze his balls until he cries out in agony. He lets go of the railing and brings his hands down to protect himself, and I yell as loud as I can. "*Goooooo!*"

By some miracle it works. He's so distracted by the pain he scrambles to his feet and steps across the gap onto the girder, sending the staircase shaking loose as he goes. I shuffle forward as he drops down to hug the steel, and just as I stand to step across the chasm I feel the world give way beneath me.

Time seems to slow to a crawl. It's a strange feeling. My stomach flutters as the support beneath my feet simply stops being there, and for a moment it feels as if the world has forgotten about the laws of gravity. I hang unsupported in mid air, a gap of air between my feet and the rapidly accelerating staircase, and I feel a strange, brief rush of dizzying elation before time comes rushing back with a vengeance. Gravity returns, and I feel the ground far below sucking at my feet, pulling me down to meet it. The last thought that passes through my mind as I begin to fall is simple:

What the fuck is that?

And then I feel myself yanked to a halt. I look up and find myself safe in the meaty grip of a bizarre angel. An angel with a mullet, a scruffy beard and a T-shirt with Kevin Bacon's face painted in bacon strips.

Bishop strains with my weight, shifting himself on the girder to steady me. "Promise me one thing, Tom," he growls, "or I swear to the Lord God I'll let you fall." He takes a deep breath and lets out an angry sigh. "You will *never* touch my balls again unless I damn well ask you to. Is there an understanding between us?"

I can feel my sanity slipping away. Maybe it's the height. Maybe it's the fact that I just watched a bridge collapse around me. Maybe it's the sight I just saw far below. For whatever reason I can't help myself break into a fit of the giggles. I can barely catch my breath, but I finally manage to get it out. "It's a deal. Pull me up."

Bishop lifts me easily with one arm, depositing me on the wide girder where I lean over and hug it for dear life, terrified that I'll laugh so much I'll fall off.

"What's so God damned funny?" Bishop demands, holding a hand over his balls and scowling at me.

"Look down, Bishop. Look at the water," I manage, gasping for air. "Tell me God isn't fucking with us."

Bishop peers nervously over the edge of the girder and finally sees why I've lost it.

Fifty yards below us thousands of tons of shattered concrete, steel supports and the few cars that remained on the bridge have plunged to the depths of the Narrows. Most of the wreckage sank straight to the bottom, but on the way it hit something that doesn't belong.

It hit a net.

Fifty yards beneath us the black, cold water of the Narrows churns and froths like a scene from the end of Titanic. In the darkness countless infected thrash about in the water. Many are tangled in the remains of the net. Many more were crushed by the falling bridge and buried beneath tons of concrete on the riverbed. I look downriver, and in the fading light I see the churning white foam kicked up by thousands of struggling bodies. Thousands of infected floating freely, released from their prison. Many of them will be carried out by the current, I'm sure.

Many of them will bloat and rot far out to sea, without ever setting foot on land again.

But some of them won't. In the dim light I can already see dozens of bodies struggle from the water. Maybe hundreds, dragging themselves to shore like rats.

Bishop plants his forehead on the cold steel girder and closes his eyes. "It's not over, is it?"

I shake my head and watch the land. The power is still running on Staten Island, and as the automatic street lights flicker on street by street they cast their glow on the heaving, wriggling shore, the narrow beach hidden beneath the dark crowds of infected crawling to land.

"No, Bishop." My laughter has gone now. "I think this may just be the beginning."

•፻•

:::24:::

THE SIGHT OF guns is comforting. We're in the back of a covered truck with an armed soldier – a real soldier, not a terrified cadet like Karl, or a sociopathic asshole like Sergeant Laurence – speaking into his radio in incomprehensible military lingo as the truck rumbles down the deserted highway. The sound of radio chatter almost lulls me to sleep, but Bishop nudges me in the side and mutters a few words to make sure I stay awake.

The medic shined a bright light in my eyes when we dragged our dripping bodies up the shore and found the military roadblock at the bridge toll booths, and he warned me that I probably have a concussion. He poured an irresponsibly large pile of Tylenol into my hands and told Bishop to keep me awake until we reached the camp.

I warned the soldiers at the roadblock about the infected reaching shore, and felt a weight lift from my mind as they assured me they had the situation under control. A 'mop-up crew' was working its way along the shore, taking out anything that moved. In fact, they told us, they were about to open fire on us until Bishop yelled at them as we approached.

I wouldn't have blamed them. Bishop looked half OK, but it would be hard to guess I wasn't infected at a glance. I caught sight of my reflection in the window of a toll booth, and if I was armed I'd have pulled the trigger without a second thought. My face was covered with blood, and my hair was plastered to my head. I barely recognized myself, but even if I'd been clean I would have noticed the difference.

It's in the eyes. I noticed them as soon as I saw my reflection. I've seen those eyes once before, looking out at me over a cold bottle of Singha at a rickety table in a bar in Hua Hin, Thailand. They're the eyes of Paul McQueen. They're eyes that have seen things we weren't meant to see. Things nobody should *have* to see. They're the eyes of someone who's lost too much.

I pull my cigarettes from my pocket, slip a damp one from the pack and try to light it, but the wick of the lighter is too wet to catch. The

Zippo just sparks in the dark interior of the truck.

"You got one of those for me?" The young soldier asks. He slips a box of matches from a chest pocket and lights mine, then gratefully accepts a smoke with a crafty smile. "Don't tell on me, OK?" he chuckles, cupping the cigarette and ducking in his seat to make sure the driver of the truck behind can't see. "End of the world, and we're still not allowed to smoke on duty."

The truck turns off the freeway and onto a curved slip road, and I gaze out of the back in wonder. Beside the road I see buildings. Houses, stores, restaurants and gas stations, all with their lights on as if this was just a regular night. There are even a few cars on the roads, just driving along at regular speeds.

I can't fathom it. Ten miles away New York is a smoldering ruin, but here life is just humming along like always. There might even be people out there who don't know what's going on yet. People who stopped to fill up the car or grab a bite to eat after a day on the road, completely oblivious to the fact that the world as they know it is over. I envy them these few blissful moments of ignorance. I feel jealous that they get to to enjoy a little more time believing that tomorrow will hold no more surprises than a new episode of Game of Thrones.

To my right a new sight looms. Row upon row of military aircraft line up alongside passenger jets, behind which sit banks of olive green tents bathed in floodlights. It takes me a moment to figure out where we are, and my guess is confirmed when we pass beneath a large sign: *Welcome to Newark International Airport.*

"Refugee camp?" I ask, flicking my ash casually out the back of the truck as if I see vast military camps every day.

The soldier nods and smiles. "Yep. I guess this is where we'll be calling home for a while. The airspace is closed, so you'll be living right on the runway. Pretty cool, huh?" His smile fades. "I mean not cool. Just... well, you know what I mean."

Bishop climbs to the back of the truck as we turn through an open security gate and drive onto the vast runway. He stares out at the scene like a giddy kid, mouth open and eyes wide as we pass dozens of rows of long tents, their open doors revealing dozens of camp beds in each. The tents never seem to end. I stop counting as we pass the twentieth row, each of them at least five deep. By the look of it each tent must hold at least a hundred people, so just those tents I've seen so far are enough to house 10,000, and still the truck passes ever more.

"How many people got out?" I ask, my voice weak.

The soldier flicks his butt out the back of the truck and shakes his head. "Some. Not as many as we hoped. We're setting up three of these places around the state, but I guess they won't be more than half full. It all just happened too quickly, you know?"

The truck rolls to a halt beside a tent emblazoned with a red cross, and the soldier nods towards the door. "They'll take care of you guys from here. Looks like you'll need a few stitches."

I reach up to my head and wince as my fingers reach the gash on my forehead. I keep forgetting about it. "So, what happens now?"

"Now?" The soldier shrugs and looks out over the endless bank of tents floodlit in the darkness. "Your guess is as good as mine, buddy. But I don't think it's all over." He jumps down from the truck and reaches out a hand. "Something tells me it's gonna get a lot worse before it get better."

I hop down to the asphalt, clenching my teeth at the pain in my legs, and wait for Bishop to climb down behind me. "Worse?" I look back in the direction of New York. In the dim moonlight I can still see the tower of smoke climbing high into the sky from the ruined city. "How could it get worse?"

The soldier shrugs, climbs back beneath the canvas canopy of the truck and taps the side until the driver begins to move. "Don't tempt fate, buddy. Good luck."

"Yeah," I whisper, almost to myself. As the truck pulls away I feel Bishop's arm slip around my shoulder to support me, and he pulls me in the direction of the medical tent. In the distance I see rows of trucks pull onto the runway, each of them carrying what few survivors could be found.

How can this possibly get any worse?

•ᵒ•

BOOK TWO

•ᵥ•

CORDYCEPS

One Month On, A Nation Expects

Published May 4th, 2019 to the New York
Times website
Byline: Editorial Staff

IN WHAT HAS been described as the most extensive mass migration event in the nation's history, the month since the 4/7 attacks on New York City and Washington, D.C. has seen millions flee west from the once crowded eastern seaboard, both to escape the immediate economic impact of the disaster and to allay fears of further attacks on major metropolitan centers.

An estimated 27 million refugees - almost half the population of the now quarantined northeastern region - have already escaped to sparsely populated areas of Missouri, Kentucky, Kansas and as far west as Oregon in an exodus that has quickly overwhelmed the capacity of municipal services, and local governments have been left reeling under the pressure to provide everything from emergency housing and medical care to basic food and potable water.

"We're calling Lexington 'Manhattan West'," jokes Maria Sloane, a mother of three who fled to Kentucky along with an estimated 85,000 former residents of Paterson, NJ, in what has been claimed by some to be an unnecessary economic migration. The group has been temporarily housed in an emergency camp established on the outskirts of the Daniel Boone National Forest, where efforts are under way to find a more permanent solution. "There's lots of money coming into these poor states. I don't really get why they're so mad about it."

While Sloane is correct in saying that the last month has seen an unprecedented injection of capital into struggling flyover states - both from the direct infusion of wealth from new arrivals and generous federal subsidies aimed at relieving the immense burden on regional governments - patience is beginning to wear thin among local residents, with many concerned about what will happen when the cash and good will finally runs dry.

"I don't mind the people from New York or D.C. at all," claims Boyd Wilson, manager of a bait shop on the outskirts of Lakeview Heights, KY. "Those folks really suffered. If a man loses his home I'll throw open my door and offer him a roof, no questions asked, but I just don't understand why we're expected to take in all these other people." Wilson complains that new arrivals from areas broadly unaffected by the attacks have been overfishing the local Triplett Creek, and that Cave Run Lake in the National Forest has become little more than a playground for wealthy easterners who don't respect the sacrifices made by local residents.

"Just last week I had a bunch in here looking for tips on where's the best fishing down at Phelps Branch on the Creek. That's a protected stretch, I told them. They need a special license to fish there, but they didn't give a hoot. And these were Boston folk, I could tell by their accents. There ain't no problems in Boston, far as I've heard. Why can't they just go home?"

Despite the local tensions most would admit that the United States has weathered the storm remarkably well in the aftermath of these unprecedented attacks, with leaders from the United Kingdom and much of Europe praising the difficult but decisive action taken to quell the danger, and the compassionate provision of aid to those affected, using lessons painfully learned from previous catastrophes such as Katrina and Sandy.

There have, however, been strong criticisms both at home and abroad of the heavy handed approach of law enforcement and recalled military forces, including accusations of racial profiling in Baltimore that led to the tragic loss of scores of lives in last week's food riots. There have also been ongoing constitutional questions regarding the legitimacy of the federal government in the light of President Howard's ongoing incapacity and the death of Vice President Lynch. Speaker Terrence Lassiter's accession to Acting President, while recognized as constitutionally valid at the time, has now been called into question by those who claim that the crisis is over, and argue that the reins should be handed back to a Democrat.

The Acting President's fitness to lead is no doubt further challenged by the fact that his government continues to operate from Site R, the secretive underground command post in the Raven Rock Mountain Complex north of Camp David. Detractors have called this an act of cowardice unbecoming of the office, and the fact that the Speaker was broadly disliked on both sides of the political divide even before the attacks leaves him with few allies in the corridors of power. Many commentators argue that the President's refusal to appear in public or even speak to the media in the past week severely erodes the argument that he is equipped to guide the nation through this ongoing crisis.

But what may prove the downfall of the Speaker and his government are not the tensions in the refugee-swamped central states, nor questions of the legitimacy or efficacy of his office, nor even the approaching economic disaster following a month of closed borders and stifled global trade, but the growing disquiet over the continued detention of US citizens in Newark Airport's Camp One. The camp, established on the day of the attacks to house refugees from New York City, has found itself at the center of a controversy not seen since the internment of American citizens of Japanese descent in the 1940s.

Those of us at the New York Times understand more than most the terrible realities of war. All of us lost friends, family and colleagues in the attack on New York, and all who survived the attacks, from the deputy editor in chief to the staff in the mail room, know that sacrifices must be made. We know that if our great nation is to survive these dark times we can't shy away from actions we may not consider palatable in peace time, but the time for transparency has come.

Our questions are simple and direct: will this government admit that upwards of eight thousand healthy, uninfected American citizens have been used as test subjects to develop a vaccine or cure for *Cordyceps bangkokii*? Will journalists, inspectors and other interested parties be given permission to enter Camp One to investigate these troubling claims, and will those detained at Newark Airport be permitted to speak publicly about their time there? If not, why not?

The citizens of the United States demand that these questions be answered. For too long has Speaker Lassiter's government remained silent on this urgent and pressing matter.

•ᐧ•

:::1:::

THEY MOVE CLOSER to my cabin every night. I can hear the screams grow louder, echoing off the steel cabin walls, out across the runway and all the way back to my little cell where they rattle constantly through my mind. I think they took the people two rooms over last night. I can still hear the woman screaming.

The worst thing is that I don't have the first clue what's happening to them. I don't know where they're taken, and I don't know why. All I know is they scream and fight as they're dragged from their cabins. They're sure not going home.

I don't know how long it's been, exactly. I didn't start counting until the sixth – *seventh?* – day, and it was a couple of weeks before I started scoring a mark into the wall whenever they brought dinner, like an old timey convict. The days melt into one another so there may be a few in the over under, but I'm pretty sure it's been around four weeks.

Four weeks since I lost my home. Four weeks since I last saw a TV or read a newspaper. Four weeks since I stood beneath a shower. A real shower, I mean. Not the warm, sudsy drip from a sponge moistened in the bucket I shared with Bishop and Edgar, at least until the old man was taken away. Now the two of us get the bucket all to ourselves, each turning to face the opposite wall as the other cleans himself as best he can, rinsing the soap suds into the sluice by the chemical toilet. They only fill the bucket once a day, so each day we alternate who goes first and who uses the dregs. Luxury.

They started taking blood the first couple of days. A precaution, they assured us, to make sure none of us were infected with a slow burn before they release us. 'Slow burn'. That's what they call an infection from a non-fatal injury. They say it can fester in the wound for a while before it finally works its way into the bloodstream and reaches the brain, but I don't buy it. I don't buy any of this shit. They did a head to toe examination of all of us on the first day, and they already know we don't have any wounds caused by the infected.

It didn't take long before I began to suspect they were drawing our blood to keep us worn out, sluggish and docile. It all adds up. We're anemic. The food is bland and low energy. We constantly feel sweaty and gross. It's the perfect formula to sap our will to do anything. All I want to do is lay in bed and stare at the ceiling. We're ideal prisoners.

It was the day they dragged Edgar away that I really started to worry. He was just a sweet old man from the Lower East Side, one of those guys who lived in the same rent controlled apartment for forty years, even after everyone they know has moved out. Even after a bunch of middle class hipster pricks like me moved in to replace them, buying up entire blocks and opening overpriced boutiques and Starbucks franchises, like yuppie parasites. New York used to be full of Edgars, and this guy was no different than the rest. He liked cats, he thought my generation was a little soft around the middle, and he tried to explain the rules of Bridge. He was harmless. Wouldn't hurt a fly.

That's what made it so weird to see the old man take his final breath through a bubble of blood.

Edgar was already there when Bishop and I were assigned to his room, a couple of days after we arrived when they shuffled us from the tents to long rows of prefab steel cabins with heavy walls and thick doors. He'd set himself up on the cot closest to the door, the first in two rows of four, and he'd already made his little space his own with photos of his late wife and a few books he'd been carrying in his bag when everything went to shit.

I laughed the first time I saw him. I didn't mean to, but it was just so funny to see this wizened, stoop shouldered old guy dressed in oversized army fatigues. He looked like a Captain America experiment gone wrong, peering out at us through a pair of thick milk bottle bottom glasses that made him look like an owl.

I felt bad for laughing as soon as he jumped up from his cot and tried to make us as comfortable as possible. I was supporting myself on Bishop's shoulder as we walked in, still a little weak after losing so much blood and my face stitched up like I'd taken shrapnel, and Edgar couldn't have been nicer. He even offered to move to a different cot so I could take the bed closest to the toilet by the door. He seemed relieved when I turned him down with a smile, and explained to us in graphic detail about the kidney problems that forced him to get up three times a night to use the john. Still, it was kind of him to offer.

That's just what he was: kind. In the two weeks I knew him he didn't have a bad word to say about anyone. He was pleasant with the guards, even after they told us we'd have to be confined to the cabin for our own safety. Even when they stopped letting us sit out on the runway to feel the sun on our backs. Even after they started locking the doors, and the guards started coming on shift armed with M16s rather than just standard sidearms. He just lay there and quietly read his books.

And then he started to get agitated one night a little after dinner, without any warning at all. It was as if a switch just tripped in his head out of nowhere. Nothing much was going on. I was tossing playing cards across the room into a bowl, Bishop was laying on his bed staring at the ceiling, and Edgar was quietly leafing through some dog eared old book when suddenly he slipped a bookmark between the pages, set it down, climbed out of bed and strode over to the locked door.

"I'd like to come out now," he calmly called, tapping his knuckles against the steel. "Guard? *Guard.* I said I'd like to come out now."

I heard boot soles crunch on gravel as the guard walked down the row towards our cabin, and he appeared at the door with a scowl. It was Lewis, the same guy who'd ridden into the camp on the truck with me and Bishop. Sweet kid. He kept us in cigarettes.

"Go back to bed, Mr. Klaczko," Lewis spoke softly through the chicken wire that covered the small open window in the door. "Lights out in ten."

Edgar banged hard on the door as Lewis began to walk away. "You don't understand, I need to come out! I gotta get out now. Open the door." He slammed the heel of his palm hard against the steel, shaking the door in its frame. "*Lemme out!*"

Lewis looked a little shaken at Edgar's outburst, and he kept his eyes fixed on the old man as he tugged his radio up to his mouth and called for backup. As he dropped it back down to his chest he swung his rifle off his shoulder and held it defensively, pointed towards the ground but ready to raise the barrel at any moment, as if this fragile old guy could possibly break the door open. "Back away from the door, Mr. Klaczko. Back away *now*. I won't tell you again."

Edgar didn't even seem to register Lewis' presence. He just kept punching against the locked door, yelling to be let out until his voice broke into a plaintive cry. It was only when he started tugging at the chicken wire that I rolled myself off the bed and walked over to help, and by the time I reached the door Edgar had gripped it so tight his fingers were bloody.

"Come on, Edgar, it's OK," I said in a soothing voice, reaching out to his bony shoulder in an effort to gently pull him back towards his cot. I didn't see the elbow coming. Didn't even feel it as he drove it hard into my nose like a piston. The next thing I knew I was on my ass, my ears ringing and my vision blurred with tears, my bloody nose squashed against my face like an overripe tomato.

I think I may even have passed out for a moment, like a pussy. I couldn't really tell, but all I know is that one second the door was firmly locked, Edgar still tugging desperately at the chicken wire with his bloodied, clawed fingers, and the next it was wide open and the cabin was swarmed with soldiers. They weren't soldiers like Lewis, the fresh-faced young private in carefully pressed fatigues who acted more like an overworked hotel concierge than a grunt, but terrifying black clad fuckers wearing anonymous face masks and knives strapped to their thighs. They looked like the kind of guys who'd go for a piss in tactical formation.

I remember the blow. Edgar rushed for the open door, yelling in a voice that had gone far beyond words. It was just a mournful, keening wail, as if he already knew he'd never reach the freedom he so desperately craved, broken off when the guy standing beside Lewis took a step forward, swung his gun around and drove the butt firmly into the old man's face. Maybe I only imagined hearing the crunch of bone and cartilage. I don't know. What I do know is that Edgar, an 84 year old bag of bones clothed in pale, papery skin, fell to the ground beside me like a sack of potatoes. For a moment a bubble of blood grew on his lips as he let out a breath, and then it burst into a trickle that ran down his gray, wrinkled cheek.

He didn't breathe again. I watched him for a long moment in the stunned silence and his chest didn't move. The thick blue vein in his throat didn't pulse, and his body was still. He wasn't just out cold. There was no coming back from where he'd gone.

One of the soldiers grabbed me by the hair and dragged me towards the back of the room while another trained his rifle on Bishop, still frozen on his cot. In front of me a couple more hooked their arms beneath Edgar's and dragged him out of the room while the rest backed out slowly, their guns still raised, filing backwards through the door and locking it quickly behind them.

We didn't see Lewis again after that night. He was replaced by a group of soldiers we hadn't seen before, each of whom spent an hour or so guarding the cabin door until a workman came along in the morning and switched the bloodied chicken wire in the window with a sheet of steel.

That was the last time Bishop and I felt the breeze. That damned steel plate blocked off our last connection with the outside world, and for the last two weeks we've been stuck in this hot, humid, stinking sweat box with nothing but Edgar's collection of old photographs, a stack of his dog eared books and, over by the door, visible from every corner of the room and weighing on us both even when we're not looking at it, a patch of carpet stained dark with his blood.

•Ϋ•

:::2:::
May 12th(?) 2019

IT TAKES ME a moment for my brain to get into gear when I hear the voice. "Hey, Tom?" I turn to Bishop's cot, surprised to hear him speak. He hasn't made a sound since burping after breakfast this morning.

"Yeah, what's up?" My own voice cracks a little. My throat is dry and scratchy, and I realize I also haven't spoken for hours. It feels good to hear something other than the wind buffeting the sides of the cabin.

"I've been thinking," Bishop continues, his words plodding out slowly in a tone I've come to recognize as meaning he's about to say something stupid, "ain't it weird that, y'know, lots of famous people have probably turned into those things?"

Huh. Compared to his usual nonsense that's not all that bad. "Yeah, I guess. I haven't really thought about it, but yeah, I supposed some of them must have."

Bishop raises himself up on his elbow to face me. "It's weird, right? I mean, just imagine you're walking down the street somewhere in Manhattan, just minding your own business, heading out to buy a pack of smokes, and, like... I don't know, John Lennon or some shit comes running around the corner all batshit crazy, and you're like '*holy crap*, I'm gonna have to kill John Lennon!' It'd be weird, y'know? Like, imagine if he was your favorite singer and you didn't know if you could kill him, and you're wondering if you should just let him get you. Y'know, outta respect or something."

I peer over at Bishop and try to read his expression. Even after all this time locked up together I can't quite figure out if he's really this dumb or some kind of expert troll, just playing with me for kicks.

"You know John Lennon died, right?"

Bishop's eyes grow wide with surprise. "No shit! In the attack?"

"In the— no, like thirty years ago! You never heard that? He got shot outside his apartment. It was global news!"

Bishop sighs and drops back to his cot. "Well God damn, ain't that a kick in the sack? I really liked that guy." He stares at the ceiling for a long moment as I watch him, looking for a telltale smile that might give it away that he's kidding, then he starts to sing under his breath. *"All my bags are packed, I'm ready to go... I'm standin' here outside your door... I hate to–* "

"Are you fucking with me, Bishop?" I demand, halfway between amused and mad.

"What? No! What do you mean?"

I swing my legs off the bed and stare at him, determined to figure this out once and for all. "I mean you're singing a fucking John Denver song. He died years ago, too. Now, are you messing with me?"

Bishop frowns so hard his eyebrows almost meet in the middle. "So who was the guy in Full House?"

"John Stamos. Not a singer. He's... fuck it, he's dead too. All your favorite Johns are dead. All the Johns are dead. There are no more Johns. Now go to sleep, you jackass."

I push myself off the cot, fumble in the jacket pocket of my fatigues for my cigarettes and sigh as I open the half crushed pack. I only have three left. Lewis stopped delivering smokes when he was taken off guard rotation after the Edgar incident, and the new guys refuse to bring us anything other than food and water. I had half a carton stashed under my bed back then, but unless the guards suddenly decide to get real friendly Bishop and I will both be climbing the walls by tomorrow.

I light up the battered, wrinkled Marlboro, take a deep pull and blow the smoke towards the spinning extractor fan in the wall beside the door, wishing I could follow the smoke outside as the fan grabs it and whisks it away. Wishing I could feel the breeze. That I could get the fuck out of here, away from that patch of blood and the still, sweaty, stifling air. That I could find out what the hell's going on outside these walls, and why we're still locked up in here.

I can't deny that the last month has taken its toll on both of us. Neither of us talk much any more. Neither of us can sleep through the night. Bishop seems to be handling it a little better than me - he seems blessed with a blissful lack of imagination that insulates him from the horror - but even he isn't his usual chatty self. When he bothers to speak his thoughts are usually about death these days.

As for me, I can't help but play a constant game of 'if only.' *If only* I hadn't trusted Sergeant Laurence, Kate might still be alive. *If only* we hadn't met Arnold we might have driven straight to the bridge instead of the park, and Kate might still be alive. *If only* I hadn't given up my obsession with the warning of the attacks I would have taken us out of the city that week, and Kate might still be alive. Hell, *if only* I'd just followed through on my plan to learn how to be a real man I might have bought some shack out in the woods, far from danger, living off the fat of the land. I'd have never met Kate, and I wouldn't give a damn if she were alive or dead.

But those thoughts all lead me back here to the grim, inevitable conclusion. I can obsess about a million what ifs, but the only thing that matters is the reality. I didn't do any of those things. I was dumb, lazy, feckless and irresponsible, and now I'm trapped in a steel box and Kate is just another corpse buried in the ruins of New York.

I blow another plume of smoke into the fan and feel a cold sweat beading my brow as I notice the layer of dust built up around the blades. I'd swear it grows thicker by the day, and I can't help but imagine that it's ash from the city, blowing our way whenever the wind shifts, carrying tiny particles of a million burned, rotting corpses towards us. We're surrounded by it, breathing more of it in with each breath, shifting the balance in our bodies just a little more each day from alive to dead as the dust builds up in our lungs, choking us. It makes me —

Hang on.

"Bishop," I whisper, turning my head so I can better hear the distorted sounds filtering through the whirring fan blades. "Did you just hear an explosion?"

•?•

:::3:::

WELCOME TO NEWARK International *Airport.*

The green sign still marks the entrance but it's now obscured by another, more forbidding notice that stands in front, its black letters printed against a red background.

You are now entering Camp One. Entry permitted to authorized personnel only. Deadly force will be used beyond this point.

The sniper takes a slow breath to calm his nerves, exhaling through pursed lips, waiting for his thumping heart to slow.

"Just take your time, Warren. We've got all night. We can wait as long as it takes. Do you need anything?"

He looks up from the scope with an impatient scowl. "I need you to shut up and let me focus, Vee, OK? I've never committed treason before, so I'd like a minute to get used to the idea."

Victoria Reyes nods silently, biting her tongue as Warren shifts uncomfortably on the asphalt, returns to the scope and delicately adjusts the reticle.

The ghostly image of the guard glows green in the scope, illuminated by the light inside the guard post. It should be an easy shot with his trusty M40A5. Just 200 yards or so to a well lit, unobstructed target on a level plane, with nothing more to worry about than a gentle, steady tailwind. A novice could make this shot on his first attempt with a well-calibrated rifle - and Warren tends to his like a father to his son - but still his hands tremble. Once he squeezes the trigger there's no going back. He'll be a traitor to his country, and a traitor to the Corps. Seven years of service to - and a lifetime of love *for* - the United States will be wiped out in an instant. He'd never be able to explain this to his father, rest his soul.

He takes another breath and clears his mind. There's no point worrying about it any more. He knows what he has to do, and he knows this is the right thing, even if it feels wrong. The decision was made days ago, and the facts remain the same now as they were then.

A final breath. His pulse slows, and he finally finds his way to that cool, focused part of his mind he keeps locked away from the rest. The simple, analytical place that doesn't care about anything but wind speed, distance to target, air temperature and humidity. He exhales, pauses, gently squeezes the trigger...

The guard drops out of sight a moment later. A clean head shot through the open window. Warren smoothly pulls back the rifle, snaps the cap back on the scope and surveys the scene. In the distance off to the right he watches a couple of guards patrolling the outer perimeter, heading away from the entrance. They keep up their slow pace along the outer fence. They didn't hear the shot. He knows from watching them over the past few nights they've become complacent and lazy, and they won't be back for at least twenty minutes. Maybe longer, if they decide to stop for a smoke along the way.

"OK, let's move," he whispers, slipping the rifle over his shoulder and hopping the low wall that was hiding them from view. Vee takes the lead, sticking close to the cover of the wall with her M16 at the ready, her finger hovering close to the trigger. Security has been light in the area thanks to the fact that almost everyone who lived within fifty miles of New York is either dead or hunkered down in camps hundreds of miles to the west, but there are still occasional random patrols on the service roads that surround the airport. This is no time to get overconfident.

Vee reaches the guard post first and ducks her head through the door to make sure the guard is down for good, and Warren follows her in to take the pistol and radio from the guy's body. There's no remorse now. No guilt. What's done is done.

Warren twists the volume dial on the radio to its lowest setting and clips it to his jacket collar, keeping one ear listening for chatter as they move deeper into the airport complex. Neither Vee nor Warren bother to speak. There's no need for it. They've both seen the satellite photos, and they both know exactly where they're headed: the runway.

He breathes a sigh of relief as they reach a maintenance building on the road to the main terminal building and find just what the photos suggested would be waiting for them. A bank of electric courtesy vehicles are parked up in an open garage bay, all hooked up to recharging stations that have long since run out of power, and from a row of hooks on the wall hang bunches of keys attached to chunky bright yellow fobs. Vee grabs one at random and tries each vehicle until the third starts up with a quiet electric hum.

"Thank Christ for that," Warren sighs happily. "I wasn't looking forward to setting the charges close up." He hops into the passenger seat and sets down his rifle while Vee slides into the driver's seat and pulls the cart from the bay.

The hum of her motor and the sound of rubber on asphalt are the only things that break the silence as the cart rolls through the darkness along the service road that runs around the east end of the main terminal building. It's far from the quickest route to the runway, but it's the only one that isn't bathed in bright floodlights and regularly patrolled, an oversight Warren knows will cost the assholes running the base dearly. This is what happens when you pull out dedicated, well trained soldiers and replace them with private thugs who are paid by the hour: you get fucked.

A mesh gate bursts open as they power through it and out onto the apron, the black asphalt crowded with hastily abandoned service vehicles that litter the area in the shadow of the silent terminal. Thousands of prepackaged airline meals rot in delivery trucks that have long since lost their refrigeration. Luggage trains snake between the planes, their contents strewn across the ground where they were abandoned in the rush for the ground staff to escape.

Even after a month this shit still amazes Warren. It seems crazy that if the mood struck he could pull over and spend a couple of hours picking through the belongings of a thousand passengers, helping himself to laptops, tablets, cellphones, cash and jewelry that have been sitting here unattended for a month, like the world's best yard sale. Back in the first week he actually did grab a few tempting shiny objects while sweeping abandoned homes and stores with the cleanup crews on Staten Island. It was fun for a while, but it didn't take long before he realized there was just no point in owning luxury shit any more.

It was a commercial that brought it home to him, back at the end of the first week when the networks were still running regular programming as if they were trying to convince themselves that the world could never *really* go to shit as long as reruns of Everybody Loves Raymond ran as scheduled in the TV guide.

Warren was back at base, shoveling a rank jambalaya MRE down his throat, trying to ignore the stink of death that clung like tar to his clothes and worked its way up his nose, when a commercial for Omega wristwatches caught his eye. Black and white, real classy shit.

Some buff guy with thick hair and just the right amount of stubble rocked up to a jetty to find a hot chick waiting for him on the deck of his yacht. She seemed to be enjoying spontaneous multiple orgasms at the very thought of this smug asshole climbing onto the boat, then the camera moved in to show his wrist. Omega Seamaster. Regular aspirational bullshit. Buy this watch and your life can be just as awesome as this.

Warren looked down at his own wrist and saw the exact same fucking watch. Brushed stainless steel, automatic movement, beautifully smooth chronograph. $4,500 of luxury, and he'd taken it from the wrist of a guy who was lying dead beside a classic Bugatti parked in the driveway of his palatial home, beaten to death by a woman who was probably his wife. Warren had put her on the ground with two shots from 100 yards, then he'd put a bullet in the guy's head just to be safe.

The watch hadn't done much for that guy. It hadn't allowed him entry beyond the velvet rope into the exclusive, perfect, endless hedonistic life he'd been promised by the commercial. It probably hadn't made women go wild with desire at the very thought of him. It had just made his chubby, torn up corpse a more attractive target for looters. All that aspirational shit's done. Over. You want to aspire to something? Get a decent gun, and aspire to still be alive in the morning.

The cart rolls silently out towards the runway, weaving between abandoned jets that had been waiting for a takeoff slot when the airspace was closed. The doors are all wide open, each of them spilling out bright yellow deflated emergency slides. Each of them carrying the names of airlines that haven't landed in the States for a month, and probably never will again: Emirates, Qantas and British Airways, all more than happy to abandon millions of dollars of aircraft and equipment if it means they can help keep this shit from spreading any further.

Of course, that's exactly what the pricks running this camp *want* to happen. That's the only reason this fucking place exists. That's why Vee and Warren are taking such a risk.

"OK, you ready for this?" asks Vee, holding the steering wheel steady with her knees as she tugs a large block of C-4 from her pack and pushes a blasting cap into the mass.

"Ready as I'll ever be," Warren replies, taking the C-4 from her hand and securing it firmly to the dash. He prepares himself to roll as Vee guides the cart towards the target. She sets the perfect approach angle, and Warren swings his rifle against his chest as they draw closer to the cover of an abandoned fire truck.

They both roll as one away from the vehicle, quickly pulling themselves to their feet and ducking behind the truck as the electric cart continues on towards the target, the accelerator wedged to the floor. Vee grasps the remote firing detonator in one hand and steadies her M16 with the other, waiting for the right moment.

Under the harsh floodlights lining the runway the courtesy vehicle rides silent, straight and true towards the first of three banks of dark green prefab cabins that extend at least a half mile down the runway. There are hundreds of them, maybe even a thousand, all of them powered by a tightly packed cluster of hybrid solar-diesel generators humming away at one end. The cart approaches them. Fifty yards. Forty. Thirty. Warren whispers a prayer as the cart begins to pull a little to the left. Twenty. Ten. It's slightly off target, but it looks like it'll still strike close enough to count.

Vee flips the cap on the detonator and squeezes the trigger.

All hell breaks loose. The rain-soaked black surface of the runway glows for a brief moment with the reflected flash of the explosion, and a fraction of a second later the truck rocks to the side as the shock wave passes and the noise washes over them. Vee and Warren wait for the roar to pass, peer around the side of the truck and smile when they see they've achieved their goal.

The bank of generators lies in ruins. The burned out wreckage of the cart smolders, while around it lie piles of twisted steel and shattered solar cells.

The floodlights flicker and fail for a moment as they switch to their own emergency solar charged backups, returning at half power and casting the runway in an eerie half light. It's dim, but in the ghostly glow Warren sees the result of the destruction.

The electronically locked doors at the front of each cabin swing slowly open under their own weight.

•⋎•

:::4:::

I STARE AT the open door in disbelief, wondering for a moment if my mind hasn't finally cracked under the pressure. I haven't seen the door open without an armed guard standing behind it in two weeks. I'd almost forgotten what the empty runway behind it even looked like.

It's only the burned down cigarette between my fingers that drags me back to the moment. I drop the butt to the steel floor and turn back to Bishop, sitting at the edge of his cot in the sudden darkness, staring open mouthed at the door as if he's waiting for me to confirm that he's not imagining it.

"Wait there," I whisper, holding my hand out to keep him on the bed. "Lemme check it out." I don't want us to go rushing out only to find ourselves pushed back in at gunpoint. I don't think ether of us could face that. Not after taking our first breath of fresh air in two weeks. I edge closer to the door, sticking by the wall until I can just about see out onto the runway.

"*Fuck!*" I jump back as the sound of gunfire breaks the silence. Muzzle flashes reflect off the dark steel of the door, and I hear the rapid drumbeat of automatic weapons fire striking the side of a nearby cabin. Whoever's firing, it's close.

It's also panicked. The rate of fire suggests someone burning through his magazine far too quickly. These aren't the quick, controlled bursts of a trained soldier. They're the frantic, last ditch shots of someone who knows he's about to die.

"Get back, Tom," hisses Bishop, rolling behind the cover of his cot. "Don't go out there!"

Yeah, no kidding. I don't know what's going on outside our door, but it doesn't matter. There's no way in hell we could ever make it across the hundreds of yards of open space outside the cabin. There's zero cover, and picking us off would be like shooting fish in a barrel. It's probably safer to take shelter at the back of the room and wait for the chaos to end.

I'm halfway across the room when I hear the sound echoing between the cabins.

Snarling. Groaning. Rasping breath.

I freeze mid-step, holding my breath as I listen for the sound again. That's a sound I've heard before. It's a sound forever burned into my memory, and I've spent the last month hoping against hope I'd never have to hear it again. It's the sound of approaching death.

"Bishop," I whisper, scanning the room for anything I could use as a weapon, "we need to get the fuck out of here, *now*." I almost expect to have to coax him out from his hiding place but I'm surprised to see him stand, lift his bed easily onto its side and begin to unscrew one of the thick steel legs from the frame. It comes loose in just a few seconds, and he tosses it over to me before grabbing another.

"I figured we might need to use these for a breakout," he shrugs, noticing my surprise. "I think they're full of sand or something. Could make a good cosh, you know? I noticed they screwed off a few days ago."

I swing the pipe experimentally, surprised at the weight. Bishop could be right. There's definitely something inside the hollow tube, and it feels solid enough to at least get in a good crack if it comes to it.

"Good thinking, Bishop. OK, you good to go?" I ask, still surprised that he isn't cowering in the corner.

"Does the Pope shit in the woods?" He tugs on his jacket and makes for the door. "I've been good to go for a God damned month. Let's get the hell out of here."

Outside the door the floodlights spaced between each cabin flicker dimly, struggling to maintain their power. Small pools of light illuminate the walls of the cabins, but between them deep shadows hide God knows what on this moonless night. I flinch as a shot rings out somewhere behind me, and in the darkness I hear frightened yells and hissed whispers from the people still hidden in the cabins. Nobody else seems to have dared emerge yet, and for a moment I wonder if we should be proud of being the first to escape or worried that we're the only people dumb enough to abandon the relative safety for a dark runway peppered with gunfire and the sounds of the dead.

It only takes a moment for my question to be answered. As Bishop and I crouch in the shadow of our cabin door a shape emerges into the light just a few yards away. It's a man.

Correction: it *was* a man, once.

Now... not so much. As the figure moves into the dim light it becomes obvious he's infected. He stands in a hospital gown, streaked with blood and trailing IV lines from both arms. He has about six inches on me, and his arms look almost as thick as my legs. There's no way I could take him down without a gun, and even if I had one I'd probably miss when this hulking monster came barreling towards us.

He turns quickly in the small pool of light, swinging his head back and forth as if he's sniffing the air for a target, and as he turns towards us and the light catches his face it's all I can do to keep myself from gasping. He's been mutilated almost beyond recognition. He drools from a gummy, toothless mouth, and his infected eye sockets weep with pus. It's hard to tell in the half light but it looks as if someone took a soldering iron to his eyeballs. The milky, misshapen, useless burst orbs stare out blindly towards us, almost as if he can still see us crouching in the darkness. *Did he do that to himself?*

He takes a step towards us, perhaps sensing our presence somehow. Beside me I feel Bishop tense to run, and I quickly grip his arm and squeeze as hard as I can. *No. Don't move.* I shake my head and point towards the guy's ruined eyes. I know he can't see us. If we just stay quiet and still we might be able to wait until–

A scream echoes from a cabin in the next row. In an instant the man breaks into a silent run straight towards it, ricocheting blindly off the wall of the cabin then tracing its sides with his hand, searching for a way in until he finally reaches the open door. The scream rings out again as someone inside tries far too late to pull it closed. All along the row I hear similar screams, ended by the groans of the infected. I start to run. I don't need to hear people die.

I run without thinking, just trying to get the fuck away from here in case there are more infected nearby. I break from the row of cabins, across the empty asphalt and out onto the wet, cool grass between the runway and the service roads leading back to the terminal; that strange, fallow no man's land you watch as you wait for your plane to taxi back to the gate, dotted with numbered markers that presumably mean something to the pilot.

My feet sink an inch or so in the soft, wet mud as I run, an odd sensation after walking for a month on the firm steel floor of the cabin. I feel like I'm stepping back on dry land after a long spell at sea, or like I'm stuck in one of those nightmares in which the air is as thick as molasses, and I'm struggling to flee while something terrifying draws closer and closer with each sucking step.

For a moment I panic as I sense a presence behind me. I hear movement and heavy breathing, and when I risk a quick glance behind I almost laugh out loud when I see the red faced Bishop struggling to keep up. In my panic I'd almost forgotten he was with me. I open my mouth to tell him to slow down for a moment, but before the first word escapes my mouth I trip on something solid, unseen in the darkness, and tumble forward and down a steep slope that suddenly appears before me.

I roll down the slippery slope, tumbling over a couple of times before I land hard, face first in something soft and moist. I try to raise myself up but my hands sink wrist deep in wet slurry. I feel like I'm sinking in it. Drowning. Being pulled down into black quicksand. I tug my hands from the grasping, sucking mud and scramble about for a grip on something solid, and after a moment my fingers meet something familiar but entirely unexpected. I probe around, confused.

A gaping mouth. Lips. Teeth. A chin covered in rough stubble.

I snatch my hand back in revulsion and clutch it against my chest, blindly checking for bite marks with my other hand. I open my eyes wide and try to adjust to the lack of light, but the pitch blackness seems even deeper down here, as if there's something blocking even the dim shapes of the clouds above. I'm blind.

I gingerly touch my hand to the ground beneath me again, and immediately realize what I'm touching. I know where I am. I know what they've done.

I scramble wildly out of the ditch, dragging myself up the wet, slippery slope using the short steel pole from the bed as a kind of ice pick, driving it into ground that feels far too firm to be soil. When I finally reach the lip of the slope and feel solid earth beneath my hands I find Bishop standing at the top, his lower lip quivering as he looks down at the dark shapes beneath him.

There's a roof of camouflaged netting held above the pit, suspended on stakes that surround it, holding it in place to hide it from view. Now the smell hits me fully. It's on my clothes, covering my hands and in my mouth. It's everywhere, and I know it's a stink that will take more than a shower to remove. It will live in my memory forever.

Hidden beneath the netting in the pitch darkness lie hundreds of bodies, all of them clad in the same blue hospital gowns as the infected man we saw at the cabin. A few of the bodies have been dumped towards the top of the slope, close to the edge of the netting where a little light can reach them. They're all the same. Puncture wounds in the arms from IV lines.

Eyes poked out. Teeth yanked from their mouths.

"What the hell is this, Tom?" Bishop asks, his voice wobbling on the verge of tears. "What happened to them?"

"They were guinea pigs."

We both spin around at the sound of the voice behind us. In the darkness the figure is barely visible, kitted out in a dark green military uniform, her face blackened with grease paint.

"Who the fuck are you?" I demand, feeling stupid even as I raise the pipe in case I need to fight her off. She just tilts her head and swings her M16 down from her shoulder as if to say *just try it, asshole.*

"We came to save these sorry bastards," she says, looking down into the pit with disgust. "Looks like we left it too late." She turns away from us and calls back over her shoulder. "Found it, Warren. You're not gonna like it."

Another figure emerges from the darkness in the direction of the runway, hidden from view by the distant glow of the floodlights behind him until he's almost on top of us. He's dressed the same as the woman, but he has a long rifle slung over his shoulder. As he reaches the pit he slows and stares at me and Bishop.

"Two guys. Seriously, two fucking guys made it?"

The woman nods. "Don't beat yourself up. We could have come two nights ago and rescued fifty, but it's just as likely we would have been shot at the door and hundreds more would have died. Besides, it's our fault. We should have guessed they'd have infected locked up in the same damned boxes."

Warren shakes his head and looks me up and down like he's judging a disappointing show dog. He snorts derisively and spits before turning away from the pit and setting off towards the terminal. As he turns away he mutters in disgust. "One of you guys better fucking cure cancer."

•⊺•

:::5:::

THE PISTOL FEELS heavy in my hand. Heavier than I remember. It feels like I'm carrying a half brick, but I don't mind the weight. I'm just enjoying the feeling of safety it gives me, knowing that if something comes rushing towards me I won't have to wait until the last moment and hope I time the swing well enough to put it down with my short stick. I may not be a great shot, but at least now I'll have to chance to deal with a threat before I can feel its breath on my face.

"You ever fired one of those?" the woman asks, doubtfully.

"Yeah, of course," I reply, with a confidence that suggests I spend every weekend down at the range, then I reconsider. What's the point in trying to bullshit a soldier? "I mean, not for a long time. Just once, actually. I spent a day at an army base in Mongolia and they let me play around with a couple of their guns." I struggle to remember long-forgotten details. "I think the pistol I used was called a Makarov. Or is it Kamarov? And I tried a sniper rifle." I nod towards the guy, Warren. "Though I guess you're all set for a sniper. I also drove a tank for a while."

She smiles and nods condescendingly. "Uh huh. OK, well I'll let you know if we need you to drive any tanks for us. In the meantime, keep the safety on and don't point that thing at anything you don't want dead. Understand? Good boy."

I nod, my cheeks hot with embarrassment. I never much cared that I wasn't a guy's guy before the last month. Shit, I was a journalist. I made my living with a pen and a laptop, and I only went into that game because I didn't want to do a real job. I long ago came to peace with the idea that I'd never set panties on fire with my masculinity, and it's only now I realize that I should have made at least a little effort to learn how to be useful now that words aren't needed any more. I feel like a third wheel for the whole world, like a telegraph operator working at Google.

"I'm Vee, by the way. Victoria Reyes. The guy with the bad attitude is Warren Campbell. You?"

"Tom. Freeman. And the big guy is Bishop."

She looks over at the lumbering giant walking ten steps away with a peaceful, vacant expression on his face. "First name? Last name?"

I shake my head. "Just Bishop. Trust me, don't ask."

She narrows her eyes curiously. "What do you mean, don't ask?"

"Seriously, you don't want to poke that hornet's nest. Just call him Bishop, OK?"

I can tell by the puzzled smile on her face that she won't drop it. She walks across my path until she's close enough to whisper. "Hey Bishop, what's this I hear about your name?"

Bishop spins on me with rage in his eyes and bellows. "Damn it, Tom, you promised you wouldn't tell anybody!"

"*Will you guys keep it the fuck down?*" hisses Warren, crouching behind the barrier at the side of the road, scanning around for signs of movement. "We're not out of the woods yet."

Vee whispers, trying to calm Bishop. "It's OK, it's OK, I was just kidding. Tom didn't tell me anything. It was just a joke."

Bishop clenches and unclenches his fists, looking between me and Vee as if he's trying to sense a lie. Eventually he relaxes. "OK, that's alright then. Just don't tell, OK? You promised not to tell."

I nod and whisper back. "Sure, buddy, I won't tell. It's OK." Vee walks back across me, and I drop my voice even lower. "I'll tell you later."

We continue in silence for the next ten minutes until we finally reach our getaway vehicle. I was expecting something like Sergeant Laurence's Stryker, or at least some kind of military Jeep, and I'm a little surprised when Warren stops beside a beat up old Toyota, pops the trunk and pulls out a soft carry case for his sniper rifle.

"Wow, I see we're riding in style."

Vee snorts. "It's got wheels, an engine and a tank full of gas. Good enough for us." She tugs open the rear door and nods at Bishop, who slides in before Warren follows him. "You're riding shotgun, cowboy. Warren needs to play with his wife for a while in the back."

Warren lets out a sarcastic laugh, settles himself in the rear seat and sets about stripping down his rifle. "You couldn't possibly understand the deep relationship a sniper forms with his rifle, you dumb grunt. Now get in and try not to crash."

I hop in the front passenger seat and take a look at my gun as Vee starts the engine and tears away onto the highway. I still don't really know what I'm looking at, but I see the words Pietro Beretta engraved in the side of the barrel. I've at least *heard* of Berettas, even though I don't know squat about guns. I squint to read the smaller letters beside the name of the gun, and a moment later I jerk forward as the car squeals to a halt.

"Gimme that!" Vee scolds, pulling the gun from my hands. "You had the fucking thing pointed right at my head. I told you, only ever point this at something you want to stop moving." She holds it up to the courtesy light and sees it's safe, then hands it back to me." Always assume it's loaded, and always assume the safety's off. I've been through too much shit to be taken out by friendly fire." She puts the car back in gear and pulls away. "Oh, and don't drop it. That belonged to my husband."

Despite my embarrassment I sense a certain tone in her voice. "Is he...?"

"He doesn't need it any more," she replies curtly, and I get the feeling it's a subject I wouldn't want to press. I fall silent and stare out the window at a world I haven't seen for a month. It all looks very different now.

We're heading south on a broad, empty highway. Almost empty, anyway. Every couple hundred yards by the side of the road lies a pile of wrecked cars that look like they were bulldozed out of the way. I vaguely remember seeing some abandoned vehicles on the road when we first arrived at the airport, so I guess the path was cleared when the base at the airport was expanded and resupplied.

The power's out now, as far as the eye can see. When I last passed this way it felt almost as if life was going on as usual. The streetlights were on, and businesses still appeared to be open on the roads that crossed beneath the highway. It almost felt like the world was normal beyond New York, and we'd escaped from nothing but a bad dream. Now it looks as if the nightmare followed us out. Every building looks abandoned, and a fair number of them have been burned out. I can't imagine that there could be anyone still alive down there, but–

"Hey, did you see that?" I ask, spinning around to Vee. "There was someone moving around down there!"

She doesn't even bother to look. "Yeah, wouldn't surprise me. There are still a few infected around here. A few looters. Maybe a few idiots who think this is a big scam so the government can take their property. They'll be dead soon enough if they're too dumb to leave."

"Jesus." I stare down at the roads as we fly by overhead, gawping in amazement at the desolation. I've got so many questions, I don't know where to begin. "OK, you gotta catch us up. We've been locked in a box for a month. What's going on?"

Vee tugs a pack of cigarettes from her pocket, pulls one out between her lips and offers the pack around. I grab one gratefully, accept her light and enjoy the first pull as I wait for her answer.

"Well," she says, taking her hands from the wheel to cup the flame as she lights hers, "we're fucked. Absolutely, positively screwed with our pants on."

Warren chuckles in the back seat. "Man, you guys'll wish you stayed in your little box. At least you got three square meals in there."

Vee frowns in the rear view mirror then looks back to the road. "You've been at the camp since this whole shitstorm started, yeah?" I nod. "So you know New York is toast?"

I nod again. "Bishop and I were there. We saw it up close. Only just got out alive."

"Oh man, what a sight that must have been." I notice she's got a faint smile on her face, but she wipes it off when she sees my scowl. "Sorry,

I don't want to make light of it, but it must have been something else to watch it happen." She senses the mood and moves on. "Sorry. Anyway, couple hours later they gave D.C. the same treatment. We thought we'd caught it in time, wiped all of those motherfuckers out, but then we heard about the President."

She cracks open the window and taps out her ash. "When they decided to raze the capital Howard and the VP were down in the White House bunker. I don't know exactly what happened, but I guess they couldn't get to Andrews AFB. The whole city was such a clusterfuck there was no way they could get a motorcade through the streets without riding behind a tank, and they probably couldn't rendezvous with Marine One either. All I know for sure is that they tried to get out to the north by road just before the bombs fell.

"They didn't make it. Maybe the motorcade got caught in the tail end of the blast, who knows, but VP Lynch was definitely killed at the scene. As for the President... well, all they told us was that she was injured. They say she's been in a medically induced coma for the last month. I'm guessing she got bit, but they don't want to admit someone from her security team had to put down the President with a bullet. Whatever really happened, we know that most of the

Secret Service detail was taken out by infected, and this was outside the blast zone. We don't know how many there are, but we know we didn't mop them all up like we planned. The infection has spread far beyond New York and D.C. Most of the military has been pulled back to guard the edge of the quarantine zone, and this whole chunk of the country is like the wild west. Anyway, after D.C. went dark they put that asshole Lassiter in charge."

"Lassiter?" I almost spit the name. "I hate that guy."

Vee forces out a bitter laugh. "Yeah, you didn't like him when he was just a religious nut who thought anyone who didn't go to his church deserved to burn in hell. You should see him now."

"Come on, how could he get any worse than he already was?" I laugh. Before the attacks the Speaker was already a political punchline. He was one of those guys who made wild, nonsense claims like women only got raped because they were being punished for their sins, and gays are responsible for stock market crashes. He was a lunatic who embarrassed moderate Republicans, and he only held onto his job because he had dirt on every politician who'd dared set foot in Washington for the last thirty years. Well, that and the fact that the Republicans never dared challenge him in the primaries, and his district hadn't come within twenty points of electing a Democrat since buckled hats were the height of style.

Warren looks up from his gun. "How could he get worse? Well, if we hadn't come save your ass tonight you would have been about 24 hours from finding out." He spits on the barrel and starts polishing it with a rag. "Lassiter was gonna have you killed."

•⸙•

:::6:::
Eight Days Earlier

WARREN PUSHES HIS meal around the tray with a look of disgust, as if it could possibly taste any worse than the average meal he'd been eating every day since he enlisted. "This food is shit."

Vee looks up from her notebook. "Yeah, I think you mentioned that once or twice, Warren."

He drops his fork in the tray and puts it on the dash. "No, I mean *really* shit. Even worse than usual. Like... I don't know, I think it's off." He scoops up a forkful and holds it out. "Here, try it."

"I don't want to try your food, Warren."

"Just *try* it."

She snaps her notebook closed and glowers at him. "Warren, it's the end of the fucking world. Get used to bad food or go hang yourself with your belt. I don't really care which, but if you keep complaining I'm going to feed you that whole fucking tray."

Warren sulks at his fork. "Hey, I was just trying to make conversation."

"Well don't." She opens her book again and pretends to read the handwritten scrawl for a minute, painfully aware of Warren's downhearted look. "Sorry," she reluctantly mutters. "I'm just worried about Karl. He should have been back ten minutes ago."

Warren tosses his tray out the window and winds it back up, licking his fingers. "You got nothing to worry about, Vee. Karl could take down a rhino. He'll be fine."

Vee plays with her radio for a second, checking she's receiving properly. "If you loved anything other than that damned rifle you'd understand, Warren. You never stop worrying. Not for a single minute."

Warren gently pats the rifle wrapped in its soft case on his lap. "Yup, well I guess I'll never find out. Old Nadine would never let me take up with another woman." He smiles. "See, me and her? We have this bond you just don't get with regular love. We're always there for each other, come hell or high water. She's never let me down as long as she's been with me. That's real love, Vee. It's simpler than your human love. Beautifully uncomplicated." He strokes the case lovingly, and pauses for a moment. "I have to admit, though, as a relationship it's lacking a little in the sex department."

Vee laughs. "Come on, Warren. Don't try to tell me you've never– " Her thought is cut off by a hiss from the radio, followed by a voice.

"You've got infected incoming on your six, guys." Vee visibly relaxes at the sound of her husband's voice. "I'm coming in fast, and I wouldn't say no to a little backup. Over."

Vee grabs her M16 as Warren slips his rifle from its case, and within moments they're in position, Warren standing through the sunroof with his gun mounted on a bipod and Vee racing back along the sidewalk to find herself a solid firing position to cover Karl's approach.

He comes around the corner at a sprint, in one hand his Beretta and in the other a grenade, the pin pulled. Moments after he appears a flock of infected come racing after him, appearing around the corner in a closely packed group.

"Grenade, five o'clock, twenty yards," instructs Vee into her radio. She watches as Karl tosses it back and slightly to the right without looking. It lands just ahead of the pack and explodes as they pass over, sending three of them straight to the ground and leaving two more running at half speed, their legs damaged. Still seven more are in pursuit, at least until Vee and Warren open fire.

Warren takes out three in quick succession, calmly firing as if he's under no pressure at all, counting out his breaths and squeezing the trigger like he's playing a video game. Two head shots and one in the chest, a lucky shot that takes out the spinal cord on the way out.

Now the flock is down to four, and they enter Vee's firing range as Karl moves aside to give her a clear angle. She rests her elbow on the trunk of the car in front of her, carefully takes aim and squeezes off a few rounds from her M16. Three more infected go down one after the other as they're hit in rapid, controlled sprays.

Karl is just a couple of car lengths away now, with a single chaser remaining along with two more limping far behind. Warren takes out the two injured almost as an afterthought, while Vee allows Karl the pleasure of whipping around and taking out the final one, a skinny woman in a dirty pink t-shirt, with his Beretta. A single shot to the head is all it takes to put her on the ground.

Karl turns back to Vee and smiles, relieved. "If you guys didn't save me any of that shitty casserole there'll be hell to pay. I haven't eaten a thing since this morning. Hey Warren, can you fetch me some of that swill?"

Vee slings her gun over her shoulder and turns back towards the car just as a warning cry rings out from Warren. She turns back to Karl and watches in horror as the world slips into slow motion.

Karl's head shot wasn't accurate enough. It only grazed the woman, sending her to the ground without finishing her off. Even as Vee starts to swing her M16 back down she knows she can't move quickly enough. Karl's gun is already holstered at his hip, and Warren has begun to lower his rifle back into the car.

She catches Karl on his bare arm in mid-turn. It doesn't even look as if she's going for the bite. She just happens to catch him with her teeth as she lunges forward, and the infected will never pass up an opportunity. She bites down hard and tries to twist her neck to tear away a chunk of flesh.

Karl's closed fist comes down hard on her shoulder, sending her sprawling to the ground. A kick with a heavy boot spins her onto her back. He slides his Beretta from the holster and puts three shots between her eyes.

Vee can't speak. She can barely move. She didn't have a clear view but she only has to look at Karl's slumped shoulders to know what happened, and when he turns around and she sees his face her worst fears are confirmed.

He looks down at his bloodied arm. Pin pricks of blood blossom on the bite mark a couple of inches beneath his rolled up sleeve. Karl wipes them away, and moments later they appear again. It's only a tiny bite, barely more than a graze. It wouldn't even need stitches, but Vee knows that's not the point.

"We have orders," Karl mutters, tugging a crumpled envelope from his pants pocket. He sets it down on the asphalt in front of him, smiles at Vee and whispers, "I love you."

She doesn't try to stop him. They both know what needs to be done. They both made a pact back at the beginning, and she knows he's even more stubborn than her. *Never infected.* That was the deal. When the time came they'd die the right way, on their own terms. Clean. Quick.

She doesn't speak as he raises the Beretta to his mouth. She holds her closed fist over her heart and closes her eyes until she hears the shot, and doesn't open them again until she hears the body of her husband hit the ground.

She promised him she wouldn't cry.

•▼•

:::7:::

IT'S A COUPLE of hours before Vee manages to speak. She sits in silence in the driver's seat of the car as Warren takes watch through the sunroof, guarding the perimeter with his rifle. No infected come.

He almost wished they would. Maybe it would be a little easier if Vee had something to take out her anger on. Something she could beat with the butt of her gun until she stopped seeing Karl's face. Until she could stop thinking about his body bundled up in a tarp in the trunk of the car.

The sun is almost setting when Warren feels a tug on his leg. He looks down through the sunroof and sees Vee's red-rimmed eyes looking up at him, holding a blood stained sheet of paper in her hand.

"Our orders," she croaks, her voice dry and and scratchy. "We're just Lassiter's private army now." Her lip curls with hate. "That's what Karl died for."

Warren takes the paper from her loose grip, pulls it up and smooths it out on the roof of the car.

Supply of test subjects at Camp One critical. Round up any remaining residents of Zone Fourteen for delivery to Major Armitage. All constitutional rights suspended. Priority One.

It may have seemed fairly innocent had they not already heard the rumors about Camp One. They'd been circulating through the east coast ranks for a couple of weeks now, and while at first they'd sounded crazy it now seemed like they couldn't be anything but completely true.

Camp One had begun as a simple temporary refugee camp, a place where the survivors of New York could be housed while the military swept the outskirts of the city and ensured the outbreak had been contained. Vee herself had delivered survivors to the camp in the first few days. She'd felt proud with every truckload that she'd done her part to save the lives of innocents.

Then the news of Lassiter's accession broke, and the orders began to change. The military proper was pulled out of the camp, replaced by a few high ranking officials supported by private security forces. Vee received orders to accompany a resupply convoy that seemed more suited to a prison or a biotech lab than a refugee camp. Hundreds of secure prefab cells outfitted with electromagnetic locks. Medical equipment that seemed designed more for experimentation than for treating the wounded. Shackles. Secure beds. Absurd volumes of anesthesia

Outside the camp the tone of the orders began to change. In the beginning their orders were simply to assist survivors and to help them reach the camp if they didn't feel safe in their homes. Now the orders became more explicit, and much more worrying. They were ordered to compel survivors to the camp. They were even issued tranquilizer guns, and authorized to use them against anyone unwilling to go voluntarily.

The numbers kept adding up. In the first two weeks following the attacks Vee personally delivered several hundred civilians to Camp One, and she knew her truck had been just one of dozens working in the area. Thousands were delivered, and none had ever been seen to leave. The rumors shifted and morphed like a game of Telephone, but when a guard finally contacted a friend outside the camp the truth became clear.

Lassiter was trying to weaponize the contagion. He wasn't trying to cure it. Wasn't trying to find a vaccine. He was simply trying to find a way to use the infection for his own purposes.

And he was using civilians as test subjects.

He'd always seemed like the kind of guy who'd want to ride alongside the four horsemen of the apocalypse. Even before the attacks it had been an open secret in Washington that Lassiter was a religious zealot of the worst kind, a man who'd spent his life just waiting for the opportunity to score a decisive victory over his enemies. He was the sort of guy who believed - *truly* believed, with every ounce of his being - that he was God's messenger. It was a poisonous belief that excused any amount of evil carried out in his name.

He'd been dug into the capital ecosystem like a tick for decades, but both his allies and opponents had always managed to find ways to keep anything really dangerous far from his desk, in the same way that Supreme Court Justices delay the important decisions when it looks like one of their number might have started on the long road towards senility. He just couldn't be trusted.

And now there was nobody left to hold him back. He'd found himself at the top of the pile, and everybody who knew him - hell, anybody who even had the slightest interest in politics - knew what that meant. It meant he was free to be the dictator he'd always dreamed of becoming.

Warren reads the order a second time, then a third. He lifts his rifle from the roof and slips down to the front passenger seat. Vee still stares out the front window at something that isn't there, and never will be again.

"What do you wanna do?" he asks quietly. He's already decided to follow Vee's lead. He trusts her with his life, and she's already proved she's good for it many times over. Whatever she decides will be the right call.

She stays silent for a long moment, turning her head from the window down to the bloody paper in his hands.

"Did I ever tell you how Karl and I met?" she asks, almost in a whisper.

Warren shakes his head. "No, I don't think so."

She smiles as she remembers. "We were stationed together in Zeraa, a nothin' little smudge on the map about twenty clicks south of Aleppo. This was a couple of years ago, right at the start of the ground assaults. Not sure if you were on active duty back then.

"We had intel that ISIL were transporting chemical weapons along the back roads to try to take back the city. Really nasty shit. The intel seemed pretty solid. Enough to authorize a strike, anyhow, but I wasn't so sure. Something about it just didn't feel right to me, but it wasn't my call. I could make a recommendation but... well, you know how that shit works." She lights a cigarette and take a long, slow drag. "Karl was my new CO, just arrived that week. He had his orders and I had mine, but I argued with him. Flat out refused to lead the strike. He could have had me court-martialed, but instead he reported that an equipment failure on one of the support drones forced a delay.

"Turns out it was a wedding party. Ground forces stopped the motorcade and checked the vehicles before they reached the city. There were fourteen kids. Two pregnant women. About a dozen elderly people, and they weren't carrying so much as a peashooter between them." She flicks the ash from her cigarette and takes a drag, making the embers glow bright red.

"I disobeyed the first order he ever gave me. I'll disobey the last." She takes the paper from Warren's hand and holds the cigarette to it until the flame catches. "He wouldn't want this. He wouldn't want us helping some lunatic President spread this shit to his enemies. That's not the country he signed up to serve. That's not the country I want this to become.

"Now, Warren, you can come with me or I can drop you off close to the base. It's up to you, but if you come with me I need you to know something." She winds down the window and tosses out the burning paper, throwing her cigarette after it.

"I intend to misbehave."

•⁊•

:::8:::

I LISTEN IN rapt attention as Vee tells the story, chain smoking with one eye on the road and the other looking out for infected.

"Wow," I say, looking down at the gun in my hand and suddenly understanding why Vee was so precious about it. "So you guys deserted."

She shrugs her shoulders and blows out a plume of smoke. "If that's the way you want to look at it, sure. I don't see it that way."

Warren pipes up from the back of the car. "You have to ask yourself who you really serve. Is it your immediate superior? The President? I don't think it's either. Call me naive, but when I signed up it was to serve my country, not just one man on a power trip. I happily signed on the dotted line and agreed to give my life for the United States. I never agreed to go to war against my own people. None of us did."

Vee nods. "He's right. The way I see it the real deserters are those who stayed. They've abandoned the people they promised to protect, and now they're just following orders." Another drag on the cigarette. Another angry plume of smoke. "It's not like we haven't seen this shit before. My grandpa had to go to Europe to fight a bunch of guys who were just following orders."

I can't argue, but I don't know what to say. I just nod, stay silent, and light another cigarette.

"Edgar was there."

I turn in my seat and see Bishop shifting in his seat. I thought he'd been sleeping, but it seems he was just listening with his eyes closed.

"How do you mean?" I ask.

"Edgar." Bishop repeats. "He was in one of those, umm, camps in Europe. Remember?"

I'd almost forgotten about that. Before he died Edgar had told us the story. I'd only been half listening at the time, since I really didn't want to hear shit like that considering our situation, but he'd told us he came from a little town just outside Kraków, Poland. He was just a baby when the German occupation began, and his first memories were of life in the Kraków ghetto. Sometime around 1942 he'd been moved to Plaszow, then two years later transferred to Flossenburg in Bavaria. By the time the camp was liberated in '45 he was ten years old, his family was gone, and the only things he owned were the threadbare clothes on his back.

"Edgar was our friend," Bishop rumbles, his voice filled with anger. "They hit him in the face with a gun and killed him. They didn't have to do that. He just didn't want to be locked up any more."

Vee turns to me with fire in her eyes. "Doesn't that make you mad? Doesn't it make you want to just reach down their throats and tear out their lungs?"

I nod. "Of course it does. I'm fucking furious, but what can we do? The camp's gone. Everyone's dead."

From the back seat I hear a dull click as Warren slots ammo into his magazine. "No. Hardly any of them are. We only got the guys who guarded the prison. The fuckers who built the place are still out there, probably already planning another. So, first priority," he says, "we find somewhere to sleep, and you can learn how to use that gun you're holding so I don't have to carry your ass across the country. Then we can get you and the big guy to Columbus, and we can blow the fucking lid on what Lassiter's been doing."

"Columbus? What's in Columbus?"

Vee chimes in. "Columbus is the first decent sized city outside the quarantine zone. Most of the big cities have been evacuated, but there's still some media working out of Columbus. Couple of radio stations and what's left of the big New York and D.C. papers set up there after the attacks. We have to at least try. If I know Lassiter he won't give up after just one little setback. He'll set up another camp, then another, then another. He'll kill as many people as it takes to win his insane war, and we owe it all the people in that fucking mass grave to give people a chance to fight back." She maneuvers the car around a pile of wrecks and guns the engine. "So, are you coming along for the ride?"

I look back at Bishop, who nods furiously. "Well, I guess somebody has to keep old Lennie here out of trouble. I'm in."

"Lennie?" Vee asks. "That's Bishop's name?"

I shake my head. "No, that's not— it's a joke. *Of Mice and Men?* George and Lennie? Alfalfa? Rabbits? Ringing any bells?" I'm met by blank faces all round. "Not a book crowd, huh? OK, fuck it. Let's go take down a President."

•▼•

:::9:::

TERRENCE LASSITER EMERGES from the
chapel with an expression of profound calm, in
stark contrast to the vein-popping rage he'd felt
as he walked in. His visits to the chapel were
always invigorating. Even after weeks without
feeling the warmth of the sun through the
windows of his own church, and even though he
hadn't seen his dear family since he'd left the
surface, no matter how troubled he felt as he
entered he always emerged from his private
sanctuary at peace, his resolve renewed.

He'd be the first to admit that the last month
had been... trying, to say the least. The vast
expansion of his responsibilities had been almost
overwhelming, but it was a challenge he'd faced
several times before. The first was when he felt
the calling to become a minister as a much
younger man. Overnight his flock expanded

from four - his wife and darling children - to many hundreds. Then, just a few short years later, he'd been called on once again to represent the first congressional district of Arkansas and once more his flock grew, that time to hundreds of thousands.

His promotion to Speaker at the age of 67 was even greater, and he saw it as a chance to speak to an even larger congregation. Not just to the men and women who served with him in the House but to each and every one of the millions of American citizens they represented. After three years in the position he'd assumed it was God's intention that he rise no further. That this would be where he could serve his Lord best.

He'd been wrong. Oh, how he'd underestimated the will of the Lord. He'd never imagined He would bless him with yet more bounty, nor demand of him an even greater sacrifice, but Terrence Lassiter knew in his heart that he was equal to the challenge. He knew he could answer the call, just as he always had before.

He'd never presume to understand God's ineffable motivations, of course, but in moments of quiet reflection over the last few weeks he often wondered if he'd not been cast in the role of Gideon from the Book of Judges. Gideon's tale had always been one of his favorite Old Testament stories, and it had always been a crowd pleaser when he preached it before his congregation.

Gideon was tasked by the Lord to free the Israelites, who had turned away from Yahweh and chosen to worship false gods, from a Midianite army 135,000 men strong. To serve His will Gideon amassed his own army of 32,000, but the Lord said they were too many. With so many men the Israelites might claim that they had been saved not by the Lord but simply by a mighty army, so God instructed Gideon to send all who wished to leave home. 22,000 left, and 10,000 remained.

Still God said this was too many. How could the Israelites be certain that it was God's will that they be saved from the Midianites? Still they may claim it was only Gideon's army that had freed them.

Gideon, eager to bring glory upon God, winnowed down his forces yet further until only 300 remained. He was afraid that such a small force may not triumph against the Midianite hordes, but he put his trust in the Lord. God, always true to his word, allowed those 300 a great victory, freeing the Israelites from their siege.

Lassiter had considered this story many times since he'd found himself thrust into the Presidency, and each time he felt closer and closer to understanding God's wishes for him. Like Gideon, Lassiter had begun with a mighty army. On his first day in office he'd controlled the massed forces of the entire United States military, the greatest fighting force in the history of the planet, and surely the equal to any earthly foe.

God, in his boundless wisdom, had decided that a victory using such awesome power would be insufficient to convince his deniers - not just the Israelites this time, but the many millions of deviants, blasphemers and followers of false prophets around the world, all of whom who failed to recognize the supremacy of God.

And so He saw fit to weaken the forces at Lassiter's command so as to better display that the victory, when it came, would be God's will. First came the loss of Roberts, the Secretary of Defense, who refused to understand the obvious need to research the infection that had overrun the United States. His resolve was weak, and Lassiter had no choice but to banish him to the surface above Site R. Perhaps if he chose to turn to God he may be allowed to live, and Lassiter would be among the first to offer him forgiveness.

With Roberts' departure it seemed prudent to put direct operational control of the military back into the hands of the Joint Chiefs of Staff, men who had spent a lifetime following orders, and who truly understood that painful sacrifices must sometimes be made for the greater good. He assumed they'd understand the need to carry out vital research at Camp One; that the loss of a few thousand test subjects was more than outweighed by the ability to wield such influence over the wider world. Like Roberts, however, these men lacked the necessary resolve, and saw fit to resign their commissions rather than carry out their Commander in Chief's orders. They too were banished to the surface.

More resignations came, and then more, until eventually Lassiter saw that simple banishment was impractical. The civilian traitors were confined to the holding cells of the complex, while the military commanders were justly executed to pay for their treachery.

Finally the bleeding began to stop. When his remaining staff understood the harsh consequences of disloyalty he was pleased to see how quickly they fell in line. Lassiter felt terrible for instilling in them such fear and he'd asked for guidance and forgiveness during many of his visits to the chapel, but he knew that - in time - the men and women working under him would understand that he had been correct, and that they were working towards a righteous cause.

Now, as Lassiter steps through the door of the situation room hidden three hundred feet beneath the surface of Raven Rock Mountain, he reflects that perhaps the Lord may finally consider his forces small enough to score a decisively righteous victory. Without the aid of the Secretary of Defense and the Joint Chiefs his command of the military is greatly weakened, with only a loyal few remaining to carry out his orders. The traitors have followed in the footsteps of Gideon's 22,000, returning home and forcing the Air Force and the Navy to stand down and reject all orders from his office. Much of the Army remains overseas, effectively stranded and unable to help the nation in its hour of need.

If Lassiter's faith wasn't quite so strong he might consider himself forsaken by his Lord, but - like the angel who appeared to Gideon and assured him that he was carrying out God's work - just as so many were abandoning him an unlikely ally arose to stiffen the President's resolve: Samuel Whelan, the Director of the Central Intelligence Agency.

It was Whelan who found the solution to Lassiter's military crisis, drawing on the vast network of covert operatives that were his prewar stock in trade. It was he who suggested that the President extend certain promises to those operatives to ensure their loyalty. Promises of cash, of tracts of land in the quarantine zone and, for those military commanders who had remained loyal, a promise of promotion to political office once the crisis was over, to fill the many seats vacated by the cowards and traitors who had fled.

It was Whelan who helped Lassiter realize that the loss of the eastern states presented a tremendous opportunity. That far from a disaster the infection had simply wiped the slate clean on a country that had moved too far from God.

Whelan had been his savior. The President was under no illusions that the crafty, scheming old spymaster was a righteous man and he knew that once this crisis was over he'd need to be justly dealt with, but for now he made a useful if unlikely ally. With his help Lassiter would remake the United States in God's image, and it would be truly glorious.

"Mr. President, there's a problem."

Lassiter's chest swells for a moment at the sound of the term of office, just as it has each time he's heard it over the last month. He allows himself a brief moment of pleasure, then adds it to the long list of sins he'll need to ask forgiveness for on his next visit to the chapel.

"What is it now, Mr, Whelan?" He takes a seat at the end of the long table, several seats from Whelan, and bristles inwardly at the fact that the Director failed to stand with the proper respect as he entered the room. That infraction is added to the bottom of a very different, much longer list.

Whelan turns to the wall-mounted screen, a map of the United States, and presses a button on the intercom. "Can you show me grid seven?" The map immediately zooms in from the overview until the northeast fills the screen, narrows down until Lassiter recognizes New York, then zooms further until he sees the outline of Newark Airport.

"About an hour ago we lost contact with Camp One. Major Armitage failed to make his scheduled check-in, so we repositioned the satellite to see if we could get an idea of what was going on. This is Camp One at 10PM, and this," he presses a key on his console, and the image immediately switches, "is Camp One on the last pass about twenty minutes ago. You're looking at an infrared image to see past the cloud cover."

"Oh, good grief," sighs Lassiter, sinking into his seat. On screen a false color image appears to show a thick column of smoke extending north from the airport, while a dull red spot at the south end of the runway shows the residual heat from what looks like an explosion. "What do we think happened? An attack? An accident?"

Whelan chews his pencil for a moment before answering. "It was an attack. And not by infected, either. We've just received word from a unit sent to investigate that several guards were found dead at the scene. Sniper and small arms fire. And it looks like they took out the generators on site using military grade explosives."

"Traitors," curses Lassiter. "They'll be the death of us. Any casualties?"

Whelan steels himself for the outburst of rage he knows to expect. "Yes, sir. I'm sorry to say our losses were total. It seems the explosion disabled the locks on the holding cells, and a number of infected were released along with the remaining test subjects. The camp was overrun."

Lassiter stares at the screen for a moment, as if trying to pick out the attackers in the image. Whelan remains silent, waiting for the President to lash out at him as if this was his fault, but the usual attack doesn't come. Instead Lassiter simply removes his glasses, kneads the bridge of his nose with his fingers and looks back at Whelan.

"Are your teams in position?"

"Yes, sir."

"And they have the required stockpiles?"

Whelan ponders the question for a moment. "It'll be touch and go. We could use a few weeks to synthesize more, but... yes, I believe they may have enough, Mr. President."

Lassiter stands, pushing back his chair. "We go today. No more waiting. Understood?"

Whelan lifts the phone in front of him to connect to his field control unit. "Yes, I understand, sir. Umm, you have to give the order. I'm sorry, it's just a formality."

"Operation Crop Dust, Mr Whelan. I'm giving you the go order. Make it happen."

At that the President replaces his glasses, turns on his heel and strolls out of the room as if he and Whelan have just enjoyed nothing but a casual conversation. Nobody who didn't understand how Lassiter's mind worked would ever guess that he'd just casually ordered the largest and most ambitious air strike in the history of the human race.

•⸎•

:::10:::

VEE RUBS HER eyes and stifles a yawn, stretching her arms to loosen her tight muscles. "You don't need to sleep?" she asks.

I shake my head and push the magazine into its slot until I feel it click. "Nah. I've been sleeping for a month. I don't know how you guys sleep out here, anyway. Aren't you worried we'll be attacked?"

Vee shakes her head. "Nah, not so much. We're usually pretty safe a few floors up, so long as we don't attract attention. Most of them can't climb stairs so well now they've started to, you know, dry out and stuff. Honestly, they're not much of a danger unless they're fresh or they've eaten recently. Besides, it's a cost benefit analysis thing. We don't sleep tonight, we make a dumb mistake and get ourselves killed tomorrow. You gotta weigh up the risks."

I lift myself awkwardly from the carpeted floor and find my way in the darkness over to the window. It's too dark outside to see much from up on the fourth floor of this abandoned office building on the outskirts of a small town off Highway 78, but down at street level I'm sure I can see a couple of shapes moving slowly in the shadows. "What *are* they?"

"How do you mean?"

"I mean what makes them tick? Why do they try to kill?"

Vee gives me a surprised look. "Shit, you don't know? Man, you really have been stuck in a box, haven't you?" She reaches in her duffel bag and tugs out a couple of candy bars. "Here, eat something, you need the sugar," she says, tossing me a Milky Way.

"It's a fungus," she explains, tearing open her wrapper. "*Cordyceps bangkokii*, they call it. You ever heard of *Cordyceps*?"

I shake my head as I happily chew. I'd almost forgotten what chocolate tastes like.

"First couple of weeks the news talked about nothing else. I think I could probably teach a damned course on it by now." She chuckles and tosses her candy wrapper to the floor. "There's a species of fungus called... umm, *Ophiocordyceps unilateralis*. It's found in the tropical forests of Thailand and Brazil, I think. I once saw a piece on it in an old David Attenborough nature documentary, and even back then I though this shit was creepy as hell. I don't know exactly how it works, but it's a type of fungus that attacks carpenter ants, and turns them into some kind of... well, I guess you could call them zombies. They just lose control. The *Cordyceps* compels them to climb the nearest tree, find a leaf and clamp on hard with their mandibles, then this shit starts to multiply inside them. After a few days the ants die and the fungus breaks through their exoskeleton and grows a long, gross tube that releases spores that drift down to the ground and land on more ants, and the whole disgusting process starts again. Circle of life, right?" She shivers with revulsion.

"Anyway, some genius must have heard about this stuff and decided it'd be a great idea to see if they could tweak it enough that it infects humans. I don't know who it was, and I *really* don't know why they decided to do something so obviously dumb, but it looks like they succeeded. Shit, they didn't just succeed. They made this stuff even worse. *Cordyceps bangkokii* is just something else. Whoever played around with it knew exactly what they were doing. It's a near perfect organism, as long as your goal is to fuck up everyone's day.

"All it takes is a single spore in your blood. A scratch. A bite. A fleck of spit in your eye. That's all you need. Once it's inside you it feeds on your blood and multiplies faster than you can believe. I'm talking from one to billions in a matter of minutes, like your blood is a fucking all you can eat buffet. The spores follow your bloodstream up to your brain, and that's where the fun really begins. They just turn everything to mush. All your higher functions. Your thoughts, your memories, everything that makes you *you*, all gone. The only thing it leaves is the brain stem and just enough little bits of gray matter to keep you on your feet and moving."

She reaches for her cigarettes, taps one out of the pack and plays with it for a moment before lighting it. "Once the fungus has control its only goal is to make you pass it on to the next host. It keeps you alive like a life support machine. You're still breathing. Your heart's still beating, though it doesn't matter to the fungus if you're technically alive or dead. As long as your central nervous system is still working it can just guide you around like a meat puppet.

"Far as I can tell, the only thing these things feel is rage and hunger. They caught a few of them back in the first week before everything really went to shit, and they ran some tests on them. Turns out they've got about fifty times as much adrenaline rushing through them as an average person. They're permanently locked in fight or flight mode, and they always choose fight."

I look down at the street again, and suddenly it looks even more forbidding down there. The shapes lurking in the dark are just vehicles, mindless creatures compelled with every fiber of their being to chase us down and pass on the infection. They were already terrifying but now, somehow, they seem even more so. We're not just fighting individuals, but a force of nature itself.

How can we possibly beat nature?

"Earlier you said they've started to dry out. What did you mean?"

Vee lets out a chuckle. "Ah, now that's where we have the upper hand. This *Cordyceps* shit is clever, but it ain't perfect. I've been chasing these things down for a month now and I've yet to see a single one of them take a drink. I don't know for sure, but I think it destroys whatever part of the brain is responsible for basic self preservation. I guess they can't tell when they're thirsty any more, so they just don't drink until they die of dehydration."

"Huh, kinda like dolphins," I say.

Vee gives me a confused look. "You're gonna have to expand on that, Tom. Dolphins?"

"Yeah. See, dolphins can't survive on sea water. It'd kill them just like it'd kill us, so they draw all the water they need from the food they eat. In the wild that works out fine. It's just the way they evolved, so they don't know any different. The problem is that when they're in captivity they'll happily drink fresh water if they can get access to it, but then they won't eat for a week. So long as nobody notices they'll just keep happily drinking water until they eventually starve to death. They don't know the difference between thirst and hunger. Their brains just aren't wired up for it."

Vee nods. "Yeah, OK, that kinda makes sense. So if the fungus has destroyed the part of the brain that tells us when we're thirsty– "

"– the hypothalamus," I interrupt, happy that there's finally something I know about this fucked up situation that Vee doesn't.

"Right, the hypo... whatever. If that's gone these guys will just keep eating and won't bother to drink, and as long as they can't get the fluid they need from human flesh they'll eventually just die out."

"That sounds about right." I think back to something Vee said a moment ago. "Then again, you said the infected have a shitload of adrenaline running through them. The hypothalamus is responsible for regulating the adrenal glands, so maybe *Cordyceps* doesn't destroy it but just repurposes it. You know, turns that whole section of the brain into a loudhailer to yell at the adrenal glands to produce more and more. I'm just guessing. I'm not a scientist."

"You might be right," agrees Vee, lifting herself up with a grunt and joining me at the window. She looks down at the shapes moving beneath with a grimace. "I guess it doesn't really matter what's going on in their heads. As long as they're not getting enough water from their food they're living on borrowed time. We just have to wait them out. Just get through it one day at a time, and wait for the very last one of those fuckers to dry up and keel over. Then we take back the country and bury Lassiter beneath the pile of the corpses he made."

"You really think it'll be that simple? Do you really believe we can survive this?"

She nods. "We've survived this long. So long as we can stop more people getting infected I don't see why we can't get through it. Shit, you and Bishop got out of New York, right? If you can live through that you're pretty much invincible." She turns to me and lowers her voice. "Hey, that reminds me. You promised to tell me about Bishop's name. What's the big deal?"

I glance towards the door and lower my voice. "OK, I'll tell you, but you have to promise not to let him know. He's crazy sensitive about it. It's not a big deal, but you know how people can be weird about things like that." I try to keep the smile from my face. "He's called Forrest."

Vee grins. "Like– "

"Yeah, like Gump. And he's a slow, friendly guy from Alabama. You can guess what it was like growing up."

"Jesus, poor guy." She falls silent for a moment, then grins again. "Damn, I really hope we won't need to run from any infected tomorrow. I don't think I could keep myself from yelling... well, y'know."

I try to stifle a laugh as Warren rushes through the door, breathing heavily, holding his wind up lamp back away from the door so it doesn't shine out through the window. "Hey, guys. I think you need to come and listen to the radio." I stop laughing as soon as I see his expression. "I think something's happening in Columbus."

.∀.

:::11:::

THE PILOT GRINS broadly as he sees the lights of the city appear on the horizon through his windshield. He's been grinning constantly since the call came through two hours ago, and to be honest his lips are starting to ache a little now, but he just can't help himself. This is far and away the biggest night of his life. This is the night he becomes a hero, not only to Mandy and the kids but to every man, woman and child in Columbus.

Tonight the name Eric Peterson will go down in history. He may only be a small, insignificant cog in the great nation saving machine, but tonight his name will join those of a thousand other brave pilots who selflessly signed up for the President's volunteer air corps; brave pilots who are right now flying towards their own cities all across the country, all of them carrying a precious cargo.

Eric feels almost dizzy with pride. He can already imagine the hero's welcome awaiting him back at the airfield. He can imagine never having to pay for a drink again in the local bars, and being showered with praise by the assholes who used to mock him. He can imagine a tasteful marble monument, somewhere prominent in the rebuilt capital, with his name engraved on it; something he can show the grandkids one day. *See, kids, grandpa really was a hero in the war. He wasn't just the drunk idiot everyone thought he was.*

He can *definitely* imagine the welcome he'll receive when he gets home. For once, maybe, Mandy will look at him with pride rather than shame. For once she might be thinking of *him* when they make love. That'd make a nice change. Hell, maybe he'll get a little attention from some of the young girls at the bar, the ones who lean suggestively over the pool table and walk around in knotted shirts that show off their flat bellies. He wouldn't *do* anything with them, of course. It'd just be nice to know the option's there.

No. Scratch that last part. He'll need to set an example for the kids. Leering at young women doesn't fit with the heroic image racing through his head.

Eric Peterson, a humble, salt of the earth Ohio crop duster who did his part to save his country from annihilation. A man who stood up to be counted when the going got tough. A skilled pilot who dared all to save the lives of the hundreds of thousands cowering fearfully below.

Eric Peterson, *American Hero*.

Yeah. It has a nice ring to it.

He grips the stick of his trusty old American made Piper Pawnee, throttles down and drops his altitude slowly towards the 200 foot target. It'll be a challenging dump so close to the deck, maneuvering between the thirty or so buildings in the city that top that height, but he knows he's a capable pilot. He's confident he can glide safely between the skyscrapers for the three passes it'll take to cover the center of the city.

The sprawling suburbs of Columbus pass beneath him as he approaches. Somewhere down there Mandy has tucked the kids in bed and settled down to watch her shows. She doesn't know he's up here. He didn't have time to call her before he was pulled from the bar, bundled into a black SUV and whisked to the hangar. She probably thinks he's still getting hammered at McCluskey's with the guys right now. She's probably cursing his name, but she'll change her tune when she hears what he's done. When he walks in, sober and clear eyed, and tells her he's saved the city.

Here it is. He sees the narrow ribbon of the 270 pass beneath him, and he tugs the red tank release lever beside the stick. He can't see the fine mist spray from the ass of the plane, but he can hear the hydraulics whir as the nozzle opens. He can feel the upward pressure tugging at the stick as the scrappy little Piper lightens its heavy load.

He skirts the city center, pulls east towards Bexley and Whitehall then curves back around in a lazy arc, bringing it in for another pass, another spray. Out towards Valleyview and Upper Arlington then back once more. All those fancy houses he could never hope to afford. All those city folk who looked down their noses at him and wrote him off as a dumb hick. They'll all owe him their lives come the morning. Everyone will know his name.

He's flying so low he can see the people down in the streets below clear as day as they emerge from their homes and lean out their windows to see what's causing the racket above. They're probably cursing him right now. They have to get up for work in a few hours, and Eric's engines just woke the kids and set off the dog. A few of them are probably even calling the airfield to complain about the nuisance. Come the morning they'll be singing a different tune.

Would a ticker tape parade be asking too much? He doesn't know if they even do those any more, but it'd be real nice to sit in the back of a convertible, riding slowly through the city as thousands of people chant his name.

It takes a half hour of dusting before the tank runs almost dry. The gauge has been busted a few years, but he cuts it off when it feels like he has maybe five percent left. That should be more than enough.

This next part of the job is kind of off script, but he has one final special delivery to make before returning to the airfield. He guides the little Piper southwest out of the city back towards Bolton Field, but angles it so it'll take him just a couple of miles to the west. The lights begin to fade out here in the boondocks, but he doesn't need much light to find this particular target. He knows this place like the back of his hand. He could find it with his eyes closed.

There it is, a mile or so west of the cookie cutter suburban sprawl of New Rome. The unlit, unpaved track cuts a clear path between the overgrown fields and there, half hidden in a grove of willow trees at the very end of the trail, he spots the dirty white roof of his small home. The rusted wreck of an old pickup out front in a mass of crabgrass. The tire swing he put in for Dan rocking back and forth in the breeze. Out front the porch light is on, and he can almost imagine Mandy sitting out there watching her little portable set while she waits for him to return home.

Once again Eric drops to the deck, bringing his little plane down so low he almost grazes the treetops, and with a broad smile he tugs the red lever as he passes over, emptying the last of the tank directly above his wife and three sleeping children.

They'll be so proud of him. They'll be so proud of their old man when they wake up in the morning.

They'll be so, *so* proud to learn he saved the very last drops of vaccine for them.

•T•

:::12:::

THE RADIO CRACKLES as Warren adjusts the dial, searching back and forth in the dim light glowing from his lamp until he finally regains the signal.

"– see them from the window of our technician's booth. We have her out there right now checking out street level, but I can't actually get visual confirmation myself without leaving the studio. Kathy? Kathy, are you still with us, hon?"

Quick, shallow breathing emits from the speakers before the DJ returns. He speaks with the same clipped, affected radio newscaster voice everyone seems to use, but it does little to hide his panic. It takes me a few seconds to realize it's Barry Brooks - the Big Double Bee - a nationwide drive time DJ I've listened to for years. It seems strange to hear him talk about something serious, since his usual fare tends to lean towards wacky politics and celebrity gossip.

"OK, I don't seem to have Kathy right now, but I can only assume she's still in the building. I'll get an update for you just as soon as she returns to her booth but for now, to recap for listeners just tuning in, all I can say is that something troubling appears to be going on in the streets below our studio up on the twelfth floor of the LeVeque Tower on Broad Street. We... ah, we don't want to alarm listeners unduly so I really don't want to speculate on what exactly is the cause of the unrest, but I can tell you that there have been ongoing protests concerning the influx of refugees into the state in recent weeks that have threatened to spill over into violence. Obviously I don't want to make light of this... ah, or in any way diminish or dismiss the complaints of the protesters, but I'm sure all our listeners are with me in hoping that the unrest on the streets below is a simple protest and not... ah, OK, we have a caller on the line. I don't have Kathy to route the calls but I'm gonna try to put it on air. Caller, can you hear me?"

The voice comes through muffled and muddy, but audible. "Yeah I can hear you, Barry. Am I on?" It's a woman. She sounds terrified.

"You're coming through loud and clear, caller. Now, can you tell us where you are? Is anything going on in your location?"

"Barry, yeah, I'm just across the river from you in Franklinton about six blocks from the science museum. I'm real scared, Barry. I don't know what to do."

Barry lowers his voice to a comforting tone. "You're perfectly safe, caller, we're all right here with you. Now why don't you tell me your name, and try to tell me a little about what's happening on your side of the river?"

She sniffs. "It's Pam," she says, tears in her voice. "I was just, umm, I was about to get ready for bed about a half hour ago but then I heard a loud noise outside, like an engine or something, you know? So I went outside to try to figure out what was making all that racket and I saw a plane fly overhead. Real low, you know, like *too* low? It was headed over in your direction, and for a minute I just thought, *oh my gosh*, it's gonna hit one of the buildings, but it just went between them and then headed back out of town. But when it passed over the river I saw that it was... I don't know, *venting* something? There was something white coming out the back of the plane and drifting towards the ground, and just a few minutes later I started to hear screams out in the street. I was about to go look when I switched on the radio and heard you talking about some trouble."

Barry's voice is full of concern now. "Pam, are you somewhere safe? Don't go out to the street, Pam. Right now we just don't know what's happening, but I don't want you risking your safety out there. Are you safe, Pam?"

"Yeah, I'm in the upstairs bathroom right now, Barry, but I have to go fetch my daughter from her room. I'm gonna try to take a quick look out the window while I'm– oh honey, thank God. Come on inside, honey. Come on, it's safe in here. My gosh, you're burning up!"

"Pam, what's going on there? Talk to me, Pam."

A few loud clicks and muffled thumps come through the speaker, as if Pam set the phone down on the floor. After a moment her voice returns, more distant now. "Oh, honey, you've soaked right through your nightgown. It's OK, don't worry about it. Come on, come to momma. There's a good girl... No, honey, that's too hard. No. Stop it, honey. Stop it! Honey, *stop...*"

"Pam? Talk to me, Pam. What's happening?"

It sounds like the phone skates across the floor before a loud bang, maybe the sound of it hitting the wall, but the background noise is barely audible over the scream. It's ear splitting, and a long moment passes before Barry manages to cut off the call.

"Oh God, I'm sorry, listeners, I couldn't... I didn't know how to, ah..." Barry falls silent for a moment before continuing. "OK, I'm gonna see if I can figure out how to go mobile. I need to see what's going on in the street. Bear with me a second, I'm just... Look, if you're listening right now I'm begging you not to leave your homes. Just... just lock all your doors and windows and get to the most secure room in your house. Obviously we don't really know what's happening, but if this is airborne we're... just stay indoors and wait for help, OK?"

The sound cuts out for about twenty seconds. Dead air, not even static, then it suddenly returns with a confused jumble of echoing sounds.

"I don't know if I'm still on the air. I think I've got this rig wired up right, but I'm no technician. If you can still hear me I've just left the studio on the twelfth floor, and I'm headed to the windows overlooking Broad Street. I'm, ah... it's pretty dark in here, but I think I can make it across. OK, I'm here in the office of, ah... I think this is the Daystar broadcast studio. Here's the window..."

He falls silent for another moment. "OK, listeners, I'm looking down on Broad Street right now, and I have to tell you I don't see a thing. I'm leaning out the window and I've got a good clear view of City Hall to the west and the statehouse to the east, and it looks to me like the streets are pretty empty. I'm hoping that means... ah, I don't even want to say it, but right now I'm hoping this is just some kind of sick hoax, and if it is I have to say it's in remarkably poor taste. I'd hope my listeners wouldn't– *Jesus!*"

For a few seconds we hear nothing but Barry's panicked breathing.

"*Somebody jumped!*" His calm, collected radio voice has gone now. "Somebody jumped, or, or, or was pushed, or something. I just saw a person fall right past my window and down to the street. I can't see where they landed or what happened but... Oh mother of God, there's more of them! Friends, I'm looking over at the Doubletree Hotel just a block to the south of the studio and I'm seeing jumpers from the parking structure." Barry's voice seems to slur a little, like he's had a couple of drinks. "They're... oh God, they're just leaping from the garage levels, four, five floors above the street. Some of them are... Jesus, some of them are getting back up again. They're just... they're getting up from the ground and they're chasing the... oh no, something's..." He sounds completely drunk now. "I can see it on the window. Little, umm... little... I'm having a little trouble here. Can't... can't think of the, umm... the words. It's... little, umm, droplets." For a few moments all we hear is his breathing, them his voice returns a final time. Small. Quiet. Sad.

"Oh no."

He drifts off, and for the length of a dozen heartbeats there's nothing but a rustling sound. The mic against clothing? Then more heavy breathing. Deep. Irregular.

Now a noise that sounds like the inside of a wind tunnel, a rushing roar.

Now a dull thud.

Now nothing. Silence.

•⸙•

:::13:::

SAMUEL WHELAN SITS slumped over the long rosewood table in the situation room, head in hands, avoiding the sight of the big screen on the wall. Every few seconds a new red dot blooms on the map. Albuquerque. Bakersfield. Salt Lake City. Seattle. Each new dot represents a successful strike. Each dot means a puny little crop duster, a massive DC10 or a Bell 205 forest fire helicopter has successfully dropped its load on an unsuspecting city. Each dot represents chaos. Violence. Tens of thousands more dead and infected.

Each new dot brings with it a loud beep, and Whelan cringes with each one as if it brings him physical pain.

This was his plan. It was his brainchild, twisted and bastardized until it had become the exact opposite of what he'd intended. A thousand or so civilian, former military and emergency services pilots, each volunteering whatever craft they had available to save the country. He'd worked for weeks to corral them, getting the word out to fire departments, flight schools and private airfields across the nation to orchestrate what may be the single largest airstrike in the history of the planet.

The strike was supposed to save the country, and Whelan would have gone down in history as the architect of that miracle. Samuel Barnes Whelan, a man who'd spent his entire career tirelessly fighting for the interests of his nation. This would have been his crowning glory, the ultimate bloodless coup, as countless cities were bathed in a lifesaving vaccine that stopped *Cordyceps bangkokii* in its tracks and took back the nation from the infection.

And then he told Lassiter about it.

Whelan spins in his chair just quickly enough to grab the trash can before vomiting. A little splashes on his suit pants but he manages to catch most of it. He spits, wipes his mouth with the back of his sleeve and turns away from the screen once again, but not before noticing the red dot over Des Moines. His home town, gone in an instant.

Terrence fucking Lassiter.

Whelan came up through the ranks as a field agent in the Eighties. He'd spent years running dangerous missions all across the globe, and his service record was so heavily redacted it was basically just a binder of black paper with his name on the front page. He'd come face to face with everyone from Afghan Mujahideen to North Korean spies to Colombian cartel kingpins. He'd fought the worst of the worst, serious bad guys, and he'd lived to tell the tale.

In all those years as a field agent, a desk warrior and a shrewd political operator in the Washington machine he'd never come across anyone as dangerous as Terrence Lassiter. He'd heard the stories, of course. Everyone in DC had heard the stories. Lassiter was a lunatic. A fanatic. An honest to goodness religious nut, as unhinged as the worst cult leader. You couldn't trust him as far as you could throw him, and he'd happily feed you and your entire family to the lions if it helped him take a single step closer to his goals.

But everyone talked like that in DC about everyone else. Everyone threw hyperbolic insults back and forth, and everyone on the other side of the aisle was made out to be Satan personified. That was just the reality in the capital, and the problem is that it all became a little like the way people misused the word 'literally' when they really meant 'figuratively', and they did it so much that eventually even the dictionary gave up the battle as lost.

When everyone in DC describes everyone else as Satan, how the fuck can you tell when the *real* Satan comes along? The warnings have all been devalued and watered down. They don't mean anything any more, so you just tune them out.

Lassiter is truly insane. Whelan knows that now, but it's far too late.

When he arrived from Langley on the first day everyone warned him. *Watch out for that Lassiter,* they said. *He's a power hungry son of a bitch.* Of course he ignored them. People had said the same about every President from Reagan to Howard, and most of them had turned out to be fine at the end of the day. Sure, some were a little too eager to send other people's kids to war, and others were a little too gung-ho about socialized medicine, but at the end of the day they were all just typical politicians. You wouldn't trust them to hold your wallet, but you never worried they'd line you up against the wall and give the order to fire.

It took eleven days for Whelan to finally learn the truth, and the truth came with a bullet, but once Lassiter started ordering the executions of 'traitors and defectors', as he called them, it was already far too late to get away. By that point Whelan was just riding the tiger. If he tried to leave he'd find himself before a firing squad, and that wasn't an option. Whelan was a born survivor.

No, the only viable option was to stick it out. To try to guide Lassiter as best he could in the right direction. Maybe - just maybe, and he could barely even countenance the idea - find enough allies at Site R to muster a coup. To take Lassiter out, and install a President who wasn't so obviously insane.

Operation Crop Dust was meant to be his way out. It was meant to get everyone back up to the surface where the cold light of day might allow them to regain some perspective and escape the warping influence of their plainly untethered commander in chief.

And so he'd played along with Lassiter's madness. He'd nodded and smiled like someone trying to placate an armed lunatic when Lassiter described to him his vision of a 'pure' United States. When he explained that *Cordyceps* had been a blessing in disguise. That it would allow them to clear out the deadwood, rid themselves of the cancer of liberal politics and return the nation to its rightful place as God's own country. Lassiter envisioned a vast evacuation effort in which a hand-picked group of the truly righteous were protected from the infection and safely hidden away while the rest of the country - the liberals, atheists, minorities, homosexuals and anyone else Lassiter deemed unworthy of life - tore each other apart, after which the righteous would arise from the ashes and begin to rebuild.

It was plain to any fool that the plan was utterly abhorrent. It was pure evil but it was also completely impractical, and a great way to keep Lassiter occupied while Whelan worked around him. Lassiter could waste his time orchestrating his insane little scheme to turn the United States into his delusional wet dream, and it would buy Whelan time to find a real, plausible solution that would save the country.

He'd spent the first week as Lassiter's right hand man liaising with the doctors and scientists working at Camp One. Unlike many he actually *did* agree that it might be worth sacrificing a few thousand innocents if it meant saving the nation. He didn't like the idea - far from it - but he was a realist. He lived in a world of hard choices, and he knew from long experience that sometimes there simply weren't any good solutions. Sometimes you just had to settle for the one that promised the least degree of harm.

Site R's point man at the camp was a man named Major Ronald Armitage. He was an accomplished scientist, the Deputy Director of DARPA, the Defense Advanced Research Projects Agency, and he assured Whelan that his team would be able to find a solution. They were pursuing an extremely promising path with a newly developed clinical vaccine against *Candida*, a fungus that causes often fatal invasive infections in immuno-suppressed patients. The vaccine ruptures and breaks down the cell walls of *Candida* spores, preventing them from latching onto blood cells and blocking them from accessing the energy they need to reproduce. Before the attacks the vaccine had already been through two years of successful human trials, and it was just waiting on FDA approval.

Armitage had said there was an excellent chance the *Candida* vaccine could be fairly easily re-engineered to target *Cordyceps bangkokii*. Both fungi were extremely similar in structure and behavior, and with a little fine tuning the vaccine could be just as effective against the new threat. What's more, Armitage already knew that the *Candida* vaccine could be effectively aerosolized and was hardy enough to survive long spells outside the body, which meant it should be possible to deliver it directly to large populations by air drop. It was a beautifully elegant solution. The only things that stood in the way of immunizing the entire population against *Cordyceps* were funding, resources and time, and Whelan was more than happy to grant all three.

He failed to understand two important things. The first was that Lassiter, while delusional, wasn't nearly as blind to reality as Whelan assumed. The second was that Lassiter was also in contact with Major Armitage, and he was issuing him very different orders.

While Armitage worked to develop his vaccine, on Lassiter's orders he'd also set aside a large number of refugees to use as... the best term may be *Cordyceps* factories. Hundreds were immobilized, deliberately infected with the fungus and harvested as it multiplied within their bodies, before being dispatched and discarded in mass graves when the fungus had burned through all available energy. The stockpiles of Cordyceps were then unwittingly transported around the nation by private security forces, FEMA and what little remained of the armed forces.

When Whelan relayed the go order for Operation Crop Dust he'd been under the impression that they were delivering the vaccine. Armitage had assured him it was ready, and was being stockpiled and distributed. He'd lied to him, on Lassiter's orders.

Samuel Barnes Whelan had, about two hours earlier, unwittingly ordered the slaughter of millions of his fellow Americans. He'd sentenced millions to death with a single phone call, and thanks to Lassiter's lies he'd snatched defeat from the jaws of victory.

That's why, on the lustrous rosewood table in front of him, just beside the phone he used to relay the order, sits a small folding knife, and beside it two clear glass vials. They're just tiny things, not much larger than a sample sized bottle of cologne. There aren't even any markings on them. There's nothing at all to suggest what's inside.

He steels himself for a moment before turning to the wall screen, takes a look at the countless dots still spreading across the United States, and says a silent prayer for the many millions of people he unwittingly condemned. He knows he'll never be able to truly atone for his sins, but while those he killed will never know it he'd like to think they'd approve of what comes next.

Whelan takes a sip of water, pushes back his chair, slips the knife in his pocket and closes his fist carefully over one of the vials. He straightens his tie, steps to the air conditioning duct at the wall, opens the cap and pours the other through the grating. He knows the system will carry the contents efficiently around the complex within an hour or so.

The other vial is just for him.

He walks to the door and nods politely to the guard on the way out. At this time of night the hallways are virtually empty, the lights dimmed to simulate the same kind of day/night cycle as up on the surface, but he can see from the glow at the foot of the door that the chapel lights are burning bright. Lassiter's in there, praying to a God he truly believes with all his heart would condone his actions.

Whelan pushes open the door and steps through into the light. It's only his second time in the chapel. He's not a particularly religious man. It's difficult to keep the faith in his line of work, and what tattered scraps of belief remained after all these years were decisively burned away over the last month. He doesn't fear eternal judgment. He just wants an end to the suffering.

Lassiter rests on his knees by the front row of pews, silently praying and oblivious to Whelan's presence. He doesn't hear Whelan approach until it's far too late.

Samuel Barnes Whelan was trained in close combat as a CIA field agent. It may have been twenty years since he last needed to draw on that training, but it's like riding a bicycle. You never really forget. Lassiter turns at the sound of Whelan's loafers squeaking on the tile floor. His eyes widen in fear as he sees the hate radiating from his right hand man, but before he can open his mouth to cry out Whelan thrusts the heel of his palm into Lassiter's throat.

The old man falls back and wheezes, struggling to breathe. It will be difficult, but he'll be able to take in enough air to stay alive. That's important to Whelan. He wants Lassiter awake and aware. He just doesn't want him to be able to call for a guard.

Lassiter tries to scramble to his feet, clutching the marble pulpit with his bony fingers. Whelan slips the folding knife from his pocket, leans down, takes hold of Lassiter's right calf and calmly slices his Achilles' tendon. The President lets out a wheezing breath, trying to scream but unable to get it out. Whelan ignores him, grips his left leg and repeats the process.

"Don't try to talk," he says, his voice low and calm. "It's time to listen, Terrence." He looks down into Lassiter's wide, terrified, bloodshot eyes, staring at his own useless feet as blood seeps from the wounds. "Don't worry, you won't bleed to death. I know what I'm doing."

Whelan lowers himself into a pew and crosses one leg over the other. "Now, do you know what's going to happen next? No? Well,

Terrence, you're going to die." He rests his hand on his thigh, palm facing up, takes the bloodied knife and runs a long line across his hand, wincing with the pain. Lassiter stares at the cut with tears in his eyes, his mouth opening and closing silently.

"You know you'll be the first man I ever killed, Terrence. Directly, at least. You know, face to face. All those years as an agent and I never had to take a life. Never had to slip poison into a drink. Never had to take out a double agent. I know, right? I wasn't exactly James Bond." He opens his fist and shows Lassiter the glass vial. "Tonight you made me kill millions, and none of them will be clean deaths."

He tosses the vial into his cut hand and crushes it in his fist. A little blood runs down his wrist and stains his white shirt sleeve red. "Millions of terrified people, Terrence. Chased. Beaten to death. Torn to shreds by their own loved ones. So," he says, relaxing in the pew," I think it's only fair that their commander in chief joins them."

Whelan blinks a couple of times and shakes his head. He can already feel the effects of the *Cordyceps* coursing through his veins. He feels lightheaded and a little sleepy, just as he does whenever he sits in a meeting after a scotch at lunch. "It's kicking in, Terrence. Not long to wait now. It'll all be over soon."

Lassiter reaches up to the pulpit and grabs at the corner of a copy of the Bible until it falls down to his chest. He hugs it close, as if it might offer some kind of protection. Whelan chuckles. "You really thought you were serving God, Terrence? You really thought God wanted you to kill millions of His people? No, Terrence, you weren't serving God. You were only serving yourself. God would be disgusted with you. He'd be ashamed to have let a self-righteous maggot like you soil his creation." He feels a tingling in his limbs, and a touch of vertigo kicks in. "He's going to let you die down here in the darkness, Terrence. You'll never feel the sun on your face again. That's your reward, Terrence. That's your punishment... Oh... I feel it. It's time, Terrence. I hope you're ready to face whatever comes next."

Beside the door of the situation room the young guard stands to attention, struggling to stay awake in the half light. For the last half hour he's been counting the floor tiles, trying to stay alert by working out the volume of water it would take to flood the hallway up to the ceiling, assuming the floor tiles are six inches to a side. So far he's–

He has his gun out of its holster moments after hearing the scream. It sounds like a wounded animal, more a roar than a scream. He rushes in the direction of the chapel, bursting through the door just in time to see Samuel Whelan lower his head to the body in front of the pulpit. He freezes in terror as Whelan takes a bite, and comes back up with a length of stringy, bloody flesh stretching from his teeth down to the body.

The guard puts him down in two shots, the first through his back and the second a clean shot through the back of the head. Whelan slumps to the ground like a rag doll, and the guard rushes forward and turns white as a sheet as he sees the President beneath him.

He mumbles a few words into his radio, and moments later a siren begins to wail through the facility, echoing through the halls, locking down each section of the site and allowing only guards free movement. He'll just wait at the door and keep the room secure until backup arrives. He'll –

Beneath Whelan's body the President begins to stir. It's just a twitch at first, but then he struggles to pull himself up. The guard rushes back towards the pulpit, desperately struggling to remember the first aid training he was given during basic. How do you treat a neck wound?

Apply pressure, right? Raise the head above the body?

He's only a few feet from the President when he realizes first aid won't do any good.

President Terrence Lassiter opens and closes his mouth, letting out a strained snarl from his collapsed throat. He locks his bloodshot eyes on the guard and reaches his hands out towards him, desperately trying to attack but held back by the weight of Whelan's body covering his legs.

The guard raises his gun without a second thought and calmly puts a bullet through the President's left eye. The man slumps to the ground, and as he falls the Bible slips from his chest and lands with a splash in the spreading pool of blood surrounding his head like a halo.

•🟊•

:::14:::

WARREN HUNTS THROUGH the AM band with a somber expression, visibly tensing whenever he finds something other than static. He's wearing earphones to pick up the weaker, more distant signals, and reporting to us whenever he finds something. In the last hour he's tuned into more than a dozen broadcasters from all across the country - KAAY out of Little Rock; KVOX, Fargo; WMVP, Chicago, to name a few - and they're each reporting the same thing. There's been a widespread outbreak in every state we've heard from, and while we can scarcely believe it it seems to have been intentional. Five of the stations reported sightings of aircraft above towns and cities before everything went to shit.

Bishop has been weeping in the corner for the last twenty minutes, and I don't blame him at all. A little while ago Warren picked up a faint signal from WJOX, a 50kW sports radio station out of Birmingham, Alabama, his home town. The DJ reported in a thick, slow southern drawl that a DC10 had dropped what looked like water across a huge swathe of the city, including the broadcast studio itself. We held the signal for ten minutes, and by the time it finally cut out the DJ was begging for help as the infected swarmed in from the street through the broken window.

Bishop's family is long gone, thank God, but I still understand how he feels. I felt the exact same way when I stood on the Verrazano Narrows bridge and looked back at the ruins of Brooklyn. It's not so much the destruction. That's just the most obvious aspect of the tragedy.

No, the biggest tragedy is learning that everything you ever knew is forever gone. It's the thought that no matter how long you live you really can't ever go home again. The city might still remain. Bishop's old high school might still stand, and his childhood home might look just the same as it always did. The same rusty gate out front. The same creaking floorboard on the third step up the staircase. The same old tire swing in the back yard. But none of it matters without the people. Without the people they're just buildings.

So now, like me, he's set adrift. Even if we can somehow survive this, whatever it is. Even if we can get through it unharmed until the very last of the infected die away, where is there to go? To where would we return after our victory? Soldiers at least get to go home after surviving a brutal war, but for us there's nowhere to return to. We've not only lost our future, but our connection to the past.

"Tom?" Warren tugs at my sleeve. "Help me out here, man, this signal's real weak. Here, take an ear." He hands over one of his earbuds, and carefully plays with the dial to try to hunt down the signal. I can hear a voice, just barely. "You hearing that?"

I nod, and press the earbud deeper into my ear in an effort to pick it up more clearly.

"– the order from up top a couple hours ago, but something didn't seem right so we held off."

"That's it, Warren. I got it, don't touch the dial."

Another voice comes through. Sounds like she's from somewhere out west. "Captain, when you say you got orders, where exactly did they come from? Is there still a command structure in place?"

"Well not really, ma'am, at least not as far as I know. The way I understand it the orders come direct from the President. Or, you know, someone at the base near Camp David, anyhow. All I know is that we've been speaking to a man by the name of Whelan these past two weeks. I'm told he's the boss at the CIA, and he had all the right authorization codes to order an airdrop, so we went along with it."

The woman returns. "And can you tell us exactly what happened tonight, in your own words?"

"Yes, ma'am. I came on shift 'bout two hours ago to find we'd received a shipment of vaccine from... well, I don't know, to tell the truth, but it was delivered in a kinda gas truck by folks who identified themselves as army, and they had all the right ID, so we let 'em fill three of our Bambi buckets. They handed me orders to make the drop at midnight local time, and– "

"I'm sorry, Captain, Bambi buckets?"

"That's right, ma'am. That's what we call the, ah, the water containers we use to make drops over wildfires. They're just collapsible open topped buckets. We usually dip them down into Kirby Lake to fill 'em up, dump them on a fire then head back to fill 'em up again." He coughs. "So anyway, they gave me orders to make all three drops at the same time over Abilene, which is... well, I don't know, something about it didn't scan quite right, then I noticed the guys pumping the vaccine were wearing respirators. Just didn't seem above board, you know?"

"And Captain," the woman asks, "did you question the orders at the time?"

"No, ma'am, I didn't. There was just something off about them, you know, and the way things have been recently I didn't want to find myself in a fight with a bunch of tooled up creeps, you know? So yeah, I just took the orders and sent them on their way, then I tried to put in a call in to Whelan over there at Site R, but I couldn't get through to the switchboard until gone half past midnight, when they told me that all orders were rescinded until further notice. They wouldn't tell me what the hell was goin' on, but they just warned me to stay the hell away from those Bambi buckets. Of course, then we started to hear about what was going on elsewhere. All I can say is thank Christ we held off. I just don't think I could have lived with myself if I'd dropped that stuff on my family. Doesn't bear thinking about, does it?"

"It doesn't, Captain. I want to thank you for taking the time to speak with us tonight, and I'm sure everyone in Abilene thanks you for your caution. God bless, Captain."

"Well, thank you, ma'am, I appreciate it.

"That was Captain Roy Walken of the Abilene Fire Department, whose brave actions tonight surely saved the lives of more than a hundred thousand residents of Abilene, Texas." She pauses for a moment, as if to collect her thoughts, and lets out a heavy sigh. "Folks, it's been a rough night here in the Lone Star State, and all across the country. We don't know much, and details are still emerging by the minute, but we know that the nation has been dealt an almost killing blow with widespread attacks on dozens of cities and hundreds of towns from coast to coast. We're also hearing rumors - and I'd like to make it clear that they are, at present, unconfirmed - that an attempted coup at the government facility Site R has resulted in the death of Acting President Lassiter. We're doing everything we can to firm up that information for you right now, but right now we can't seem to raise contact with the facility. As it stands we're..." The voice suddenly fades out.

"What did you do? Get it back!" I demand.

Warren shrugs. "I didn't do anything, the battery died." He sighs. "I got some more in the car, but unless somebody wants to ring the dinner bell for the dozen or so hungry fuckers down on the street it'll have to wait until morning."

Over in the corner Vee's trying to coax Bishop out of his depression with a candy bar, and strangely enough it seems to be doing the trick. He's stopped crying, at least. "Hey, guys?" I call out quietly. Vee looks up while Bishop struggles with the wrapper of a Three Musketeers bar. "Word is the President's dead."

I don't know what I expected. Joy? Relief? I've no idea, but I didn't expect anger. Vee looks furious, as if she's personally offended that she won't get the chance to kill him herself. She makes a fist and punches the wall beside Bishop, making the big guy flinch away from her and drop his candy bar. "Fucking piece of shit coward prick, dying in his bunker like a God damned cut price Hitler. I wanted to string him up above a pit full of infected, hand a knife to the families of everyone who died in that camp and watch him beg for fucking mercy. *Jesus*," she sighs and slumps against the wall beside Bishop.

Warren and I exchange a look. "Warren, let's never get on her bad side, OK?"

He chuckles. "Hey, you don't have to tell me, brother. Couple weeks ago she pushed a guy off the roof of a 7-Eleven for bleeding on her boots."

"Infected, right?"

He shrugs and gives me a sly smile. "Well, she said he was, but..."

"He was infected," Vee testily insists. "I just really loved those boots, OK? Had to throw the damned things out once they got covered in infected blood." She looks down at her heavy standard issue boots and breaks the slightest hint of a smile. "This apocalypse has been murder on my wardrobe."

Warren smiles and tucks the dead radio back in his duffel. "Well kids, I'd love to stay up all night and regale you with gory stories about the trail of dead Lieutenant Reyes has left in her wake, but I think it's a good idea for us all to get a little shut eye. Come morning we have to make some big decisions, and I don't want you guys all cranky and uptight while we're planning how to stay alive." He lifts himself from the floor and hikes his rifle up over his shoulder. "I'll take first watch."

I glance at my wrist, as if the time of night really matters any more. "I think I'll join you for a while if you don't mind. Don't think I'll be able to get much sleep, knowing what's outside."

Warren nods. "Yeah, it takes a little getting used to, I'll grant you that. Come on, I think I've got a little scotch in my pack. That should help knock you out."

"You good, Vee?" I look over to Reyes to find her smiling, leaning against Bishop's large, pillow-like shoulders. "Yeah, go ahead. This might be the best night's sleep I'll get in weeks. Bishop here's like a big teddy bear."

Bishop flashes a cheerful grin, his mouth surrounded with a ring of melted chocolate, and shuffles his ass forward until he's resting comfortably against the wall. "Huh huh," he chuckles, closing his eyes. "Teddy bear."

"Good night, guys." I grab my jacket, switch off the lamp, and follow Warren down the corridor back to the front of the building, glad for the opportunity to take a little fresh air.

"After a month locked in that box this is something I'll never take for granted again," I say, heading straight for the window.

"What's that?"

"Air. Just... fresh damned air, whenever I feel like taking a breath. You don't miss the breeze on your face until it's gone, you know? All I want to do now is go live in the middle of a big, open field and just live under the stars, feeling the breeze."

Warren smiles. "Me, I just wanna get a nice little yacht and find some island somewhere. I don't care where, as long as it doesn't stink of dead people." He tugs a bottle from the depths of his duffel and tosses it over. Lagavulin, 16 years old. "Thanks." I nod appreciatively. "Hey, this is good stuff."

"Yeah? I boosted it from a liquor store out in Valley Lake. I'm not a big liquor drinker, to be honest. I just grabbed the bottle with the biggest price tag."

"Good call." I unscrew the cap and take a long swig, enjoying the warmth as it coats the sides of my throat like honey. "This is my drink, when I can afford to switch from beer." I hand it back, and try to resist the urge to laugh at Warren's expression as he takes a gulp of the burning liquor.

"Jesus," he groans, wiping his mouth. "People drink this shit for fun? Gimme a cold beer any day of the week."

I take the bottle back from him. "It's an acquired taste, but if you ever want to get drunk again I'd advise you to acquire it. I get the feeling the future isn't so bright for cold beer." I take another swig and lower myself down against the wall by the window. I'm already feeling the whiskey kick in after a month without touching a drop. "So what's your story, Warren? How'd you end up on the wrong end of the apocalypse?"

He grabs an office chair in the darkness, rolling it over by the window so he can see out to the street. "My story? Well, it doesn't take much telling. Typical army brat. I spent a lot of time following my dad around the world as a kid. Little time in Germany. Couple of years at Okinawa. *Far* too much time in Guam. Soldiering is the family business, so when the time came I joined up. Trained as a sniper at Fort Benning, then it was straight off to Afghanistan, then Syria. Three tours, 107 confirmed kills." He reaches over and takes back the bottle. "I never really cared for it, to be honest. I always wanted to be a firefighter, but what are you gonna do? Turns out I'm just really good at killing people from far away." He winces again at the burn, then sighs. "Anyway, I took an IED hit near Damascus just back in March. They shipped me off back home, and I'd just about had the last piece of shrapnel pulled out of my ass in Maryland when everything started to go south. I checked myself out, found a ride north, hooked up with Vee's unit from Fort Dix and the rest is history. We spent the last month on cleanup duty, trying and failing to get some kind of handle on this mess."

Another pull, another wince. "Gah! That shit's awful." He hands it back again. "We bugged out after Vee's husband was killed last week, when we found out what was really going on at Camp One. Figured it was best to carry on solo after we realized who we were really fighting for." He falls silent and takes a long look out the window, scanning the street below. "What about you? What did you do before all this shit?"

I pull out my cigarettes. "Do you mind if I...?" Warren shakes his head, and I light up. "Well, before all this I guess I was a professional drifter, if we're being honest." I take another swig, and I'm surprised to realize I'm already getting pretty drunk. "I was a freelance journalist. I traveled around the world picking up work here and there. Mostly small stuff, you know, local papers, airline magazines, that kinda thing. I wasn't great, but I made enough cash that I could live pretty well in Asia and avoid growing up for as long as possible.

"I was in Thailand last year, just a couple of months after the first attack. You remember that guy Paul McQueen? The Aussie guy who survived it? I knew him. Just by chance he and I used to be drinking buddies in Ulaanbaatar, Mongolia, and when he decided to tell his story he reached out to me. I guess I might have talked up my career a little after a few beers one time, and he thought I was some kind of serious newsman. You know, rather than a guy who wrote articles like *15 Budget Breaks in Sweden* for Scandinavian Airlines' in-flight magazine.

"That got me a feature in Time Magazine. My first big story, and it ended with an old friend killing himself." I take a long drag on the Marlboro, and watch the smoke curl away in the dim moonlight. "After that I guess I went a little off the rails for a while. Came home to New York and spent months obsessing about that warning. You remember it, that weird handwritten message from the Sons of the Father? That thing scared me. I got caught up in all kinds of conspiracy theories, trying to prove it was genuine, but I didn't know how. I guess I went a little too far down the rabbit hole. Started to lose track of what was real." I can tell I'm slurring my words a little now.

"Then one day I met a girl. Kate. Just a regular girl, nothing all that special about her. I wasn't in love with her. Didn't really have all that much in common with her, to be honest, but she was *safe*. I figured if I just acted liked I was in love I might magically end up leading some kind of normal life. You know, move in with her. Get a rescue dog. Argue about which IKEA bookcase best suits our personalities. I managed to fool myself for months." I take another long swig and pass the already half empty bottle up to Warren.

"Don't let me have any more of that." I stub out my cigarette on the carpet and continue. "When New York went to shit we got caught up right in the middle of it. We ended up at a park in Brooklyn, just... just *rammed* with people. Thousands of them, all terrified and confused. When we heard there were bombs on the way we tried to get out, and... well, the details aren't important, but it all went wrong. Kate died."

I look up at the weaving image of Warren at the window and take a deep breath. "You know the first thought that went through my head when I realized she'd been killed? I was *relieved*. I was fucking relieved that I didn't have to play at being a regular person any more. *Jesus fucking Christ*, I'm going to hell."

Warren takes a sip from the bottle and remains diplomatically silent.

"That's what's been rattling around my head for the last month. Stuck in that box, wondering why an asshole like me deserved to live while a sweet girl like Kate deserved to die. Where's the justice in that? She was too good for me. She loved me, and I couldn't even keep her safe." I reach for my pack of smokes, then remember I just put one out. "Anyway... I don't know why I'm here. I don't know why I survived and she didn't, and I don't have the first fucking clue how I can ever redeem myself."

My mind finally clears long enough for me to realize I'm heaping my innermost worries on someone I've only known for a few hours. I look around in the darkness for my jacket and pull over my legs. "Umm... I think I need to rest my eyes a little."

"Yeah, I think that's probably a good idea, Tom. Don't worry, I'll hold the fort. You just get some sleep. You'll feel much better in the morning."

"Yeah. Yeah, it'll all be better in the morning. Thanks, Warren. You're a good guy." I roll to the side, tuck my legs up towards my chest and pull the jacket a little further up. "Better in the morning," I mutter to myself.

The darkness only takes a few moments to close in.

•┇•

:::15:::

IT HAD BEEN three days since a car last went by, and he was growing impatient. He was hungry. He was tired. He hadn't been laid in more than a week. If he didn't find someone soon he'd die before they let him back in. Jesus, he might never get laid again.

The community was pretty simple. You get to sleep somewhere safe and warm, and maybe you get the chance to take a turn with one of the women every once in a while, but only if you deliver the goods. Bring in loot to share and you get to stay. Come home empty handed and you're on your own. Sounds like a perfect system. Fair work for fair pay. No damned welfare queens suckling at the teat of hard working folk like Roy. No scroungers taking what was rightfully his. No assholes to abuse the generosity of good, honest, decent people.

It was just what he'd been hoping for all these years. It was what he'd prayed for whenever someone shared yet another story on Facebook about some entitled asshole buying lobster with his food stamps, or a damned immigrant family being handed a free home bigger than his just because the mom couldn't stop firing out kids. Roy had been over the moon when he finally got his wish. Work hard and you're on easy street. Slack off and you're out on your ass. No free rides. That's the way it should be. We can't afford to support folk who don't pull their weight. You don't want to work? Tough shit.

The community had been pretty great in the beginning, back when the quarantine zone was first established. The place was set up pretty quickly after people started evacuating, and with only thirty or so residents its needs were simple. Guns, food, and clean water. Maybe a little medicine, just in case. With millions of fugees fleeing to the west and no cops on the streets the pickings were easy. Roy worked just a couple hours a day. He'd get up, head out, raid an abandoned Walmart, and he'd be back home before lunch with a trunk full of canned soup and a few crates of vodka.

Then it all began to change. The community grew, and it started taking in people who had real skills. The doc arrived, and he was exempt from looting. A couple of plumbers came in, and they got the same treatment 'cause they knew how to keep the showers working with some fancy pumps. An electrician showed up - a damned wetback, at that - and he was given a pass 'cause he knew how to set up solar power up on the roof so they didn't have to run the generators day and night. And the women, of course. They were let in for free so long as they were willing to give it up every so often.

It was only a few weeks before there were ten times as many mouths to feed. More than four hundred people behind the walls, and suddenly they decided old Roy wasn't doing his part. "You only got a hundred tins today, Roy?" they'd say, looking down their noses like the fancy assholes sitting at the top of the pile always did to good, honest people like him. "We got hundreds of mouths to feed in here, man. We need at least a thousand tins every day just to keep folks fed. You're gonna have to go out again."

He tried to keep it up for a while. Worked four, five hours a day collecting loot. Tried to find new stores that hadn't already been picked clean. Tried to lug enough crap home that he'd get a pat on the head and the satisfaction of a job well done, but it was never enough for those bastards. They always wanted more. They always wanted to exploit his hard work just a little too much.

So... yeah. Suddenly good old Roy found himself surplus to requirements, just like he had in every damned job for the last ten years. There were fifty folk out looting for the community, and they said he was the laziest. They said he drank more'n he brought back, and he was taking more'n his share of food and smokes. They said he took too much time with the women, and if he wanted more he'd have to work harder to earn it.

Of course it was bullshit. Roy pulled his weight just like everyone else. He broke his back to provide for his new family, but like always folks like Roy just weren't appreciated. There was always some asshole up at the top who'd try to take advantage of simple hard working folk like him.

The last straw came one day when he'd just finished up with one of the girls, sometime around lunchtime. He was just about to wash up and go on a looting run when the top guy - some jumped up prick who called himself the Chief - stormed in and grabbed hold of his collar. He dragged Roy down to the front door, threw his bag out into the street and tossed Roy after it. Kept going on about how they needed the beds for people who worked hard for them. Wouldn't even listen when Roy said he was just heading out the door to go to work.

He still wanted back in, though. Even after just a week he was already tired of sleeping with one eye open. He was tired of washing with cold bottled water. He was tired of having to find somewhere to rest each night where he knew they couldn't get at him. Everything was better at the community, even if it was run by silver spoon pricks who wouldn't know a day of hard work if it married their sister.

Then he figured out what he could bring to the table. He figured out how he could get back through the door.

There were a little more than four hundred people in the community when he left, but only around forty women. When everyone ran away to the west it was mostly the guys who stayed behind. People with families were long gone. You're not gonna keep your wife and kids in Pennsylvania when there are crazy infected fuckers running around the place, so of course they were the first to go, tearing away in their sensible SUVs with SpongeBob playing on the screens in the back of the seats.

The guys who stuck around were mostly young, ambitious types. Guys with vision and balls. Guys who could see the opportunities presented by the quarantine zone. They were mostly single, and of course they all liked to get laid.

Now, some of those forty women in the community were a little too old, or a lot too young. The law didn't hold much weight any more but the Chief had made it pretty damned clear from day one that nobody was to touch the kids and grandmas. That only left one woman for every twenty or so men, and by the time they kicked Roy out the girls were already whining about being worked too hard for their keep.

So... yeah. There was Roy's way back in. They'd have to open the doors for him if he brought back a fresh, tasty piece of pussy to share around. They'd slap him on the back and call him a hero. Maybe he'd earn himself a couple weeks grace. A couple weeks to sit back and relax in safety before they started asking more from him. A couple weeks to try out the rest of the girls. Hell, maybe they'd be so grateful he took some work off their plate they'd throw him a little extra.

But there was a problem. He didn't know where to find any fucking women.

He'd been out on the road for a week, and he'd yet to see a single chick. He'd looked high and low, scouring houses out in the sticks, visiting all the old FEMA camps to see if there were any stragglers left behind. He found plenty of guys and plenty more infected, but no pussy.

Then he had a brainwave. The highway.

The 78 was pretty much the only east-west highway still clear. Most of the other routes got snarled up with breakdowns and pile ups the first few days when all the fugees fled west, but the 78 wasn't so bad. It came from the direction of New York, and... well, most of the folks from New York were already dead.

So Roy decided to camp out. He stocked up on food and water, found himself a pair of binoculars and set himself up on a hill close to a curve in the highway where cars would have to slow down to pass a pile of wrecks. He figured eventually he'd get lucky. Eventually a couple of stragglers would decide the east was too risky, and they'd try to make it out west by the highway. There had to be a few women left, and when they came by he'd pounce. It was a solid plan, and he was pretty damned proud of himself for dreaming it up.

Then three days went by.

Three days without a single car. Three days staring down at an empty road, sleeping up a tree with a branch sticking into his spine just in case any infected came by at night. Three days without a wash, and a day since his cigarettes had run out. He was about ready to call it quits, drive back to the community and just beg them to open the doors. He'd clean toilets. He'd scrub dishes. He'd go out looting ten, twelve hours a day. He'd do just about anything if it meant he could sleep in safety again.

He'd decided to make a move as soon as the sun came up after his fourth night in the tree. He'd stop in at a Target he'd seen close to the highway and return with a car stocked to the roof with goodies. Candy, cigarettes, booze and enough tinned food to feed an army. He'd camp outside for a week if necessary, pleading with them to open the doors. It was all set.

It was sometime around one in the morning when he heard the engine. For a moment he thought he was imagining it. The only sounds he'd heard in days were the wind, the groans of the infected and the report from his own pistol as he burned through his dwindling supply of ammo. He rolled down the window, cocked his ear and held his breath as he listened for it.

There it was, right on the edge of his hearing, drifting in and out as the wind carried it. He scrambled quickly from his car and climbed to the roof, grabbing his binoculars as he went. It took him a moment to find it but there it was, an old, beat up Toyota puttering slowly through the wrecks.

And there was a woman driving.

He could barely believe his luck. He hadn't seen a woman out in the wild for about three weeks, and to be honest it was really weird to see one just sitting in a car, driving around like she wasn't an endangered species.

Not only was it a woman but she looked pretty hot, far as he could tell. Slim, nice lips, decent set of tits. It wasn't so easy to see in the darkness but she looked like she might be a Spic. Roy didn't really go for Mexican chicks, but he knew a lot of people went crazy for the exotic types. She'd go down a storm back at the community. They didn't get all that many of them in rural Pennsylvania, and most of the women back at the community were white as snow apart from one light-skinned black chick with a smart mouth and a fat ass. The folks back home'd just eat up that sweet Latina pussy, so long as she was one of the clean ones.

He scanned the rest of the car through his binoculars, and he was a little put off by the fact that there were a few guys in the car. The big guy in the back looked like he could be trouble. No telling with the other two. They both looked smaller than Roy, but who knows? Sometimes those wiry guys could throw a solid punch. Might be a good idea to take all three of them out if the chance came up.

He jumped back in the car and gunned the engine, fishtailing it with the lights off until he finally skidded his way down onto a dusty track that ran alongside the highway a while. He tried to keep his speed under control. He was getting a little too excited, and he knew the Toyota would easily outpace him once it worked its way through the wrecks. If he could just get to the next on ramp before it vanished he might be able to trail them until they took a break.

His heart leaped to his throat when he saw the car peel off the highway at the next exit. It was coming right towards him, so he cut off the engine and sat in wait while it rolled slowly into the next town. He followed carefully, making sure he didn't get too close, until they parked up in front of an old office block and started unpacking their car.

Mm hmm, she was hot. He got a much better view once she stepped out of the car, and he definitely wasn't disappointed. She was one of those cute, spunky Michelle Rodriguez types. All tough on the surface with her heavy, shapeless army gear, but he could tell she'd be sweet and warm as apple pie underneath. There was definitely a cute little ass hiding beneath those fatigues, and even though he wasn't a big fan of the wetbacks he'd love to hold her down and spend a little time getting to know her. Hell, it was a long drive back to the community. Maybe he'd be able to find somewhere safe and quiet along the way to break her in for a while before he shared her with the rest of the guys.

He gave it a couple hours before making his move. He was eager to go earlier, but the sound of the Toyota had attracted a few infected to the street and he had to wait for them to wander away. Couldn't fire off the weapon without letting the girl know he was coming, so he had to be patient.

Finally the last of them drifted off down the street, and Roy made his move. He left the car where it was parked - it was a busted up old wreck anyhow - and skirted the buildings until he reached the car, grinning when he saw they'd left the keys in the ignition. Perfect.

Roy pulled out his pistol and checked the magazine. Only two shots left. Not enough to take out all three of the guys, but if could be enough to get the upper hand if it came to it. He slipped quietly through the open front door of the building, careful to stick to the silence of the carpet, and slowly began to make his way up the stairs.

Boy, they'd be proud of him when he got this sweet little piece of ass back to the community.

•🝓•

:::16:::

I OPEN MY eyes slowly, and immediately look around in the darkness for the cat that took a shit in my mouth.

The headache hits me right away. After a month without a drink and nothing lining my stomach but a candy bar the liquor coursed through my blood like poison, and now it's mounting a full frontal assault directly behind my left eye. It feels like my brain swelled two sizes in my sleep, and it's trying to escape through the socket.

By the window Warren lies asleep, resting against the sill, his arm draped over the stock of his rifle. On the floor beside him the bottle of Lagavulin has fallen on its side, and Warren's olive green duffel now rests in the middle of a patch of sticky carpet. I kick my jacket from my body, climb shakily to my feet and grab the bag, searching through it until I find a bottle of water and a blister pack of paracetamol. Thank God for the well-prepared.

My bladder starts calling out to me as soon as I finish the water, and in the dim blue pre-dawn glow I clumsily make my way out of the room to the bathroom at the far end of the hallway. It's pitch black inside, so I grab a trash can and prop open the door before stumbling to the urinal, fumbling with my pants and releasing a pungent, worryingly dark stream of piss. I make a mental note to drink as much water as I can find today. They only gave us a small glass with each meal at the camp, so Bishop and I are probably both pretty severely dehydrated.

I'm shaking off when I hear the moan, and I freeze instantly. The hairs on the back of my neck stand on end, and I realize how stupid it was to leave the Beretta in my jacket pocket by the window. I'm standing in a room with only one exit, cock out, unarmed and hungover. The moan comes again, closer this time, along with the sound of wet, rasping breath. I zip up and scan the room for a weapon, but the only thing that isn't screwed down is the flimsy plastic trash can. I tiptoe to the door and grab it anyway. Maybe I can wedge it over the head of anyone who enters, blinding them long enough to get past and run back to my gun.

The moan is just outside the door now, a few steps down the hall. I flip the trash can, and I'm ready to pounce when the moan turns to soft weeping. *What the fuck?* I risk a quick peek around the door.

"Bishop, what the hell happened?" The big guy is leaning with one hand against the wall, clutching his nose and crying with pain. Tears stream down his face, and his swollen nose is a mess of blood and bubbling mucus. "Jesus, come here. Let's get you cleaned up."

Bishop nods and lets me guide him to the washbasin. I turn the faucet and wait, and it takes a moment of creaking and bubbling from the pipes before I remember the water isn't running any more. All that escapes from the faucet is a thin trickle of brackish brown liquid, so I pull Bishop over to a stall and sit him down while I lift the lid from the cistern.

He winces and moans as I wash the blood from his face, trying to squirm out of the way as I splash him. "Hold still, Bishop," I order, but still he twists away from me like a kid.

"It hurts too bad," he cries, digging his chin into his armpit so I can't reach his nose.

"OK, no more water. Lemme just get a look at your nose, man." He shakes his head and tucks it deeper. "Just lemme look at it, and I'll get you some painkillers."

After a moment's thought he finally untucks his chin and turns towards me, looking down with crossed eyes at his bloody nose. "It's real bad, Tom. I think it's broken."

"Yeah, no shit." There's a large bulge sticking out of the right side, and the tip is curved about a quarter inch to the left. I can tell by his voice and the blood and mucus bubbling from one nostril that the other is completely blocked. I know what I have to do. I've reset my own nose twice before, and I know he'll thank me in about ten minutes when the pain begins to fade.

Before Bishop figures out what I'm doing I reach out, press both thumbs firmly into the sides of his nose and pull down. With a dull, wet click the bones and cartilage shift straight, and Bishop jerks back against the cistern with a snorting cough that sends a massive amount of blood spraying across both of us.

"*Fuck!*" he yells, blowing a strand of phlegmy blood onto his shirt. "What the hell did you do that for?"

I reach behind him and rinse my hands in the cistern, then rush to the towel dispenser and grab enough paper to wipe myself down. "I fixed it," I gasp, trying to hold back the puke climbing my throat at the sight of the wet, gooey red phlegm dripping from my shirt. I grab another wad of towels and pass them to him. "Now stop whining and tell me what happened."

Bishop wipes his face and sniffs away the tears. "I thought it was a bad dream, Tom. I just thought I was imagining it, then I woke up with this," he says, pointing at his swollen face.

"What do you mean? How did it happen?"

He sniffs again. "A man came in, sometime in the night. I just woke up and he was right there in front of me with his gun. I thought he was gonna shoot me but he just turned it around and hit me in the nose and I fell down. Then he hit me on top of my head." He tilts his head towards me and gingerly pushes aside his hair. There's an angry purple lump just above his hairline. "I must have passed out, because next thing I knew it was starting to get light out in the hallway and Vee was gone."

It takes a few moments for this to sink in. "Vee's gone?"

Bishop nods mournfully. "Uh huh. Her bag's still here, but she took her gun with her."

I lean down and grab him by the shoulders. "Bishop, the man. Did he take Vee?"

He shrugs, and the tears begin again as he rubs the lump on his head. "I don't know, Tom. He knocked me out, you know?"

"OK, just... just don't do anything. I'm going to get Warren."

My hangover is completely forgotten as I rush back down the hallway, poking my head into Bishop and Vee's small room as I go. Bishop was right. Her gun is nowhere to be seen, but her bag is right where she left it by the wall.

I continue on until I reach the front of the building, where Warren is clutching his head and popping painkillers from the blister pack I left on the floor. "Man, that stuff's brutal." He nods towards the spilled Lagavulin in the floor. "I'm sticking to beer from now on, even if I can't find a cold one." He looks up at me with bloodshot eyes. "Jesus, what happened?"

I look down at my bloody shirt and wave it away. "Doesn't matter. Vee's been taken. Some guy came in the night and knocked Bishop out. She's gone, but her stuff's still here."

Warren's face turns gray as I speak, and his eyes flit guiltily to the empty bottle on the floor. "Jesus, I should have been awake."

"We can blame ourselves later," I say, grabbing my jacket and checking the gun is still there. "For now let's just concentrate on getting her back."

Warren nods, hefts his rifle from the windowsill and scoops his stuff into his duffel bag before following me out the door. Along the way we find Bishop moping in the hallway, and after grabbing Vee's bag the three of us move quietly down through the building, checking along the way that we're alone.

It's only when we reach the ground floor that we realize how fucked we really are. Through the propped open glass door I see a dozen infected milling in the street... and one of them is standing in the empty spot where we parked the car.

"I don't suppose you have a spare vehicle in that duffel, Warren?" I nod out the door to the empty space.

Warren looks out, and when he turns back I can see he's smiling. "No, I don't," he says, rooting through Vee's bag, "but I do have a homing beacon." He pulls out a chunky black device that looks like an iPhone and a walkie talkie had a kid. "Sat phone," he says, clicking the thick, stumpy rubber antenna into place. "My battery died last week, but Vee still has a bit of charge. Aaaaaaand..." He taps the screen a couple times, frowning. "Yep, here it is. Big mistake, you dumb bastard. Karl's phone was still in the trunk with the rest of his stuff." He flips the phone around, and I can see a blue dot flashing on the screen against a faint map. It's moving west along what looks like Highway 78.

"OK, shut it down." I point to the red battery warning in the corner. "Save the power. We can power it back up when we have a car. Speaking of which, any idea how we're gonna get past these guys outside?"

Warren shrugs the rifle off his shoulder. "How do you think? You know how to turn your safety off?"

I slip the Beretta from my jacket pocket and flip the catch with my thumb. "Got it. Bishop, get ready to hold this door when we shout, OK? Warren, I'll give you backup from here. Try to keep it quiet."

Bishop nods, and Warren sees what I'm getting at. He takes a knee by the door and checks his gun while I take up position just behind him. "Good thinking, kid. We'll make a soldier of you yet."

Six of the dozen are on the ground before the first of them notices us. Warren's rifle reports echo through the street and the infected swing around wildly, hunting for the source of the sound as their brothers drop to the deck. Once one of them notices us, though, it only takes a few seconds for the rest to pick it up and come charging in.

It's been almost a decade since I last fired a gun. I'd forgotten how the noise fills your entire world when the gun is only at arm's length, but I don't flinch. I hold it steady and squeeze off rounds until the magazine runs empty and the slide springs back, and by the time I'm squeezing the trigger on air there are four more infected down.

The final two are just a few yards away now. I'm empty and Warren can't seem to slide the bolt forward on his M40. I barely hear him yell above the ringing in my ears, but Bishop barrels forward from behind us and wedges himself against the door at the very moment the two crash into it. The door rattles in its frame and a spiderweb appears in the toughened glass, but it doesn't shatter.

"Hold the door!" I yell, releasing my magazine to the ground before I slot the fresh one in. I feel the click as it seats, pull back the slide and step forward, nodding at Bishop to move aside. He wedges his foot against the door, relaxes his shoulder a little and gives me a couple inches space. The sound of the Beretta firing through the gap in the door is deafening. Bishop flinches and steps away, allowing it to swing open, but the two infected are already down.

My hands are shaking and I feel lightheaded, looking down at the dozen bodies lying in the street before us. Most of them look like they've been infected a while. They're thin and sinewy, their clothes ragged and dirty, but the final two -

the two I shot at close range - look like they only turned recently. One of them looks to be a teenage boy, maybe sixteen or so.

I'm still staring down at the kid when Warren takes the Beretta from my hand, pulls back the slide to check the chamber, and calmly puts a bullet in his head. "You only winged him," he says. "Gotta watch out for that. Other than that, pretty solid performance for your first time." He looks around at the carnage and nods with approval. "OK, let's start checking cars. Every infected for a mile heard that racket, and I don't wanna be around when they come for a look see."

•፶•

:::17:::

ROY WINCES IN the driver's seat, shifting uncomfortably and choking back panicked tears. Just an hour ago he felt like he was on the verge of his greatest triumph. He'd have a hot piece of ass tied up in the back of his new car, he'd be on the way back to safety at the community, and if the mood struck he'd pull over and break in that cute Latino bitch before sharing her around.

All that happened as planned, but if he could go back and do it again he'd walk back to his shitty wreck of a car, gun the engine and get the hell out of there. No piece of ass is worth this much pain. Even the safety of the community isn't worth what's happening in his pants.

The bitch kicked him. Hard. She woke at the sound of Roy's gun clocking out the big guy, and she kicked out before he even realized she had her eyes open. The thick, heavy heel of her dumbass army boots crushed his left testicle against his pelvic bone - he was probably imagining it, but he'd swear he heard it burst - and then she dragged her foot down his thigh and did all sorts of damage to his cock.

He looks down at his open pants and starts gibbering frantically. It's... it's just a fucking mess. His left ball is swollen up like a hard boiled egg. His scrotum is stretched tight as a drum, and he can't even hold his legs closed for fear that the lightest brush against his skin will result in fresh waves of agony. As for his cock... Jesus, it looks like someone took a belt sander to it. A roll of torn skin hangs loose, and the blood gushing from the wound has glued it like a Post-It note to his right thigh.

He doesn't dare touch anything. The pain didn't kick in until after he'd knocked her out with the butt of the gun, but as soon as the message from his groin reached his brain he almost puked from the agony. It was all he could do to drag her down to the car without passing out. He'd almost killed her there and then, but just before he gave in to his rage and put his last two bullets in her skull he had a rare attack of common sense. He realized he'd need a doctor if he was ever going to be able to fuck again, and the only doc he knew lived at the community. Fighting the strongest urge to slaughter the bitch he tied her up, bundled her into the trunk of the Toyota and painfully eased into the driver's seat.

Roy looks down again and begins to weep as he sees a trickle of blood pour from his pee hole. He's no doctor, but he knows that ain't good. Blood from there means he's all torn up inside. This isn't a wound that'll be right as rain after just a few stitches. This means surgery. Anesthesia. Pain drugs. Bed rest. He's pretty sure they'll let him back in with the girl, but will one piece of pussy be enough to earn him a month of the doc's time? It's touch and go.

By the time he sees the sign for Harrisburg he feels cold and weak, and in the rear view mirror his face looks drawn and pale. He can't tell how much blood he's already lost, but the seat beneath his ass is soaking wet and ice cold. He glances down and starts to shake when he sees the torn skin on his cock looks dusky, and his swollen left nut has started to turn a terrifying shade of purple. He doesn't even want to guess what that means, but an unpleasant word has been rattling around his mind for the last forty miles: amputation.

The end of the world didn't faze Roy at all. He'd never had anything to begin with, so he had nothing to lose. All the collapse of society had done was drag everyone back down to his level, and Roy counted that as a win. Roy, 1. World, 0. This, though... this thing between his legs, it's the one thing that didn't cost anything. The one thing the government couldn't tax, the one thing that brought him joy, and that bitch in the trunk tried to take it away from him.

As soon as he recovers he'll make her pay for every bit of the pain she's caused, punch by punch. Once he's done with her she'll beg him to kill her, but he won't give her the relief. He'll ruin her, and then he'll shove her broken body out into the street for the infected to play with.

Finally he reaches the Harrisburg exit, and he almost smiles as he pulls the car into the city and heads down the familiar streets towards the community. The pain has begun to radiate down his left leg, and he can tell he won't last much longer without medical attention. The doc had better be awake and sober.

A road flare spins a few times in the air before landing on the street about fifty yards ahead of him, spitting out a stream of red sparks. He slows, approaching the blockade carefully. He knows they don't have any problem opening fire on strangers, but he knows they usually wait until they establish whether a new arrival is a threat before taking aim. He drops his speed to a crawl and flashes his lights, waving slowly out the window. He almost weeps with relief when they wave him in closer, and then his blood runs cold when he sees the guard's expression harden as he recognizes Roy. He turns the car around and carefully backs up as close as he dares, just in case they decide to start shooting.

"Hell no. Head right back the way you came, Roy. You know you're not welcome here." The guard hikes up his rifle and points it down from his perch on top of the blockade.

"*Woah, woah, woah*, it ain't like before," Roy pleads, pushing open the door. "I brought a... a, a peace offering for you guys. Trust me, you're gonna love it." He climbs out of the car, remembering too late that his pants are still unzipped and the mess of his crotch is on display. The guard turns away in disgust. "Never mind that. I just had a bit of trouble on the way, the doc'll fix me right up. Now look what I brought you guys." He limps slowly to the back of the car and pops the trunk, and the guard breaks into a cautious smile when he sees what's inside.

Vee lies on her side, her legs tightly bound at the knees and feet, her arms strapped painfully behind her back. Her mouth is bound with Roy's jean jacket, one of the arms pushed between her lips and tied around the back of her head. She bucks and struggles, but Roy knows how to tie a solid knot. It'd take days for her to work her way free, and she only woke up a half hour ago.

Roy looks up at the guard and nods towards the rusted yellow school bus blocking the blockade entrance. "So... you think we might be able to deal?"

The guard doesn't speak. He just looks behind him, waves a hand and vanishes from sight. Moments later the school bus begins to silently move, dragged backwards by some unseen pulley system until there's just enough room for the Toyota to pull through the gap. Several armed men pour like soldier ants through the opening, taking up defensive positions as Roy carefully climbs back into the car and reverses through the gap. They stay vigilant, watching for infected until the car is safely through, then as one they withdraw to safety, training their weapons on the opening until the moment the bus returns to block the way.

Nothing breaches the walls of the community. In the old days it was the most exclusive hotel in the city. $200 would buy you a night in one of its cheapest beds. Today, though, the price is much higher. If you want to live within the secure walls of the Harrisburg

Hilton you'll need to pledge your life to the Chief.

⁎⁎⁎

:::18:::

WARREN LOOKS UP from his scope. "Absolute tactical shit for brains. Idiot civilians can't do anything right." He looks over at me. "Sorry, no offense, Tom. It's just... I mean, Jesus H Christ, what kind of idiot sets up a defensive position in a building at a damned four way intersection? And how dumb do you have to be to leave the tall buildings around you unprotected? It's amateur hour in Harrisburg."

It's hard to argue with his assessment. We're sitting beside our ambulance on the sixth floor of the Market Square garage, across the street from the Crowne Plaza Hotel and just two blocks from Warren's homing beacon. I can see the obvious weaknesses in the compound's defenses. I don't have the first clue about military tactics, but I know we can see - and could fire, if we wanted to - into every window on the front of the building. We might not have a clear shot into any of the rooms at this angle, but we could give everyone inside a damned good fright.

The Harrisburg Hilton seems to be the only building in the compound. We slowly coasted a few blocks around it as we arrived in the city, and by the looks of it there are strong, well defended blockades built from wrecked cars on each of the roads around the building, with guards stationed on walkways at the top of each one. It seems like it'd be nigh on impossible to breach the place by road without being cut down by the guards, but the compound is hardly airtight. The Hilton is surrounded on three sides by buildings that loom over it, and apart from having the doors bricked up they're all easily accessible to anyone who really wanted to get in.

"I could take out most of the guards from right here," Warren mutters, sighting down his scope, his finger well clear of the trigger. I can see four atop the two blockades visible from the garage, all dressed in civilian clothing and carrying a random assortment of guns. From the vantage point of the garage even I could probably take them out myself before they made it back across the open ground to the hotel. It really doesn't seem like a secure site.

"Is that the plan?" I ask, suddenly nervous.

Warren shakes his head. "Waste of ammo. We came across a couple of places like this in the last few weeks. Damn things started popping up everywhere soon as the cops pulled out." He sighs and pulls his rifle back over the edge. "They're damn near all run by dumbass survivalists who think they're playing some kind of video game. Not your hardcore guys, mind you. The real hardcore survivalists had their bunkers ready and waiting years ago. These guys are your part timers. Weekend warriors, y'know? They subscribe to the magazines, but they're mostly just losers who couldn't hack it in the real world." He peers over the edge. "They're well provisioned, though, and if they're anything like the others we've seen they'll have enough guns and ammo to take out a small country. Nah, a full frontal assault won't do us any good against these particular assholes. We just don't have the numbers."

A shot rings out from the nearest blockade, echoing down the street. We both duck our heads beneath the wall and prepare for more. For a moment I can only hear the sound of my own heart beating in my throat, each pulse as loud as a shot, but nothing comes. It's thirty seconds before I finally dare raise my head, and almost immediately another shot blasts out, its echo bouncing off the walls of the tall buildings surrounding us. For the first time I consider that we didn't plan our escape from the garage, and as far as I know there's only a single exit. If the compound sends out scouts to find us we'll be sitting ducks.

As I glance over the wall and down to the street, though, I catch something out of the corner of my eye before I duck back down. Six floors below us a small group of infected wander towards the blockade, seemingly unaware that they're drifting towards death. From the top of the blockade a guard rests his rifle on the roof of a pickup, carefully sighting through his scope before taking potshots at the creatures. I raise my head again, and even from this distance I can see that his gun is trained on the street and not us. Another shot comes, a woman falls to the ground as if her legs have been swept out from under her, and the seed of a plan begins to form in my mind.

"Warren," I whisper, nodding down to the doomed herd beneath us, "what kind of numbers do we need?"

•⸼•

:::19:::

VEE SPITS THE taste of Roy's musky sweat from her mouth the moment the denim gag leaves her mouth, and she struggles for a moment to hold back the vomit until she can finally take a deep breath.

"I'll fucking kill you," she gasps, straining against the ropes binding her arms and legs. "Let me the fuck out of here, now!"

The man looming over her holds up his hands to calm her, reaching down to her ankles to loosen the straps. "Please, please, ma'am, don't struggle. We mean you no harm." He quickly moves away from her legs as her ankles work loose from the rope, avoiding the flailing kick she telegraphed from a mile away. "Please, you have to believe me, I don't mean to hurt you." He carefully tugs loose the knot between her wrists and takes a few quick steps back as she finally frees herself.

Vee rolls herself off the bed quickly, backing into the corner and scanning the room as her captor cowers away. It looks like some kind of hotel room; comfortable but sterile, without any obvious weapons within reaching distance. "Why the fuck did you take me prisoner?"

The man lets out a soft chuckle and shakes his head. "I didn't. I can only apologize, ma'am, on behalf of Roy. He was one of our less... disciplined residents. We didn't quite see eye to eye on a number of subjects, and we had no choice but to exile him after it became clear he didn't fit in with our little community." He looks behind him as the back of his knees hit a stool, and he calmly takes a seat. "I'm afraid Roy somehow got it into his head that we'd welcome him back with open arms if he brought us a peace offering, and I'm sorry to say that he intended you to be that offering. I'm so sorry for everything that's happened to you. Please... I assure you I'm not your enemy."

Vee feels the injured rage begin to drain from her, a sensation she doesn't really appreciate. She's happy to learn that her situation may not be as dire as she feared, but she feels a little cheated that she won't get the chance to have her revenge right away. She's been dreaming of that perfect punch since the moment she woke up in the trunk of the car, and the urge to throw it anyway is almost overwhelming.

Still... she can't deny that there's something oddly comforting about the man before her. Despite his quick, fearful withdrawal as he loosened her ropes it's clear he's in command here. There's something about the relaxed way he sits on the little beige stool by the dressing table that tells her he owns this room. Hell, he seems like he'd own every room he walked into. He seems so... so confident. Self-possessed. If she didn't know better she'd say he was accustomed to command. Military, maybe?

He's even a little good looking, she realizes. Well built. A little gray in his cropped dark hair. Old enough to look a little rough around the edges, but young enough to retain the sort of boyish looks that let Patrick Dempsey walk into a few roles his acting skills didn't warrant.

"Don't forget that I favor my left leg." he says, smiling. "An old war wound? A memento from a bar fight? Childhood polio?"

Vee blushes as she realizes he can read her just as well as she can read him. "Old habit."

He chuckles and lifts himself to his feet. "Don't worry about it, I size up everyone I meet, too. Doesn't matter, though. The old rules don't mean anything any more. You think you can do a Sherlock Holmes and figure out that I'm a high school math teacher because I have a chalk mark on my sleeve and my loafers haven't been polished for three weeks?" He slips out a full pack of cigarettes and runs his thumb around the foil until he finds the break. "Couple weeks back I met a math teacher with four dozen kills to his name. Day after that I saw a Marine so scared he put a bullet in the roof of his mouth." He finally tears the foil from the pack, opens it up and then reconsiders. "I don't think you can judge a book by its cover any more."

Vee smiles for the first time. She pats her pockets for her own cigarettes, finds she's been stripped of her belongings and happily accepts the tossed pack from the man. "Thanks. I'm Victoria. What do I call you?"

He smiles. "Call me the Chief." He sees Vee about to open her mouth and cuts her off. "Yeah, just the Chief. I'm ex-military, like you probably guessed. If this shit ever comes good and we get back to some semblance of normal I don't want my name dragged through the mud, you know? It'd be nice if I could just slip quietly out the back door, head back to base and pretend none of this ever happened. I don't think my superiors would be all that thrilled to learn I abandoned my post and started up my own little kingdom,"

Vee laughs as she lights her cigarette. "You and me both. I called it a day a little more than a week ago, but I doubt I'd ever go back even if everything went back to normal tomorrow morning. Too many bad memories. If I get through this I'm looking for a fresh start." Something occurs to her. "So, what happened to the guy who brought me here? I want to spend a little alone time with him, if it's OK with you. He needs to be taught a lesson, and I'm eager to teach it."

The Chief smiles and shakes his head. "I wish I could help, but that isn't the way we do things here. We don't kill within our walls. Our only punishment is exile, but as I understand you already inflicted injuries that will amount to the same thing once he leaves our protection. In fact..." He stands and strolls over to the window. "Yes, there he is. If you'd like to watch?"

Vee cautiously walks towards the window as the Chief raises his walkie talkie. "Yeah, it's me," he says. "Send the fucker out."

Vee looks out the window and sees she's a couple of floors above street level. She's looking down on the front of the building where an area has been cleared between the high roadblocks penning in the compound. A dozen or so armed men loiter in the street, and as she watches one of them breaks from the pack, walks towards the front door and, a moment later, returns dragging a struggling man. Even from four floors up she can tell it's Roy. He limps and struggles with the wounds she inflicted with her boot, and he clearly lacks the strength to put up a fight.

Another guard walks around to the back of the beat up yellow school bus that serves as the gate for the largest roadblock. He grabs a couple of loose cables, hooks them up to a car battery sitting on the ground and hits a button that starts an electric winch, tugging a cable taut and pulling the bus back until there's just enough room for a man to fit through the gap.

The Chief pushes open the window, and suddenly she can hear Roy's weeping and pleading. From this distance she can't make out the words, but it's clear he's begging the guards to let him stay. They don't respond. They barely even look at him. The guard who pulled him from the building simply drags him to the opening like a disobedient child, and unceremoniously shoves him out onto the street beyond the road block before a group of guards push the school bus forward until the gap is closed.

Now Roy seems insensible. He drops to the ground and tries to slide under the bus, but it becomes clear when he reemerges that there's something blocking the way. He then tries to climb the cars, but after just a few moments he falls back, exhausted and crying with pain. The front of his jeans are stained dark with blood, and even his hands are red with it.

A guard climbs slowly to the top of the roadblock, and for a moment he calmly surveys the street into the distance until he finds what he's searching for. About two hundred yards down the road a small group of infected mill around aimlessly, seemingly unaware of the presence of the living at the other end of the street. The guard slips two fingers between his lips and lets out a shrill, loud whistle, and immediately the infected snap up their heads and hunt for the source of the sound.

Vee feels her stomach turn over as they begin to run. There are four of them, all in the late stages as far as she can tell from this distance. They're too far gone to manage a full sprint, but their speed doesn't matter at this point. Roy is blocked in on all sides: the roadblock behind him, boarded up buildings to either side and the infected shambling towards him from ahead. Maybe if he was at full strength he'd have a chance of evading them, but it's clear he couldn't fight off a cold right now.

Now the group are just a hundred yards away, and Vee catches the sound of their snarls on the breeze. Inhuman. Hungry. Desperate. They look emaciated, like they haven't eaten in weeks, and they couldn't be more eager to help themselves to an easy meal.

"Stop this," she says, grabbing the Chief by the arm. "Nobody should have to die like that." She's as surprised as anyone by her words. She'd happily kill Roy by her own hand if she had the chance. She's put a bullet in his skull without a shred of guilt, but this is different. This isn't just execution. This is torture.

The Chief shrugs her off and concentrates on the scene below. "We have rules, Victoria. Roy broke those rules, and now he has to pay the price." He turns to her, and she's shocked to see that every scrap of the friendly, charming man she'd seen just a moment ago has vanished, replaced by something else. Something cold and calculating, almost reptilian. "I told him not to come back. This is what happens when my people disobey me."

The Chief is *enjoying* this.

The infected are just a few steps away now. Vee desperately wants to turn away but she just can't. Her eyes are locked on the scene, and she can't help but imagine her husband standing there as teeth tore into his flesh. She can't help but remember every one of her friends taken by the infected over the last hellish month. She can't turn away, and she can't close her eyes.

Roy falls to his knees, weeping and resigned to his fate. He doesn't even try to run. He knows there's no hope as the infected close in.

The first one reaches him now. It's a young man dressed in the torn, dirty rags of an oversized gray suit. He looks to be about eighteen years old. Boyish and fresh faced, probably on the way to his first real job when the infection took hold. He's missing his left arm up to the shoulder, but a spur of bone around eight inches long still remains. As he descends on Roy the bone swings around like a phantom limb, as if the boy isn't aware that the arm is no longer there and still tries to punch with it.

He's clumsy and uncoordinated, and when the second member of the group, an older woman completely naked and missing chunks of flesh from her torso, barrels into him from behind he tumbles forward onto Roy. The boy tries to steady himself with the missing arm, and as he falls the sharp spur of bone pierces Roy's stomach and vanishes inside his body. Roy lets out a piercing scream and tries to struggle away, but as he scrambles backwards the bone simply tears his midriff open wider. The final two infected reach him now, and they see his ripped open stomach as nothing but a buffet.

Vee feels bile rise to her throat as all four infected reach into Roy's body and begin to pull their share of his intestines out to feast. They drag the slippery pink tubes to their mouths, ignoring Roy's weak screams and kicking legs as they chew into the rubbery mass. They squabble over him, each of them jealously guarding their meal from the others. Each of them grab the offal from each other's hands, pulling it away, dragging more and more from Roy's body until the asphalt around him is swimming in blood, flesh and half digested slurry.

Still Roy is alive. Still he weakly cries out with agony, his eyes wide open and staring in horror at the glistening offal that spills from him. He holds out a weak hand to push his attackers away, but the youngest boy simply grabs the hand by the wrist and bites down on a finger, gnawing through the flesh until he reaches the bone.

Vee finally manages to tear her eyes away from the scene, her legs weak and her stomach turning, but the Chief continues to stare, smiling until one of the infected finally reaches deep within Roy's chest cavity and tugs until the wet, pink mass of a lung tears from his body. Finally his cries stop, and the only sounds that remain are the snarls of the dead and the moist slurping of their feast.

Vee steadies herself against the wall and flinches as five silenced shots ring out. She turns back to see the infected fall to the ground, their mouths still full of Roy. The fifth shot obliterated Roy's face, ensuring that he won't return to take his vengeance on the guards.

The Chief nods with satisfaction, turns on his heel and makes his way towards the door as Vee stares down at the pile of bodies beyond the roadblock. "You'll be happy here with us, Victoria. The women here are... quite comfortable, so long as they understand their role. I'm sure you understand that I can't release you now you've seen our operation, not now I know you're military." He stops at the door, and places his hand on the butt of the gun holstered at his waist when he sees Vee take a step towards him. She stops. "And if we can't make you happy, well..." He leaves the sentence hanging in the air.

"Rest up now. I'll have some food sent up for you shortly, and then you can start work." He looks her up and down with cold eyes. "We have a lot of men here I'm sure are eager to make your acquaintance."

•⸎•

:::20:::

BISHOP'S SWEATY HANDS slip on the steering wheel, he's so nervous as the ambulance cruises slowly through the streets of Harrisburg. Warren sits beside him calling out directions as we approach each intersection, and I sit in the back and look out the open door at the growing crowd of infected giving chase.

"A little faster," I call out, nervously gripping the Beretta as one of them comes within ten paces of the vehicle. I just pray we don't reach a blockage in the road. If we have to stop for any reason a swarm of infected will flood into the back of the ambulance, and my clever little plan with be the last I ever make.

"Coming up on a big herd," Warren calls out from the front. "Bishop, give it a little gas." The ambulance jerks as it speeds up, and as we drive beside a large open square I feel myself shiver at the sight of scores of infected locking onto our movement and launching themselves into a run. They follow us like the tail of a comet, dragging behind us for a hundred yards as we crawl through the streets just a little too quickly for them to catch up. It's a chilling sight.

I feel my heart thump in my chest as I recognize the street we're on. We're almost back at the garage now. Just a few hundred more yards and it'll be game time. Either the plan will work perfectly or we'll be trapped with no escape as hundreds of infected tear us to pieces.

In the passenger seat Warren grips the bipod he uses for his rifle, extending the telescopic legs until they reach the required length. He'll have to judge the distance right, or he'll still be fiddling with it as the dead catch us.

"OK, you guys ready?" he calls out. I nod, and Bishop simply grips the steering wheel tighter. "You ready, Bishop?" Finally he nods and speeds up until there's a hundred yards or so between the ambulance and the quickest of the swarm. That should be enough to keep them chasing, but it should also be enough to give us the time to work before they catch us.

Bishop turns the corner at speed, and for a moment it feels as if the vehicle lifts onto two wheels as we jerkily skid onto the street running towards the largest roadblock. Warren rests his hand on Bishop's shoulder to calm him, and when he finally pulls to a halt he jumps out of the ambulance as if it's on fire. I do the same, leaping out of the back and sprinting with Bishop to the dark entrance of the parking garage, while Warren tugs on the emergency brake and jams the legs of the bipod between the frame of the driver's seat and the gas pedal, pinning it to the ground. The engine lets out a tortured whine as the revs build up, and moments later Warren releases the brake and leaps out of the vehicle as it begins to move.

It's already three car lengths away by the time Warren reaches the garage, and moments after he rolls behind a low wall to conceal himself the first of the infected races around the corner, spots the accelerating ambulance and tears towards it. The rest of the swarm quickly follows. Hundreds of them pour around the corner and continue on, and none of us dare watch in case they notice us hiding.

For a long, painful moment I hold my breath and squeeze my eyes closed, terrified that the mad thumping of my heart would kill me stone dead there and then as hundreds of stinking infected swarm by just a few yards away on the other side of the wall. I flinch when I hear gunshots, and after twenty seconds I finally dare poke my head over the wall to see what's happening.

The last of the swarm has passed us. In the distance the ambulance continues to accelerate towards the roadblock, veering a little off course with torque steer but still pointed in the right direction. I can hear the panicked yells of the guards as they fire wildly at the front window of the ambulance, presumably trying to kill a driver who isn't there. Bullets ricochet from the vehicle, but it plows on regardless.

The ambulance hits the school bus at speed, striking it close to the back and shunting the rear wheels ten feet to the right before the engine finally dies and the power fades. It's more than enough. A wide gap has opened in the roadblock, and within just a few moments the swarm of infected reach it at a dead sprint.

The guards are in disarray. A dozen or so hide out at the top of the barriers and fire down into the swarm, but they may as well be firing into water. For every infected they put down three more replace them, and it isn't long before the strongest of them begin to climb the wrecked cars until they reach the terrified living.

We waste no time now the guards are too busy being eaten to notice us. Bishop, Warren and I sprint as fast as we can across the empty street on what's now the 'safe' side of the largest roadblock, and when we reach it we take a right and quickly climb to the top of the secondary barrier blocking the road the runs along the side wall of the hotel. This one isn't manned, but beyond it in the empty no man's land lies a service entrance and a delivery bay, its rolling shutter wide open and unguarded.

Warren leads the way, his rifle slung over his shoulder and his pistol clutched in one hand. In the other he holds his sat phone, its battery indicator blinking warning flashes but still carrying enough juice to show us the location of its twin. With a little luck it will lead us to Vee, and we can all get the fuck out of here.

"Should be just up ahead," Warren whispers, stepping through a door beside the delivery bay that leads into a large storage room filled to the ceiling with sheets, towels, bathrobes and anything else fluffy and white enough to proudly carry the Hilton name. We sneak through the aisles with our guns raised, stepping carefully to avoid making too much of a noise on the tile floor, until we reach the far wall and realize the room is empty.

Almost empty, anyway. Propped against a stack of towels lies an M16, and beside it a small duffel bag. Warren takes a knee beside it and fumbles within until he pulls out a boxy sat phone. "This is Karl's bag," he sighs, dropping the phone back inside. "They must have brought in everything from the trunk. But where the fuck did they take Vee?"

Bishop points to a door hidden between two aisles. "Maybe she's through there," he suggests, stepping towards it. Before Warren can warn him to stop he tugs it open, and beyond its frame the world is going to hell.

"Bar the doors, now!" comes a panicked voice followed by an unintelligible protest. "Because I fucking said so! They're already dead! Now bar the fucking door!"

I creep to the door and look out on what I immediately realize is the hotel lobby. The storage room opens behind the concierge desk, and across the wide, airy room a dozen or more men struggle to lock down the revolving door at the front of the building. They try to slot a locking pin into the marble floor to prevent the door from turning, but they can't seem to get it in. I creep out a little further and hide behind the desk, and I can see why right away.

A crowd of infected force themselves against one of the panes of glass in the door, desperately trying to push their way through. Just ahead of them in the section of the door sealed closed stands a man. Alive, and armed with a pistol. Through the glass I hear him plead to the men on the inside to let him in, but they just continue to struggle with the lock. They know that if they allow the guard to enter they'll only be a single pane between them and the infected, and it looks like they're willing to sacrifice their friend for the sake of that extra pane.

I turn back to the storage room and beckon Warren and Bishop closer. "Come on, while they're distracted." They both drop into a crouch and run behind the desk, then Warren silently points towards the staircase to the left of the lobby and makes his move. We both follow.

As we reach the foot of the stairs I hear a single gunshot. I drop to the ground and freeze, but no more shots come. It's only when I hear the voice that I realize that the shot wasn't intended for me.

"You fucking asshole, you shot Josh!"

I turn in time to see the man trapped within the revolving door slump against the glass and slide to the ground. A guard kitted out in bulky riot gear pulls back his pistol from the narrow gap in the door and holsters it. "Better him than us," he says, turning away. "If we'd let him in the rest would be inside soon enough. Now you, you, you," he points to three guys in the group. "Get upstairs and start picking those fuckers off from the windows before they break through."

The three chosen men nod and turn towards the staircase. Towards us.

I move with a speed I didn't know I possessed until I'm hidden behind a wide marble column, and as the men reach the staircase and leap up two steps at a time I realize Warren and Bishop are no longer there. I can't see where they went, but they must have run as soon as they heard the shot.

For a moment I stand with my back pressed against the column, unsure what the hell I should be doing, but eventually I figure there's no going back. The men still in the lobby will eventually head this way, and if they're willing to shoot one of their own without a second thought I don't want to find out what they'd do to me. Up ahead at the top of the flight I see a sign: an arrow pointing to the left, followed by room numbers. Just to the right of it hangs an emergency map with the locations of the fire exits. If I can't get out the way I came maybe there's another route that's less crowded with armed guards and the dead.

I take a deep breath, tighten my grip on the Beretta and push myself away from the column, bounding up the stairs as fast as I can. I don't breathe again until I round the corner and find myself at the beginning of a long, empty corridor, flanked on both sides with an endless row of doors.

•👁•

:::21:::

VEE STANDS BY the window, looking out over the compound and trying to formulate a plan. Down at street level the area behind the roadblocks is packed with guards, almost all of them armed, and she has a clear view down three of the four streets leading away from the hotel. They're all free of obstacles with a clear line of sight off into the distance. Even if she could somehow find a way to climb down from the open window there's no way she'd ever make it to safety without being picked off. It'd be like shooting fish in a barrel for the guards armed with sniper rifles.

No, there has to be another way. but she's damned if she can see it. The Chief locked the door securely on his way out, and unless she wants to try to overpower the next person to come through the door - unarmed, at that - she's not getting out through there either.

She's staring back at the locked door when she hears a commotion through the window. Panicked yelling, shouted orders and the sharp rattle of automatic gunfire. She rushes back just in time to see the school bus jump to the side, forced out of the way by a speeding ambulance plowing into its side. Her blood runs cold as she sees what's running behind it. Hundreds of infected catch up with the ambulance as its ruined radiator vents steam against the side of the crushed bus. Some swarm over it, fighting to get at whoever was inside, while many more flood through the gap and into the compound. The first few fall as a hail of bullets tears through their bodies, but for every one that falls many more swarm through. There aren't enough guards to take them down quickly enough. They weren't prepared, and it's only moments before the first falls in a mass of grabbing hands and biting teeth. She turns away with a look of disgust as a young boy dips down towards the struggling guard's face, moments later coming back up with an eye between his teeth, still attached to the screaming guard by a length of wet, stringy flesh.

Vee turns away and scans the room urgently as the swarm begins to turn to the front door of the building. If they're coming inside there's no way she'll allow herself to stay trapped in a locked room until they take her. *Never infected.* That was the rule. If she dies, she dies fucking fighting.

"Think, Victoria, *think,*" she whispers to herself as she surveys the room. It's pretty basic, just a simple double bed and a small dressing table at its foot. There's nothing solid enough to even consider attempting to break open the door. She stalks through to the small bathroom, and immediately an idea hits her. The lid of the toilet cistern looks heavy enough to use to destroy the door handle. Maybe - just maybe - if she hits it hard enough she can loosen the lock and manage to open the door.

She grabs the heavy lid, rushes back to the door, raises the thick porcelain above her head and brings it down with all her power onto the brushed steel handle. The porcelain shatters into a dozen pieces with the force of the blow and Vee staggers backwards, flinching away and raising her arm to protect herself from the flying shards.

She opens her eyes and lowers her arm.

Nothing. The handle is still there, barely even scratched by the shattering porcelain.

Fuck.

She refuses to give up, rushing back into the bathroom to come up with plan B. *Maybe... maybe... ah, there it is.*

She climbs onto the lip of the bathtub and grabs at the long steel shower rod, lowering herself down to test its strength against her weight. Maybe she'll be able to use it as a support to shimmy across the gap between her window and one of the rooms to either side. It's a long shot, but it's better than waiting here to die.

She braces herself against the wall, plants her feet firmly on the edge of the tub and pushes up with all her strength, forcing the the rod to break away from the bolt securing it to the tile wall. It moves a little but doesn't break, so she pulls down with all her weight before pushing once again. The tile around the rod begins to crack, and she blinks dust from her eyes as the rod begins to loosen from its mooring.

With a final firm push the rod is freed, and without any more resistance it shoots up towards the ceiling. Thick clouds of white dust shower down onto her, and she slips from the lip of the tub and cracks her head on the basin as she falls. The pain is intense, and she fights to remain conscious as a ringing builds in her ears and her vision grows muddy with colored spots, dust and tears.

After a few moments she shakes her head and forces herself to her feet. She feels a trickle of blood run down the back of her neck, but there's no time to worry about that right now. She climbs back onto the edge of the tub, reaches out to grab the freed rod, looks up and...

And her lips spread in a broad grin.

"Thank God for cost cutting," she whispers to herself, smiling up at the ceiling. When the rod came loose it pushed against the plain white ceiling she'd assumed was solid and unbreakable, but now she looks up and sees a wide hole broken through cheap half inch sheet rock that even now crumbles around the edges. In the darkness above she can see wooden support beams set wide enough to climb between, and beyond them the dim glow of lights that must be coming from the hallway on the other side of the wall.

With the shower rod to help she makes quick work of widening the hole, and after just a few moments she grabs a beam in each hand and lifts herself into the dark crawlspace above. In the half light she crawls on hands and knees until she reaches the beam that marks the edge of the room. She climbs over, clenches her fists into a ball and pounds down on the sheet rock beneath her until it collapses. The crawlspace floods with light from the hallway below, and she grabs a beam and easily lowers herself to freedom.

"Vee!" A surprised voice cries out behind her.

•🦋•

:::22:::

JACOB MOORE STANDS with his back pressed against the concierge desk, praying for the others to return while there's still time. Everyone else ran upstairs to take potshots at the infected from above, leaving him alone with nothing to protect himself but his dad's old Mossberg 500 shotgun. He stares through the revolving door with wide, tear filled eyes at the swarm of infected still beating against the glass, and at one in particular: his dad.

Jacob had been due to go on guard duty with his father. He should have been out there, but he'd been caught short and rushed off to the bathroom just ten minutes before the swarm breached the perimeter. He'd watched through the glass as a group of them had descended on his dad, and his feet had been frozen to the ground as he watched them crack his bones until his arms hung loose in their sockets. As one of them leaned down and clamped its jaws over his dad's face he'd felt the warmth spread in his pants, but still he'd been unable to move. Even if he could have gotten through the door to save him he'd have been powerless. He was frozen with fear, and now that fear was multiplied beyond counting.

His dad's face is contorted with rage, barely recognizable as he pounds madly against the glass. His right cheek is missing, and his dentures have slipped so far to the side that they're almost falling out of the gap. Blood gushes down his dirty white shirt, drooling down his chin and spraying against the bulging window as he yells wordlessly.

The glass is breaking under the weight of the infected. With each pounding fist it shatters a little more, the tiny fractures spreading ever closer to the frame. Jacob knows that at any moment the whole door will shatter, and once that happens he's dead. There's no way he can take out more than a couple with the two 00 buckshot shells in the Mossberg.

He also know he can't fire on his father. He can't fire on the man who saved him when his mother turned; the man who dragged him to the car and gunned the engine until they were far away from the house... far away from the bodies of his mother, brother and sisters.

He knows his dad's gone. He's scared, but he's not stupid. He knows the creature pounding at the glass isn't really his old man any more. Even so, even as the window bulges in just a little more he knows he won't be able to pull the trigger. He won't be able to fire, knowing that the shot will take away the last member of his family.

He closes his eyes when he hears the glass finally give way. He squeezes them tight when he hears the groans and pants of the infected, and swings the shotgun around as he hears their footfalls on the tile. The barrel slips awkwardly between his lips, chipping a tooth in his haste, but he ignores the pain. He reaches down and his fingers hunt for the trigger. His thumb closes over it, and he pulls down while holding the barrel steady against the roof of his mouth with his tongue.

He isn't fast enough. His attacker knocks his hand away from the trigger before he can fire, and he loses his grip on the gun as he's pushed backwards over the concierge desk. He falls to the ground, his eyes open, and looming above him he sees his father, bloodstained and wild eyed, lunge down towards him with clenched fists.

The boy stays conscious for... who knows how long? Nobody alive is there to see it, and nobody alive cares about his pain. He feels every blow. Every bite. He feels it as his father gouges his left eye deep into his skull with his thumb. He feels his own eyeball burst, and his mouth opens in a silent scream until the pain is so great he slips away.

There's no more pain. He doesn't feel the punches any more. He doesn't feel it as the rest of the infected find him and begin to feast. The spores in their saliva race through his bloodstream, but by the time they take hold there isn't enough left of Jacob to bring back.

Daniel Moore stands from the remains of his son when there's nothing left to eat. He's still hungry, and he knows there are many more meals waiting for him here.

He moves towards the staircase.

•ᵀ•

:::23:::

I CAN'T BELIEVE my luck. One moment I was racing down the hallway in search of the fire escape, and the next I heard a loud bang behind me. I turned around just in time to see a pane of sheet rock fall to the ground, closely followed by a pair of legs. When Vee dropped softly to the ground I could barely believe what I was seeing.

"What the fuck are you doing there?" I demand, half expecting her to vanish like the figment of my imagination I'm sure she is.

Vee dismisses the question with a shake of her head. "Long story, don't worry about it. Did you assholes let a bunch of infected inside?"

Nope, she's real. "Umm... yeah. It was the only way to get you out of here. We needed a distraction to get past the guards."

Vee snaps her head around at the sound of screams in the distance. They're coming from inside the building. "Great distraction, genius. Where are the guys?"

I shrug. "We got separated in the lobby. I think they headed up this way, though. You wanna go look for them?"

She shakes her head. "This place must be twenty floors, we'd never find them. No, Warren knows what he's doing. Soon as he hears those screams he'll know to head for the door. You got a weapon for me?"

"Shit, sorry, I think we left it downstairs." I hold out my Beretta. "You want this back?"

"Uh uh, you keep it," she replies. "I'll make do." She turns to the wall and pulls a fire extinguisher from its bracket, then scans the emergency exit map beside it. "That's where you were headed?" She juts her chin towards the fire escape at the end of the hall. I nod. "No good. I got a look at the fire escape on the way in, and it leads right back to the front of the building. No..." She looks back at the map and points to an exit on the other side of the building. "This one leads across to the parking garage next door. Maybe it's still in one piece."

I look back with dread at the way I came. It leads back towards the lobby staircase. Worse, it's the direction from which the screams came just a moment ago. I'd rather take my chances climbing down to the infected swarms at the front of the building than head back that way.

"I hope you know what you're doing, Vee. I'll lead the way but watch my back, OK?" I set off along the hallway at a slow jog, and moments later my fears are confirmed. Two men appear on the staircase from above, one running and one tumbling head over heels. The fallen man sprawls on the floor for a moment before regaining his footing, and he continues down towards the lobby just moments before a group of infected race down in pursuit. Vee and I press our backs against the door of the closest room, forcing ourselves into a hiding space just a few inches deep, but the infected don't seem to notice us.

We continue on after a few deep breaths, and as we reach the top of the staircase I risk a look down into the lobby. The two men are nowhere to be seen, but we hear the echo of snarls and screams reverberate across the marble and up the stairs. Something tells me down isn't a good option. Ahead seems clear enough, though, and the fire escape is close. I just pray it's passable. Apart from a few rooms leading off the hallway there would be no escape if we found ourselves trapped down there.

Vee takes the lead, sensing my hesitation, and I quickly follow when I realize I'm out in the open, visible to anyone who might come down the stairs right now. I run to catch up and regain safety in numbers, and I reach her just as she presses her shoulder against the fire escape and pushes open the door.

I catch hold of her just in time, grabbing at the back of her collar as she loses her footing and starts to tumble out the door. She loses her grip on the fire extinguisher, and it falls through the air until it clangs on the asphalt two floors below. The noise attracts a group of infected who look up and begin to snarl and growl at the two of us far above their reach.

The fire escape is gone, sheared away where it should meet the wall. All that's left is the bolts that used to connect it, but beyond them blackened, jagged steel is the only evidence that the staircase was welded until the steel came free.

"Shit!" Vee yells, pulling herself back in through the door. "Fucking idiots could have just blocked it at ground level."

The fire escape used to run down to the narrow alley between the hotel and the parking structure next door, and from the look of the sheared steel on the opposite wall about ten feet away from us it looks like it also served as a walkway connecting the two buildings. Just a few steps or a single leap away, tantalizingly close, the entrance to the garage looks like a wide open mouth. It's a little below us, maybe a couple of feet lower than the hallway, and it looks like we might just be able to make it.

"You think you can make that jump?" Vee asks, already taking a few steps back.

"Ummm... I don't know. Maybe. I'm... shit, I'm not sure."

She pushes me gently aside. "Well, it's either that way or back out the front door, and I don't wanna get eaten today. Just follow my lead, OK? If I can make it so can you." She takes a couple of deep breaths, swings her arms back and forth and breaks into a run towards the door. I barely dare to watch, but I force myself. She leaps from the very edge, thrusting both arms forward as soon as she leaves the ground.

For a moment it looks as if she'll fall far short. I almost yell out, as if there's anything I could possibly do to save her if she missed, but before I can open my mouth her feet connect with the concrete on the other side. She falls forward into a graceful roll, and before I know it she's back on her feet and breathing easy.

"Come on, your turn," she says, beckoning me forward. I feel like my feet are cemented to the ground, but when I hear another scream echo down the hallway behind me I know there's only one real option. I take a few paces back, drop into a runner's starting position and, after a few more seconds of painful indecision, launch myself off the block towards the edge.

"Tom!" I hear the yell from behind me just as my feet are about to leave the ground. It's too late to pull back, and my jump loses power as my mind yells at me to stop and turn. I sail through the air, but before I'm halfway across the chasm it's clear I won't make it all the way.

My ribs bash against the concrete on the other side, knocking the wind out of me, and I start to slip back as my weight pulls me over the edge. I scrabble at the ground but there's nothing to grab hold of, and my heart lifts to my throat as I feel myself tip over the edge.

I'm barely even aware of Vee grabbing me by the arm. I don't know what's going on, but I feel my fall arrested just enough that I can scrape my feet against the wall and regain some purchase. I open my eyes, look up and see Vee straining against my weight, her small frame struggling to hold me steady, and from unknown reserves of energy I kick myself up against the wall until I feel the ridge of my aching ribs scrape across the edge and move my weight onto solid ground. I turn and roll, desperately moving until finally I feel the ground beneath my feet.

"Warren, get down here!" I hear Vee yell. I look back at the hotel and see him standing at the open doorway that now seems impossibly distant. It takes me a moment to realize it was Warren yelling my name that distracted me at the crucial moment.

I have no idea how we both made it across, and I don't dare take a breath as Warren takes just a few short steps back, sprints forward and athletically leaps across the gap. He lands a solid two feet into the garage, as if the gap was nothing but an easy step.

"Where's Bishop?" I ask, struggling to catch my breath. Warren looks down at me.

"Fuck, I thought he was with you. How did you lose track of him?"

I feel the anger rise. "I didn't lose track of him. I thought the two of you had left me!"

"OK, OK, no point in us bouncing each other off the walls," Warren replies, trying to calm us both. "What are we gonna do? We can't just leave him in there. He's not even armed."

I look back at the door we jumped from. There's no way any of us could ever make it back. It's a good two feet higher than us, and it'd take a superhuman effort to reach it without falling. Besides that, even if we could leap over and grab the frame before falling the wall is covered in jagged steel from the destroyed fire escape. We'd be stabbed for sure.

It's a few seconds before I register the sound of the footsteps. Loud, heavy clomps bouncing off the walls of the alleyway like a slow drumbeat, followed soon enough by deep, panting breaths.

Bishop appears at the door on the other side of the alley, and he scans around for a moment before he notices us on the other side. Before he speaks a word his eyes catch the long drop to the ground below, and his face turns white. "Oh, fuck," he sighs, looking like he's on the edge of tears. "I can't jump that far, you guys."

I pull myself to my feet and call out to him across the void. "You can, Bishop. I thought the same thing but I made it." I don't mention that I almost didn't. "It looks further than it is. Just take a good run up and then throw yourself across. Come on, buddy, you have to try."

Bishop's eyes well with tears, but he seems to trust me. He wipes his eyes and nods. "OK, I'll try. Just gimme a second to get ready, OK?"

The shot comes out of nowhere. We all hear it, but we all look in different directions. Vee and Warren look down into the alleyway and I look behind me back into the garage, but it's not until we see Bishop that we learn the truth.

The big guy looks down at his chest, at the dirty fatigues he's been wearing for days. It's hard to see against the dark camo, but a growing patch of blood spreads across his jacket like a blooming flower.

"Oh," he says simply, his voice little more than a whisper. He touches his jacket and his hand comes away red before he plants it against the door frame to support himself. His legs tremble for a moment, and without another sound he falls slowly forward and tumbles face first into the alleyway.

In the alley beneath the snarls grow louder as Bishop lands hard on a dumpster, rolls off and tumbles into the middle of the pack. Before we can tell if he's alive or dead they close in over him, grabbing at his clothes and tugging at his arms and legs. I pray the fall killed him, but as the infected loom over him I hear a weak, desperate whimper. A gap forms between his attackers, and for a moment I see Bishop's eyes, wide open and terrified. I may be imagining it but he seems to meet my gaze.

I don't take the time to think. I already know what needs to be done. I take a tight grip on my Beretta, point it down at the alley and squeeze the trigger, putting a lucky shot through Bishop's cheek. I won't let him return as one of those things.

For a moment there's a stunned silence. None of us wants to be the first to speak. We wouldn't know what to say. We're just numb. So numb that it occurs to none of us that whoever shot Bishop may still be here.

Almost in slow motion Warren drops to the ground as I watch. His mouth opens wide with shock, and it takes a moment for me to realize he's taken a hit in the leg. Vee thinks more quickly than me, and before he hits the deck she grabs him and drags him away from the entrance, behind the cover of a parked car.

I look up, and I suddenly feel like I'm in a nightmare I've had a dozen times over. The shooter stands above me and across the alleyway, grinning, a pistol in his hand. I watch as he calmly reloads as if he's completely unconcerned that we pose a threat.

Without any conscious thought at all I lift my hand, point my Beretta at the door and squeeze off shots until the magazine is empty. The man ducks quickly back inside at the first shot, and every one of my bullets buries itself harmlessly in the drywall of the hallway.

My arm drops to my side, and I stare at the empty door. My mind is barely working at half speed, and I don't even try to resist when Vee grabs me by the collar and drags me behind the car. It doesn't matter. None of this could possibly be real.

"Fucking *wake up*, Tom!" she yells, slapping me in the face. "You have to help me with Warren!"

I move as if I'm in a trance. Vee hooks an arm beneath one of Warren's shoulders and I do the same, pulling him away deeper into the garage as he grits his teeth through the pain. It's not until we all collapse, exhausted, at the far end of the structure that I begin to wake up.

"That fucking asshole, I'm gonna take his balls!" Vee exclaims, punching a car door.

Warren pushes himself painfully up until he's sitting up against the side of the car. He grabs at his trouser leg and tears it to the knee, inspecting the wound. He feels the back of his calf and sighs. "Through and through, I'll live. Now who the fuck was that?"

Vee hisses through clenched teeth. "He calls himself the Chief. He's the fucker who locked me up. Wanted to use me as a sex toy for his little fucking group. I'm gonna kill him."

I hear my own voice, but I'm barely aware I'm speaking. It still feels like a dream, and I can't quite believe what I just saw.

"His name isn't the Chief." I look back across the garage to the hotel as if I might still see him standing there smiling in the doorway. "And you're not going to kill him, Vee. I am."

Vee looks at me as if I've lost it. "What are you talking about? That's the fucker who runs the place. Calls himself the Chief."

I shake my head. "I know him by a different name." I look down at my spent gun and wish I had more ammo. If I had the fucking nuclear codes in front of me I'd use them if it meant he'd be dead. "His name is Sergeant Laurence," I say, staring back at the hotel. "I met him in New York. He's the man who killed my girlfriend. Shot her in the chest and drove over her body."

I look back at Vee, and she can tell by the fire in my eyes that I'm completely sane, and completely serious. "And now he's killed Bishop. Enough." I nod towards Warren's injured leg. "We're going to get Warren's leg fixed up, then we're going to find more ammo. Then I'm going to kill that bastard."

In the distance I hear the howls of the infected echo from the streets below. For a month those sounds have stuck terror in my heart and sent me cowering into the shadows. Not any more. Now the dead will become my allies, bound by a shared cause.

There are worse things out there than the infected.

And I'm going to kill them all.

•⁊•

BOOK THREE

.▼.

VACCINE

:::1:::

DEAR JACK,

AS I write this I don't know where you are. I don't even know for sure if you're still alive, but my heart tells me that you and your mom are safe and sound. Mom was always much smarter than me – as I'm sure she'll remind you often when you're old enough to ask her – and I know she has what it takes to keep you safe.

I wish I could see you both right now. The thought that you're out there waiting for me to come home is the only thing that gives me the strength to put one foot in front of the other. The hope that I'll one day see your face again gets me up in the morning, and the dream of hugging you and your mom is the only thing I look forward to when I fall asleep. It hurts so much to be away from you that sometimes I feel like I can't go on, but I know you need me to be strong.

Writing these letters helps a little. Even though you can't read them it feels like I'm reaching out to you. Just for a moment it feels like you're right here beside me, and that's enough to get me through the day.

I want to be honest with you, Jack. I need you to know the truth about what's happened in the last few weeks.

I've done terrible things. I stood by and allowed awful, unforgivable, evil things to take place at Camp One, and I want you to know that I'm truly sorry. I'm sorry I couldn't be a better role model for you. I'm sorry I couldn't be the man I hoped to be. I'm sorry I couldn't find in myself the courage and strength I know you possess.

I know there's no excuse, but I want you to know that when it all started I was sure I was doing the right thing. I didn't set out to do harm. I thought I was fighting on the side of the good guys, protecting people from the infection, but when I learned the truth it took a long time – *too* long – for me to stand up for what's right. I'll never forgive myself for what I did, and I know I can never be forgiven for running away and leaving those poor people behind. I just hope that what comes next helps erase a little of the red from my ledger. Not all of it, but maybe just a little. Maybe enough.

I remember all the names of the people in my sector. I'll remember them until my dying day. These are the people I promised to keep safe. These are the names of the decent, innocent people I abandoned. I want you to remember them, Jack. Remember their names, and say a prayer for them whenever you can. They deserved better. They deserve to be remembered for the sacrifice they made, and they deserved to have been protected by someone braver than me.

Polly Rice
Robert Grant
Amanda Leigh Montgomery
Forrest Bishop
Edgar Klaczko
Thomas Freeman
Stephanie Burrell
Harold Lawson
Rose McKinney

These are the nine people I was assigned to guard. I knew them. I made friends with them and brought them their meals. I smiled at them even after I learned what was happening. Even after I'd seen the bodies in the pit. I kept the doors locked even after I learned that I wasn't protecting them but holding them prisoner.

Even when I knew they were going to die.

When I saw Edgar killed I knew I couldn't take it any more, but I didn't have the courage to try to save the rest. I ran like a coward.

I want to tell you, Jack, that I've been given a chance to redeem myself. A very brave young lady has given me something that could help save us all. I have a long way to travel and the road ahead is dangerous, but I'll do my best to make it. I'll try to make you proud, son.

I miss you both so much.

Forever your loving father,

Lewis Rhodes

.˸.

:::2:::

LEWIS CAREFULLY FOLDS the sheet of paper over his knee and presses a sharp score down the middle with his thumb, folding it once more before tucking it between the pages of his notebook and stretching an elastic band tight around the thick bundle. He wipes a tear from his cheek, kisses his index finger and touches it tenderly to a creased, slightly out of focus photo of a baby boy tucked at the front of the book. Behind the boy a tired looking Rhodes beams a dazzling smile, pointing proudly to the words on his blue t-shirt that read '*World's #1 Dad*'. He either hasn't noticed or doesn't care about the line of spit up running down from his shoulder.

It's been two days since he fled Camp One. Two days since the mousy, nervous Czech mycologist whose name he could never quite pronounce cornered him in the mess. Two days since she pressed the Petri dish and notebook into his hands, told him her story and begged him to leave, her voice dripping with fear.

He hadn't needed much convincing. Without a second thought he'd slipped the little plastic disc in his pocket, grabbed his pack and hopped into the back of one of the dirty green military trucks that had just dropped off a fresh load of unsuspecting refugees to their new cabins. He was already prepared to go at the drop of a hat – he'd been looking for an excuse to flee since the moment he saw the old man, Edgar Klaczko, hit the ground – but the doctor gave him the excuse he needed to run without feeling like quite so much of a coward. She made him feel like he was running *towards* something, and not just away.

He'd been surprised at just how easy it had been to leave the camp. Nobody bothered to check the back of the truck on the way out, but just in case he'd hunkered down low behind the fluttering canvas flap, pressing his cheek against the cold steel floor thick with the dried mud from hundreds of boots, until he could no longer see the tails of the planes poking out over the buildings.

He'd started to count as soon as the final plane vanished from sight, and when he reached one thousand he hopped off the back and sprinted for the roadside as the truck slowed to pass a pile of mangled wrecks on the highway. There he hid, crouched behind a pile of twisted steel that had once been a Cadillac, until the sound of the engine dwindled in the distance.

It had only taken an hour or so before he found a Civic with the keys still in the ignition. Full tank, half a pallet of bottled water in the trunk and a Tom Petty CD in the stereo. Score. All he had to do was pull the beaten body of its former owner from the driver's seat and roll down the windows until the smell started to fade. The steering wheel was tacky with dried blood and the inside of the windshield was stained with pink flecks of spray that wouldn't rub off beneath a fingernail, but apart from that the car was pretty much still in showroom condition.

Nobody had come looking for him. To be honest he felt a little slighted by the fact that there hadn't been so much as a moment's radio chatter mentioning his disappearance, even after he didn't show up for two guard shifts in a row. It was a weird feeling. The last couple of weeks had been the defining experience of his life, but nobody seemed to notice or care that he'd deserted. It was all a little... well, anti-climactic, to tell the truth. He'd half expected them to mount a manhunt and drag him back to the camp. In fact, he wouldn't have been at all surprised if they'd put him in one of the cabins he'd been guarding. At least it would have been justice of a sort.

Still, he's not complaining. With nobody chasing there's no need to keep such a close eye on the rear view, and instead he can focus on reaching the address scrawled in the notebook tucked in his pocket. It'll be a long and dangerous journey, and even if he makes it in one piece there's no way of knowing if there'll be anyone waiting for him when he arrives. It really seems hard to believe the facility will still be up and running by the time he gets there. The mycologist assured him he'd find a staff of dozens still working when he reaches his destination, but really? After all that's happened? It just seems a little unbelievable. Everything's fallen apart just a little too fast. It feels like the brake lines have been cut on the whole country, and there's nobody left up at the top to fix them before they reach the edge of the cliff.

That's the really strange thing about all of this. Just a few weeks ago Lewis – like everyone else – spent his mornings with the newspaper shaking his head in dismay at the state of the US government. Out of control obstructionism. Multi-million dollar vote buying boondoggles.

Insults and lies thrown back and forth across the aisle. Politicians more interested in stoking the fires of the latest scandal than actually getting shit done, and a media that seemed eager to encourage them for the sake of clicks and ratings rather than step in and try to referee the shouting matches. Lewis had been as frustrated with the state of politics as anyone. He thought things couldn't get much worse, but now? *Jesus.* Now he'd happily cast his vote and hand out fliers for every one of those infuriating assholes, Republican *and* Democrat, if they'd just come back and right the ship.

He'd still want to slap them all silly, of course, but he wanted them back all the same. He'd never realized just how important they were, even when they were wasting time sponsoring bills to make the rainbow trout the state fish of Vermont, or boasting at the top of their voices about how much they support the troops while quietly voting down a funding bill for veteran healthcare.

See, it turns out all the politicians really needed to do was *be* there. Just... just fucking show up, claim their fancy lunches on their generous expense accounts and do their little song and dance on C-SPAN. Who would have thought that was the most important thing? Who would have thought that the *illusion* was what mattered?

That's what the government was, at the end of the day: an illusion. Hell, it had always been an illusion. All around the world society only keeps ticking over when the people at the bottom believe the folks at the top are keeping a close eye on them. It's the only reason people pay their taxes and take out the trash before they go to bed on a Sunday. People don't do any of that shit because they're civic minded. They don't do it just because they want to be good citizens. They do it because they know that if they don't pay their taxes they'll be screwed without lube by the IRS. They do it because if they don't take out the trash on the right day they'll find a citation in their mailbox from the county. Society runs on fear.

Things went to shit pretty damned quickly when people started to realize that mom and dad weren't watching any more; when people saw D.C. razed to the ground, and when they watched what was left of the government scurry away like frightened children to their underground bunker at Raven Rock. That was the moment when, beyond the panic about the infected running through the streets, people started to throw up their hands and ask *why the fuck am I still recycling?* It's tough to give a shit about rinsing out your tin cans when the people in charge are hiding safely underground and the water doesn't run from your faucets any more.

These are the thoughts that run through Lewis' mind as he tucks his notepad into his jacket pocket, takes a quick glance at the fuel gauge – the needle hovers around a quarter tank – and starts up the car. It's not really the infected he's afraid of. He has his pistol, a healthy stock of ammo and enough boot camp drilling to keep an eye on his six. The infected make a lot of noise when they come running, and their movements aren't exactly difficult to predict, so the only reason to be afraid of them is if you're too dumb to drive away or clumsy enough to run yourself into a corner. And frankly, if you find yourself trapped by a creature blessed with the coordination of Stephen Hawking and the intelligence of a Black Friday midnight shopper you almost deserve to die.

No, what really scares him is the *lawlessness*. That's the real threat, and it's what people should really be worried about as they're fleeing the infected. Lewis is kept awake at night by the thought of the countless crazy fuckers between here and Nevada who've been quick to realize that all the old rules don't need to apply to them any more. Sociopaths. Rapists. Murderers. All those folks who were only ever kept in line by the worry that society would punish them for their sins, who've now learned that they can let their freak flag fly without fear. They can take what they want, do what they want and fuck who they want, and the only people who can hope to stop them are those with more firepower and a better aim.

It seems crazy to think that he can possibly find his way through this madhouse all the way to Vegas. He was sheltered from the worst of it back at the Camp, but even there he heard reports about vast tracts of the quarantine zone suddenly going dark without explanation. Well armed units would enter a region to look for survivors and never return, and nor did any search parties sent in to retrieve them. They couldn't spare the manpower to investigate further, but the theory was that gangs of survivors had begun to carve out their own little fiefdoms all across the east, guarding their territory jealously and attacking anyone who dared breach their perimeter. If the reports were true the quarantine zone has become the wild west, and nobody who roams blindly through the region is safe from attack.

In this terrifying lawless reality Nevada might as well be somewhere beyond the moon. Lewis can't imagine how he'll ever make it in one piece, but he has to at least give it his best shot. If Tish and Jack are still alive somewhere out there he owes it to them to try. He owes it to everyone. If everything goes to plan he could bring an end to this nightmare, and maybe one day he'll even be able to forgive himself for leaving those poor folks behind at the Camp.

He rubs his eyes, cracks open the window and pulls slowly off the gravel shoulder and back onto the winding highway. He's about two hours beyond exhausted and there's still a long way to go before he'll allow himself to take a rest, but for now he's enjoying the freedom of the open road.

As the Civic gains speed he smiles and takes a deep breath of the fresh air, a welcome relief after a couple of weeks of inhaling the thick, choking dust and smoke drifting over from the smoldering ruins of New York. Every breath of it caught in the back of his throat, filling his lungs until he woke each morning coughing like an old smoker, hacking up a wet, black plug of sticky phlegm from the depths of his throat. After breathing the dead, stale air of the city for so long he'd forgotten how incredible the countryside air smelled. So fresh and sweet, almost like–

"*Oh, for the love of–*" He hurries to roll up the window and slap closed the air vents as a putrid stink suddenly wafts into the car. It's almost indescribable, like a butcher's counter after a month long power cut during a heatwave. Lewis gags and holds his hand over his mouth and nose, and as he rounds the next bend in the road he sees through watering eyes the source of the fetid, rotting odor.

Beside the highway a broad green pasture stretches off into the distance, a beautiful hillside that puts him in mind of the old Windows background. At any other time he might have stopped and gazed at its beauty for a while, maybe regretting the fact that he wasn't riding with his family in the car and a picnic basket in the trunk, but not today. Now the pristine rural idyll is ruined by the sight of countless hulking mounds packed so tightly together that the grass is almost invisible.

They're cows. Hundreds of them, all dead. Eviscerated. Torn to pieces. Lewis slows to a crawl and gapes in amazement at the carnage. He can see thick clouds of black flies buzzing over the cadavers, and the closest mounds just a few dozen yards away on the other side of the wire fence seem to be *writhing*. It's only when he pulls in for a closer look that he can see they're swarming with maggots, millions of them feasting on the spilled, rotting entrails.

He shivers and steps firmly on the gas. It's hard to imagine what could have brought so many of those massive creatures to their knees.

Certainly not just a few infected. No, that kind of slaughter would take hundreds of them. Thousands, maybe, flooding the pasture in an unstoppable swarm, like locusts stripping a field to the roots.

He feels goosebumps prick at the skin of his arms as he pictures the sight. An endless mass of infected racing towards their ignorant, docile prey. The panic spreading through the herd as they realized what was happening. The hopelessness of their plight, penned in by impassible fences, helpless as the swarm reached them, biting and tearing through thick, rough hides to tug out the warm, slippery offal within. The terror of not understanding death; of not knowing if the agony would eventually end. The blackness must have come as a blessing after that horror.

For a moment Lewis eases off the gas as it occurs to him that the swarm might be ahead of him. They might be waiting around the next turn, blocking the highway. He might run right into them, and there's no way in hell he could drive through a swarm of that size. They'd drag him from the car and tear him to pieces before he even had time to scream.

His mind is still awash with images of the immense swarm tearing into the herd when something catches his attention in the corner of his eye, indistinct against the setting sun obscuring the road ahead. It comes up fast, and he doesn't have time to react before driving over it. The tires squeal and the car veers wildly to the left, and it's only instinct that allows Lewis to straighten up before he plows into the concrete median barrier. By some miracle he manages to stay on the road, and after a few moments and a hundred yards of butt clenching deceleration he manages to bring the bucking, veering vehicle to a halt. For a moment he sits silently clutching the sticky steering wheel, the only sound the gentle ticking of the stalled, cooling engine.

He already knows what he's going to find before he climbs from the car, but it doesn't stop him from slamming the hood with a clenched fist when his suspicions are confirmed. Two flat tires, each of them still boasting a generous handful of the nails that punctured deep into the tread. He looks back at the road behind him, and in the fading light he can just about make out a wooden garden trellis extended across the carriageway, no doubt the source of the nails.

Lewis sighs and reaches for the pistol tucked into his hip holster. This was no accident. The trellis looks like a homemade Stinger, a row of caltrops designed to ruin the day of any driver dumb enough to pass over it, and unless he's long dead the owner might still be nearby waiting to spring an ambush.

He moves slowly to the back of the car, warily scanning his surroundings as he pops the trunk and grabs his backpack. He knows he couldn't possibly be in a weaker position. The highway winds through the surrounding fields in a broad recessed gully, penned in on both sides by high ground that offers excellent options for concealment. As far as the next turn in the road the ribbon of asphalt is lined with trees and thick hedges. A hundred men could be hunkered down in the undergrowth, and he wouldn't know they were there until the moment they wanted to be seen.

There's nothing for it. He knows full well that the only thing behind him for ten miles is the thick, cloying stink of countless maggot-ridden livestock. The last exit was miles back, and when he passed it all he'd seen in the distance was a small village full of burned out homes and an abandoned roadside diner with shattered windows, no doubt long ago picked clean by looters. Maybe the next off ramp will be more promising. Maybe there'll be a car he could steal. Maybe there'll even be somewhere he could sleep safely for the night. If the dimming orb of the setting sun is anything to go by he'll be needing shelter soon, unless he wants to walk through the night and take his chances with the infected prowling unseen in the darkness.

He's only taken a few steps from the crippled car when he hears the throaty roar of an approaching engine carried on the shifting breeze. His eyes dart to the grass verge on either side of the highway, but a quick glance tells him he won't make it to cover before he's spotted. The road bends to the left just a hundred yards ahead, and his instincts tell him the car must be just a few seconds from coming into view.

Moving with uncanny speed and grace Lewis bounds back to his car and slides beneath it on his belly just as the vehicle rounds the bend. He knows it's far from ideal cover, but it's better than nothing. If the approaching driver is particularly dumb he might be able to take him out with his pistol before he's seen, if it comes to it. He awkwardly cranes his neck to look forward as the vehicle appears, and what he sees almost takes his breath away.

It isn't a car. It doesn't even come close. The vehicle slowly approaching is a fully kitted out Stryker armored vehicle, an eight wheeled monster plated in thick armor and equipped with all the latest offensive weaponry. Lewis has never even seen one on US soil before, and it looks massively out of place on this pleasant, tranquil stretch of Pennsylvania rural highway bathed in the warm orange glow of the setting sun.

The tactical vehicle slowly trundles towards him before pulling to a grumbling stop a couple of car lengths ahead. Lewis looks down at his standard issue Beretta M9 and rethinks his plan to try to take out the driver. The .50-cal M2 mounted on the roof of the Stryker could reduce him to a moist pink smear on the asphalt before he could get off more than a couple of shots, without the operator ever having to show his face. As he watches the .50-cal swings around towards him, electronically controlled by the unseen operator safely ensconced behind the Stryker's ceramic armor plating.

"Hold your fire!" he yells. "I'm coming out!"

He slowly, awkwardly slides out from beneath the car, holding his pistol by the slide to avoid any misunderstandings that might leave him with a few unwanted air vents in his body. When he's clear of the car he stands, slowly holsters his weapon with exaggerated motions and dusts off his fatigues. For a moment he wonders if he should place the pistol on the ground and step back, but he figures it makes little difference whether or not he's armed. Not with that M2 trained on him.

His heart races as the rear hatch of the

Stryker creaks open and bounces against the body with a metallic clang, followed by the sound of boots hitting the asphalt. A man appears, walking slowly and casually from the back of the Stryker. Military dress, but unkempt. Some kind of absurdly overbuilt civilian assault rifle on a strap slung over his shoulder. A week of rough stubble on his chin and an unlit cigarette between his lips. A deserter? A survivalist? Does it even matter?

The new arrival reaches into his breast pocket and pulls out a Zippo. For a moment he watches Lewis as if appraising him, and the only sound is the clink of the lighter lid and the strike of the flint. He takes a long pull on the cigarette and releases a thick cloud of smoke through pursed lips.

"Just you?" the man asks, peering around as if Lewis' buddies might pop up from the bushes.

Lewis nods. "Yeah, I'm alone."

He points to Lewis' fatigues. "Deserter?"

Lewis nods again, reluctantly. "I guess so."

The man approaches, and Lewis doesn't resist when he takes the backpack from his hand. He unclips the strap and roots around, finding little more than ammo, bottled water and MREs. He doesn't bother to check the outer pockets, so he doesn't find Lewis' precious cargo.

"You won't get far with that little

peashooter," he says, nodding to the holstered M9. "I've seen some of them keep going with three 9 mil rounds in their skulls. We'll have to get you something a little more Texan if you're gonna come with us."

Lewis frowns, confused. "Come with you?"

The man smiles, slips two fingers between his lips and lets out a piercing whistle. Almost immediately a man decked out in dark camo and greasepaint emerges from the undergrowth by the side of the road, only becoming visible when he steps out from the long grass. He slings a sniper rifle over his shoulder and begins to trot down towards them.

The man turns away from Lewis and begins to walk back to the Stryker. "Kid, I need men, and you just got conscripted. *Vamanos.*" He takes a few more steps then turns back when he doesn't hear Lewis move. He looks around at the highway, darkening already as the sun drops beneath the horizon, and shrugs. "Unless you feel like taking your chances out here? Your call."

Lewis hesitates for a moment. He doesn't want to do anything that would delay his mission, but it looks like he doesn't have much of a choice. Alone on foot at night he stands little chance of survival. Besides, the guy is still holding his backpack, and without that he can't go on.

He takes a deep breath and steps towards the Stryker.

•ϒ•

:::3:::

A SHRILL RINGING fills my ears, moving from one side to the other and back again as the pain blossoms in my red, quickly swelling cheek.

"*Why the fuck did you hit me?*" I demand, glaring up at Vee as I lift myself awkwardly up on my elbows from the oil-stained concrete floor where I landed hard just a moment ago.

Vee meets my glare and sends it back with twice the anger, then reaches down and snatches the pistol from my hand. "To save you from getting yourself killed, Tom." She waves the gun. "You're empty. What were you gonna do, storm in there and kill them all with hurtful insults?"

I sit silently for a moment, probing my mouth with the tip of my tongue. I can taste the sharp, coppery edge of blood, and I'd swear my teeth aren't supposed to wiggle like this as I press my tongue against them. "I was... I just wanted to..." I close my mouth when I realize there's no way to end the sentence without sounding like a fucking idiot.

Vee's absolutely right. I don't know what I was planning to do. The moment I recognized Sergeant Laurence all that mattered to me was making him not be alive any more. I didn't care how. All I knew was that I needed to get back to the hotel and end the fucker, and putting a bullet in Bishop to save him from the infected had been the last straw. I just grabbed my Beretta and started marching towards the door, and that's when Vee decided she needed to put my ass on the floor.

If I'd been thinking clearly I would have realized how ridiculously dumb my 'plan' sounded. A clueless kid with a useless gun running through a crowd of infected to hunt down a trained, well armed soldier who'd proved many times over that he wouldn't hesitate for a second before putting a bullet in me? It was an insane idea. I'd be lucky to make it to the front door of the hotel, never mind all the way to Laurence.

"Sorry," I mumble, lifting myself from the ground and wiping the greasy dust from my pants. "Thanks. I, ummm... thanks. I wasn't thinking straight."

Vee reaches down to Warren's duffel, finds a

fresh clip in an outer pocket and slides it into place before handing the Beretta back to me. "We're in this together, OK? I want to kill that slimy bastard just as much as you, but if we try to do it without first engaging our brains we'll all end up dead, and he wins. Understand?"

I nod. "Yeah, I understand. So... what now?"

Echoing off the concrete walls of the garage Warren's voice booms out angrily. "If you ladies are done bickering you might remember I got shot a few minutes ago, and these holes tend to leak. Vee, do you have any... ummm, you know..." He looks like he's beginning to blush, and he drops his voice. "Sanitary products?"

Vee's expression stays blank for a moment before she catches on. "You mean tampons? *Jesus*, Warren, you're not buying weed in the back of a bar, you can call them what they are." Warren's cheeks flush a deeper shade of red. "Yeah, I have tampons." She reaches into her breast pocket and pulls out a couple. "What is it with you guys? One mention of a woman's menstrual cycle and you all turn into shy school boys. Here."

Warren catches the plastic wrapped plugs, then reaches into his pack and pulls out a small bottle of rubbing alcohol. "You know the old joke," he mumbles, trying to cover his embarrassment. "I don't trust anything that bleeds for five days and doesn't die." He unscrews the alcohol and holds it above the entry wound in his calf, but hesitates before pouring.

Vee shakes her head, crouches down and grabs the bottle from his hand. "Grow up, you big baby. On three." Warren nods and braces himself, but Vee immediately pours the alcohol on the wound without counting.

"*Jesus!*" Warren hisses through clenched teeth. "You said on three, damn it!"

Vee ignores him and continues to irrigate the wound until the blood has cleared, then snatches a tampon from Warren's hand. She tears the plastic wrapping away with her teeth and gently pushes it into the wound until it's firmly plugged, and ignores his protests as she repeats the process for the exit wound at the back. "Tom, pass me the gauze from Warren's bag." She points to the duffel and impatiently snaps her bloody fingers as I search through the random crap until I find the small green first aid kit pouch. Eventually I find a roll of bandages and a few sterilized cotton pads, and Vee wraps the leg in just a few moments.

"Looks to have missed everything important, you lucky bastard," she says, standing and taking Warren by the hand. "Just a scratch, really. Let's see if you can put some weight on it."

I rush forward and help Warren climb to his feet, his back pressed against the side of a car, until he's finally standing and gingerly testing his weight on the leg. He winces. "I won't be running any marathons any time soon, but I should be OK to walk." He takes a few short steps, his teeth clenching as if he's being tased with every step, but he stays on his feet.

"We have a few morphine syrettes if you need them," I say, rifling through the first aid kit.

Warren shakes his head. "Not a good idea if we want to get out of here alive. You don't need to be carrying my stoned ass through the streets. Don't worry, I'll be fine." He forces a smile, but it's clear he's in the kind of pain that would leave me a weeping wreck.

For a moment I can't help but feel an almost overwhelming sense of self pity. I hate to admit it, but out of the three of us it's painfully clear I'm by far the least well equipped to survive this. I feel like the guy called in to make up the numbers on a softball team when one of the players with actual talent can't make it. Warren can bravely shake off a hole in his leg and Vee can patch it up like a pro, and meanwhile I'm the jackass who can't think straight and tries to storm off without ammo. *Why am I even here?* I'm not helping. I couldn't save Kate, and I couldn't save Bishop. If I'm not careful I'll get these two killed as well. I have to do better. I have to *be* better.

"We need to leave." I mutter the words quietly, reluctantly. The last thing I want to do is allow Laurence to take another breath, but I can't ask these two to follow me on a suicide mission. "There's no way we can take out Laurence. Not with Warren's leg and my shitty aim. We gotta just suck it up and survive."

Warren nods eagerly. "He's right, I'm no good to fight right now. If I go limping in there like this I'll be dead before we get through the lobby."

Vee looks unsure. She clenches her fists as she thinks. I know she wants to kill the guy just as much as I do, but finally she seems to allow common sense to overcome her lust for revenge. "OK," she sighs. "We can come back when we're better prepared." She grabs Warren's bag and begins to angrily shove our dwindling supplies back inside, and Warren slowly leans over and picks up his gun. "Tom, can you go see if you can find us an old model car? It's a long shot, but if there's something more than twenty years old here I might be able to hot wire it."

"Sure," I reply, looking around without much optimism. The garage seems to be packed to the rafters with new SUVs, a few Teslas and a bunch of high priced European models, Mercs and BMWs. Not exactly the kind of place I'd expect to find a shitty old beater without all the electronic gadgetry that stops people from just splicing the ignition wires and firing up the engine, but I'll look all the same. Who knows, there might be a few classics parked up somewhere. I walk quickly down the row, raising myself up on my toes to get a better view across the level.

I'm maybe fifty yards away when I hear the shot.

From the corner of my eye I see the figure appear at the top of the concrete ramp from the next level down. He comes up running, and he seems surprised to see me standing there just a few car lengths away. As another figure follows behind him he reaches for his holster and clumsily tugs out his pistol, and by the time he gets off a shot I've darted to the cover of an enormous black SUV. In my panic my ears barely register the sound of the shot, but I feel the glass from the shattered side window come raining down over me like hail. The next shot hits the Prius parked beside me, kicking up a spark as it punches a tiny hole through the fender.

My hands are shaking so much I can barely hold my own Beretta. I fumble to disengage the safety, and I cast my eyes around desperately for an escape route. I'm maybe twenty cars south of Warren and Vee, but between here and there is a hell of a lot of open space. I could try to crawl beneath the cars but I figure that would make me an easy target for anyone who–

Fuck.

I swear I feel the bullet pass by me as I quickly sidestep behind the relative safety of the tire. The shooter was thinking just a few moments behind me, and if I hadn't stepped to the side I'd have a bullet in my leg just like Warren right now. Another shot comes, and this one buries itself in the tire wall and sends the SUV tilting to the side as it quickly deflates.

"Vee!" I yell out, as if she and Warren aren't already aware of the gunshots echoing across the garage. "*Fucking help me!*"

Just moments later I see movement in their direction. Vee flits across the gap between the cars, Warren's rifle slung over her shoulder, and rolls to the ground just an instant before a hail of gunfire peppers the concrete where she was just standing. From here I can see her recover from the roll and wedge herself between a car and the outer wall of the garage, but there's no way she can be of much help from where she is. She could never get the long rifle into position before the attackers aimed their pistols.

"Drop your weapons!" The voice booms out from just a few cars away. "You! Guy behind the car! Put that pistol on the ground and kick it out towards me. Lady! Toss out the rifle!"

I cling onto the gun for dear life, but in the distance I see Vee slump her shoulders, turn in her tight space and slide the rifle out into the open. I can't believe she'd give up so easy, but I can only assume Warren still has a pistol and a plan.

"Don't make me come back there, boy," the man growls in my direction. "It won't end well for you if you're looking for a gunfight. Why don't you follow your girlfriend's good example and toss that thing out to me?"

The gun doesn't want to leave my hand. Without any input from my brain my fingers clutch tightly to the grip, but I know I can't take out two guys. Hell, I'd probably struggle to manage one from this position. Against all my instincts I force myself to relax my grip and slide the Beretta across the asphalt and away from the car.

I hear footsteps approaching. I feel my heart thumping in my chest, five beats for each step, until the figure appears around the front of the car.

He's just a little guy. Receding hairline. Thick glasses. A bit of a paunch beneath his dirty plaid shirt. He looks like someone's dad. If this was a regular day I'd pass him in the street without a second glance, but right now he has his gun trained on me, and there's a darkness in his eyes that tells me he's waited his entire life for the opportunity to feel this kind of control over another person. Something that tells me he's just begging for an excuse to pull the trigger.

"Stand up." He spits out the order bluntly, knowing I'm completely at his mercy, and there's a faint flicker of a sadistic smile on his face as I slowly comply. I can tell he's enjoying this, just as he'd enjoy a hunt. He enjoys the power he has over me, and the fear in my eyes as he twitches his trigger finger suggestively.

"Go get the girl," he calls over my shoulder, and I hear the shuffling of feet behind me. "We're gonna take her back to the Chief and have a little fun. And hey," he adds as an afterthought, "don't fuck up her face. Gotta keep her pretty."

"What are you gonna do with this one?" the man behind me asks.

I hold my breath for a moment as the man before me waves his pistol slowly up and down. Eventually he speaks. "Just another mouth to feed." Without any warning he lifts his gun to my chest and squeezes the trigger. I flinch as I hear the shot.

The man looks down in silent shock at the red patch spreading across the chest of his plaid shirt. His hand loosens from the gun, and it slips from his fingers as a second shot hits the exact same spot and sends him slumping to a heap on the floor.

"Turn around." I barely hear the voice behind me. My ears are ringing from the shots at close quarters, and I'm surprised to still be breathing. I look down at myself, half expecting to see my own little patch of blood, but I seem to be unharmed.

"I said turn around," the man orders once again, and this time it filters through to my conscious mind. I force my legs to obey and slowly swing around to face him. He stands just a few yards from me, his gun raised and still smoking from the shots. He's dressed in worn fatigues, and over his face he wears a black ski mask. "You want a cigarette?" he asks, reaching into his breast pocket and pulling out a crumpled pack of Marlboros. "This is your brand, right?"

I frown, confused. *What the fuck?* "How do you know?"

The man takes a step forward and holds the pack closer, and I nervously slip one from the pack. He lowers his gun, and as he reaches up to pull off the mask I break into a broad smile.

"I figure I owe you a few packs by now, right?"

•⁊•

:::4:::

PRIVATE LEWIS RHODES beams from ear to ear as he crouches over Warren, rewrapping his leg after a much more thorough cleaning than he and Vee had given it. He explains that he'd been training as a field medic when New York fell. In fact, so had most of the guards at Camp One.

"I'm glad I can tick you off my list, Tom," he says, cigarette bobbing up and down between his lips as he speaks. "Those names were weighing pretty damned heavy on me after I left. I figured you'd all be dead by now." He takes a drag and blows a cloud of smoke to the ceiling. "What about everyone else? Bishop? The guys in the other cabins? Did anyone else get out?"

His smile slowly fades as I describe what happened over the last couple of days. Warren and Vee's attack on the camp. The doors unlocking. The infected running loose, attacking the survivors. Finding the mass grave in the darkness. Everything up until Bishop's death, when a tear rolls down Lewis' cheek as I point to the gap in the wall just a dozen or so cars away. He quietly stands and walks to the edge, looking down at Bishop's body. I don't join him. I can't face seeing my friend like that again.

After a few minutes Lewis returns with pink, bloodshot eyes, slumps to the ground and explains how he came to be here. How he fled from the camp shortly after Edgar was killed, and how he was ambushed by the Chief in his Stryker. He tells us that he was brought back to the community and ordered to work guard duty twelve hours each day in return for safety and a few warm meals. He insists that he hated being there, that he knew that the Chief was an evil son of a bitch, and he felt terrible for what was happening to the women in the compound. Vee tenses up as he describes the floor they're confined to, and that they're forced to 'work' for their keep. He doesn't describe the work they're doing, but it doesn't take a genius to guess.

"Why didn't you just run?" demands Vee. "In fact," her voice turns angry now, "why the fuck didn't you try to do something for those poor women?"

Lewis sighs sadly. "I'm sorry. Believe me, I am. I'd love to set them free, but it's more complicated than that." He looks over at me. "Tom, you remember the bodies you found at Camp One? Did you notice they were all wearing surgical gowns?" I nod. I'll never forget that image. "That wasn't just a refugee camp, Tom. You guys were being used for medical trials. The doctors were trying to develop a vaccine. They wanted to stop this thing before it spread to the rest of the country. That's why–"

"That's *bullshit*," Vee interjects angrily. "You weren't developing a vaccine, you were using them to grow more fucking *Cordyceps*. Believe me, we've heard all about the attacks on the cities. We know exactly what you people did."

Lewis shakes his head firmly. "*No*! That wasn't... I mean, yeah, they were doing that too. I'm not gonna pretend there wasn't some bad shit going on there, and I hate that I worked for those bastards, but there were some good people there too. They were trying to fix this thing and save everyone." He looks away from Vee and drops his gaze to the ground. "They just couldn't make enough of the cure in time."

Warren lifts his head. "What do you mean, cure?"

"That's what I'm trying to tell you," Lewis replies. "They *succeeded*. There's a vaccine. We could inoculate everyone left in the country, then all we'd have to do is wait for the infected to die off. That's why I left the camp in the end. One of the doctors knew about the... you know, the *other* plan. She knew the President wanted to attack someone, and she needed me to get the vaccine out to try to stop it. I was trying to get it to a CDC lab near Vegas when I was caught by the Chief. That's why I'm still here. That's why I couldn't free those women, and I couldn't run away. The Chief has the vaccine locked up in that damned truck of his. I've been waiting for the chance to get back in there and save it before I run."

Warren lowers his voice. "You heard...?" He leaves the sentence hanging in mid air.

"About the attacks? Yeah, I heard." Lewis lowers his head. "We have radios. I guess I left it too late."

We all ponder this for a moment. It seems amazing that there could be a cure to this thing right there in the next building over. I can hardly believe that we might be able to save the rest of the country. That we might be able to actually survive this, if only we could–

"Wait a minute," I say, prodding at the idea like a loose tooth. "What's the point of a vaccine when these things are going to die off anyway? They'll just starve eventually, right? They're not immortal. Why can't we just hole up in a bunker with some MREs and a barrel of water and wait for them all to drop dead?"

Lewis turns pale as he shakes his head. "You don't understand," he says quietly. "We can't just wait this thing out. When those things out there die it's only the beginning. Remember back when I first dropped you at Newark?" I nod, but I barely remember. It feels like a lifetime ago now. "You asked me how this could possibly get worse, and I warned you not to tempt fate." He sighs and pinches the bridge of his nose between his fingers.

"Well, it's about to get a *lot* worse."

•ᵛ•

The following documents have been classified Top Secret 1.4(b).

Note A: *fig. 1 (redacted from this document) comprises an image released into the public domain by NASA JPL against the strongest objections of concerned parties. Recommend we revisit the JPL security issue soonest.*

Agent comment: *Guys, this has gone beyond a joke. Administrator Franks needs to have his leash tugged a little harder if he keeps doing this. Eventually the wrong people are going to join the dots, and do we really want this kind of info available in Pyongyang? Moscow? Damascus? We need some semblance of oversight here. Can we get on this ASAFP?* – PA

Figure 1: Satellite image of Bangkok region, 2018

Courtesy NASA/JPL-Caltech

Document 1: Comment (Armitage, R) :

The attached image (redacted) of Bangkok, surrounding regions and the Northern coast of the Gulf of Thailand was taken remotely from the International Space Station, May 17, 2018. While appearing unremarkable at first glance, the cloud formations in the leftmost quadrant were later analyzed using NIR-red spectroscopy, and though the formations themselves revealed no aberrant data it was found that the surrounding haze was indeed largely comprised of the spore plume we feared.

Concentrations within the plume were relatively low, with peaks of just 4,000 spores/m(3) at its core. For comparison, benign fungal spore plumes in the US during summer months have been measured at peaks of over 200,000 spores/m(3). Furthermore, the meteorological parameters of the region present ideal conditions for the formation of plumes, given the high humidity, strong winds and lack of rainfall in recent weeks. It is to be hoped that such plumes would not ordinarily be able to form elsewhere.

I would, however, caution against premature celebration. There are several factors I believe should be taken into account:

a) We are as yet in the dark about the concentrations necessary for infection, and have been unable to study live subjects nor obtain spore samples directly. If a single spore is sufficient for colonization we're facing a potentially disastrous situation.

b) The subsequent silver iodide cloud seeding procedure performed by the Thai authorities to disperse the plume no doubt introduced spores into the Chao Praya River, either directly or indirectly. We do not know the survival requirements of *Cordyceps bangkokii*, though examination of related benign fungal species suggests it would be capable of surviving for prolonged periods in water. In any event it's clear that cloud seeding alone would be an unwise strategy in the event of a US outbreak.

c) While the May 28 firebombing of Bangkok was, in my belief, the best possible course of action it unfortunately left us unable to procure further data on spore production, and it should be noted that the number of infected present in the city before that time was low, perhaps only in the thousands, following the fire that swept Silom and surrounding areas. In the case of a full blown outbreak unhampered by external influences, the increased spore production may result in plumes considerably larger and denser that those observed in the skies above Bangkok. If this were the case it's possible we could be facing a potential extinction level event.

Recommendations: in the event of a US outbreak it's my professional opinion that the best course of action is, quite simply, extreme prejudice. The needs of the many outweigh the needs of the few, and we should try to accustom ourselves to the idea that it may be necessary to sacrifice large population centers in the protection of the population at large.

Sincerely,

Major Ronald Armitage, Deputy Director, DARPA

·▼·

Document 2: *Audio transcript of Cordyceps bangkokii fruiting event*, Bangkok, date unknown*

*Audio has been translated into English from the original Thai. Words for which there is no direct translation have been highlighted in italics (approximate translation provided in parentheses).

Participants:

1: Dr. Methee Sukonramuk (male), Director of Epidemiology, Bumrungrad Hospital (Hua Hin secondment)

2: Dr. Kanniga Natthanicha (female), Head of Research, PK Group

3: Unidentified male, referred to as Decha (military)

Decha (D): (Engine sounds) Now entering Asok junction from north. Please advise. (Radio chatter, unintelligible). OK, doctors, we're cleared for approach. Remember your instructions, and follow my orders to the letter.

Dr. Sukonramuk (S): Understood. Kai, are you OK?

Dr Natthanicha (N): I'm OK, I'm just embarrassed. Please don't tell anyone I puked in my suit.

S: I've told you not to worry about it, *Khun*

(respectful term of address) Kai. Anyone would feel ill after seeing that. There's no need to be embarrassed. Now, do you think you're OK to go on? Can you see well enough through the visor?

N: *Ka* (may mean yes or OK). I want to take a look at that one over there.

D: (Further garbled radio transmission) Doctor, they're asking that you point your camera towards anything you describe. Can you please show them the body?

N turns headset camera towards Asok junction. Multiple corpses are visible in various states of decomposition across the wide roadway, but in the center of the image lies an apparently fresh body that nevertheless appears to be in an advanced state of decomposition, with gases bloating the stomach of the thin, almost skeletal cadaver to the point that the skin has begun to tear and slough away.

N: Can't be more than a few hours gone. What do you think is causing it?

S: Autolysis, maybe? I don't know, but it's all I can think of. You have your instruments?

N: Uh huh. Decha, shout if you see anything approach. (Speaks to S) Come on, let's get this over with.

Camera shakes and blurs as N climbs from the vehicle and approaches the corpse. Heavy breathing sounds from within environmental isolation suit. Camera stabilizes as N reaches corpse, and pans slowly from feet to head.

S: You see the lack of decomposition of the subcutaneal fat? (S crouches in shot and points out a deep, clean wound in the cheek) I'd swear this was inflicted recently if I didn't know better. No putrefaction. No signs of infection. It's as if foreign bacteria haven't been able to gain a (unknown Thai word, possibly translates as 'toehold'). I'm going to take a sample.

N holds camera steady as S cuts a small section of flesh from the cheek with a scalpel.

S: It feels almost desiccated. See how there's no interstitial fluid at the incision? If he wasn't infected I'd suggest this man died of dehydration. He's just... well, he's drained. I think we should take a brain biopsy. (sounds of retching from N) I'm sorry, would you like to turn away?

N: (Heavy breathing) No, doctor, go ahead. I'll be OK.

S produces a small electric drill from his kit and sets about boring a hole in the skull of the corpse. Camera pans around quickly as N checks surroundings before returning to corpse.

S: (Drill pierces skull and sinks deep into cavity) Oops, that was a little far. Doesn't seem to be much resistance there. Oh well, it's not like he'll be needing this brain any longer.

S removes drill bit with difficulty, then drops it to the ground in surprise.

S: *Yet mae!* (closest translation is 'motherfucker') What the hell is that?

Sounds of D approaching from rear.

D: What is it, doctor? Are you OK?

S: It's... Look. Khun Kai, come, come. We should record this.

The camera moves closer to the head of the corpse, where a spongy white mass has emerged from the bore hole. It extends vertically from the hole at a slow but noticeable rate, protruding until it becomes a long, firm shaft.

N: (horrified, retching) What is it?

S: (crouches to corpse and pokes shaft with glove) It appears to be some kind of... some kind of stroma. Umm... the, err, the fungus we spoke about. This looks like the shaft of a flowering body. I'm sorry, I'm not sure if those are the right words. This isn't my area of expertise.

S and N step back quickly as two more stromae emerge from the eyes of the corpse, squeezing the orbs against the cheek as they expand, and N makes a panicked sound as the torso of the corpse begins to split, exposing a white mass beneath its torn, ragged clothing.

D: Doctors, I think it would be wise to leave right away. Right now, doctors.

N: Yes, can we please go? Methee, please?

S: (Shaking head) Not yet. We need a sample of this for the lab. Just a few more minutes, please.

D: Doctor, I have to insist. We shouldn't be near this thing.

N's camera focuses on the first stroma as its growth slows. In less than 30 seconds it grows to approximately four inches in length and two in girth, its pressure expanding the bore hole in the skull of the corpse as it grows. S lowers himself towards the stroma as a small bulge quickly forms on its tip, and as he peers at it the bulge suddenly splits open, sending S jumping back in surprise. The light catches a small cloud of fine particles as they emerge from the bulge.

N: (Panicked) What was that?

D: (Speaking over N, angry) We need to leave now, that's an order!

S: I don't know what it is. Some kind of powder. Oh shit, it's on my visor.

The camera pans around quickly and blurs the image as further stromae begin to erupt on the body, enveloping the group in an expanding cloud.

D: Now, doctors! Don't make me force you.

N turns back towards the vehicle and runs until she reaches the door. Behind her D and S approach quickly, climbing into the vehicle as the white mass quickly produces dozens of thick stromae that each let off another puff as they reach their full extent.

Superfluous segment removed for brevity. Please refer to extended notes for unexpurgated account.

D: (Speaking into radio) Approaching blockade. Please prepare decontamination showers and advise on protocols.

30 seconds pass without reply.

D: (Into radio) (Thai military designation for 'home' or 'base') Repeat, please advise. We have the blockade in sight.

Further 30 seconds without communication.

N: Is there a problem, Decha?

D: No... No, Khun Kai, it's just I can't reach them on the radio. It's OK, we're almost there.

N's camera shows indistinct image of a large military roadblock approximately one hundred yards ahead of the vehicle. Flashes of gunfire are visible, and the camera moves quickly to point to the rear passenger foot well. The camera mic captures the sound of continuous gunfire and breaking glass, and the feed cuts out abruptly with a loud crashing noise.

End of transcript.

•┇•

Document 3: *Fragment of internal memorandum sent from Phan To (Lieutenant Colonel) Prasert Maneephet to Phon Ek (General) Dusit Kantawat, National Council for Peace and Order. Intercepted 05/25/18*

(fragment not recovered) ... far beyond the security perimeter. We now believe that at least some of the later incidents may have been the result of the introduction of spores into the water system, most notably the infection of the village of Na Kluea close to Khlong Sapphasamit, a tributary of the Chao Praya River. It should be noted that Na Kluea took from the local khlong both its communal water supply and water for irrigation purposes, all of which was treated upriver before consumption. Na Kluea lay 15km outside the Bangkok security perimeter, and no attacks were reported to officials ahead of the outbreak.

The remoteness of the village has so far allowed us to keep news of its destruction from public knowledge, but on a personal note I'd like you to know that several members of my wife's family were among the 2,300 residents destroyed in the aftermath, along with my mia noi (*Note: 'minor wife' or mistress*).

The discovery that the infection can be

carried downriver presents urgent questions, including that of our cloud seeding strategy to disperse spore plumes. These plumes are predicted to grow in both frequency and density as more of the infected succumb, and as of now it is entirely unclear as to whether our strategies are preventing the spread of the spores or simply returning them to be dispersed by other means.

It is now my belief that it will not be possible to recover Krungthep (*Note: local name for Bangkok*). The presence of spores in even small concentrations would no doubt put any future residents at risk, and we simply cannot afford to sustain another outbreak. Furthermore, the longer we allow the current situation to persist the greater the risk grows of spore plumes reaching more distant populated areas.

It is my recommendation that Krungthep be destroyed at the earliest opportunity.

Song phra charoen ying yuen nan (*Note: 'Long live the King. May his days be without number'*)

Phan To Prasert Maneephet, 25/05/2561 (*Note: Buddhist calendar date*)

•༚•

:::5:::

I GRIP THE ragged scraps of paper like a past due power bill, hoping with each word I read that the next will offer a glimmer of hope, but nothing comes. When I finally finish I hand them back to Lewis, who tucks them back between the pages of his bulging notebook.

"So..." I mutter, without a clue what to say next.

Lewis nods. "Yeah." He slips the notebook into his jacket pocket and sighs. "There's no escaping this. Not now. Maybe... I don't know, maybe back when only the east was infected, maybe we could have got lucky. Maybe the air currents would have taken the plumes out to sea or something, but now..." He shakes his head. "This shit's everywhere. Wherever we go it'll catch us. Shit, even if the rest of the world is infection free it might not stay that way for long. They say sand from the Sahara can make it all the way to the States on the wind, so when a couple hundred million infected start to produce spores..."

"How long do we have?" Vee asks, suddenly businesslike.

Lewis shrugs. "What do you mean? How long until...?"

"Until the infected start... I don't know, whatever you call it. Fruiting, or whatever."

"Ah, right. Well, I don't know for sure. I'm just a private, ma'am. I've only got high school science, but I spoke a little to Doctor Zlama... damn, I can never pronounce it." His voice slows as he concentrates. "Doctor Zlamaljelito. She was one of the, umm, what's the word for, y'know, a fungus scientist?" He frowns for a moment. "Mycologist, that's it. She was one of the head mycologists working at the camp. I didn't know what she was talking about half the time, but she said the speed of the reproductive cycle depends on the energy available. It, umm, breaks down fat and muscle for energy, but the... hang on, she gave me some of her notes." He digs in his pocket for his notebook again, then flips through until he finds the right page. "Here, read this. I only understand about half of it, but maybe you'll have better luck."

I take the notebook and squint to read the small, scrawled handwriting. It looks like it was

written in a hurry, and it takes a moment before
I can begin to make out the chicken scratch.

•ᵥ•

Cordyceps bangkokii appears unable to sporulate in an excessively nutrient rich environment, and will instead continue to grow vegetatively into undifferentiated mycelium until such a time as all available nutrients have been exhausted. In order to hasten the arrival of the fruiting phase we found it necessary to deprive infected subjects of nutrients.

In those subjects for whom we provided an accelerated course of intravenous glucose solution or even solid food (raw meat or equivalent) we found that the infection continued to grow in mass to the point at which the host body could no longer survive, often resulting in spontaneous eruption of the undifferentiated mass from within the host. As this free mass lacked the required energy to progress to the fruiting stage and manifest perithecia it was essentially useless for harvesting, and was immediately incinerated.

Through a process of trial and error we have determined that subjects deprived of nutrients will rapidly incubate the undifferentiated mycelium until their reserves are spent, at which point they progress to a docile, immobile state before biological functions cease and the fruiting phase begins. In layman's terms, the reproductive cycle of *Cordyceps* requires its carriers to starve to death in order to move to the next stage. We theorize that this is the reason the infected refrain from consuming the flesh of many of their victims.

While there is no firm timetable for this (given variations in body mass, initial concentration of *bangkokii*, etc.) we have found that subjects in ideal lab conditions can progress to the fruiting stage in as little as four days after initial infection, though it should be noted that such conditions will rarely be present in the 'wild'. Indeed, we estimate that the usual time from infection to fruiting under normal conditions will be approximately five to six weeks, depending on local conditions and the initial health of the subject.

We have also discovered, based on both the recovered Thai data and our own experimental results, that *bangkokii* requires the presence of UV light to initiate the process of sporulation. Under normal conditions this will be achieved by the puncturing of decomposing soft tissues by the expanding stromae, leading to the unusually rapid development of perithecia quickly followed by the mechanically explosive dispersal of spores, but we have found that the effect can be hastened by manually puncturing the flesh and applying artificial UV light. To that end we have installed appropriate equipment in all harvesting chambers, and have accelerated our production by 17%.

Dr. Marika Zlamaljelito

•⸬•

:::6:::

I PASS THE paper to Vee, and wait as she and Warren struggle through the technical language.

"Five to six weeks," Warren whispers. "*Jesus.*"

I light a cigarette as I wait, turning all this information over in my head. So. It takes five or six weeks (she couldn't be more precise?) for the infection to burn through the body and reach the reproductive stage. I reach to my pocket out of habit to grab my iPhone and check the date – it's weird that I'm still doing that – then remember there's nothing there but my gun and cigarettes.

"Anyone know the date?" I ask. Vee and Warren ignore me, but Lewis pushes back his sleeve and checks his watch.

"May 14th, I think," he replies with an almost guilty tone, as if this is all his fault.

I nod and lapse into thought, trying to remember the old rhyme. *Thirty days hath September, April, June and November...*

"OK, so the outbreak began on, what, April 7th? That makes it, umm..." I start counting the weeks off on my fingers, "14th, 21st, 28th, 5th, 12th... Five weeks and two days since the first people were infected? Oh *fuck*."

Almost without thinking I tug the collar of my jacket up over my mouth, suddenly imagining the air to be full of deadly spores. All around me I see dust motes dance in the dim light of the garage. I've never thought twice about them before, but now each speck catching the light seems like a potential threat.

"Don't worry," says Lewis, smiling a little at my reaction. "We killed most of the first wave, remember? A handful made it out of New York and D.C. before the bombings, but it was a week or so before the outbreak really picked up steam again. By that point anyone with a scrap of common sense had run west as fast as they could move, and a lot of the infected were taken out by the military when it was still up and running." He waves his hand up and down as he makes an estimate. "I'd say we have a million or so infected in the east right now. Maybe a quarter of them are due to start popping any minute, but the rest might have a couple weeks before they fruit. You'd be damned unlucky to inhale any spores just yet."

"Only a quarter, huh? A quarter of a million

infected ready to burst? That doesn't sound very comforting, Lewis. It sounds pretty fucking terrifying."

Lewis grins a little. "The east is a big place, Tom. Think about it. A quarter million is, what, one infected every couple of square miles? So long as we don't run into any of the fuckers ready to fruit we should be OK, and in the meantime we should hightail it west as fast as we can move. Get out ahead of this shit and cook up a huge batch of vaccine."

Vee finally finishes reading the mycologist's report, closes the notebook and tosses it back towards Lewis. "So," she says, "what's your plan, great savior? We need to get hold of this vaccine, right, and that creepy fucker with his little harem has it locked away? Are we to assume you have a grand plan to get it back from him?"

The grin on Lewis' face flickers a little under Vee's harsh gaze, but I can see there's a little mischief in his eyes. "Yeah, I have a plan, but I don't think you're gonna love it." He reaches deep into his jacket pocket and fumbles around for a moment before pulling out a bundle of plastic cable ties.

"You guys have seen Star Wars, right?"

•⁊•

∴7∴

SERGEANT LAURENCE STANDS at the window of the fourth floor suite, looking out over the destroyed barricade below. His men are struggling to tow the wrecked school bus back across the opening. They're making progress, but even from this distance he can tell by the way they move that their confidence is shot to hell.

Just an hour ago the men in his community were certain they were safe behind the impregnable walls their Chief had built for them. They strutted around the compound like they owned the city, but now their eyes dart fearfully around as they fight to regain some semblance of security. A single fucking ambulance had been enough to shake everything he'd built to its foundations, and for the first time since he claimed the hotel Laurence feels like the tide has turned against him.

From four floors up his men look like ants scurrying around aimlessly after losing their scent trail, suddenly confused and skittish where before they'd been certain of their direction. Laurence knows just how they feel. Worry and doubt gnaws at him, and a knot grows in the pit of his stomach.

He turns around and grimaces at the sight of the room. They haven't even seen what's happened up here yet. The moment the first man steps into the suite and discovers the truth it could all be over. The barricades can be rebuilt and the dead and infected guards can be quickly replaced, but the women... the women were much more valuable.

At the Sergeant's feet lies the broken body of one of his more reliable guards. He'd never bothered to remember the names of most of the grunts but this one had become a friend, as much as Laurence was capable of making real friends. Daniel Moore was his name. He'd been a good man. Always showed up for his shifts on time. Didn't drink more than he should. Didn't bother to use the women. He was just a slow, unimaginative, reliable old boy who happily toed the line so long as it meant his son was safe.

Laurence hadn't enjoyed killing him, but he'd been left with little choice when he discovered what he'd done. It's just a shame Moore's death had come too late. He'd already done his damage by the time Laurence had returned from shooting that fat fuck across the alleyway.

He turns away from the window and feels his anger rising at the sight of the whores. Just an hour ago this had been his favorite suite in the hotel. It was the heart of his operation, and the source of his control over the men scurrying around in the street below. Eighteen women laying in their cots, each of them shackled to the rope that ran around the wall, each of them gagged so they couldn't spit their hateful insults at the men as they took their rewards for service.

It had been a nice little set up. The men had set up shower curtains between each cot for a little privacy, and every couple of days they'd been allowed to take a half hour or so out of the women in trade for their hard work. It kept them in line. In fact it was the *only* thing that had kept them in line. Without the promise of pussy Laurence had no leverage. No power.

Now... Well, now it's all over. Daniel had seen to that. He'd beaten seven of them to death before he'd decided he was hungry and dug into the girls with his chipped, blood stained dentures. The white shower curtains are spattered with so much blood the suite looks like the bathroom in the fucking Bates Motel.

He didn't get them all. Ten more of the women writhe in their cots as they struggle against the rope, hissing and groaning through their thick gags. Their eyes are locked on Laurence with just as much hatred as they'd showed him when he tied them up, but now the hatred isn't personal. Now it's just mindless loathing for anything that breathes. Anything that thinks. Anything that isn't infected.

He wonders for a moment if the men might still be happy to use them. Two of the women are definitely lost causes, that's for sure. Daniel tore at one of their bellies in his attack, and even the horniest fucker wouldn't be able to keep his pecker up at the sight of exposed entrails. The other barely has a face left. Her gag was pulled away as Daniel ate her cheek, and two rows of pink, blood stained chiclet teeth are exposed on one side of her face. She snaps at him hungrily, but that's nothing new. She'd snapped at him the day he'd tied her to the wall and told his men to have their fun.

All may not be lost, though. Maybe one of the men would be willing to be a guinea pig, just to see if it's possible to fuck the infected women without catching the infection himself. Hell, maybe they'd be happy to just rubber up and not worry about it. It *could* work, so long as he tied their arms down a little more securely. Laurence knows the men in the compound aren't... sophisticated. They'll do pretty much anything if it means they can get laid, and if they'd be happy to lower their standards he could keep them on board for at least a couple more weeks. Maybe even long enough to send out teams to bring some live women back to replace the dead.

The sound of weeping softens his anger a little. Crouching beside her bed in the corner of the suite the single surviving girl looks up at him with a confused mix of fear, hatred and hope.

Laurence had learned at a young age to identify the emotions that telegraphed across the faces of the people he met. It was a valuable skill for someone like him to develop. He'd always been well aware that the cold, unfeeling darkness that lurked in the depths of his heart meant that he wasn't put together the same way as regular people, but right now he just can't make out what the girl is feeling. He'd saved her from Daniel just as he was about to take a bite out of her thigh, for which she should be grateful, but he was also the man who'd chained her to the wall yesterday. Laurence can only really deal with one emotion at a time, and this girl seems to have four or five flitting across her face at the same moment. It's confusing, and she's making him feel distinctly uncomfortable.

"Stop crying," he orders with a stern voice. She ignores him and continues weeping while staring up at him, so he waves his gun in her direction and speaks louder. "I said *stop crying*."

That works. She ducks her head further beneath the cover of the bed, pulling her arms as far away from the rope as she can.

Maybe this girl will be his savior, if the men won't agree to use the infected. He stands over her and gives her an appraising look. She's quite attractive now she's been cleaned up a little. Long blond hair and a little pixie nose. Slim waist. Decent tits, if a little on the small side. He doesn't know her name.

When the girl stumbled across the community two days ago she'd been almost feral. Her hair had been little more than a mass of greasy knots, and her clothes were so dirty and ragged the men had almost shot her as she'd approached the blockade. Laurence didn't particularly care – he didn't really give the tiniest fuck about the lives of anyone in the community so long as he was comfortable – but the girl's story had been horrific enough that he'd allowed her a day to rest up before he tied her up with the others and let her know that she'd only have one job for the rest of her life.

If Laurence had been a different man he might have pitied her. He might have decided that she'd been through enough, and let her leave after a good meal, but he *wasn't* a different man. He knew *exactly* what he was.

Laurence was a man whose mother had never let him have another dog as a kid. Not after what happened to the first. He was a man who remembered the parents of the other kids giving him odd looks in the street, and wondering if it had anything to do with the glassy smile he always flashed them; the smile that he could never quite manage to carry all the way to his eyes. He was a man who'd joined the army because it had offered him the chance to do things that would have landed him in jail in the civilian world.

With what little humanity he possessed he'd managed to muster a passing scrap of pity for the girl, but it had only lasted a day. He needed women. It was the only way he could maintain control, and if that meant putting her to work 24 hours a day he'd let the men fuck her until she was dead.

He looks back towards the girl crouching in the shadow of the bed and smiles that same glassy smile. She doesn't know it yet but she might just be his savior. She'll work harder than any of the other girls ever did. He'll let the men take their turns with the infected, if they'll have them, but this one will be saved only for the most loyal. Only for those men who manage to keep the others in line. She'll be their special treat, and she'll keep the community on an even keel until they can restock the cots with more live women.

It'll *work*. He's *sure* of it. He's been through tougher scrapes than this.

A yell from down below drags his gaze away from the girl. Some kind of commotion in the street below. He strides back to the window and blocks out the groans of the infected as he looks down at his battered but intact barricades.

In the street beyond a small group walks in single file towards the gap in the blockade. It takes Laurence a few seconds to pick out his own man, the young black guy he picked up on the highway. The rest of them...

Ah. His grin widens as he recognizes them.

The guard points a rifle at the backs of the three prisoners, their hands bound in front of them. One of them is the young guy he vaguely remembers but can't quite place. The other walks with a stiff limp, slowing with each few steps until the guard prods him in the back with the rifle.

The third is the woman who'd been brought in this morning.

Maybe things aren't quite as bad as they seem.

•⁊•

:::8:::

"JESUS, WILL YOU cool it with the gun?" Warren mutters angrily under his breath.

Lewis prods him in the back once more, pushing him forward with the barrel until he stumbles painfully on his injured leg. "Sorry, Chewbacca" he whispers, "I have to make it look convincing. Just a little further and I'll stop."

Warren balls his hands into fists as I turn back to face him, and I shoot him a silent look that begs him to just play along for a little longer. I get the feeling his injury has taken its toll on his patience.

"Prisoners coming in!" Lewis yells towards the barricade. "Stand aside!"

Through the gap opened by the ambulance a few faces appear, all of them angry.

"Where's Dwight?" one of them calls out, idly laying his hand on the stock of the rifle resting against his leg.

Lewis pauses for a moment before answering, and I hold my breath. "Infected got him. I had to take care of it."

I let out a sigh of relief. I don't know these men, but by their expressions I don't think we'd have survived if they thought we'd killed their friend ourselves. They seem angry but satisfied with the answer, and nobody moves for their gun as we enter the compound. I sense at least a few of their eyes falling on Vee walking ahead of me, and I get the impression they might be a little too interested in her to care too much about why Lewis is returning alone.

"Where's the Chief?" Lewis asks, shoving Warren roughly forward to make sure we don't end up stuck down here.

A few of the men shrug, and as Lewis pushes us towards the front door of the hotel a shrill whistle makes us look up. A face appears from a window a few floors up, and as soon as I recognize Laurence I look down at the ground. I've no idea if he recognizes me, but I'd prefer not to let him take a close look until we're in the same room.

"406," Laurence calls down to Lewis. "Bring 'em on up."

Lewis pushes us through the front door without another word, and thankfully we find the lobby empty of men. Living men, anyway. Over by the concierge desk seven or eight bodies have been dumped in a pile. The mottled white marble floor is slippery with blood, and for a moment I can't help but feel a pang of guilt that we're responsible for putting those bodies there. It was my idea to break the barricade, and it's my fault their blood was spilled. We don't know anything about these people. They're led by a murderous asshole, but they might be decent enough.

My guilt quickly evaporates when Lewis whispers to us, "406 is where he keeps the girls."

Ah, yes. Decent people don't have their own little rape room in their home. *Fuck 'em.*

Now we're out of sight of the men Lewis quickly hustles us up the staircase to the second floor, and as soon as we reach the hallway he loosens the cable ties around our wrists, pulls our pistols from the waistband of his pants and hands them back to us, though he keeps hold of Warren's rifle. "OK," he says, "just follow my lead. Remember, we need him alive. No shooting until we get the keys to the Stryker. Vee, you—"

He falls silent at the sound of footsteps on the stairs above, and Vee and I quickly tuck our guns in our waistbands moments before a man appears in the hallway, carrying over his shoulder the body of a young man, leaving a trail of blood on the carpet in his wake.

"Are these the guys?" he growls, lowering the body carefully to the ground.

Lewis nods. "Taking them up to meet the Chief." He tries to usher us back towards the staircase, but the man steps in front of Vee as she tries to pass.

"Not so fast there," he says, holding a meaty hand against Vee's chest. He looks to have maybe four inches on her, and he comes up close to her face as he speaks. "See this guy here?"

Vee doesn't look at the body on the floor but instead locks eyes with the man, who stares right back at her.

"I said did you see this guy? Look at him. *Look at him.*" Vee finally breaks his gaze and her eyes flit momentarily to the corpse. "His name was Billy."

"Come on, Geoff," pleads Lewis. "Don't go starting something you'll regret."

Geoff ignores him. "This guy... he was my neighbor. We came in together. He saved my life more times than I can remember, and you know what I had to do a half hour ago? Can you guess? Go on, take a wild guess." He's right up in Vee's face now, pressing her back against the wall, his spittle showering her face as he angrily spits out his words.

"Geoff, fucking *leave it*," Lewis insists, but Geoff looks as if he doesn't even hear him.

"I had to put a bullet in his head when he tried to claw out my eyes. I had to watch him get attacked by five of those psychos, and then I had to watch him stand right back up and join in fighting for the other team. You ever had to watch a friend die?" Vee keeps her eyes locked on him. "You ever seen the light go out in your buddy's eyes as they bleed to death?" She stays silent. "I guess that's a no. Well, let's see how you like it, bitch."

In one smooth movement he spins on his heel, grabs Warren by the collar, reaches down to a sheath on his thigh and pulls out a large serrated hunting knife. Everything seems to slow down as the blade moves towards Warren's stomach, and my mind kicks into overdrive. I can see that Lewis won't be able to bring the rifle around quickly enough. I know Vee won't be able to wrestle him away before he manages to plunge the knife in. Almost without the thought passing through my conscious mind I know that I'm the only one of us in a position to do anything, and my body starts to move without any sort of input from a mind that would no doubt prefer to turn and run if it had the chance to cast the deciding vote.

I feel myself leaping forward, and I watch almost as a spectator as I tuck my head against my chest and meet Geoff's waist shoulder first. He outweighs me by maybe thirty pounds but I catch him off balance on his left side as he swings the knife in from the right, and as soon as I barrel into him I feel his legs give way beneath him.

We both fall to the carpet, and my suddenly heightened senses pick up the movement of the blade as it twists in to face Geoff as he tumbles. The moment we hit the deck I feel the resistance beneath me as the hilt anchors itself on the ground and the tip of the blade slips through his skin and grinds against the bone as it finds the narrow gap between two ribs.

I roll away quickly, desperate to put myself beyond arm's reach just in case I'm wrong. Just in case I only imagined the knife piercing Geoff's body, and just in case he's ready to turn it on me. I roll onto my front and scrabble at the thin, scratchy carpet for purchase, and I don't stop crawling until I know I'm well out of reach.

I can barely hear anything above the thumping of my own heart, but one noise that manages to drown out the din is the sound of rasping breath. It sounds just like the labored breath of the infected, but this sound is coming from just a few yards away.

I turn back towards Geoff and understand right away. The long hunting knife is buried halfway to the hilt in his chest, jutting out at an angle where it slipped between the ribs and punctured the soft tissue of his lung. He lies on his back and desperately struggles for air, gasping as his face turns pink, but I can see that whatever oxygen he manages to gulp in won't go where it's needed. Around the blade the blood bubbles as air escapes through the wound, deflating his lung much more quickly than he can gulp mouthfuls of air. He grits his teeth against the pain, and his eyes cast around desperately for someone who might help him. Nobody moves.

Once again the guilt grips me as I watch him gasp and struggle. I know I did what I had to do, but I know just as strongly that I'm responsible for his pain. I'm responsible for the terror in his eyes, and the knowledge that's he's about to die. The guilt hits me hard for a moment, and I almost find myself rushing back to help him until I remind myself once again of the room upstairs. The room he must have visited many times. It's not enough to rid myself of this feeling entirely, but it takes the edge off.

I watch as Warren crouches over the gasping man, kneels on both his arms to keep him from struggling, clamps a hand over his mouth and pulls the knife from his chest, and I turn away just in time so I don't have to see him draw the blade smoothly across Geoff's throat to put him out of his misery. All I hear is a soft, muffled whimper as the man fades away, and I don't turn back until I can no longer hear his feet kicking weakly against the carpet.

"Thanks, Tom," Warren sighs, pulling himself to his feet. "I owe you one." His hands are covered in blood, and he leans back down to wipe them clean on Geoff's shirt.

I wave it off, and after a few half hearted mumbles I manage to squeeze a few words through my suddenly parched throat. "I think that makes us even. Umm, should we...?" I nod at the two bodies bleeding into the carpet and point at an open suite door to the side of the hallway.

Between the four of us we manage to drag them both into the empty suite, where Warren pats down Geoff's body until he finds the pistol in his shoulder holster. Vee takes the knife, unclips the sheath from Geoff's thigh and, after cleaning his blood from the blade as best she can, tucks it inside her jacket.

"Y'know, that was pretty damned brave," Vee says, patting me on the shoulder as we return to the staircase and begin to climb. "It takes a lot of guts to take on a guy that size."

I flash a weak smile and try to stop my hands from trembling. "Thanks. I don't feel all that brave." I can still remember how Geoff's fall slowed beneath me as the knife blade slid into him, and I reflexively reach up to my own chest as a shiver passes through me.

I never expected this. I've shot infected before. Hell, I shot Bishop in the head while he was still alive, but even that horror didn't feel all that immediate, and it was nowhere near as visceral. I squeezed the trigger, a reaction was set off, the bullet was ejected and somewhere off in the distance death happened. It's easy to rationalize it; to distance myself from the act and pretend I was just a small part of the process. This, though... this feels *different*. I tackled Geoff, he fell on his knife and I felt the blade slide into his body. I may not have been holding it in my hand but it was my weight that forced it between his ribs and into his lung.

I don't regret it. If I had to do it again I hope I'd do the same thing. It's just... well, I'm just glad Vee took the knife. I don't want it anywhere near me.

I try to get my breathing under control as we climb the stairs, and as I ascend I bury my hands in my pockets so nobody sees how much they're shaking. My heart rate only grows quicker as we approach the fourth floor. I know there will be more death to come, and the thought of it makes me want to puke. I just want to be somewhere safe, just for an hour or two. Somewhere I can close my eyes and pretend the world hasn't gone to shit. I wish–

"OK, hold up," Lewis interrupts my train of thought. "I gotta tie you up again." Vee begins to protest and Lewis holds up his hand. "I know, I know, but we need to get in close. There are a couple dozen innocent women in 406, remember? If we go in guns blazing they'll all end up dead. We gotta be smart about this, OK?" Vee scowls for a moment, then holds her wrists together and allows Lewis to cinch the cable tie around them before moving onto Warren and me.

"OK, you can reach your guns, but try as hard as shit not to until you have a clear shot, OK? The Chief will be armed, and if you don't take him out with your first shot you won't get the chance at a second. Trust me." He gives us a final once over, straightening our clothes so the bulges of our guns aren't visible at our waists. "You guys good to go?"

Vee and Warren nod right away, followed moments later by my own weak agreement, and we proceed up the final few steps to the fourth floor hallway. It's empty of men but for a body way off at the far end, and as Lewis steps to the front of the group we can only hear our own soft footsteps on the carpet as we approach 406.

"Chief?" Lewis calls out as he taps on the door to the suite. "I'm coming in."

As he reaches down to the handle the door suddenly swings open, and Lewis takes a step back as Laurence pops his head out. "Is it just you?" he asks, his eyes darting from side to side to scan the hallway. Lewis nods. "OK, bring 'em in."

Laurence steps back inside the room and swings the door wide open to allow us in, and the sight that greets me makes my stomach turn.

Ranged around the walls of the large suite lie a couple dozen stained single beds, each of them separated by makeshift rails on which hang bloodstained white plastic curtains. As we walk deeper into the room each bed reveals a new scene of carnage, and my eyes flit from one to the next despite my wish to close them tight to block out the horror.

The women are all shackled to a single rope hanging at waist height around the wall, connected by the same plastic cable ties that bind our own hands. A handful are obviously dead, but the rest hiss at us as we pass, struggling to break free of the rope as they try to lunge at us.

I reluctantly step further into the room and almost gag when I see one particular infected woman on the left side of the room. She's writhing on the bed, twisting back and forth, her skin red raw at the wrists where she yanks at the cable tie, but that's far from her worst injury. With each jerking motion the intestines spilling from her belly twitch and roll across the bed, draped across the bloodstained mattress as if she's the subject of a gruesome anatomy class. Laurence strolls past her without interest as the bile rises in my throat, and I can't help but double over and puke on the carpet as the smell hits me. My diaphragm spasms as the vomit splashes on the floor, and I lean against the corner of the bed just inches from the feet of the woman as I continue to puke.

I don't even notice what's happening until it's too late. Laurence reaches the window and turns back towards me, and through blurred, watering eyes I can see a look of confused surprise on his face. Behind me I hear Lewis gasp, and as I turn towards him I see him lift Warren's rifle. I spin around again, and now I see Laurence throw himself behind the cover of the bed by the window as Lewis opens fire, and the glass in one of the windows explodes out in a million shards as his wild shot misses its mark.

My eyes clear, and as I look down I see it on

the floor. It's my gun. I didn't even feel it slipping from my waistband as I leaned over to puke.

I gave the fucking game away.

Without another thought I drop myself to the ground and shuffle behind the nearest bed, where Warren and Vee are already crouched in the small space. Vee awkwardly reaches into her jacket and pulls out the knife, and Warren and I hold out our hands so she can slice the ties with the serrated blade.

"Real smooth, Tom," Vee scolds as Warren takes the knife and cuts her tie. The shower curtain above us balloons out as a shot punches through it. "Where's Lewis?" she demands, ducking as another shot bursts through the curtain and buries itself in the wall above.

"*Fuck*, I'm sorry." I wipe my mouth with the back of my hand and look around, flinching when I see I'm just inches from the spilled intestines of the woman in the bed above us. She strains in her effort to break free, and a cold, fleshy tube flicks against my cheek. I almost jump out from behind the cover of the bed, but somehow manage to stop myself at its foot.

That's when I see Lewis.

•⁊•

:::9:::

WHAT A FUCKING disaster.

Lewis kicks at the grasping hands clawing at his feet as he climbs up onto the bed. He knows his boots are more than thick enough to keep him protected, but it doesn't stop the shiver running down his spine as he feels the fingers scratching at the leather.

He steps up and grabs at the closest rail until he's balanced on the rope running around the wall. Already he's regretting the plan he hatched in the few moments he had to think. With his hands stretched above him he grips the flimsy frames from which the shower curtains hang, and painfully slowly he makes his way across the beds towards the window as the guys draw the Chief's fire towards their side of the room.

He can't see much from up here, lost in the rows of white, and all he can do is pray the

Chief will stay over by the window until he can reach him. He's desperate to shout out to Vee and Warren to provide a little fire to pin him down, but he knows he can't give away his position. All he can do is put one foot carefully in front of the other.

A hand reaches up and grabs at the laces of his left boot, and as he pulls away the knot comes untied and hangs down, well within reach of the infected women. With the next step he feels the oversized boot loosen on his foot, and with horror he feels it begin to slip off with another.

Fuck. What am I gonna do now?

The rope hangs tight against the wall, but beneath his weight there's still far more slack than he'd like. It bows down towards the infected and allows them much more freedom of movement, and he knows it's only a matter of time before one of them manages to twist around and raise herself within biting distance. He can't afford to take the time to retie his boot, and even if he could he'd never be able to keep his balance.

Oh well, fuck it. Only a couple more beds.

With the next step the infected woman beneath him tugs at his dangling laces and pulls the boot from his foot. For a second or two it hangs on his toe, and moments before it falls he takes the opportunity to do some damage. With careful balance he drives his foot down into the woman's face with enough force to send her reeling, and he quickly slips past her and pushes his way past the next curtain.

Finally he hears shots coming from the direction of the guys, and a shuffling sound from behind the next curtain tells him that the Chief has retreated behind the bed.

"You know you can't escape, right?" yells Warren. "You got nowhere to go, you son of a bitch. Why don't you just give it up?"

Yeah, that's right, thinks Lewis. *Keep making noise.* He's been around the Chief long enough to know he'll fight to the last round, but he's thankful for the distraction all the same. Just a few more steps now.

"Son, I hope you have plenty of ammo," the Chief replies, laughing manically. "The second you get off your last shot I'm gonna feed all of you to these bitches feet first."

Lewis balances carefully on the rope, thankful that the woman in the next bed is already dead. Her hands hang loosely from the rope, and as he passes over her he quietly lowers himself to the ground, praying that he isn't visible through the curtain that separates him from the Chief.

With great care he peeks behind the white

curtain and breathes a sigh of relief when he sees that the final bed is empty. He can't quite see the Chief, but he can hear from his quick, shallow breathing that he's hiding somewhere at the foot of the bed. Slowly, deliberately he reaches to his hip and pulls out his pistol, draws back the slide and...

Oh, fuck.

He releases the clip, praying with all his might as he slides it out, but his worst fears are confirmed. He's empty.

Another few shots come from the other end of the room, and for a moment he wonders if it might be better just to sit tight and wait for the guys to make a move, but it only takes a moment to abandon that idea. His first rifle shot through the window would surely have alerted the guards outside that something was going on. If they're lucky they have just a few minutes before the first of them arrive.

Lewis returns his gun to its holster, reaches to his belt and pulls out the telescopic nightstick he was issued at Camp One. It's only a lightweight thing, designed more to menace than to injure, but it might be enough to give him the edge. He slides it out to its full length and locks it into position, then carefully creeps to the wall and prepares to make his move.

One breath.

Two.

Three.

The Chief leans around the edge of the bed and squeezes off a shot, and Lewis pounces while he's distracted. He pulls back the curtain, leaps across the bed in two steps and throws himself at the crouching man, barreling into him with all his weight. The Chief looks shocked, taken completely by surprise, and by the time he regroups Lewis has him pinned, his knee in his back and his arms pinning the Chief's, leaving him only able to point his pistol at the wall.

"I got him!" he yells. "*Cease fire!*"

It takes Lewis a moment to notice the girl as he holds the Chief firmly in place. Ahead of him, unseen until now, a young woman cowers between the bed and the window, her hands attached by cable tie to the end of the rope where it's tied to a steel loop hammered into the wall. She stares out at him in terror, and it's not until it's too late that Lewis realizes her fear isn't directed at him. It's directed at the Chief's gun, pointing straight at her.

Lewis lunges for the pistol but it's too late. The Chief squeezes the trigger. Lewis makes a grab for the gun, but the moment he releases the Chief's arm the man beneath him manages to twist around despite his weight, throwing Lewis off. The gun spins around.

The Chief squeezes again.

•◥•

:::10:::

"NO!"

I'M JUST two beds away when the second shot rings out. The world once again falls into horrific slow motion, but this time I can't move fast enough to do anything about it. Lewis, sprawled against the side of the bed, doubles over as the shot hits him. He looks more surprised than anything else. For a second or two I wonder if the shot missed, until the message finally reaches his brain and he slumps to the ground.

Vee comes running past as I stand there in shock, my gun hanging loosely by my side, and I barely blink as she squeezes off two shots into Sergeant Laurence. The first strikes him in the shoulder, the impact forcing him to drop his gun to the ground. The second catches him in the neck, grazing by and sending him to the floor, clutching at the wound.

"Warren, get Lewis out of here!" she yells, crouching down as she reaches Laurence and pressing the muzzle of her gun into his back. She pats him down until she finds a set of keys in his pants pocket, grabs them and tosses them to Warren. She looks up. "Oh Jesus... Tom? Take care of this one."

The sound of my name snaps me to attention, and as Warren grabs Lewis under the arms and drags him slowly towards the door I rush forward. As I pass the blood drenched curtain I see something I was never expecting. A woman. Alive. Her face is streaked with tears and her eyes are wide with fear, but otherwise she seems unharmed.

"Are you OK?" I ask, carefully stepping past Laurence and reaching down to take her hand.

She nods, hesitates, then reaches up to me. As she moves the rope between her wrists slips away, falling from her at its ragged, broken end. In the wall behind her I see a small bullet hole beside a steel loop, through which the other severed end of the rope is attached.

"Umm, Vee?" I lower my voice, as if speaking too loud might make it more real, "I think we need to get out of here right now. Look." I point to the broken end of the rope. Inch by inch it climbs the side of the bed.

Vee takes a second to understand what it means. "Oh, for the love of... OK, looks like we'll have to make this short and sweet." She looks up at me. "Is there anything you'd like to say to this fucker?"

I lift the girl to her feet, push her in the direction of the door then nod at Vee. "Yeah," I say, lowering myself into a squat just far enough from Laurence that I know he can't reach me. "Look at me," I say, waiting for him to turn his head. "Remember me?"

Laurence clasps his hand tightly over the wound in his neck, and when he opens his mouth I see blood on his lips. He gasps before speaking through gritted teeth. "Yeah. You're the pussy from the parking lot."

I shake my head angrily. "No! Do you remember me from before? From New York?" I don't know why it matters so much to me, but I can feel my rage bubble to the surface at the blank look on his face.

"Kid, I got no fucking idea who you are." He gasps, a line of blood dribbling down his cheek.

I can't believe it. I know I look pretty much the same as I did a month ago. The world has become unrecognizable but I haven't. There's no way he doesn't remember me. "New York, you evil fuck. You tried to kill me." I can hear my voice rising, and my finger twitches up to the trigger of my gun. "You shot my girlfriend. You remember Kate? You shot her in the chest and left her to die in the middle of the fucking street!"

Vee casts a wary eye to the rope. "Tom, time to go. Wrap it up."

I ignore her, locking eyes with Laurence as he looks at me with what appears to me genuine ignorance. Eventually he smiles and looks away, as if I'm not worthy of his attention. "Kid, I shot a lot of girls." He lets out a chuckle, spraying the carpet with specks of blood. "What makes you think yours was special?"

"Tom..." I hear the warning tone in Vee's voice as she looks around at the room.

This isn't quite the cathartic release I was looking for, but fuck it. It'll do the job. I lean in close to Laurence, wait until he locks eyes with me once more, and I squeeze off two shots, one in each thigh. He grimaces with pain and bares his teeth.

"You'll remember these girls," I whisper into his ear and point at the beds. "Vee, let's go."

I keep my gun trained on him as Vee stands, and we back out quickly. With each step the rope running around the room gains more slack as ten infected women tug it loose, and as we reach the door the woman closest to the severed end finally works herself free. She rolls from the bed, her hands still bound, and quickly pulls herself to her feet as she notices Laurence on the floor.

"Please," Laurence manages to call out, an edge of fear suddenly in his voice. "*Don't leave me with them!*"

There's nothing more to say. Vee backs out of the room and I follow, closing the door on Laurence just as the first infected woman reaches him. She falls to her knees above him, her teeth bared.

The thin door does nothing to block out the screams.

•┳•

:::11:::

Two Days Earlier

"WHY DIDN'T YOU eat the cop, Joe?"

Joe snarls in response. He isn't much of a conversationalist.

"Seriously, Joe, I'm really wondering. Why the fuck didn't you take a bite out of him when he was fresh? He can't have been dead more than a couple of hours. Shit, he was probably still warm and tasty. What are you, a picky eater?"

Another snarl. Joe does like to drone on.

"Don't tell me you're one of those assholes who demands gluten free shit in restaurants, Joe. Come on, buddy, fess up. You sure look just like one of those pricks."

Kaylee looks up through the bars of the cell and shoots a hateful glare at the man leaning against them. "You wouldn't want to eat me, Joe. I'm packed full of gluten. Stuffed to the gills with delicious gluten. I'm not organic, either. One bite of me and you'll shit yourself inside out, you nasty little prick." She laughs out loud as a snatch of Fight Club comes back to her, and she begins to yell. "*You don't know where I've been, Joe! You don't know where I've been!*"

Her voice echoes claustrophobically off the wall just a couple of yards away, and she squeezes her eyes closed as the first hint of another approaching panic attack sets her teeth on edge. The last one almost made her swing open the door and try to run. She pinches her eyes tight until colored spots appear in her vision, and doesn't open them again until her breathing starts to settle down.

Joe isn't the guy's real name. She doesn't know his real name, but she needed to call him something once she'd started recycling all the curse words she knew after the third day. 'Pestilent asshole' just wasn't cutting it any more, and after a few days on her own she felt like she needed a buddy. Joe sounded like a nice, friendly name. It sounded like the name of a guy who wouldn't try to eat her. Good old Joe.

Kaylee stands from the narrow bed and silently paces back and forth for a few minutes. It's not quite enough to calm her completely, but the movement helps just enough to keep her from losing it. If it wasn't for the tiny little window set high in the wall she would have gone crazy days ago. That little beam of sunlight passing across the floor for a few hours each day is just enough to remind her that the world continues to exist outside. The earth continues to orbit the sun.

Today, though, the approaching sunlight is more than just a distant ray of hope. After nine days trapped in this ten by eight cell with no food and nothing to drink but the water in the toilet bowl, the moment those rays hit the wall will be the moment Kaylee will finally escape this stinking, rotting hellhole. Today she'll breathe fresh air for the first time since the moment the cops locked the cell door. Hell, it might be for the last time. She has no clue what's going on beyond the walls of the jail, but if she dies today she'll at least die with the sun on her back.

"You have no idea what's coming, Joe," she mumbles, flashing a hint of a smile through her dry, cracked lips. "Your snarling days are over, buddy."

Joe snarls again. Always with the snarling. He just stands there, mouth open, drooling, snapping and snarling at her as if he thinks today might be the day he can magically squeeze through the bars. It's almost as if he isn't even listening to her.

Kaylee slumps back to the bed and looks beyond Joe to the desk down the hallway. She tries not to look at the cop still resting in his chair with the revolver on the floor by his side, but it's tricky for two reasons. For one thing it's his fault she got stuck here in the first place. It's hard to tell by the way his head tilted to the right after he shot himself, but she recognizes him as the booking officer who locked her up that first night.

Jesus, that night. What a disaster.

She'd been out at a party billed as End of the Worldapalooza, some concert a bunch of frat guys decided to throw when word of the evacuation came down. She'd planned to stay home and pack a few things, but one of her idiot friends was desperate to lose her V card before society went to shit. She insisted she needed to have sex before the water was cut off, because she couldn't bear to go to the refugee camp without being able to shower herself off after fucking. She'd convinced Kaylee to come along and – like always – Kaylee had told herself that she was capable of having 'just one drink' at a party. Hey, there's a first time for everything, right?

The cops pulled her over around 5AM the following morning. She had no idea where her friend had gone and no memory of the last few hours, but what she did have was a blood alcohol content of 0.15, a half empty bottle of Patron on the passenger seat and, in the pocket of her jeans, a baggy of something she absolutely couldn't pretend was baking soda. They threw her in the drunk tank to sleep it off, and the guy out in the hallway missing the back of his skull was the cop who booked her in.

When she woke up around lunchtime she figured she'd slept through the evacuation. There was no way of knowing exactly what happened, but she guessed that it was the booking officer's job to clear out the cells before getting the hell out of Dodge, and for whatever reason he'd decided to eat his gun instead. Before he went, though, he'd been kind enough to put the key in the door so she could get out. She guessed he figured she'd wake up, see him, find the key and take care of herself. Fucker probably thought he was being kind.

He just hadn't counted on Joe being there when Kaylee finally woke up to the worst morning of her life: a wicked tequila hangover, the end of the world and an infected bastard gnashing at the bars of her cell.

That was nine days ago.

This, though, isn't the main reason she doesn't like looking at the cop. Over the last nine days of hell she's pretty much forgiven the cowardly bastard for not making sure she got out safe, and the sight of the key in the door has been a great comfort. He screwed up, but at least he meant well. No, the main reason she doesn't like looking in that particular direction is simple.

The cop brought a snack with him the day he decided to kill himself.

On the desk beside him sits a Snickers bar and a bag of Cool Ranch Doritos, and for nine days they've been all she's dreamed about. She's woken up every morning licking imaginary Dorito dust from her lips. She's spent hours fantasizing about that first bite of the Snickers. She's dreamed about the chocolate, slightly melted in the warm room, coating her tongue, and the delicious resistance of the peanuts and nougat between her teeth. After nine days it's almost become a fucking sexual thing, just as much about the tactile pleasure of the food as the flavor, and she suspects that if she makes it through this alive she'll spend the rest of her days dealing with some extremely complicated feelings whenever she visits a 7-Eleven.

As she sits and stares at the candy she realizes the sun is beginning to rise. It'll be a while before the sunlight hits the wall, but out the window the little patch of sky has already shifted from black to dark blue. Just a little longer and she'll get to eat. Finally the gnawing pain in her belly will be soothed, and she'll be free to head to the nearest store and grab everything she's been craving for the last nine days. Spray cheese. Pastrami. Marshmallow fluff. *Oh Jesus*, a whole jar of pickled onions.

"It's almost time, Joe," she says, pulling out the skinny pillow from behind her and tugging off the pillowcase. "You're gonna be dead soon." She finds the corners of the case where she's already torn through the cotton by rubbing it against the sharp edge of the bed frame, and she feels a little rush of satisfaction as she tears the case lengthwise to make a yard long strip of fabric. Another half hour of patient sawing at the corner of the bed leaves her with four lengths of cotton, each of them a yard long and about a hand's width, and she patiently sets about knotting them together until she has a long, thin rope that can take a decent amount of tension. Finally she ties a thick knot at one end. It's not as heavy as she'd imagined, but it should do the job.

The idea had only come to her the previous night, and now she's kicking herself for waiting so long. For all this time she'd pinned her hopes on rescue, and she'd told herself time and again that there was nothing in the bare, spartan cell that could help her fight off Joe when she finally left. The bed and toilet were both secured firmly to the ground, and the bed itself had no sheets or blanket. Literally the only thing in the room she could pick up was the pillow, and it had taken her all this time to figure out how to use it as a weapon.

Out the window the sky looks a little lighter. The sun isn't quite up, but she's done waiting. It's light enough beyond the cell to see Joe clearly, and she doesn't need more than that.

She wants to eat that damned Snickers.

"It's time now, Joe," she says, noticing her voice is suddenly weak and wavering with the nerves. In her chest she can feel her heart flutter, but her path is set. If she doesn't eat now she won't have enough energy to try to get out later. It's make or break time. "Come on, buddy. You wanna eat me, right?" She walks over to the wall on the opposite side of the room to the cell door and Joe slowly follows, snapping at her through the bars, excited by her movement. His arms reach through the bars a little too close for comfort and Kaylee takes a quick step back, a sudden chill shivering down her spine. If he grabs her hair it'll be game over.

After a few deep breaths she steps forward again, carefully lowering herself out of reach of Joe's grasping hands. He swings wildly down to her but he doesn't seem to remember how to crouch. He just leans against the bars and reaches to around waist level, allowing Kaylee to slide in close to the bars and push the knotted end of the rope through.

Joe suddenly steps to the side, focusing his attention on the makeshift rope instead of her, and Kaylee makes her move before his awkward shuffle catches up to her. Reaching through the bars she tosses the knotted end to the side, passing the rope behind Joe's legs, and quickly drags it back through the bars before he can step out of the way. She grabs both ends and pulls the rope tight around his knees, dragging his legs against the bars before she quickly ties the ends in a tight knot.

Joe begins to howl as Kaylee shuffle back and lifts herself from the ground. His face contorts into a confused grimace when he finds himself unable to move his legs, and he wobbles from side to side for a moment before suddenly falling backwards, bent at the knees, and cracks his head on the tile floor.

Kaylee's hands are shaking as she hurries to the door and takes hold of the key, and at the sound of the door creaking open she barely notices the tears cutting lines through the grime on her face, nor the gulping sobs escaping her throat. She crosses the hallway in a daze, ignoring the dead cop to reach over and grab the

Snickers and chips, and in moments she's torn open the brown wrapper and crammed the chocolate bar whole into her mouth.

It's the best thing she's ever tasted. The best experience she's ever had. Her taste buds are almost overwhelmed, and as she blissfully chews the nougat and soft, melted chocolate her hands tremble with the joy of that feeling she missed so much. It's something she never really thought about, and something she swears to herself she'll never take for granted again, this joy of eating. It's... it's incredible.

The pack of Doritos follows closely after the chocolate, along with – bliss! – a stale jelly donut that was sitting in a Dunkin' Donuts box obscured by a stack of files. The sugar rush hits her right away, and for a brief moment she feels invincible, followed immediately by a violent bout of vomiting on the booking officer's desk. She braces herself on the edge and waits for the nausea to pass, ashamed of herself for wolfing down the food all at once.

A snarl from Joe shakes her back from her glassy eyed stupor, and she suddenly realizes she's now exposed for the first time in nine days. There are no bars to hide behind now, and she can't afford to drift off. She needs food – real food – and somewhere safe to rest up as she evaluates the situation. She grabs the revolver from the floor and pushes out the... what do you call it, the wheel? She doesn't know guns, but she knows what she's looking at well enough to realize that the bullet that went through the cop's head was the last one in there. Still, she thinks, the butt might make for a pretty good cudgel until she can find a better weapon. She knows she doesn't really have the strength to fight, but it feels good to hold the gun even if it's useless.

Joe's whining over by the cell door sends needles driving into her brain. She's been listening to it for what feels like forever, but before now it was coming from the other side of the bars. It drove her crazy but she knew he was harmless. Now they're both on the same side of the door, though, the snarling and gnashing takes on a much more threatening tone.

Kaylee looks down at the gun. Surely it wouldn't take too much force to bludgeon Joe to death, right? He's immobilized and he doesn't seem to have much coordination now he's on the floor with one arm awkwardly pinned beneath him. Just a few blows to the head with the heavy steel butt should be enough to put him out of his misery...

... but she can't bring herself to do it. He's *real* now. She gave him a damned name. It'd almost be like... Jesus, she can't imagine she's thinking like this... It'd almost be like killing a friend. She sighs.

"You got off light, Joe," she mutters quietly. "You're just lucky I'm cool."

She turns her back on him and walks slowly down the hallway, remembering her drunken route into the station days earlier. When she comes to a door with a security card reader she panics for a moment, but sighs with relief to find it swings open now the power's out. Beyond the door she finds the front desk, and beyond that the automatic sliding doors leading out into the street. These are clamped firmly closed – probably the only reason her cell wasn't swarming with infected – but they judder slowly open when she uses the last of her energy reserves to pry them apart.

The world outside is... normal. The streets are empty, of course, but there's nothing that would suggest that the nation has collapsed and zombies rule the earth. It could almost be just another quiet Sunday morning in Harrisburg, after the late night drunks have stumbled home but before the weekend shoppers begin to fill the streets. It's eerie, and the still air does little to help the mood.

Across the street a hot dog cart sits unattended, and a few pigeons peck hungrily at the remains of the stale buns scattered across the asphalt. Off to the south a small dog rounds a corner, takes one look at Kaylee and immediately turns and runs in the other direction. To the north...

To the north, far in the distance, Kaylee squints to see some kind of blockage in the street. It looks like a bright yellow school bus parked across the middle of the road. She takes a few steps towards it, stops and squints again. Yeah, it's definitely a school bus, and there seems to be something built up around it like a wall, though it's impossible to tell at this distance in the early morning half light.

She hesitates for a moment. After nine days in solitary she really doesn't want to go stumbling blindly into a dangerous situation, but her rumbling stomach overrules her. The thing looks likes a roadblock. Maybe it's the entrance to some sort of refugee camp. Maybe they have food. Safety. People she can talk to. People who'll actually reply with words, and not just violent snarls.

She knows she doesn't have much energy left. The bitter taste of bile in her mouth is the only memory she has of the candy, and the brackish toilet water she's been drinking for days wasn't nearly enough to quench her thirst. Any minute now she'll collapse from exhaustion, and if there's a chance she might find some sort of safety on the other side of that bus she has to take the risk. She takes a dozen steps towards the bus...

... A bullet ricochets off the asphalt a few steps to her right, and she drops to the deck. "*Please!*" she yells, casting her eyes about for the closest cover. "*Don't shoot!*"

Her voice is dry and croaky and she fears it hasn't carried over the distance to the bus. She coughs and yells again, a little louder this time. She can't move for terror, and she expects the killing shot to come at any moment.

In the distance a shrill whistle sounds, and in the still air she hears the sound of voices carrying back and forth, questioning and answering. She can only make out a fraction of the conversation, but the final calls comes through crystal clear.

"I think it's a woman."

"Bring her in."

•⁊•

:::12:::

ALL I CAN hear is my wheezing breath, our echoing footfalls on the service staircase and the sound of Lewis' jacket rustling against my right ear, his weight heavy on my shoulder. Ahead of us Warren clears a path, rounding each corner with his rifle leading the way, and behind Vee covers our rear with her pistol, wary of the sound of Laurence's men reaching 406 and discovering what's happened to him. The young woman we found sticks close to Warren, silent and wide eyed but apparently more comfortable in the presence of the biggest gun. We all run just a little faster as we hear the guards open fire on the infected.

Climbing the five flights down to the basement parking level seems to take an eternity. Lewis is far from heavyset but I'm in no shape to carry 150 pounds of dead weight over my shoulder, and by the time we hit the basement I can feel the days of grime glued to my skin sealed in beneath a fresh layer of sweat. My fatigues chafe against my armpits and crotch, and my hair sticks to my forehead. I'd give a year of my life in return for a shower and a change of clothes.

It's only when we hit the parking lot and Lewis weakly taps me on the back that I realize why I feel so uncomfortable. He mumbles for me to set him down, and as I gently lower him to the bare cement floor I feel his clothes peel away from mine like velcro. There's so much blood he almost slips out of my hands. I'm covered in it from shoulder to waist, and to my untrained eye it looks like more blood than a man can safely spare.

"*Jesus!*" I yell, cursing myself immediately when I see the stricken look on Lewis' face. His eyes are sunken and his skin ashy. If his lips weren't moving I'd swear he was already dead.

"Tom," he whispers as he weakly beckons me closer with a hand. "You gotta..." His eyes roll up as if he's falling asleep, but he pulls himself back with the last of his energy. "You gotta take the lead on this now." His hand pats at his jacket, coming away bloodier with each touch until he finds the flap to his chest pocket and reaches in. He pulls out his elastic bound notebook and holds it out to me.

"Take it," he whispers, pressing it into my open hands. "Go to the back page."

Vee appears beside me, drops to her knees, lifts Lewis' shirt and runs her hands across his bloodied skin, searching for the entry wound. "Hold on, Lewis, we're gonna take care of you. Warren!" she yells, "bring the morphine."

Lewis tries to bat her hand away, but he lacks the strength to do anything but wave weakly. "No, no, don't worry about it." His voice emerges as little more than a whisper. "I can't feel a thing. Tom, come closer." I kneel down beside him and lean in, holding the book open where he asked, and I try to ignore the thick coppery smell of blood that fills my nostrils. Lewis reaches out and touches the page, leaving a bloody fingerprint behind. "You gotta get there, Tom. All of you guys, you gotta get there. The vaccine is in my bag in the Stryker."

I look down at the book and read the scrawled handwriting. It's a street address somewhere in Nevada.

"What's there, Lewis? What are we supposed to do?"

His hand slips down to his waist as he tries vainly to fight off Vee. She's tearing through his pants with her knife, pulling the hole in the fabric wider to locate the entry wound. "No no no, stop it. I'm done, don't worry about it." He looks up at me and cracks a faint smile. "Never thought I'd be trying to stop a beautiful woman from tearing off my pants." He tries to laugh, but descends into a coughing fit instead.

I grab his shoulder and wait for him to catch his breath. "Come on Lewis, stay with us. What's in Nevada? What do we have to do?"

His eyes are losing focus now, and he's clearly fighting hard to stay conscious. "It's the last... the last CDC lab. Hoover Dam, you know? There's still... I think there's still some people there. They know I'm coming." He reaches up to me and grabs my collar with surprising force, pulling me in closer. "You have to put the vaccine in their hands, Tom. Just put it in their hands and they'll take care of the rest. Promise me, Tom." His eyes focus on me, and for a moment they burn with intensity. "*Promise me!*"

"I promise," I reply, meeting his gaze. "Don't worry, Lewis, I'll get it to them."

At Lewis' waist Vee sighs, and when I catch her eye she shakes her head. I feel Lewis' hand loosen its grip on my collar and slip away. With his last ounce of strength he reaches out to touch the photo stuck to the front of the notebook, staining the picture of his own face with a bloody fingerprint.

"My boy," he whispers, his voice now little more than a breath. His eyes begin to close, and I have to lean in close to hear his final words.

"Tell him I tried my best." His hand falls limply to his side, and after a few seconds I realize his chest is no longer rising and falling. He's gone.

Vee lifts herself to her feet and hurls her knife angrily to the floor. "*Fuck!*" Her hands are drenched to the wrists in blood, and she wipes them on her jacket until her front is stained dark. She looks down at herself and sees the mess she's made, then turns away from the body. "It severed his femoral artery. There was nothing I could have done, he was dead the second the bullet hit him."

"You tried, that's the important thing," I reply. I've no idea if that's the right thing to say, but she nods and turns back towards me. "Yeah," she sighs. "Fuck. An inch either side and he'd just have been limping for a while." She stares at the pool of blood slowly creeping away from Lewis' body, and when I look down I notice I'm standing in the middle of it. I take a quick step back, as if it's somehow disrespectful to disturb it.

The silence is broken by echoed shouts coming from the stairwell. They're still distant, maybe a few floors above us, but we know it won't take the guards long to find us. A splash of blood every few yards leads all the way to Lewis' body, like a trail of breadcrumbs.

"Come on," I say, tucking the notebook in

my jacket pocket, "we have to get out of here. Where did Warren and the girl go?"

Vee opens her mouth, but before she can speak the roar of an engine answers her question. With a squeal of tires the immense Stryker turns the corner, its bright headlights blinding us as the vehicle approaches, and I feel my body tense. Over the last month I'd almost succeeded in blocking out the terrible memory of this damned vehicle, but now it all comes flooding back. The muzzle flash from the dark interior. Kate falling back, landing in a heap on the street. The lifeless look in her eyes, and her glassy gaze staring blindly up at the sky. The tires crushing her body.

I shiver despite the heat, and my hands clench in tight fists before a wave of calm suddenly washes over me. I haven't had time to process what happened in the last few minutes, and I can't help but smile when I remember that the man responsible for all this pain is a few floors above me, his body torn and broken by the people he hurt. I don't think I'm a vengeful person, but I won't apologize for this feeling. I'm not ashamed. Some people deserve to die.

The Stryker pulls up alongside us, and before it comes to a stop the rear hatch swings open with the same creak I remember from New York. Vee rushes to the back and I follow slowly, reluctantly, almost as if I imagine Sergeant Laurence will be waiting there for me. I finally shuffle to the back of the hulking vehicle and find nothing but the new girl offering a hand to climb into the rear cabin, but before I lift myself up I don't miss the dent in the side of the Jerry can mounted to the rear by the hatch. Without thinking I lift my hand to my head and rub the spot where I hit that damned thing.

Up front Warren turns in the driver's seat as I swing the hatch closed behind me. "Lewis?" he asks. I shake my head, and Warren turns back to the controls and sighs. "Damn shame. So, where are we–"

We all flinch at the sound of shots ricocheting off the armored exterior. Warren floors it, and I tumble backwards at the Stryker bolts forward through the parking level. I can't see out the window but I swear I can feel a couple of slight jolts, as if we're barreling into people.

The new girl unsteadily stumbles to the front of the vehicle as we emerge from the parking lot and sunlight suddenly floods the cabin, and I follow close behind. "This thing's armored, right?" she asks.

Warren nods. "Don't worry, they could shoot all day and we'd be perfectly safe in here."

"No, that's not what I mean," she replies. She

points out the narrow slit windscreen at something I can't see. "I mean is it tough enough for that?"

Warren grins and mutters under his breath, "I like the way this one thinks." He pulls to a sudden stop, turns back to me and Vee with a cheerful smile plastered on his face and raises his voice above the guttural roar of the engine. "Hold onto something, guys. We're leaving a little farewell gift."

I scramble to the front, grab the back of Warren's seat and peer through the narrow window, and as soon as I figure out what I'm looking at a smile appears on my face.

Warren guns the engine, straightens up the Stryker and plants his foot hard on the gas. Through the window I see a few men scramble to get out of the way. A few more stand fast and try to fire on us, their shots swatted away like mosquitoes from our toughened bullet resistant window. Nothing can stop us as we gain speed and barrel towards our target.

We're thirty yards away now. Twenty. Ten.

With a deafening crash the heavily armored vehicle tears through the bright yellow school bus in the center of the compound's largest roadblock like wet tissue paper. The rear axle of the bus shears away from the rest of it, and as we race across the open space in front of the hotel we drag a section of the bus along with us, the broken, twisted bench seats hanging from the gash we tore through the vehicle. It sticks to us until we hit another, smaller roadblock, batting aside the stack of cars like a 16 pound bowling ball toppling racked pins.

The smile is still plastered across my face as I spin around and see Vee push the rear hatch halfway open to survey the wreckage. Behind us the remaining guards scurry desperately around the front of the compound, some yelling orders at each other while others stare open mouthed at the two gaping holes in their barricades. Warren picks up speed, and as we race away from the hotel we see the first groups of infected emerging curiously from the side streets, no doubt attracted by the sound of our engines. As we pass they try to chase, but when they realize we're moving too quickly they begin to turn back to a closer target. The sound of yelling pulls them back towards the hotel, which quickly gives way to the sound of gunfire, which only attracts yet more infected from the shadows. Dozens of them. Hundreds.

Maybe some of the men will survive, if they're smart enough to run.

·T·

:::13:::

THE STRYKER GROWLS north through the low rise city sprawl for ten blocks before Warren swings the wheel left and guides the hulking vehicle towards the Harvey Taylor bridge. He easily shunts aside a pair of cop cars parked up to serve as a barrier, their tires squealing in protest as they slide sideways, then guides us slowly out across the broad, lazy Susquehanna.

Beyond the cop cars the bridge is clear of traffic. It stretches half a mile across the river with a clear view to either side, so when Warren pulls the Stryker to a stop in the middle we quickly crack open the rear hatch and climb out to regroup. Off in the distance I can still hear the sound of gunfire, but from the occasional lonely pops it sounds like there are only a couple of guys still shooting. Fuck 'em.

The new girl hops down from the back,

stretches and starts to massage her wrists, the skin raw from the chafing of the cable ties. For a long moment she gazes upriver at leafy Independence Island, her face tilted towards the sun, smiling, before she finally turns back to find the three of us staring at her.

"Oh," she says, smiling casually as if she didn't have a care in the world, "thanks for, umm... all that." She points vaguely back towards the hotel. "I'm Kaylee." She gives us all a little wave. "So the world ended, huh? Bummer." At that she turns back to the river without another word.

Vee and I exchange glances. PTSD? A little crazy? Just plain dumb? Her behavior seems a little weird, but we don't have time to deal with an unhinged young woman right now. "OK guys," I say, turning to the only other people who seem to be sane right now, "Lewis said we need to get to a lab somewhere in Nevada with the..."

A thought occurs to me. I climb back into the Stryker, drop to the floor and search under the bench seats in the rear cabin until I find what I'm hunting for. Lewis' camo backpack is hidden away toward the front, and I dig through the pockets until I pull out a small plastic disc. I climb back down from the back and hand it to Warren. "This is the vaccine. Lewis told me there's a CDC lab still operational that can, I don't know, work some magic and mass produce this or something. He mentioned something about the Hoover Dam, but he wasn't making much sense at the end. I don't know what he meant."

Warren nods as he looks at the disc. It's a Petri dish containing a layer of agar jelly spotted with dozens of small black patches. "Power," he says. He glances up and notices my questioning look. "The Hoover Dam. It's hydroelectric. You remember that old documentary? What was it called, *Life After Humans* or something? No? Well, it said the dam would continue to generate power for about a year without maintenance, until the cooling pipes became too clogged up with mussels or something. I think I'm remembering that right, anyway. It's been a few years since I saw it."

My jaw drops. "You mean there's still power somewhere?"

"Oh yeah, sure," Warren nods. "I mean, I'm not saying all those neon lights in Vegas will still be shining. I'm guessing a lot of the infrastructure has started collapse now there's nobody there to balance the power load. A lot of transformers have probably blown out, but yeah, I'd guess there's still pockets of power in Nevada and California. Maybe a few other places with solar power or wind turbines. That shit'll keep going for years so long as the grid can take the load."

I feel almost giddy at the thought. I'm not sure why, but it just feels like there may be hope for the future if the lights are still on somewhere. Forget the infected. Forget the assholes like Sergeant Laurence and everyone who follows people like him. Just the thought that somewhere in the country a refrigerator is still humming away makes me think we might be able to pull ourselves back from the brink. Maybe all it takes is a cold beer and a frozen steak that hasn't started to rot. We can start there and work our way up.

"We're going," I declare, more certain of this than I've ever been of anything. "We can get the vaccine to the lab and then find a place with AC, a cold Bud and some ground beef." A grin plasters itself on my face as a thought hits me. "I can make chili. I make a fucking awesome chili."

Vee chuckles and pats me on the arm. "OK, settle down Tom. How do you think we're gonna get to Nevada from here? You really think we can make it, what, two and a half thousand miles without getting ourselves killed? We couldn't even make it out of Pennsylvania before some fucker tried to make me a slave. Bishop's dead, Lewis is dead and Warren got a bullet in his leg for his trouble. What makes you think tomorrow will be any better?"

Kaylee spreads her arms wide, basking in the sun, a peaceful smile on her face. "We could fly there," she says, then she makes a whooshing sound and thrusts her arm out ahead of her like Superman.

Vee adopts the tone of someone humoring a child. "That's a lovely idea, Kaylee. Maybe we can think about that a little later." She turns back to me and rolls her eyes. "Look, I know it's important to get to this lab, but I just don't know how we're gonna make it all that way. It's a suicide mission."

"Let's just fly there," Kaylee repeats, spreading her arms like wings. "We could be there in, like, a few hours or something."

Warren steps in. "Kaylee, please. We don't have a plane, and none of us can fly. Now, Tom, I have to agree with—"

"I can fly." Kaylee turns to face us now, suddenly lucid. "We can just go in my plane. Well, OK, not *my* plane. My dad runs a flight school. There's a plane there."

"You have access to a plane? A *real* one? Not just a toy?" Warren asks incredulously.

"Sure. It's a nice one. It's got, like, five or six seats. It goes really fast."

"And you can fly it?"

Kaylee grins. "Sure, I could fly it with my eyes closed."

Vee, Warren and I exchange doubtful looks. "And where is this plane?" Vee asks.

Kaylee points vaguely towards the south. "It's at the airfield just down the river. We can be there in about ten minutes if we leave now." Her eyes light up. "*Ooooh,* but can we stop at a 7-Eleven on the way? I've got some insane cravings going on. Deal? You find me some chocolate covered pretzels and I'll fly you anywhere you wanna go."

I lean in towards Vee and Warren and lower my voice, turning away from Kaylee. "What's the harm?" I whisper. "If she's telling the truth we're golden. If she's making shit up it's ten minutes out of our day."

They both think for a moment then nod, though of course they still look doubtful. "OK, deal," Vee says. "You wanna lead the way?"

Kaylee grins and claps her hands. "Ooooh, pretzels," she says in a sing song voice. "I'm so fucking hungry I could eat ten bags. Let's go!"

She hops excitedly into the back of the Stryker and rushes to the front seat. Warren climbs in after her and yells a warning to her to not touch the controls to the roof-mounted gun.

"You think she's crazy?" Vee asks me, her voice low.

I shake my head and smile. "I don't know. If she's really got a plane I don't care if she wants the Cookie Monster to be her co-pilot. Do you?"

•᎖•

:::14:::

THE NEXT HALF hour passes for all of us in a sort of odd, dreamlike state.

Warren slowly guides the Stryker through the leafy, picture perfect suburbs west of the Susquehanna. Endless rows of pretty houses ringed with pristine white picket fences line the wide, leafy streets, their slightly unkempt sun-dappled lawns the only indication that the owners are either gone or long dead.

Little by little the houses grow smaller and less well kept until we finally pass through the low rent neighborhoods and out into the grimy industrial district of the city, a landscape pockmarked with prefab warehouses and sprawling discount used car lots.

Warren pulls in at a convenience store beside a Burger King with shattered glass glistening across the parking lot, and for a few minutes

Kaylee skips happily through the aisles and stuffs her pockets with strawberry laces and Jelly Belly beans. When she can carry no more we guide her, protesting, back to the Stryker, and we continue until she points out a small sign by the side of the road that reads Capital City Airport.

It's only a small airfield, the main building a two floor block with broken windows that look like they were probably already broken before the world ended. There's no security to speak of but a low wire fence around the perimeter, and the Stryker pushes through it like it's a fine mist. Kaylee climbs to the front and points over Warren's shoulder to a small, run down hangar sitting out on its own about a hundred yards from the main building.

None of us but Kaylee really believe we'll find anything in there but disappointment and the punchline to a long, time wasting joke, but as we pull up beside the tall open doors of the hangar we see in the darkness within a small, sleek white plane with a sharp, pointed nose, a red tail and the words 'Baxter Flight School' emblazoned along its side.

"It's nice, right? That's my dad's." Kaylee grins at us and rushes to the back, pushing open the rear hatch and hopping down with her hands held over her bulging pockets to keep the candy from falling out. "Come on, guys!"

I stand up to leave, but Warren grabs my arm before I can move. "Hey, do you really trust this psycho at the controls of a plane?" he hisses. "How do we even know she can fly this thing?"

I shrug. "Do I trust her? No, not at all. I wouldn't trust her with plastic cutlery, but it doesn't look like we have much of a choice, right?" I pull the Petri dish from my pocket. "We have to get this to Nevada, and Vee's right. Driving there would be a suicide mission." I let out a sigh. "Look, you don't have to come if you don't want to. You can stay here and wait for the fungus to arrive, but I'd rather die taking a chance, you know?"

Warren shakes his head and frowns at me while he thinks, then eventually nods as if he's come to a decision. "Your dumb ass wouldn't make it five minutes without me. I'll come, but look..." he grabs the fabric of my jacket and pulls me in close. "Is your chili really that good or were you just kidding?"

I meet his gaze and speak slowly, in the most serious tone I can muster. "My chili will make your eyes pop out of your fucking head."

Warren lets me go and grabs his rifle. "OK then, what the fuck are we waiting for? Let's let a crazy bitch rocket us to 40,000 feet in a tin can."

As we climb from the Stryker Kaylee is

yelling instructions to Vee as she circles the plane, dropping to a squat to check the tread of the tires before she moves to the wing, unclips a cap and pushes a small glass vial against a valve.

"What are you doing?" I ask, curious.

Kaylee ignores me for a moment as she carefully studies the fluid in the vial. She seems like a different person now she's focused on a task. "Pre-flight checks," she distractedly mumbles. "I'm checking for impurities in the fuel. This bird probably hasn't been in the air in a while." She waves me away as if I'm bothering her. "Go find some new clothes for us in the back room over there. I hate to say it, but you guys all stink like old ass."

I start to walk in the direction she's pointing, then stop short when she yells out to me. "Oh, and... sorry, what's your name?"

"It's Tom. That's Warren, and she's Vee."

"Great, Tom. Can you go in the bottom drawer of the desk and bring me the little pink My Little Pony lunch box?"

"Umm, sure." I turn back and shake my head, hardly believing I'm about to let this weirdo get us off the ground. I carefully make my way through the dimly lit hangar, avoiding stacks of engine parts and discarded chairs until I find the back room, a cramped little office strewn with maps and charts, and find Vee rifling through file cabinets.

"What are you doing?" I ask, heading for the desk.

"Fetching things for little miss bananas over there," she replies. "She wants maps, charts, handbooks... I don't know, it's a long list. What job did she give you?"

I pull open the bottom drawer and pull out the box. "Ummm, a lunch box and clothes, because apparently we all stink like old ass."

Vee laughs. "Well, she's not wrong there. I wouldn't say no to a shower right about–"

"*Jesus!*" I gasp. Vee falls silent and turns to me. "OK, correction. I'm collecting the contents of the local pharmacy." The lunch box is full to bursting with pill bottles. "Lamotrigine... Xanax... Lithium... Oh, and a shitload of weed and rolling papers. Looks like Kaylee has quite the party planned."

Vee gathers her supplies and looks back at Kaylee through the window to the hangar. "Fuck. Tom, is this a dumb idea? Maybe driving isn't such a crazy plan. Not as crazy as letting an insane drug addict fly us to Vegas, anyway. Maybe we could just–"

Again she doesn't get to finish her thought. A shot echoes deafeningly off the corrugated steel walls of the hangar, and Warren comes running through the doors. "Time to go, folks! Looks like they heard our engine. Kaylee, you ready to go?"

Kaylee glances up from the vial she's pushing into yet another fuel valve. "Nope, it'll be another ten minutes. Gotta inspect the flaps and go through the instrument checks." She looks back to her vial as if she doesn't have a care in the world.

"*Guess again!*" Warren shouts, peering out the door towards the concrete apron beyond. "I want us in the air in two minutes. Make it happen!" He braces his rifle against his shoulder and squeezes off a few quick rounds then looks back to see Kaylee still gazing at the vial. "Now! Vee, Tom, get her in the fucking plane!"

I grab the lunchbox and a bundle of clothes from beside the locker, then follow Vee at a dead run towards the plane. She pulls open the door and dumps her load in the back, then runs to the wing and pulls Kaylee away.

"Hey, I need to–"

"You need to get in the fucking plane, young lady!" Vee yells, pulling down the retractable steps with one hand while dragging Kaylee to the door with the other. "Warren, come on!"

I climb in behind them and watch as Vee bundles the girl roughly to the cockpit, before Kaylee twists around to face me. "Tom, did you get my box? Please tell me you got my box!"

I hold up the pink My Little Pony lunch box triumphantly and yell out "*I got the box!*", moments later realizing this may be the single most ridiculous moment of my life.

Kaylee grins and turns to the controls. "Sweet! OK, brakes... test and set... avionics... where are you? Aha, off... circuit breakers... check... ummm, fuel shutoff valve... on. OK, guys? We gotta do a passenger check. Do you all have your seat belts fastened? Do you know the location of the nearest emergency exit?"

Vee grabs her by the shoulder and squeezes hard enough to make her yell out in pain. "Forget the fucking checklist and get us off the ground, now!"

"Jeez, OK, OK," Kaylee mutters, rubbing her shoulder. She flips a switch and the engines begin to hum behind us, and moments later she releases the brake and pushes the throttle forward a little. The plane judders for a few seconds then begins to slowly trundle forward, and I move back to the door and lean out.

"Warren, come on!" I yell, but he doesn't hear me over the engine noise. By the look on his face I'm not looking forward to what we'll see when we pass through the doors, and my confidence doesn't climb any higher when he finally turns back to us and starts sprinting for the plane.

"Go! Fucking *go!*" he cries, throwing his rifle through the door before leaping in after it.

I pull up the steps behind him, swing the door closed and twist the locking bar down, and finally the plane begins to pick up a little more speed as we move out from the dark hangar and into the sunlight. As we emerge I look out through the small windows, and a chill runs down my spine as I see what awaits us.

The broad concrete apron is swarming with infected. Dozens of them race towards the hangar while still more swarm in from the road beyond. "Kaylee, go faster!" I yell. "Where the fuck did they come from?"

Warren presses his face against the nearest window. "They must have heard our engine and followed us. We've probably been pulling them in like a fucking magnet all the way down from the bridge." He turns to the front. "Kaylee, will these guys cause us any problems? Can they tip us?"

"No!" she yells over the drone of the engine. "But if any of them get close to the jet intakes we'll... well, let's just say it won't be good news."

"Then go faster, woman!" As he speaks the fastest of the swarm reach the plane. Two of the sprinters slam violently into the side and sends us rocking, and the plane jogs up and down for a moment as the rear wheels roll over one of the fallen bodies.

"Faster!" I yell. "Why the fuck are we going so slow?"

"There's a speed limit!" Kaylee replies. "We're not allowed to taxi at more than 20 knots per hour when there are obstacles on the apron. It's in the handbook!"

"Forget the fucking handbook, the fucking world has ended! Vee, can you deal with this shit?"

Vee nods, leans over Kaylee and pushes the throttle lever all the way forward. Almost immediately the engines build to a dull, deafening roar that reaches down to our bones, and the plane accelerates with a jerk that almost knocks me off my feet.

"*No!*" Kaylee cries, "we need to taxi to the end of the runway before we can reach takeoff speed!"

I run through the plush cabin and burst into the cockpit as Kaylee reaches out to the controls to throttle back. "Wait! Kaylee, how much runway do you really need? Look at the swarm. We have to take off now or the runway'll be crawling with them."

She finally seems to realize what's going on. The narrow taxiway we're on joins the runway around halfway down its length, but the infected are now flooding in from all sides.

Some are even running, hobbling and dragging their bodies across from the other side of the airfield, out over the scrubby grass in the distance. Within moments the fastest will reach the asphalt, and once they're there we'll have no chance of a clear run down the runway.

"OK, you better hold onto something," Kaylee says, slowing us just a little. "This turn might get a little rough. Oh, and everyone get to the left of the plane."

I brace myself against the wall of the cockpit as Kaylee prepares for the turn. The runway is at least as wide as three wingspans, but even so we're looking at a turn of around 30 degrees at close to full speed. I grab the back of the pilot's seat as Kaylee steers us in, and for a brief moment my stomach turns over as we list to the side. I feel one of the rear wheels rise from the ground, and after a few seconds in which I'm certain the wing will scrape along the ground we finally begin to straighten up. The wheel crashes back to the ground, and for a moment the rear wheel on the other side of the plane digs into the soft earth beside the runway before Kaylee fights the controls and pulls the plane out of the swerve.

The first of the infected reach the asphalt as we approach, swarming in almost a solid block onto the runway far ahead of us. Kaylee pushes the throttle forward and desperately flips switches as we accelerate, and by the time she grabs the yoke they're just a couple hundred yards ahead of our nose. I grit my teeth and cling to the back of the pilot's seat as the engines roar and the infected hove ever closer. At this distance I can almost make out their faces, and it's all too easy to imagine us plowing straight into the swarm. It's easy to imagine them grabbing at the wheels as we pass, yanking us back down to the asphalt nose first, sending us into a burning heap and allowing them to climb into the wreck to drag us out. I close my eyes and squeeze the back of the chair even harder.

Finally Kaylee grips the yoke and pulls back as hard as she can. I feel the front wheel raise slowly from the ground, and after a few seconds of terror I see the runway begin to fall away beneath us. The infected stand as one, their arms raised, reaching out for us as we pass just out of reach of their fingers. Gravity tries to pull me down to the floor, and I hang on tight to the pilot's seat until I can only see clear blue sky out the front window.

"Tom," Kaylee says, her voice low, "can you do me a favor?"

"Sure," I stammer, surprised I can still form words.

"Can you go and get me my lunch box?

Bring me Xanax. And lithium." She begins to level the plane off, looks down at her instruments and banks into a gentle turn. Beneath us the runway comes back into view, and we all stare open mouthed at the sea of infected staring up at us, raising their arms as if they're trying to pluck us right out of the sky. Kaylee runs her shaking fingers through her hair and slumps back in her seat. "And, like, *all* the weed."

•⁊•

:::15:::

WE'RE CRUISING SOMEWHERE over central Illinois by the time Kaylee's medication kicks in enough to level out her mood and stop her hands from trembling.

Once we were out of sight of the airfield she climbed further then leveled off at around six thousand feet, high enough to clear any mountains we might come across before we hit the Rockies, but low enough to avoid any high altitude air currents that might push us off course.

As soon as she was satisfied we were on the correct course she stumbled back to the cabin with her lunch box of medication. Now she's reclined in one of the luxurious leather seats in the cabin while Warren takes a turn in the pilot's seat, under strict instructions to just make sure the plane stays level and not fuck around with the controls.

The Spectrum S.33 was fresh off the production line six months ago, according to Kaylee. It's equipped with an autopilot system so sophisticated it can track approaching weather patterns and adjust course to avoid storms and turbulent air, but unfortunately the system only functions with an accurate GPS signal. Warren tested it soon after Kaylee leveled out the plane but it refused to so much as start up, throwing up a connection error message on the little OLED screen beneath the master switch.

Warren's guess is that the entire GPS network has begun to fail after a month without maintenance. He explained that the network depends on constant care from the Ground Segment, a network of monitoring stations around the world that track the orbit of satellites, fractionally adjusting their course and correcting their clocks whenever they drift slightly out of sync. Even without those stations the satellites should stay in the sky for years before their orbits finally degrade, but without maintenance they're designed to automatically take themselves out of the network if they fall too far out of sync.

The idea is that the remaining satellites will plug the gaps until a failing node can be repaired or replaced, but without updates from the

Ground Segment multiple satellites must have stopped sending a signal. The network had been reliable enough to pinpoint our sat phones when Vee was taken, but apparently it's not stable enough to track the movements of a light aircraft cruising at 400mph.

It was only after Warren explained all of this that a worrying thought occurred to me. If the GPS network is controlled by stations all around the world, surely it wouldn't fail with the loss of just the US stations. Surely that must mean that the infection hadn't only affected us. Maybe the whole world was like this now. Seven billion people fleeing from monsters, desperately fighting for their lives from Sydney to London to Rio.

I don't mention my concerns to Warren – we've all got enough on our plates without piling more on – but I can't help but feel a little scared of what that realization means. For the last month I've been focused so much on the collapse of my home country that I haven't given so much as a passing thought to the rest of the world. It never occurred to me. I'd just assumed this was our problem alone. At the back of my mind I think I'd assumed that if we could survive this, if we could somehow stick it out and stay alive until the last infected fell, the governments of the rest of the world would swoop in and save the day. The UN. The Red Cross. *Medicine Sans* fucking *Frontiers*.

I imagined the rest of the world waiting in the wings, ready to make airdrops and build refugee camps. In my more pleasant daydreams I imagined a resettlement somewhere warm with its own McDonalds franchise, and I thanked God I was born in a country that had exported its culture to all corners of the world. Even if America was really over, I thought, even if we'd taken a truly killing blow from which we could never hope to recover... well, at least there were people in England who knew the recipe for Big Mac special sauce.

Deep in thought I leave the cockpit and head back to the comfortable, well furnished cabin, planting myself in a generously cushioned chair opposite Kaylee. She casually rolls a joint while barely looking down at her hands, as if she does it so often it's become muscle memory. In the ashtray beside her lie the crushed butts of another two joints, and the golden sunlight pouring in through the windows picks out the thick smoke hanging in the air.

"It's called cyclothymia," she says out of the blue, her voice a little distant and slow now the weed has begun to take effect. She notices my confused look and smiles. "The... y'know, the reason I was acting all weird and spaced out back there. It's like, I don't know, like half assed bipolar, y'know? I don't get the full blown manic episodes and long drawn out depression bipolar sufferers get, but without my medication I can get a little... kooky." She moistens the rolling paper, smooths out the joint and lights it up, filling the cabin with even more fragrant, dizzying smoke.

"To be honest I don't really remember much of the last few days. Nothing until the pills kicked in, really. It's like I was watching a movie from the back of my mind, you know?" She sees my expression, and instantly recognizes me as someone who has no idea about mental illness. "Ah, you don't know. It's OK. It's kinda hard to describe to mentally typical people. I'm OK now, anyway. A joint and my pills usually level me out pretty quickly." She looks out the window and breaks into a grin. "Fuck, I can't believe I really took off. Dad never let me do that."

I can't help but laugh. No surprise considering Kaylee's been hot boxing the cabin for the last half hour. I haven't smoked weed since college, and my head is already swimming. "You mean you've never taken off before?"

"No, not solo" she says, smirking. "Dad only let me take the stick when we were at cruising altitude. I didn't even really know what I was doing, I just copied the shit he always did when he took off."

I start to chuckle, and it takes a few tries to get the words out. "So you're telling me the first time you ever piloted a plane you were being chased by zombies? Not bad, Kaylee. Not at all fucking bad."

Kaylee bursts out laughing, and her laughter sets me off until we're both giggling uncontrollably. After a minute or so I can't even remember what we're laughing about, and I don't care. After the events of the day it just feels good to cut loose. My ribs hurt by the time Vee loses patience with us and goes to find the air circulation controls in the cockpit. Finally, after several long minutes of laughing at nothing, the fans kick in and start to dissipate the smoke fogging up the cabin.

Vee ducks back into the cabin and takes a seat beside us. "Guys, I hate to be the mom in this little family, but we really need to work out where we're going. This tin can won't stay in the air forever, and I'd really prefer it if our pilot isn't completely baked when we come in to land, OK?"

Kaylee sits up and shakes her head as if to clear the cobwebs, then tamps out the joint in the ashtray in the arm of the chair. "You're right," she says, trying to keep a smirk from her face. "Sorry, *mom*." That sets us both off giggling again, and Vee sits quietly until we both notice her stern expression. Almost immediately all the humor is sucked out of the cabin along with the smoke.

"Don't worry," Kaylee says. "I'll be straight by the time we land. Sorry about the way I've been acting, and thanks for, y'know, saving my life and everything. I wasn't really thinking clearly until now." She slaps her hands on her thighs and lifts herself out of her chair. "OK, where are we headed?"

Vee turns to me. "Tom? What's the address?"

I reach into my jacket and pull out Lewis' notebook, focusing for a moment on the bloody fingerprints before flipping to the back page. "Ummm, it says the facility is just outside Railroad Pass, Nevada. Off the 515 between Vegas and Lake Mead."

Kaylee pulls herself up from her chair, walks to the back of the cabin and settles herself down by the pile of maps and charts Vee carried on board. "Could be cutting it fine," she says, frowning. She rifles through the pile until she finds a map of the US, flattens it out on the floor and uses her index finger to measure out the route between Harrisburg and Las Vegas. "Hmmm. Damn, the scale is in kilometers, Anyone know how to convert to miles?"

"Divide by eight then multiply by five," I say immediately. I've spent so much time traveling in countries that use the metric system that I can do rough conversions in my sleep. "What's the distance?"

"3,400 kilometers"

I close my eyes and do the sum with the same speed I used to convert speed limits as soon as I spotted a cop in the distance. "That's... about 2,100 miles, give or take a few."

Kaylee grabs a thick binder beside the maps and starts flipping the pages. "Huh. OK, let's see... 2,100 miles is around 1,800 nautical miles, and the Spectrum can fly... ummm... OK, cool, this bird can fly 2,000 without refueling" She looks up at Vee. "It's all good. There's not a huge margin of error but we had a full tank at takeoff. So long as we stay on course and maintain speed we should make it to Vegas with plenty of fuel to spare. I just hope the runway's clear, because I don't have local maps for smaller airfields and I don't think I could find one by sight. If we can't land at McCarran we'll be looking at a highway touchdown, and..." she sees the color drain from Vee's cheeks. "Don't worry about it, we'll be fine."

Vee stands up without another word and stiffly returns to the cockpit. I almost feel another attack of the giggles come on, but my sense of humor vanishes when I start thinking about the fact that I'm thousands of feet in the air with a pilot who's never landed a plane before. I look out the window to distract myself from the sudden attack of nerves.

On the other side of the plane the sun is dipping towards the horizon, casting golden ovals of warm light against the wall of the cabin, and out the window the sky is already darkening while the ground below fades in the half light. In the crystal clear, unpolluted air it seems like I can see to the ends of the earth, and as I gaze down at Illinois I'm reminded of just how little of my country is really built up.

Down on the ground it's easy to forget. Before the infection arrived most of us were firmly tethered to towns and cities. They were the core of our civilization, shaping our lives, their gravity influencing the very structure of our country like lead weights on a rubber sheet. Even now, a month after the collapse of society, I can't help but think of our journey as a series of stepping stones, hopping from one city to the next until we finally reach Las Vegas. It makes little sense. There's little awaiting us in the cities but the promise of a quicker death, but despite everything I still I think of them as oases of civilization

If you stick to the roads you could cross

entire states without seeing anything but towns, cities, sprawling suburbs and the endless strip malls, fast food joints and gas stations that seem to fill every available inch between them. You might be forgiven for thinking that America had long ago lost the war with concrete and asphalt, but from up here it's clear that the country is, more than anything else, still an unspoiled land. Far below us the ground is a patchwork of every imaginable shade of green. Orderly rectangles of farmland give way to dense, sprawling forests, which themselves give way to broad, lazy rivers that trace serpentine tracks between rolling hills and through deep valleys. The towns and cities that weigh so heavily on the landscape at ground level appear few and far between from up here, mere islands of gray ugliness amidst a sea of green.

I think back to the last time I flew across the country, a late night flight from La Guardia to a friend's wedding in some nothing little town an hour or so south of Atlanta, and I remember gazing out the window and seeing nothing but light all the way to the distant horizon. Each road was a glowing ribbon, a narrow filament connecting one sprawling mass of light to the next. It seemed as if there was nowhere you could stand on the east coast without seeing an artificial light. I'd found the sight oddly comforting.

Soon after college I'd spent a year living in Mongolia, a country the size of western Europe with a population just a little larger than that of Chicago, and I'd quickly grown wary of the vast, unimaginably empty steppe. Once, while on a horse trek up near the Russian border, my horse had thrown me and bolted with most of my kit, leaving me with a broken wrist and a two day hike back to the nearest road. Winter was closing in and the temperature wasn't far above zero, but it wasn't the cold that got to me. It was the sounds I heard after dark, rustling and chattering from all directions, with no way of knowing what was making the noise. The experience had taught me to embrace the light. Light meant safety. It meant heat, and food, and help. More than anything else, light meant that there was someone there to switch it on.

Looking out the window now as the sun dips beneath the horizon I feel a chill pass through me. The setting sun used to bring with it the flickering of lights. Rows of streetlights would power up, connecting towns and cities that would glow in an almost joyous celebration of our dominion over nature. Each little comforting pinpoint would keep away the monsters that lurked in the dark, primal corners of our minds, keeping us safe until the sun once again returned.

But now there's nothing. Not even any fires large enough to see at this altitude. Now the people below know that light doesn't repel the monsters. It *attracts* them. Now there's no escape. The setting sun can't be fought. We're no longer the masters of nature, and the only thing we can do now we're just another link on the food chain is hide in the darkness and pray for the sun's return.

I shiver again, suddenly cold, and when I turn back to the warm light of the cabin I realize that Kaylee has returned to the cockpit to pilot the plane through the darkness. Warren gives up the seat and balls his hands into fists to hide the fact that they're shaking, but not before I notice.

"That was.... interesting," he says as he walks back to the cabin, a nervous grin on his face. "Never thought I'd get to fly a plane." We suddenly pulls into a climb, no doubt to avoid any sudden mountains we might slam into in the darkness, and Warren falls into the chair facing me. He looks back to the cockpit. "Vee's up there trying to learn the ropes. She says she's just interested, but I got fifty bucks that says she's terrified Kaylee's gonna space out on us before we reach Vegas." He looks around at the ashtray and open lunch box overflowing with pill bottles. "What do you think?"

I pull myself away from my thoughts of the darkness below with a start. "Hmm? Oh, you mean about Kaylee? She seems OK to me, but I'll be damned if I know. I guess we'll find out soon enough."

Warren pulls out his cigarettes, lights two and passes one forward to me. For some reason it feels wrong – but a little thrilling – to light up in the cabin. Smoking on planes went the way of the dodo years before I took my first flight, and I've spent all my life staring up at the no smoking sign next to the fasten seat belt light wondering why the warning is even necessary. The idea of smoking on a plane has always seemed as ridiculous as lighting up in the middle of a wedding service, but now? *Jesus H Christ*, it feels good. I can't imagine how shitty passengers must have felt during that first long haul flight after they outlawed in-flight smoking. This is just the *best*.

"Oh wow," I grin, blowing a cloud of smoke through my teeth, "I'd pay any amount of money to be able to do this on a regular flight."

Warren chuckles. "Tell me about it. I managed to sneak a cigarette a couple of times on military flights, and it always felt like Christmas had come early. Did you know the air was actually cleaner on commercial flights back when smoking was allowed?" I shake my head.

"Yeah, it's all a big damned con. The airlines just used the ban as an excuse to recycle the air less often because they didn't have to extract the smoke. They saved millions every year, and all we got in return was air rage and that shitty stale smell."

For a few minutes we sit in silence and enjoy our cigarettes, both of us gazing out the window at the dark landscape passing far below. Eventually Warren stubs his out and speaks. "You've been around a little, right? I mean, you spent a few years traveling?"

I nod. "Yeah, I guess so. I left the States for Asia not long after college, and I only came back a couple of times since then. Why?"

Warren pulls out another cigarette, looks at it for a few moments then thinks better of it. He sighs. "I've just been wondering how we fucked up so bad. I mean, I spent more time than I care to remember in the Middle East, and it was a fucking mess. If the infection arrived in Damascus they wouldn't last two days. Same goes for Baghdad and Kabul. Even without the wars they were a disaster, but Thailand? They were hit with this shit without any warning at all. No fucker knew what the hell was happening until Bangkok had been wiped off the map, but they managed to contain it. The country survived, and I'm trying to figure out where we went wrong and they went right. Any ideas?"

I don't say anything for a moment. I'd spent a lot of the last month wondering the same thing, and I could only really come up with one idea that sounded half way believable. "Honestly? I think it's because we have a... let's call it a healthy disrespect for authority."

Warren frowns. "How do you mean?"

"Well, I didn't spent all that long in Thailand before all the shit went down, but what I know is that it's far from the tourist paradise you'll see in the ads. I don't know the figures, but there were a couple dozen military coups in the last century alone. Every five or ten years the country goes to hell for a little while. Some faction isn't happy with the government for one reason or another, and ten minutes later there are tanks on the streets. The most recent coup was in 2014 when the army dissolved the government and took control. Curfew, martial law, press censorship, the works. They even banned that three fingered salute from the Hunger Games movies." I remember reading about that in the papers and laughing at the absurdity of the law.

"Eight years before that there was another coup. Exact same deal. The army rolled in, deposed the Prime Minister and installed a new interim government with some bullshit name. Campaign for Democratic Reform. National Council for Peace and Order. It's all the same shit. The entire country is like a game of musical chairs, but the army controls the chairs and the music." I light up another cigarette while I think. "Anyway, an old journalist friend of mine lived in Bangkok through both of these shitstorms, and he used to be amazed at the reaction from the Thais. They were so obedient it was untrue. I mean sure, you'd get the occasional protest every now and then, but for the most part when the soldiers came out on the streets everyone would just go indoors and wait quietly until they left. They were *used to it*, you see. They knew governments come and go like the seasons, and they knew the safest thing to do was just follow instructions from whoever seemed to be in charge on the day. You could have marched those people into the sea and they wouldn't start complaining until they were neck deep."

Warren laughs. "Not really our style, right?"

"No, not our style at all. We've got civil disobedience baked right into us. It's part of who we are as a people, and it always has been. We're never happier than when we're telling the government to go fuck itself, and I think that's always served us pretty well. We have a talent for protest and we're not afraid to make our voices heard, and in peacetime that's fine, but what happens when the war comes to our doorstep without any warning? What happens when the enemy is approaching, and the government finds itself trying to protect people who don't trust a word that comes out of Washington? They never had a chance. They had the infected on one side and armed citizens on the other who already had plenty of reasons not to trust them. Evacuating free people is like herding cats."

Warren nods. "You know who really would have come out of this without a scratch? The North Koreans."

"Yeah," I agree. "You know what, though? I spent a month locked in a box, and as far as I knew the government was protecting me from the infection. After living through that there's not a doubt in my mind that I'd take freedom over safety every time. Kim Jong whatever he's called might have the power to hide his people behind a million strong army, but given the choice I'd prefer the freedom to fuck up and make bad decisions. Without that it's not really freedom, know what I mean?"

"Damn right," Warren smiles, lighting another cigarette and blowing the smoke towards the ceiling. "God bless America."

It's the first time I've heard those words in a

month. Actually, now I think about it it may be the first time I've heard them in person, earnestly – rather than spoken by some politician because a pollster said it would give him a two point swing with soccer moms in the Midwest – in years, ever since I left the US. I look out the window and watch the blackness below, praying there are still some people surviving down there.

My voice cracks a little as I whisper, "God bless America."

•*•

:::16:::

JACK BENSON FOUND the job on Monster just two months before the world began to collapse around him. $14.50 an hour, with a bump to $21.25 after six months as long as he got a basic passing grade on all eight of the training modules. He'd never be a millionaire, but it beat the crap out of the $9.25 minimum wage he'd earned as a greeter at the Walmart back home in Fallon.

Munitions Handler also sounded a lot cooler than Walmart greeter, and for a 25 year old kid that was almost as important as the wage, even if it meant he had to spend his weeks in a small town of three thousand in the baking desert five hours from Vegas. Come the weekend he could make the long drive into the city with a couple of buddies and blow his wages at the tables, and in his uniform the girls seemed to respond to him a little more readily than they had when he was wearing a blue vest covered in pieces of flair. Things had been going pretty well, all told, and the move down to the Hawthorne Army Depot had finally given him something vaguely impressive to write on his resume.

If he'd known when he took the job that three months later he'd find himself firing a Stinger missile at a DC10, though, he might have preferred to stick with the blue vest.

For hours after he'd taken the shot people slapped him on the back and called him a hero. He tried to believe it, but he'd seen the wreckage. He'd seen the scorched path of destruction the plane had carved through the north wing of the Mandalay Bay before exploding into the ground floor of the Delano, bringing most of the hotel down on top of the twisted remains of the plane. Both hotels had been packed well beyond capacity. Hundreds of refugees had been killed in the wreck. Dozens more were probably still trapped beneath the rubble, alive but injured, but they'd never reach them before they died.

But Jack was a hero, apparently. That's what everyone kept saying, at least until he stopped responding.

He'd been six weeks into intensive training when the infection had arrived in the US, and for two weeks after that he barely slept. Seven day shifts, fifteen hours on, nine off. He spent every waking moment prepping mothballed vehicles and testing outdated ordnance that had been crated up and stored in the underground bunkers years ago, but there weren't nearly enough staff to get the job done.

The problem was that few had ever seriously considered the prospect of a war on US soil. For decades the military had been shaped around the Two-War Doctrine, a defense strategy designed to prepare US forces to fight two simultaneous Gulf War sized ground campaigns. A big part of that doctrine was the assumption that both wars would be overseas, and in recent years the unspoken addendum to that was 'and they'll probably both be in the Middle East.' With the hot, arid climate of Nevada, Hawthorne had been the ideal location to train soldiers bound for Iraq and Afghanistan, and later Syria, so after 9/11 the base had been repurposed as a training facility while its previous purpose, the storage and deployment of weapons and ammo to front line forces, was sidelined. When Jack got the job he became one of just a dozen munitions handlers on the whole base.

If Hawthorne had already been understaffed before, the infection only made things worse.

Hawthorne personnel never deployed overseas, so when it all went to shit the Depot was one of the few places the military could look to bolster its numbers in the east. Jack had showed up for duty one day to find the place virtually deserted. He was suddenly one of the most senior men on the base, and he wasn't even enlisted, never mind an officer. He was just a civilian kid who wanted to put aside enough money to buy a car that had more than one working tail light.

For a couple of days he'd been at a loose end. Communications with military command became erratic and confusing and then, suddenly, just stopped. It was only by watching the TV news that the remaining personnel at the Depot learned that the entire military command structure had collapsed after some kind of rebellion against the emergency government at Raven Rock. Suddenly Hawthorne was stranded, with fewer than one hundred men in charge of the world's largest ammunition and ordnance storage depot, but they didn't have any orders to follow.

The decision to deploy a team to Las Vegas had sprung out of nowhere, without a single person seeming to come up with the idea on his own, but after a little thought it started to make more and more sense. Those left behind at the depot were aimless and confused but they had access to the sort of weaponry that would fuel the wet dreams of any tinpot dictator. They might as well at least try to do some good with it. If they could just defend this little part of the country from the worst of the disaster they could be proud of a job well done.

Even in peacetime Vegas had always been an impossibly chaotic city, a gaping neon-lit drain into which countless tourists poured each day to lose their money and pick up a nasty case of crotch rot, but now – according to the sporadic news reports, at least – it seemed to be tearing itself apart at the seams. They say that any society was three square meals away from anarchy, but Vegas had always been just a steak dinner and a light snack from collapsing in on itself.

When air travel had been grounded on the day of the New York and D.C. attacks hundreds of thousands of tourists had suddenly found themselves stranded in the city, but there wasn't any sort of guiding intelligence to manage the refugee situation beyond the overworked police force and a handful of casino security guards who stayed at their posts. Overnight the city became little more than a neon lit riot, on one side thousands of terrified citizens desperate to find food, water and shelter from the scorching sun, and on the other side hoteliers who weren't eager to hand over their fortunes to a bunch of freeloaders.

And so it was that Jack rolled out of Hawthorne with around fifty men – the last three remaining officers, a small handful of enlisted men and the rest on-base civilian support – loaded down with anything they thought might be useful for crowd control and refugee support, along with a bunch of weapons they didn't expect to need but didn't feel all that comfortable leaving behind with the forty strong skeleton security team. It took nine hours for the convoy to reach the city, and when they arrived they found the tension palpable. The entire city was engaged in a tense standoff, just waiting for someone to light the fuse and set the city aflame.

Almost as soon as Jack's team established its base at McCarran Airport the refugees began flooding in looking for help. They mistook the ragtag squad from Hawthorne as part of a major disaster relief effort rather than just a handful of guys who wanted to lend a hand, and that first night they were almost overwhelmed by the demands of the needy. Every last one of their MREs had been handed out before dawn, and everyone woke up with hunger pains stabbing at their stomachs. That first morning they all suspected that leaving the relative safety of

Hawthorne may have been a terrible mistake.

Within a few days, though, they began to turn the situation around. The hoteliers trusted the military and felt better for having them patrol the streets in front of their multi-million dollar properties. They knew they couldn't win in a fight with thousands of rioters, so with the Hawthorne contingent acting as arbitrators they each agreed to take in a certain number of refugees – perhaps more than they'd have liked, but the implicit threat that the military would happily withdraw and allow the people to loot hung heavy over the negotiations, so they didn't dare to press the point.

After two weeks the small but effective Hawthorne squad, against all odds, had the maddeningly complex city running like a well oiled machine. As vulnerable as Las Vegas was to any sort of instability, being as it was a remote desert outpost completely reliant on the outside world to survive, they managed to get by after a fashion. The food stored in thousands of restaurant deep freezes and dozens of warehouses was organized and rationed by volunteers. The water kept flowing from faucets thanks to the near endless supply from Lake Mead after a harsh winter and a spring with plentiful snow melt. They even began to make provisional plans to convert the four 18 hole golf courses within a couple of miles of the Strip into farmland, just in case the crisis wasn't resolved as quickly as they hoped. The climate wasn't particularly crop friendly, but with enough irrigation they figured they could tease out a few meals.

Most importantly, Jack's team managed to dispatch a handful of civilian engineers to assist the few staff who hadn't abandoned their posts at the Hoover Dam, where they helped balance the power load to prevent the city's grid from frying. That was what really saved Vegas. People will do anything for AC in the middle of a desert.

In peacetime the hydroelectric power generated by the dam was distributed to three states and supported almost eight million people, but now the population of Vegas had ballooned to almost two million, and the national power grid had been almost irretrievably damaged thanks to weeks without proper maintenance. The inexperienced engineers didn't dare attempt to regulate the power production at the source, so in a bizarre twist it was now necessary for the residents of Vegas to use as much power as possible to keep the excess load from being dumped onto the grid and blowing transformers all the way to California.

With the government AWOL, fear and confusion rife and the infected hordes growing closer with each passing day, Las Vegas was a pleasant oasis of ice cold air conditioning, chilled water and electric light. They even ran the power hungry, blindingly bright beam of light from the top of the Luxor every night to drain the excess electricity when demand dipped. The gaudy, over the top shaft of light was now a beacon of civilization to everyone from miles around. It was a comforting sight, and a welcome reminder that not everything had been lost.

For two weeks life in the city had been running remarkably smoothly. The news coming in on the radio from the rest of the country – even those areas in the west as yet unaffected by the infection – painted a picture of a crippled nation, lurching from crisis to crisis thanks to the lack of leadership, and quickly descending into chaos. In comparison Vegas felt almost as if life was continuing as normal, after a fashion. Jack felt like he and his team had really achieved something worthwhile. They'd dragged the city back from the brink, and they'd done it without firing a single shot. Everyone from Hawthorne walked tall through the streets, and they were greeted at every doorway with smiles.

And then the news reports suddenly began to

pour in.

Last night Jack had been roused from sleep a little after midnight by a young volunteer who'd been monitoring the shortwave radio stations in neighboring states for news. The kid was panicked, and it took a sharp slap to get him to calm down enough to make sense. He said there were reports of sudden outbreaks in cities in the western states, dozens of them, flooding the airwaves from Texas to Montana. The news was confusing, but it seemed as if there had some kind of aerial assault on the cities before the outbreaks began. Maybe someone was airdropping infected and letting them run free? It didn't make any sense. Nothing about it made a lick of sense, but something was clearly going down.

Within minutes the team had fired up the computers in the air traffic control tower at McCarran, and the controllers they'd managed to corral were manning the radar desks, yelling instructions to each other as they scanned the skies for a hundred miles in every direction.

And then they found it. The plane had its transponder switched off so they couldn't identify it though the radar beacon system. There was no answer to hails, and the only information they had came from the primary radar. They didn't know the size or type of aircraft. They didn't know its altitude, and they could only guess at its speed. All they could see was a green blip on the radar screen, an unidentified threat approaching on a direct bearing to Vegas.

In the confusion nobody had been able to reach any of the three officers from Hawthorne, and all of the enlisted men were scattered across the city. Jack looked around the tower as the blip continued to approach and found everyone looking at him. Looking *to* him, expecting this 25 year old kid to make a decision based on nothing more than the fact that he'd told them he was in charge, and they'd been desperate enough to believe him.

He felt like he was in a trance as he walked down the corrugated steel staircase back to ground level. He drifted in a daze across the asphalt to the secure garage they'd set up to house the trucks and ordnance, and he searched through the stacks of hard shell olive green crates until he found the one he was looking for.

The Stinger missile system in the case was a simple tube around two yards long. It had a defective S&R switch and had been returned to Hawthorne to be safely destroyed, but Jack had decided to load it on the back of the truck all the same. In the month since it had showed up on his decommissioning roster he'd often dreamed of firing it, but now he was actually pulling it from the case he didn't feel the same enthusiasm.

For ten minutes he studied the weapon and tried to remember the firing sequence from the literature he'd skimmed weeks ago, and it was only when he heard the drone of an aircraft – the first time he'd heard a jet engine in a month – that he snapped out of it and dragged himself back to the moment. He hefted the tube onto his right shoulder and awkwardly lurched back out onto the apron in front of the garage, tugging his radio from his belt as soon as he stopped.

"Tower," he said, breathlessly, "have you raised the plane? Any word?"

The radio crackled for a moment before the reply came through. "Negative. They're still not answering our hails, and their transponder is still inactive. What do you want to do?" Even with the bad reception he could tell the voice was edgy and nervous.

Jack didn't know what to say. He still didn't know the answer to the question even as he raised the tube and snapped the chunky nickel cadmium battery into place, hearing the low hum from the targeting speaker as it locked on to the engine noise.

It was a moonlit night with just a light

dusting of low cloud, and in the distance the enormous plane was clearly visible even without its strobe or navigation lights activated. Jack had been an airplane nut as a kid, unsurprising for someone who'd grown up a stone's throw from Nellis AFB. He'd spent his childhood watching in awe and wonder as everything from F22-A Raptors to the Super Hercules to tilt rotor Ospreys roared over his house on their way to the base, shaking his windows as they passed, and as soon as he saw the distinctive third engine at the base of the vertical stabilizer he knew the approaching plane was a DC-10. He also knew that the USAF had decommissioned its remaining DC-10s in 2017, as had FedEx in 2018. The only ones still in operation in the States were three tankers leased to the US Forest Service, which still used them to fight forest fires up and down the west coast.

Suddenly the high pitched sound of an actuator rang from the Stinger's targeting speaker. The plane was losing altitude quickly, dropping towards the deck for its approach, but it didn't look like it was coming in to land. Its heading would take it across the runway at a sharp angle, west towards the Strip. In the moonlight Jack saw the belly of the plane begin to open, and suddenly he realized what was about to happen.

The hulking DC-10 was about to dump something from the tank in its belly. It would swoop down over the most heavily populated part of the city and drop its cargo, and if the news reports were to be believed it wasn't going to be a pallet of MREs.

There was nothing else he could think to do. No other way he could stop whatever horrors had befallen the other cities from reaching Vegas. The very thought of it bore an acid hole in his stomach, but he knew he had to bring down the plane. Them or us. It was just that simple.

He whispered a prayer – more for himself than for the people in the city or those approaching in the plane – and raised the tube until he could sight it through the reticle. With a squeeze of his left hand he uncaged the targeting system, and when the DC-10 looked to be around a mile from the runway he squeezed the trigger.

Nothing happened.

The plane was fast approaching, and in the bright moonlight he could see that the doors in the belly were almost fully open. Jack felt the panic grip him tight around the throat as he pressed the cage/uncage button once again, and once again felt the whir of the machinery as the targeting system moved freely. He sighted the plane once more, waiting an agonizing few seconds for the target to lock in the canoe of the reticle. He went for the trigger once again, but before squeezing this time he toggled the defective S&R switch that had sent it back to Hawthorne. Somewhere deep in the mechanism he felt a jolt as something clicked into place. He pulled the trigger, squeezed his eyes tightly closed in prayer, and three seconds later the SAM shot from the tube with a jolt, pushing the cushioned rest back against his shoulder with bruising force.

For a moment the missile seemed to hang motionless in the air before the primary motor kicked in and sent it screaming towards the target, trailing a fine line of gray vapor that drew a curved streak from the ground to the sky. In the blink of an eye the missile found its target, exploding through the left wing of the plane in a dull orange burst that looked almost dainty and weak compared to the size of the plane.

As the hulking DC-10 continued its approach it looked for a moment like it might shrug off the impact. It continued straight on course towards the Strip as if the explosion had dealt it little more than a mosquito bite, but as it loomed overhead it suddenly began to bank wildly to the right, one wing scything down towards the roof of the terminal building. Jack threw himself to the ground as the pilot struggled to pull the enormous craft back into the air, but it was clear it was going to crash. As it vanished from sight behind the terminal the engine tone rose to a scream so loud it became almost a physical presence, shaking the windows of the terminal and forcing Jack to clamp his hands over his ears to block out the pain, and then with a deafening roar the thin, wispy clouds hanging over the city glowed orange for a brief moment with the reflected light of the explosion. The terminal windows burst outwards as one, showering the asphalt below with countless glittering shards, and after what felt like an eternity the roar faded away to an eerie silence.

Somewhere in the distance, out towards the neon lit Strip, sirens began to wail.

•ⵟ•

:::17:::

JACK STARED INTO space as he half listened to the susurrus of muted conversation in the air traffic control tower, his eyes drawn out the window to an empty section of dark sky just above the passenger terminal. Beside him a cup of coffee had gone cold an hour ago, and everyone passing by seemed to slightly alter their course to avoid him since he'd lapsed into silence, as if he was wearing a sign around his neck that read 'don't even try to talk to me.'

It had been 24 hours since he'd pulled the trigger and watched the plane tear through the Strip, and still his hands were trembling. His clothes still shed dust whenever he moved, and his throat was raw and his eyes red after a day of pulling bodies from the rubble.

The hours after the DC-10 had crashed had been a muddled, terrifying mess. The bodies of two of the officers from Hawthorne were found in the remains of the Mandalay Bay. When the third, Sergeant Blythe, didn't report for duty it was pretty much assumed he was also buried somewhere in the wreckage.

By virtue of the fact that Jack was the 'hero' who'd saved the city everyone seemed to have made the unspoken decision that he was now the leader. All day they'd turned to him, expecting him to make decisions that affected the lives of all two million residents of the city, and he just wanted to grab them by their collars and give them a firm shake until they realized he was just a terrified 25 year old kid with a GED and a recreational pot habit. Fuck, he didn't even understand how plumbing worked.

Meanwhile the news reports continued to pour in on the radio. There was little doubt that this had been an attack on an unprecedented scale. Virtually every major city in the western and central states had suffered a terrible fate. They'd not been warned of what was coming. They had no idea until the planes and helicopters had already dumped their loads. The first they knew of it was when the infected hordes reached their doors. Hundreds of thousands had died. Maybe millions, and all in a single night.

Everyone within reaching distance of a radio had spent the day scouring the stations, and so far they'd only found a few other attacks that had failed. There were a couple of reports that Abilene had survived, and San Francisco was still on the air and reporting what they'd heard from elsewhere. LA was confusing. There had been around two dozen stations broadcasting two days ago, and now they were down to eleven. What's more, each of them seemed to be reporting stories completely at odds with each other. Some stations screamed that the infected were massing in the streets, while a couple of others just reported the weather and local sports results.

After listening to a few reports urging listeners to head towards cities that had escaped attack Jack made his first executive decision: he ordered the local radio station to stop broadcasting. He was a little surprised that they listened to him, to be honest, but they seemed to understand it would be for the best. Nobody wanted to imagine what would happen if the entire population of LA decided it would be a good idea to suddenly decamp to Vegas, so they powered down the transmitters and went dark within the hour.

After hours sifting through the wreckage and yet more dealing with endless questions from people who now looked to him for guidance Jack just felt numb. Since the Hawthorne squad had brought the city back under control they'd all realized just how lucky they were. They might be facing challenges, sure, but Las Vegas was as good a fortress as you could hope to find against the infected. Hundreds of miles lay between it and the next large city, and much of it was scorching, featureless, unforgiving desert. They had power and water, and food supplies that could be stretched to weeks or even months with careful rationing. Nobody wanted to say it but they'd all begun to believe they could safely ride out the storm. They could wait it out while the government wrested back control of the country, and they could emerge into the reclaimed civilization with pride.

Nobody thought that any more.

Now the game had changed. This was no longer a matter of just waiting it out. Somebody out there was trying to bring the fight to them, but they didn't have any idea who, or why. All they knew was that Las Vegas was no longer the safe haven it had been just 24 hours earlier.

After the DC-10 had come down over the Strip the Hawthorne team had leaped to action along with the local authorities. Fire crews doused the blaze around the wreckage, and teams worked around the clock to search for survivors and remove the bodies that weren't buried deep beneath the rubble. An armed squad kept a close eye on everyone who entered the perimeter set up around the wreckage, with orders to fire with extreme prejudice on anyone who displayed signs of infection, though fortunately nobody felt the need to follow that order. It seemed that whatever the plane had been carrying had been destroyed in the crash, or in the subsequent fire.

Meanwhile the squad sent civilian crews to establish lookout points ten miles out on every road leading to Vegas, with orders to raise the alarm if anyone tried to enter by land. They were loaded down with weaponry, and given permission to fire on anyone they saw as a threat without fear of repercussions.

Las Vegas was now a fortress. Nobody in, nobody out. Until they had a better grasp on what the hell was going on beyond the city they had no choice but to treat any outsider as a potential hostile. They'd worked too hard to save the city to allow anyone to threaten them. Now they–

"Jack?" An alarmed voice climbed above the hum of conversation. "Shit, looks like we got another one."

Jack pulled his attention from the window to find Vera, the matronly air traffic controller who'd been guiding planes into McCarran since the early 90s, waving him over to her radar desk. The color had drained from her face. He didn't want to look. He already knew what he'd see, and he already knew what would come next. What had to come next.

It was a green blip on the screen, just like last night, on a direct course to the city.

Vera rested a comforting hand on Jack's shoulder as he leaned over the desk. "You want me to call in one of the boys, Jack?" she asked, her voice full of concern. "You don't have to do it yourself. You've done enough."

He gently shrugged her hand away as he stood. "No... No, I can't ask anyone else." He alone knew the pain of making that call. Of shouldering the weapon, pulling the trigger and watching as the missile found its target. He knew he'd spend the rest of his life waking up in a cold sweat, the memory replaying over and over in his mind, and he knew he wouldn't wish the experience on his worst enemy.

He'd pull the trigger again. He couldn't ask anyone else.

Maybe the second time wouldn't hurt so bad.

•᛭•

:::18:::

I WAKE UP to the plane bucking in heavy turbulence, and as I clutch the armrests of my seat my thoughts immediately flash to all the rock stars who died in small aircraft. I've never flown in anything smaller than a sixty seater prop plane, and I never realized how much these tiny private jets are at the mercy of the elements. With every sudden plunge I feel like I'm driving by an articulated truck in a tiny European clown car, almost lifted from the ground by the buffeting of the air as the truck blasts by.

"What's going on?" I ask, rubbing my eyes, but when I look around the cabin I realize there's nobody there. Muffled voices come through the cockpit door. I turn and look out the window, and for a moment I think my eyes must be playing tricks on me.

Far below in the darkness I see a small patch

of light appearing intermittently through the clouds. It's not much, but it's definitely not my imagination. I squint and lean in close to the cold window, pressing my nose against the Plexiglas to get a better view, and as the clouds clear I pick out about a dozen lines of lights, tightly clustered and equally spaced, with a single much longer line stretching off to either side of the cluster before dying away in the distance. It takes me a moment to figure out what I'm looking at, but as soon as it dawns on me a broad grin breaks across my face.

It's a town. Far below us a small town sits bathed in electric light, with street lights illuminating the road in and out. Ever since Warren had suggested the west might have power I'd dreamed of seeing something like this, but I hadn't let myself really believe it might be possible until now. There may be people down there bathed in the glow of electric light. I never thought that could make me so happy.

That's another thing. It's not just light down there, but everything else it entails. Refrigeration. Microwaves. Stoves. TV and radio, AC, garage door openers, blenders and games consoles. It's civilization, or at least everything my life so far has taught me to associate with it.

I leap from my seat and stumble down the

aisle towards the cockpit, grabbing onto the headrests on the seats as we hit another pocket of turbulent air. "Guys!" I yell as I burst through the cockpit door. "Did you see the lights? There's a town down there with power!" Vee turns to me and rolls her eyes, but it's not until I look out the front window that I see why she's so unimpressed with my discovery.

Far ahead of us, partially obscured by a thick, heavy layer of cloud, a dazzling shaft of light shines from the ground and bursts towards the heavens.

It's the Luxor, the pyramid shaped casino at the heart of Las Vegas.

We've arrived.

•ᛉ•

:::19:::

JACK FEELS THE weight of the Stinger on his shoulder once again, and he wishes – not for the first time – that he'd had the time to get good and drunk this evening. The final Stinger is loaded into the tube, and he prays that he managed to seat it properly. He'd not read anything about loading the weapon in the literature he'd seen, but it seemed fairly simple. It slid in and seemed to lock in place with a heavy click. With a little luck that meant it would fire from the tube and not simply explode on his shoulder.

Last night the skies had been almost completely clear, but a front had moved in through the afternoon and covered the city in a bank of low cloud, hanging what looks like just a few hundred yards overhead like a thick blanket. The orange glow from the city's lights reflects off the base, and hidden somewhere beyond is another plane. Another threat. Another attempt to destroy the city he'd fought to protect.

From the engine tone the plane sounds like it's much smaller than the DC-10. It sounds like a small jet, and in the back of Jack's mind the thought occurs that maybe the attackers aren't as powerful as he feared. Maybe the DC-10 was their only large plane, and they never expected anyone could possibly knock it out of the sky. Maybe the approaching whine heralded the arrival of their only other plane, and maybe if he could take this one out they'd have nothing left to throw at the city.

But he still can't see it.

Jack turns slowly, pointing the aiming reticle into the clouds. He doesn't know much about the Stinger, but he knows it finds its target based on the infra-red signature of an aircraft – essentially it's a heat seeker. Maybe the clouds would disperse the signal and prevent a lock, but he panned around just in case it picked something up.

When the plane finally breaks through the low clouds Jack doesn't spot it at first. He has the Stinger pointed at the same part of the sky from which the DC-10 approached last night, but the flashing navigation lights of the new plane come in at a 90 degree angle, almost in line with the runway.

It's coming in at a lower angle, too, and Jack has to awkwardly jog to clear the corner of the terminal building as the lights vanish from sight. He awkwardly stumbles beneath the weight and accidentally squeezes the trigger, and for a few moments he freezes and holds his breath until it's clear the missile isn't going to fire before he presses the uncage button to release the guidance system. He whispers a silent prayer as the SAM remains firmly in the tube.

Slowly, carefully, he falls to one knee and brings the reticle in line with the approaching plane. The targeting speaker drops in and out as it picks up the sound of the engine, and a shrill alarm begins to sound to warn him the battery is close to dead. He'll have to make this quick.

Jack curses as the plane drifts in and out of the center of his reticle. Last night the DC-10 approached at a steady, stately pace that made it easy to hold it in his sights, but this small plane weaves from side to side in the buffeting crosswinds as it drops lower. It keeps moving out of the sights, and he can't be sure if he has a lock.

There's nothing for it. The plane looks to be only a few hundred yards from the start of the runway now, and if he doesn't fire right away it will be too late. He doesn't know what they plan to do but he sure as hell won't give them the chance to do it.

With a trembling hand he squeezes the uncage button on the front of the tube, and with a whir the targeting system activates. The plane is within spitting distance of the runway now, landing gear down and locked. He takes a deep breath, holds it for a moment and whispers a quiet prayer.

Jack Benson squeezes the trigger once again.

•٦•

:::20:::

"OK, CAN YOU just all stop talking for a
second? *Fuck!*" Kaylee takes the yoke and glares
out the window as we all fall silent. "Tom, pass
me that chart." I hand over the map in my
hand, and she tosses it back. "No, not the US
thing, the Nevada chart. Quickly!"

I rifle through the sheaf of maps, dropping
the plane's heavy handbook on my toe, and
eventually fish out the crumpled map of
Nevada. "Got it."

Kaylee grabs the map and lays it out flat
across her instruments. "OK, now let's see..."
She draws a finger across the map until she finds
Las Vegas, then reads the tiny, almost illegible
small print on the key written beside the city.
"North north east," she mumbles to herself
before grabbing the map and thrusting it back
into my hands. "This may be a bumpy landing,
guys. You guys should probably buckle up. Tom,
sit down and navigate. Vee, Warren, back in the

cabin."

I'm about to point out that Vee would make a better navigator, but something about the way Kaylee spat her name tells me that the two get on like cats in a sack. I don't really mind sitting up front, though. I came of age long after airlines stopped allowing kids to go up to the cockpit to meet the pilot, so I've never seen an approach from the co-pilot's seat before.

Kaylee's hands are shaking as she grips the yoke, and I have to tell myself I'm only imagining that I can feel the plane shake in response to her nerves. Her eyes are fixed on the beam of the Luxor out the window to the left, and I wait in silence until it finally vanishes from sight.

"OK, that's far enough, I'm going to turn into my approach now. See this compass?" She reaches down and taps the glass without looking. "I need you to tell me when we're pointing South south west, understand? Give me a little warning so I can straighten up."

I feel a lump rise in my throat as she suddenly banks the plane to the left, and my stomach turns as the ground comes into view below us out the left window. We seem dangerously low – much lower than I've ever seen a commercial plane make its approach – but I don't dare say anything for fear that I'll freak Kaylee out.

"OK, we're pointing west,' I whisper in the most calming, comforting voice I can squeeze past vocal cords that feel as taut as violin strings. "South west now." Kaylee begins to straighten out the plane. "OK, that's south south west."

The ground vanishes from view out the left window as we pull level and I take a deep, shuddering breath. I look down and realize my fingers have torn through the map, and the knuckles of my left hand are white where I'm clutching the arm rest of the chair.

Now the bright beam from the Luxor is ahead and slightly to the right, and I can tell by the way it's moving quickly across the window that we're just a mile or two from the city. Kaylee takes a trembling hand from the yoke and flicks a few switches that set unseen mechanisms into whirring motion, and with a slight jolt I feel the landing gear emerge and lock into place.

"Buckle up," she says, tapping the strap of the four point harness attached to my seat, and I struggle to clip myself in as Kaylee plunges us down so low that I'm certain we'll snag ourselves on power lines. Beneath us the dark, featureless desert gives way to the sprawling outskirts of the city. Endless clusters of bland McMansions, run down strip malls and lush golf courses flit beneath the plane, all of them lit up like Christmas trees.

Kaylee pulls back on the throttle, and my ears pop as the engine tone falls and we drop still further. Now I can see cars moving on the streets below. Not many, but enough to see that – somehow – Vegas is still functioning. People have gas and electricity. They're not rioting in the streets, and they're not too scared to ride around town in the dead of night. I can't help but feel excited at the prospect that I might get to eat a steak before the night is over.

"See that ahead?" Kaylee points directly forward out the window. "See the runway lights?" I peer ahead but can't see how she can tell one row of lights from another. "That's McCarran." A hint of a stoned smile flits across her mouth. "I damn well hope so anyway, cause that's where I'm putting her down."

She reaches up and flips a switch, and suddenly the cockpit lights go out and the world outside grows much brighter. Now I see the lights of the runway, quickly flickering on and off in sequence, guiding us to the ground. Kaylee swears under her breath when she notices we're coming in too shallow. The first of the runway lights vanish in the window and we're still well above the ground. She cringes as she pushes lightly forward on the yoke, and my stomach turns as the nose of the plane suddenly dips down directly towards the ground. I hold my breath as the runway comes racing towards us, and I can't help but let out a gasp as Kaylee pulls back on the stick and yanks up the nose just a few yards from the blinking lights. She reaches out for a switch on the instrument panel and–

And the world suddenly erupts in orange flame. I can't make out what the fuck is going on but there's an enormous explosion directly above us, exactly at the altitude we were at just a few seconds ago. My mind races as I wonder if we're exploding. Maybe Kaylee fucked up a step and one of our engines has gone. Maybe we're about to be torn apart and strewn across the runway in a trail of flames and torn steel. Maybe we've already been torn in two, and I'm living through the last seconds before we're sucked from the plane and hurled like rag dolls into the air.

All of these thoughts flit through my mind in an instant, and I barely notice Kaylee thrust forward by the explosion, pushing hard on the yoke and forcing us sharply down towards the black runway. Our front wheels squeals as they make contact before bouncing us back into the air, and moments later the rear wheels come down hard, sending a sharp, painful jolt shooting through my spine.

For a moment all I can see are the dim orange lit clouds above us before the nose comes down once more. Now our front wheels make contact again, this time permanently. We've landed at an angle to the runway, and after just a few moments the cockpit shakes like an old dryer as we careen off the asphalt and onto the dusty, uneven ground beside it. Something loud snaps with the sound of a whip, and for a moment I'm weightless as the front wheels dig into the ground and hurl us forward.

The nose plunges to the ground and crumples before us. The windows shatter outwards with the force of the impact, and the world suddenly erupts with noise as the plane gracelessly slides through the dust before finally, with the sound of tortured steel screaming in my ears, a wing breaks away from the plane. The last thing I see before blacking out is the world flipped upside down.

•ɤ•

:::21:::

I FEEL HANDS clawing at me, pulling at my clothes and tearing at my flesh. Sharp nails dig into my skin, but after a moment of shock and pain my mind just... slides away from it. It takes a back seat and lets me watch the world divorced from emotion. Even the pain fades into the background, and the gaunt, pallid faces of the infected, their jaws snapping just inches from my face and their spittle spraying my skin, bring me no fear.

I'm hanging upside down.

I feel a sense of *deja vu*. I've been here before, I'm sure of it, but last time... last time it wasn't quite the same.

The belt cuts into my skin as I hang from my seat, and I look out on New York as it burns. From my inverted point of view the bomb climbs gracefully through the clear sky, just like before, like a balloon that's slipped from the hand of a child. This time I shield my eyes before it explodes, and this time I'm spared the pain in my eyes as the blindingly bright orb expands in the sky like a second sun. It's so bright I can see pink between my fingers, where the light shines through so powerfully it makes my blood glow beneath my skin.

There weren't infected last time. Last time we were alone, just me and Bishop on the bridge. Last time we had to run.

Last time the bridge came down beneath us.

I grab at the clasp of my belt, suddenly panicked as I realize I need to run. I've only got a few minutes to reach the tower before all of this comes crashing down into the icy Narrows. I need to find the bottle jack and raise the car. I need to grab Bishop and drag him to safety.

But this time we'll need to fight past the infected. There's no way of telling how many there even are out there, clawing at me through the broken window. All I see are snapping jaws and grasping hands, reaching out to tear me from my seat.

No, wait. There's more. More explosions come, each one blindingly bright and perilously close. Each one lights up the world outside until it's so bright it hurts. I need to squeeze my eyes tight to block it out, but even with them closed

I can still see the lights, flashing before my eyes and drawing nearer as the hands and teeth close in. Clawing at me. Tearing at my flesh. Pulling me from the chair and out through the broken window into the blinding light.

I scream.

Something hits my head.

Everything goes black.

⁘

:::22:::

JACK IS ALREADY halfway to the wreck
before he realizes he's still carrying the spent
launcher on his shoulder. He stops in the pitch
darkness between the terminal and the runway
and drops the heavy tube to the ground with a
thud. He takes a moment to catch his breath,
and when he starts running again it's at a much
slower pace. A floodlight swings around from
the air traffic control tower, and as he spots a
Jeep bouncing across the ground on a direct
course for the wreckage he realizes he doesn't
want to be the first to arrive at the crash site. He
already has more than enough bad memories to
haunt him for the rest of his life without piling
on another few bodies.

The Jeep reaches the wreckage way ahead of
him, and Jack decides to hang back in the
shadows until they've removed the dead.

Nobody will miss him. He already did his job. He brought down the plane and neutralized the threat. In fact, nobody would blame him is he just fucked off to the nearest bar and helped himself to a bottle of the strongest liquor he could find. He's probably earned himself a week of R&R in the past couple of days.

After a few more moments during which both of his feet seem to want to move in two different directions he makes his decision. He'll leave. After all, it's not like he's really in charge. He's not a leader. He's just a kid who was in the right place at the right time, and now he can just melt away into the background and let someone qualified take–

A startled yell comes from somewhere close to the front of the plane, and suddenly all the flashlights swing to the broken window to the cockpit. "They're alive!" a voice cries out.

All thoughts of escaping to a bar vanish from Jack's mind as he processes this new information. *Hostages!* He never imagined in a million years they'd ever be able to actually catch one of the attackers alive. He never imagined they'd get the chance to find out just why the hell they were under attack.

He breaks into a sprint across the hard, dusty ground, his boots kicking up clouds as he tears towards the wreckage. In the wreckage of the plane he can see movement through the broken cockpit window. Two people hang upside down, trapped in their harnesses, one of them limp and lifeless while the other waves his arms in the air as if fending off invisible attackers. At this distance Jack can't make out what he's saying, but as he draws closer the incoherent yells begin to coalesce into words.

"*Bishop!*" the man cries, swatting at one of the soldiers as he approaches with his flashlight. "*Bishop, where are you?*"

As Jack finally reaches the plane three of the soldiers awkwardly climb through the window, hoisting themselves up the crumpled roof until they can carefully lift themselves over the broken glass. Two of them hold the crazed man steady while the third unclips his belt, and together they lower him to the ceiling of the cockpit and drag him back towards the window, struggling all the way.

Two more men wait on the ground to accept the wildly flailing body as he's passed down to the ground, and Jack takes a few steps back as the man starts to lash out at the soldiers. It's hard to make out what's going on in the confusion but he seems to be trying to attack the flashlights they're holding for some reason. In their beams a stream of blood shimmers from the man's forehead and he continues to yell out for Bishop, whoever that is, as they try to subdue him. It's clear he's out of his mind, and it's only when one soldier steps smartly forward and knocks him out with the butt of his rifle that some semblance of peace returns to the wreckage.

As soon as the man falls to the ground Jack hears yells coming from within the plane. There are more inside, alive, and the soldiers order them with stern voices out of the cabin. The first to appear is a limping man in fatigues, quickly followed by a woman in the same outfit, apparently uninjured. They both climb slowly out of the plane as the two soldiers remaining in the cockpit unclip the woman still hanging from her seat and lower her gently to the ground, where one man crouches down over her for a moment before turning back to the group. "This one's dead," he says, bluntly.

"What do you think, Ray?" One of the soldiers asks as he hops down from the shattered window. "Quick execution, or should we make it hurt?"

"Good question," replies Ray, the same man who knocked the raving guy out a moment earlier. "Maybe we should off a couple of them to give the last one an incentive to talk. What do you think, kill the guys and keep the girl?"

The first man chuckles as he walks slowly

around the group, aiming his rifle menacingly towards the prone body of the first man.

"*Shoulder that rifle, Private!*"

It's only after a moment of stunned silence that Jack realizes the voice was his own. The group turn and face him, squinting in the darkness to identify their colleague, before Ray lets out a dismissive laugh. "You're not in command here, Jack. We don't take orders from you."

Jack steps into the light cast by the floodlight and stares Ray down, looking more confident than he feels. "You might want to tell that to all the folks watching us from the tower, Ray. They seem to think I'm in charge, and I'd love to see what happens to the city if they see one of my men slaughter an unarmed prisoner against my orders. Make the call, Ray. Shoulder that firearm or take your shot."

For the first time Ray loses some of his swagger as he looks back towards the bright light shining in from the tower. He can't see them, but he knows that dozens of civilians are watching his every move. He also knows that the Army only rules Las Vegas by consent. Fewer than fifty men remain to govern two million, and they're only in charge because the people *allow* them to be in charge. Jack knows this, and he can see in his eyes that Ray understands it too.

"Sorry, sir," he mumbles, swinging the rifle back to his shoulder. "It's your show."

"Damn right it's my show," Jack replies, exuding confidence while he tries to stop his hands from trembling. "Load them up in the Jeep and take them back to the tower. We're gonna question them. No violence. Just questions. Then we'll decide what to do with them."

Ray nods, and moments later the rest of the squad fall in and help heft the unconscious body onto the back of the Jeep, followed by the body of the dead girl. With a nod of the head the other two slowly climb aboard, and Jack climbs in as the overloaded Jeep sets off back towards the source of the floodlight.

"You're going to wish you'd stayed away," he says, looking over at the man in fatigues. "We heard about the other cities. We know what you were trying to do."

The man returns the look with incredulity. "Jesus, that's why you shot us down?" He shakes his head firmly. "We're on the side of the angels, you damned moron." He looks down at the unconscious man, and as two of the soldiers swing their guns around on him he moves with exaggerated care to the man's jacket. "No need to fire, guys. Look." From the man's jacket pocket he pulls out a slim plastic disc that shines with the reflected light of the distant floodlight.

"This is why we came," he says, holding the disc up for all to see. "We're here to save your dumb asses."

•⁊•

:::23:::

MY HEAD HURTS.

For a moment that's the only thought that passes through my mind. I don't know where I am, and right now I don't care. All I care about is the throbbing sensation behind my hairline, and the certainty that when I reach up to touch it I'll find yet another angry lump. It seems recently I've been getting almost as many head injuries as a linebacker. I should start wearing a helmet.

I don't open my eyes at first. Instead I take a moment to listen before I let my captors know I've come to. There's not much to hear. Somewhere off to my right a few low voices murmur, and in the distance I hear angry words echo, as if they're coming from the bottom of a well. I'm outside – I can tell by the slight breeze – and I can smell cigarette smoke hanging in the air.

Finally I crack open my eyes, and I'm surprised to find the sun breaching the horizon. I must have been out for hours. Beside me the wall of a cylindrical building climbs towards a bulbous platform perched at the top. The echoed conversation reaches me through an open door, beyond which in the darkness lies a steel staircase. I can't pick out any words, but it sounds like there's some sort of debate going on inside.

I turn away from the building and shield my eyes from the rising sun. In the distance I see the wreck of the plane. From this distance it looks almost intact, like it would be fit to fly if we could just flip it over on its wheels again. I know better. I felt every bump of that landing, and I know the plane is in no better shape than I am.

I look away from the wreck, over towards the terminal building, and–

There's a body just beside me, shrouded in an oil-stained gray tarp that doesn't quite reach down to the feet. They're small, barely larger than child-sized, and clad in neon pink Nike sneakers with the Back to the Future style self lacing gimmick that was all the rage last year until everyone realized the laces pinched the skin of your feet as they tightened.

Kaylee was wearing shoes like that.

I painfully roll onto my front – my body feels like one big ache – and reach out for the edge of the tarp.

"You don't want to look, Tom."

I swing around in the direction of the voice to find Warren appearing from around the curved wall of the building. He tosses his cigarette to the ground and crushes it beneath his feet, frowning as he exhales a stream of smoke that's immediately caught by the breeze.

"Is it...?"

"Yeah, it's her," Warren nods, then averts his gaze and stares at the ground. "Vee says it was quick. Must have taken a knock to the head as we came down. She wouldn't have suffered."

I let go of the tarp and watch as the heavy fabric settles across what I can tell is Kaylee's nose. "You and Vee? Are you guys OK?"

Warren lowers himself to the ground beside me, wincing as he puts his weight on his bad leg. "I feel like I've gone ten rounds in the ring with Ali, but I'll live. Vee..." He lets out a chuckle. "She came through without so much as a scratch. I think she's too mad at the world to let it kill her." He points to the top of the building. "She's up there now, arguing with the guys in charge."

Suddenly a thought occurs to me, and I pat my pockets with a growing sense of panic until

Warren taps me on the arm. "Settle down, Vee has the vaccine. I took it out of your pocket while you were out cold. Took the notebook, too. Vee's trying to explain what the fuck's going on, and to get some of the guys to take us out to the CDC facility."

We both turn to the doorway as footsteps begin to echo down the staircase, and I fish out a battered pack of cigarettes as we wait. When I pull out my lighter I find it's empty, and a tiny hole in the base tells me it exploded during the crash. I lean back and tug down the waist of my pants, and I almost laugh when I see a small pink burn mark on my thigh.

"So... what the fuck happened in the plane? Why did we come down?" The last moments before the crash are all just a blur.

Warren takes one of my crumpled cigarettes and lights mine before his. "Looks like it was a case of mistaken identity. Seems Vegas was hit by a DC-10 in the attacks, but some hotshot took it down with a Stinger. When they saw us on the radar and we didn't answer their hails they assumed we were the second wave, so they took a shot at us. It's a miracle we're still here. If that thing had hit us full on they'd still be finding fingers and toes scattered across the runway." He nods towards the wreckage. "Anyway, the welcoming committee wasn't all that welcoming. That's why you've got that big lump on your coconut. Sounded like you were going a little crazy until one of the guys gave you a good crack in the head."

A fragment of memory bubbles up from the confusion. "Yeah, I think... I think I was hallucinating. I thought I was back in New York on the day of the attack, but this time there were infected there with me, trying to get at me." An involuntary shiver shoots down my spine. "Are there any infected here? In Vegas, I mean?"

Warren shakes his head and smiles. "Not a one, buddy. Looks like they've done a great job of keeping them out, even if they went a little overboard with the firepower. I think we can finally sleep easy without worrying about anything sneaking up on us and taking a bite. Thank God for small mercies, right?"

•⁷•

:::24:::

SERGEANT ERIS BLYTHE closes his eyes and once again tries the dumbass breathing technique his ex-wife once taught him, some yoga bullshit that was supposed to fend off her regular panic attacks. Breathe from your belly, deep down. In through the nose. Hold. Out through the mouth. In through the nose. Hold, and on and on and fucking on.

It doesn't work. He could have a bottle of tequila in his hand and a hooker's mouth around his cock and it wouldn't help him forget the fact that the air is running out. With each stinging breath of the thick, choking dust he can feel it growing thinner. He can feel each breath satisfy him a little less than the last, and he knows that some time very soon he'll take a breath and they'll be nothing there. His lungs will burn in their desperate need for oxygen, but each new breath will only bring with it dust, pain and terror.

And then he'll die. He'll die down here, buried in the darkness.

He can't fucking *believe* this is the way he's gonna check out. He'd trained his whole life to go to war and defend his country, and instead he'll die crushed beneath the collapsed remains of a gaudy Vegas hotel, slowly asphyxiating in pitch blackness.

When the building came down Eric had been trying to fall asleep on an uncomfortable canvas cot in the ground floor lobby. He had no idea what had happened but in the moments before the collapse he'd heard the roar of a jet engine approaching, and then everything went to hell. The floors above him came crashing down, and it was only thanks to dumb luck that he wasn't killed right away. The thick pillars holding up the ceiling of the lobby withstood the weight, allowing a tiny little safe pocket to form as the building collapsed like a house of cards above him. After he was knocked out by a chunk of falling concrete he woke up covered in cuts and bruises, and he suspected his collarbone was broken, but at least he wasn't pinned beneath the rubble.

Unfortunately the pocket was just that: a pocket. Two heavy slabs of concrete form the ceiling, and without tools there's no way he could ever break his way through. For the first two hours he struggled to work himself free but it was obvious it was never gonna work. The slabs weigh a ton, and from them jut several long poles of rebar that anchor themselves in the wreckage on either side of him. The rebar is the only thing stopping the pocket from collapsing in on itself, so even if he could move the slabs he'd be crushed before he could climb out.

All night he yelled for help, listening to his deadened voice bouncing back from just a few inches ahead of him. He yelled until the sound of his own voice began to scare him. For a while he lost control, scratching at the concrete until his fingers bled. He wept, alone in the darkness, and then finally accepted his fate. He realized he'd die down here. He knew he'd never see the sun again.

Eric fishes out his phone and activates the light, shining it around his modest tomb. He doesn't look at the battery indicator. Doesn't want to know how little time he has left before he'll be plunged into darkness. He just wants a quick look at the concrete above him before he begins to ration the precious light.

For the last couple of hours a strange sound has been filtering through the wreckage from above. It sounds like some kind of engine, and every few minutes there's a loud scraping noise and a tortured metallic moan. He doesn't want to raise his hopes only for them to be dashed, so he barely allows himself to entertain the idea that there might be an earth mover up there sifting through the rubble.

In any case, even if there are people above trying to reach him they'll never arrive before the air runs out. By the light of the phone he can see through a crack in the concrete above him a curved, riveted sheet of steel maybe ten yards away. He can only see a small segment of it, but it almost looks like the outer hull of an airplane. If that sound before the collapse really was an approaching plane it looks like it settled almost on top of him. It'd take days to clear it out of the way to reach him, and he can tell he won't make it to tomorrow in this thinning air.

There's that sound again. The concrete around him shakes and sheds dust as a scraping noise reaches him from far above. Something's moving up there, and—

He almost drops his phone in shock when he sees it. Far, far above, almost hidden behind the shower of dust raining down in his eyes, a shaft of sunlight has appeared. There's no way of knowing if it's twenty yards above him or a hundred, but for the first time since he awoke in the rubble he allows himself to entertain the notion that he might not die down here. New air flows in through the crack, and as he takes a deep breath he can almost feel it nourishing him more than the last.

"Help!" He cries out with renewed strength, straining his neck as if his voice will carry further if he can stretch himself just two inches closer to the surface. "*Heeeeeeeelp! I'm alive down heeeeeeere!*"

In the distance the sound of the engine cuts out, and in the sudden silence he imagines he can hear voices.

"*Heeeeeeeeeeeeeelp!*" His dry, dust choked throat cracks with the effort of projecting his voice.

This time he knows there are voices. They grow closer and less muffled until he can make out the words. "... alive down there. I swear I heard it."

"*Heeeeeeeeeeeeeelp!*" Now there are tears streaming down Eric's cheeks, cutting pink lines through the gray dust caking his skin.

"Hello?" The answering voice reaches him, and he can barely contain his excitement.

"I'm alive! Help me!"

For a moment the voice grows quiet, and Eric can no longer make out the words. A terrifying, traitorous thought passes through his mind that maybe he's just imagining it. Maybe this is simply an hallucination, the cruel last gasp of a dying, oxygen starved brain.

"Sir! Hold on, we're coming to get you! Just hold on, OK?"

Now he knows it's real. Far above something blocks the shaft of light, and as Eric squints in the darkness he can make out a face close enough that he can see the bristled, dust-laden mustache of the man yelling down. He looks like he's maybe thirty yards above him.

The face vanishes, and moments later the engine kicks up again. Eric grins broadly as the chink of sunlight grows. The earth mover drags away slabs, and before long there's a whole patch of sky visible through the gap. He can see blue sky, and when he sees a rope drop over the edge of the hole he weeps with joy. His chest aches as it convulses in big, gulping sobs as first one man and then another climbs through the hole and lower themselves steadily down towards him, heavily laden with gear and cloaked in bulky bright yellow firefighter jackets.

It takes what feels like an hour for the two men to reach him. Along the way they pull rubble aside, carefully bracing the shaft with wooden beams lowered down from above. It's painstaking work, but after an eternity they finally plant their feet on the concrete slab above him and begin the job of chipping away at it to make a hole. The mustachioed man pauses for a moment to reach down through the narrow gap, and Eric grabs his hand so firmly the man winces.

"It's okay, buddy, we'll have you out of there in just a few minutes. Just hold on a little longer, all right?"

Eric can barely speak. He can only weep as the mustachioed man withdraws his hand and continues steadily widening the hole until it's finally large enough for him to climb through. He gladly takes the hand of one of the men, and plants a foot against the crumbling concrete wall of his tomb to boost himself up.

As soon as his foot kicks against the rubble, though, something shifts around him. The pocket that saved his life kicks out a plume of dust as it collapses in on itself, and for a moment of terror Eric thinks the whole shaft will come crashing down around them. The men above him yank him sharply upwards, and his feet escape by only a few inches as the concrete collapses beneath him.

A metallic groan echoes off the walls and Eric braces himself for the pain. The crumbling, delicate walls of the shaft tremble and shed dust as the rubble settles around them, but after a few seconds the shaking stops. Eric takes a breath.

"Jesus," he whispers, afraid the the slightest

noise may disturb the wreckage. "Are we still alive?"

One of the men grabs hold of the rope as the other pulls a harness from his pack and slings it around Eric's waist. "Just hold onto the rope, OK? They'll do all the work up top. You just sit tight."

Eric nods, dazed and overwhelmed. It's only after the harness is attached and hitched to the rope that he realizes he hasn't even thanked these men for rescuing him. He feels himself welling up. His lower lip quivers, and he knows he won't be able to get the words out without bursting into tears. Instead he simply hugs them, holding them tight in a bear hug, burying his face between their shoulders as heaving sobs escape his body.

"Alright, buddy, settle down." He pulls away, and the mustachioed man grins with embarrassment. "Let's get you up there, OK?" He grabs his radio and mumbles an order for the team above to start up the winch.

Eric nods and silently mouths the words 'thank you', looking up hopefully at the patch of sky as tears stream down his face. A whirring sound filters down from far above, and with a sharp jerk Eric begins to ascend.

He's a few yards in the air when he realizes that the liquid running down his cheeks isn't all tears. As he creeps up inch by agonizing inch he notices that water is dripping down from above, and it's only when a drop catches the sunlight that he sees it's coming from the steel hull of the plane above him. A new crack seems to have formed in the last few minutes, and in the dim light Eric can see narrow rivulets of water escaping from the base of the crack and gathering in beads at the rivets that line the hull, swelling until they're so large they drip down below. He peers up at the hull just as a drop lands right in his eye.

"Hey guys," he calls out, turning to look at the men beneath him, "I think you should hurry out of there. It looks like this thing up here's leaking."

The men crane up to see him pointing at the cracked hull just as it suddenly widens. With a scream of tearing steel the crack bursts violently open, releasing a deluge of water with the force of a fire hose. For a moment Eric feels himself fall deeper into the shaft under the force of the spray, then he's knocked out of it and shoved firmly against the wall.

"Quick!" He cries out, reaching down a hand. "Grab the rope! We have to go now!" A few yards beneath him he sees the men already up to their waists in the inky, turbulent water, and they quickly scramble up the walls of the shaft to drag themselves from the deluge, their fingers digging into the crumbling, friable concrete. They climb faster than the winch hoists Eric, and after just a few seconds they're close enough to grab the rope and swing away from the walls.

They climb more slowly now under the weight of three men, but they're still moving quickly enough to pass the cracked hull of the plane. As they pass just an arm's length away from the gaping tear in the steel it becomes clear that it isn't fresh water that's rushing from the crack. The liquid looks cloudy and green-tinted, and Eric realizes it smells kinda... stale, maybe? Kinda musty, like brackish water from a stagnant pond.

He turns his attention back to the light above. The liquid doesn't matter. All he can think about is the ice cold water he'll be drinking any minute now. Gallons of the stuff, and then a cold shower, a fresh set of clothes and a nourishing meal. He'll never take the little things for granted again. He'll never...

Something feels... off. He feels dizzy all of a sudden. The shaft of light above him drifts out of focus. It seems to be spinning around, and the walls of the shaft passing by beside him seem to fade into a fog. He turns to the two men attached to the rope and sees them frowning, blinking their eyes as if they're full of dust.

"What's... umm..." the mustachioed man looks at him, but it seems as if his eyes are passing through him and focusing on something in the distance. "The, errrrm... the thing... what's with the, errrrm... y'know?" He points down at the swirling liquid filling the dark shaft beneath them. "Wet."

Eric nods. It seems to make sense, somehow, and he points along with the mustachioed man.

"Wet."

With that the two firefighters loosen their grip on the rope, and both fall back into the churning black water below. Eric looks down into the darkness but sees no thrashing. It's as if they didn't even try to swim.

With their weight gone the winch stops straining, and Eric notices the walls of the shaft move by much more quickly now. The light approaches.

Thirty seconds later Eric finally reaches the surface. He emerges into the blindingly bright light slumped and still, hanging immobile from the rope.

A young woman rushes towards him, a foil survival blanket crumpled in her arms. She yells out for help as she pulls Eric's lifeless body clear of the shaft, then orders the winch operator to let out enough slack to bring him down to the ground.

A small group crowds around as the woman leans in to check Eric's pulse and breathing, and they all whisper prayers as she crouches over his prone body and starts to administer mouth to mouth.

One breath.

Two.

Three.

Eric opens his eyes, and above him the woman breaks into a relieved smile as he begins to move. She reaches out for the survival blanket and tries to wrap it around the dust-caked, bedraggled figure beneath her, but he seems eager to stand.

The people working elsewhere in the rubble turn and stare in confusion as a piercing scream echoes around the crash site. Over by the hole where the survivor was found a group of rescue workers suddenly turn and run in every direction. A young woman stands for a moment, stumbling clumsily on the loose rubble and clutching her throat, and then she slumps to her knees and falls forward onto her face.

Beside her a man begins to stand awkwardly. He seems to be struggling with the rope attached to his waist. He runs in one direction until it jerks him back, and then he tries another direction with the same result. On his fourth try he runs straight back into the hole from which he emerged, and the rope dances across the ground until it's suddenly pulled tight.

A few of the rescue workers now turn their attention to the young woman on the ground. Katherine. She's the nice young EMT who helped organize a blood drive soon after the guys from Hawthorne arrive. Everyone likes her, and everyone wants to help.

They're only a few steps away when Katherine begins to move.

•⸙•

:::25:::

VEE APPEARS IN the doorway and flashes me a smile when she sees me up and awake. She strides towards us, tossing a couple of bottles of water our way as she arrives, and drops to the dusty ground with relief.

"Man, those stairs took it out of me," She stretches her legs out in front of her and winces as she massages her thighs. "You think they'd give a girl a break after a plane crash, right? How's the head?"

I takes a swig from the water and pour a little over my head to cool myself from the warm morning sun. "I'll live. What's the word?"

She grabs the bottle from my hand and takes a long gulp before speaking. "OK," she says, still catching her breath from the walk down, "there's good news and there's bad news. The *bad* news is that the CDC facility has been abandoned.

Jack – that's the kid in charge, Jack Benson – tells me they have the road all the way to Lake Mead locked up tight, and there's not a soul around any more. That's the bad news."

I feel my hopes slip away. We came all this way just to find nobody home? "And the good news?"

Vee brightens. "The good news is that the guys running this place seem to be pretty damned organized. After they took over the city they swept up everyone living within fifty miles of Vegas and brought them here, so there's a good chance anyone who was working at the facility is camped out somewhere in the city. One of the guys up there remembers the lab, and he's pretty sure he sent all the white coats to stay in the Luxor. That's the *other* good news, by the way. Turns out the DC-10 they brought down crashed into the Mandalay Bay, and pretty much everyone who was staying there is buried beneath a few thousand tons of concrete. Anyway, they've put out a call to the Luxor to see if they can track them down."

I feel myself relax a little. "Thank God for that. Do you still have the vaccine?"

Vee pats her pants pocket. "You better believe it. I'm not letting this thing out of my sight before–"

Her voice is suddenly drowned out by a

droning wail that fills the air, slowly rising in tone like a child's plaintive cry. I've never heard one in real life before, but it sounds to me like the air raid sirens I used to hear in old movies.

"What the fuck is that?" My voice barely carries above the racket as we jump to our feet. Warren tries to yell back but I can't hear a word, and I'm about to shout back when a group of soldiers begins to flood from the door of the air traffic control tower. They look terrified, but I'm not too concerned about that. What *does* concern me is that a small group detaches from the crowd and surrounds us, guns drawn and aimed squarely at us.

I turn to Vee. "What the fuck did you do up there?"

"Nothing to do with me," she replies, shrugging her shoulders and shooting me a worried look. "They seemed totally cool with us."

In the direction of the doorway the line of soldiers breaks to allow a man to pass through. His pistol is holstered, but that does nothing to stop him grabbing Vee by the collar and yelling angrily. "Did you do this?" he screams.

Vee looks desperately around at the men, as if searching for a direction in which to flee. "Do what? Jack, I don't know what the hell you're talking about!"

"The infected!" Jack's bright red face is right in hers now, and I worry for a moment that he's going to draw his gun in anger. I take a step forward, my arms held up.

"Woah woah woah, take a fucking breath!" I strain to make my voice heard about the noise. "What do you mean, the infected?" As I yell the last word the siren suddenly cuts out, and now my voice rings out over the airport. "What do you mean, infected?" I repeat, speaking normally again.

Jack angrily pushes Vee away and turns towards me. "The fucking infected! We just got word that there's an outbreak on the strip. Are you responsible?"

"What? Jesus, no! We've been here the whole time. We haven't been anywhere *close* to the Strip. Look, if you don't believe we're here to help you might as well just fucking shoot us now. Get it over with. Just..." I turn to Vee. "Vee, give me the vaccine."

Vee reaches into her pocket hesitantly, pulling out the Petri dish with a doubtful look on her face. "Tom, I–"

"Just give it to me, Vee." I take it from her hand and turn back to Jack. "Look, trust us or don't, It's up to you, but whatever you decide just promise me you'll get this to someone who knows how to cook up enough of it to inoculate everyone in the city. We don't have time to fuck around."

The young man looks down at my outstretched hand then stares me down, glaring into my eyes as if he's trying to look deep into my soul. For what feels like an awkward eternity I stare right back at him, until finally he takes a step back and seems to relax.

"Keep it." He looks around at the soldiers surrounding us. "Lower your weapons, guys. It's... it's OK. We're going to trust them. For now."

None of us breathe until the soldiers begin to lower their rifles, and in the silence we hear nothing but the squawk of their radios. Jack reaches for his, unclips it from his belt and brings it to his mouth. "Private Barnes, I need a sit-rep on the Strip. Can you give us a safe route from McCarran to the Luxor?" He waits through fifteen seconds of silence, then tries again. "Barnes, report your position? Come back."

Another ten seconds of silence, then the radio crackles to life. "That's a negative, sir, you have no safe route. These things... Jesus, they came outta nowhere. The Strip's fucking crawling. I have five men securing the entrances to the Luxor, but they're low on ammo and we can't hold this position for long. What are your orders, sir?"

Jack casts his eyes around the group, desperate for help, and holds the radio to his forehead as if he's coming down with a sudden migraine. "Umm..." He holds down the transmit button. "Standby, Barnes."

The response comes back immediately, the panic growing in the speaker's voice by the second. "Sir, I need orders now. We have a swarm incoming from the south. *What the fuck do you want us to do?*"

Jack brings the radio back to his lips. "Ummm... OK, umm, hold... hold your current position, Private. We'll be there as soon as–"

Vee steps smartly forward and snatches the radio from Jack's hand, and before he can so much as flinch she's speaking in a commanding tone. "Barnes, report your position."

The voice comes back. "Who the hell is this? Put Benson back on, woman."

Vee's expression darkens, and despite the heat of the morning sun I swear the air suddenly chills by a few degrees. "This is Lieutenant Victoria Reyes, Combat Aviation Brigade, 3rd Infantry Division, US Army, and I'm assuming command of this operation. Now report your fucking position, Private!"

The Private's response comes back meek as a kitten. "Yes, sir. I mean ma'am. I have two men at the north entrance, and me and two more are guarding the main entrance."

"OK, now listen carefully. The infected respond to sound and movement. They don't *think*. They don't *plan*. They only attack when they're triggered, so I need you to stop firing your weapons right now. Stop making sound, and get the hell out of sight." She pauses for a moment. "Now, the main entrance is the one with the big sphinx at the door, right?"

"Umm, yes ma'am, the lion kinda thing."

"Don't argue, Private, it's a sphinx. I need you to withdraw into the building right away. Don't bother barricading the doors, just get inside. *Quietly.* Then get anyone else on the ground floor up to the hotel levels, out of sight. Do you understand?"

"Yes, ma'am."

"Good. Now, find your men at the north entrance and order them to withdraw. Just inside the north entrance they should see a Vittorio Handbags store. Wait there with them, and stay out of fucking sight until we arrive. Do you understand?"

"Yes, ma'am, loud and clear."

"Excellent. One more thing. Do you have records of everyone who's staying in the hotel?"

A few seconds of silence pass before the voice returns. "Umm, yes, ma'am, we have them all written down in the big book in the lobby."

"Excellent. Get that book and guard it with your life. Now get to it. If I get there and find you dead I'll bring you back to life and kill you all over again, understand?"

"Yes, ma'am. Thank you, ma'am."

"Excellent. Out."

Vee tosses the radio back to a shocked Jack Benson. "I hope I'm not stepping on any toes, but you seemed like you need someone in command."

Jack shakes his head and smiles in disbelief. "Umm... no, not at all. I think we should... umm... guys, are you happy?" He looks around at his men, all of them nodding and mumbling their agreement. Jack looks back at Vee with a dazed expression. "OK, I guess you're in charge. What next, Lieutenant?"

Vee sets her jaw and looks around the airfield. "We have vehicles?" Jack nods. "OK, then let's saddle up. We're gonna go find us some scientists."

Jack Benson turns to his men and orders them to bring the Jeeps around, and I give Vee a sidelong glance.

"A handbag store?"

She narrows her eyes. "What? I've vacationed at the Luxor, and I remember thinking it'd make a good defensive location."

"You sure you don't just want a new handbag?"

She smiles as the Jeeps arrive, and as she hops aboard I hear her mutter under her breath. "Nothin' wrong with killing two birds with one stone."

•⸱•

:::26:::

THE FIRST THING I notice as we race west down Tropicana Avenue, our four Jeep convoy speeding through the streets in the shadow of the MGM Grand and the Tropicana itself, is that word of the outbreak has yet to spread beyond the Strip. There's still traffic on the street, a few trucks here and there parked up and delivering boxes of food to the hotels that serve as refugee camps. In the sprawling parking lot out front of the Tropicana several hundred people wait patiently as the trucks unload, milling around and shooting the shit.

It strikes me that Vegas is really a world unto itself, each resort acting like its own little self contained nation, each separated by vast tracts of parking. It seems hard to believe that this little world is ending just a couple of blocks away, and these people don't have the first clue of the danger running through the streets towards them.

I turn to Jack as he grabs his radio and orders the two Jeeps at the back of the convoy to peel off to the MGM and the Tropicana, and as we reach the Strip I look back and see the crowds first stand, then listen, and then begin to run.

Now we're down to two cars as we turn onto the Strip, and my heart leaps to my throat as I see the first of the infected. Out at the front entrance of the knockoff Disney castle exterior of the Excalibur a crowd of refugees struggle to fight off a hundred strong swarm of infected. At this distance it's difficult to tell who's who, but it's clear to see who's winning. One man standing beside the water feature out front of the hotel brandishes his gun and stands protectively in front of a woman and three small children. Each time his arm kicks up with the recoil one of the infected drops to the ground, but with each shot more and more of them turn their attention towards the noise. As we roll by the man fires his last shot, and I see Jack avert his eyes as the swarm barrels into the family and carries them over the wall and into the water.

"OK, Jack," Vee says, turning in her seat. Jack keeps his eyes fixed on the other side of the street. "Jack! *Look at me*, kid." Finally he turns, and I see his face is white with terror. "We need your guys to draw the infected away from the Luxor, OK? The moment we reach the north entrance Tom, Warren and I will jump out, and I need you guys to make sure none of them follow us. Do you understand what I'm saying?"

Jack nods weakly. "You don't want us to come in with you?"

"No, this is a stealth mission. While we're inside I need you to clear a path for us. Do you know how to work this?" She points to the bullhorn attached to the window frame of the Jeep. Jack nods again. "Good. I need you guys to act as... OK, this sounds worse than it is. I need you guys to act as *bait*. You gotta make as much noise as possible and draw the infected away from the Strip, OK? You have to draw them back to the airport, away from populated areas."

Jack's eyes are wide as saucers, and he looks like he's about to puke, but when Vee's palm connects with his cheek it brings a little color back to his face. "*Focus*, Jack. Man the fuck up. We can contain this, OK? These people don't all have to die."

Finally Jack manages to get a few words out. "I can't... I... I can't. *I just wanna go home.*"

"*Jesus.*" She sighs and twists in her seat again. "Warren, can you take the lead here? I need someone who won't piss his pants."

Warren climbs awkwardly from the back of

the Jeep to the rear seats. "OK, but you gotta promise me we go for a steak as soon as this is over. Scout's honor."

Vee smiles and takes the radio from Jack's unresisting hand. She passes it to me and grabs a spare from the dash for herself, tucking it onto her belt. "Deal. We'll call you as soon as we're ready to go. Until then maintain radio silence." She taps the driver on the shoulder. "OK, turn here," pointing to the junction at Reno Avenue, running between the Excalibur and the Luxor, and the driver swings into the street in a wide arc. I breathe a sigh of relief when I see no infected near the entrance to the Luxor, but I know they'll be close by.

"You ready for this?" Vee asks, pulling the driver's pistol from his holster and handing it to me.

I grab the gun and check the safety's off. "Fuck no, but let's do it anyway."

The Jeeps roll beneath the elevated walkway connecting the Luxor and the Excalibur, and under cover Vee and I climb quickly from the car before the convoy turns back into the street. As I scurry to the safety of the front door I hear Warren break into an ear-bleeding rendition of *Take Me Home, Country Roads* over the loudhailer as the cars race back towards the Strip.

It's not until I reach the glass doors of the Luxor that I see the problem.

The glass is shattered.

Beyond the doors I see movement.

They're here.

•᛭•

:::27:::

IT DIDN'T MATTER that Private Barnes and his men stayed quiet. They could have been as silent as church mice or banged pots and pans together as they withdrew into the casino, and it wouldn't have made a blind bit of difference. Beyond the shattered doors at the north entrance our ears are assaulted by electronic beeps, bells and alarms from the casino floor, and even from outside we can see the flashing lights and bright colors of the gaming machine flashing at us.

If I wasn't so terrified I'd laugh at the irony. These machines were designed down to the last inch to be irresistible to gamblers. They were created with a single purpose, to draw in dumb people; to beckon them close enough to reach out and drop a coin into the slot. I wonder whether the designers would be proud of their creations if they could see what I see now. The machines are now a dinner bell, irresistibly drawing in the infected to *eat* the gamblers.

The sprawling casino floor is packed with the infected. Every flashing light and enticing sound has pulled them in from the surrounding streets, and now they stand before the slot machines, staring and frozen, hypnotized by the sound and movement.

Vee tugs my arm to draw my attention, then leans in and whispers. "You see the handbag store?"

I follow her pointed finger until I find the concession about a hundred yards into the casino, right before the rows of slots begin. It takes me a few moments to spot something out of the ordinary. "Is that...?"

"Yeah, I think so. Poor bastard." The body of a soldier clad in fatigues lies halfway inside the store, his back twisted awkwardly over the broken window frame. I watch for a few seconds, and almost jump out of my skin when I see the man's legs suddenly twitch. It looks like he's caught on something and trying to work his way free, but it's clear from his awkward, jerking movements that he's not alive anymore. As we watch he twists his body on the frame and jerks his left leg wildly, and as he kicks out an object beside him goes sliding across the floor: a book.

"*Fuck*, we gotta get that," Vee whispers, narrowing her eyes as she looks around the casino floor. She points to a flight of escalators to the right just before the store. "Get over there, quietly." With that she stands and, without another word, begins to work her way towards the store, keeping low to avoid triggering the placid, enthralled infected.

I can feel my heart race in my chest as I break away from the front door and out over the carpeted lobby. It's only eighty yards or so to the escalators but it's all wide open space, and I can't help but imagine what would happen if the scores of infected staring at the machines suddenly turned their attention to me. One false move would be enough. One accidental sound and they'd be on me, and it wouldn't stop with them. I can only see a few dozen from here but I know there must be hundreds across the vast casino floor, all of them just waiting for something more interesting than flashing lights to chase.

Vee speeds ahead of me, moving in a stealthy crouch towards the store, and by the time I reach the escalator she's already there. I stop and watch as she slips a small knife from her belt, and without hesitation she brings it down into the eye socket of the infected soldier caught on the window frame. He stops struggling and his body goes limp, and Vee wipes her knife clean on her clothes before slipping it back in its sheath and scooping up the book from the floor.

She turns back towards me, but as she stands I notice movement inside the store. A fleeting shape moves across the broken window, and I wave madly to attract Vee's attention as she begins to scurry back towards me.

"Wait! *Don't leave me!*" A voice cries out above the din of the gaming machines, and out from the store emerges a soldier, his face a picture of terror. Vee spins around as he runs towards her, and at the same time the closest of the infected jerk their heads away from the bright lights of the slots and lock their eyes on us.

Vee turns back to me and breaks into a sprint as the infected begin to pursue, running down the aisles between the slots and pouring into the lobby in a flood of bodies. I grab hold of the rubber handhold and leap two steps at a time up the escalator, and by the time I'm halfway up I feel the steel steps shake with the weight of the infected arriving at the base.

I run, not daring to look behind me until I finally reach the top, and when I turn I'm met by a terrible sight. Vee leaps gracefully from step to step just a few yards behind me, but the soldier isn't so lucky. He's dragging behind him an injured leg, and the quickest of the infected quickly reach him on the steps. One reaches out and grabs him by the foot as he leaps. His landing leg falters and misses the edge of the next step, and he falls forward and hits the serrated edge of the steps chin first. He doesn't get a chance to recover. The infected are on him in a second and he vanishes beneath a writhing pile of bodies, punching, biting and tearing.

"*Reverse the direction!*" Vee yells out as she comes tearing past me. I stare at the controls for a moment in confusion before I notice, beside the big red emergency stop button, a green switch with an arrow pointing up and down. I flip it with shaking fingers and watch as the escalator judders to a halt and then begins to flow downwards, carrying the soldier's body and the infected feasting on it back down towards the casino floor. A few of them catch sight of me and try to chase me up, but they seem disoriented by the moving stairs and trip over their own feet in their efforts to climb. If it wasn't so terrifying I might even find it a little funny.

I find myself unable to tear my eyes from the sight. The body of the soldier is caught at the foot of the escalator, and after just as few moments the steps make their full circuit and appear back at the top. I look down at my feet and see that each step is streaked bright red with blood. One appears with a tuft of bloodied hair attached to the serrated edge and I watch, hypnotized, as it heads slowly back down to the crowd of infected waiting at the base.

"Fucking *move!*" Vee grabs my arm and drags me away just as a safety feature kicks in and brings the steps grinding to a halt, and as I turn to run I see the first of the infected begin to climb up towards us. We sprint across the deserted floor, our feet scuffing the ugly carpets as we run past a Starbucks, a McDonalds and yet more banks of beeping, colorful slot machines begging gamblers to drop a quarter in the slot and watch their worries slip away. Above us an illuminated sign points towards a bank of guest elevators, and we turn off the main concourse as the snarls of the infected carry across the floor towards us.

Vee reaches the elevators first, and she slams a bloodied palm on the call button and watches the screen above the door count down slowly from 12. Behind us the snarls grow louder... *8...* I reach out and hit the call button again in desperation, as if it might make it reach us more quickly... *5...* The first of the infected round the corner and slide across the tile floor of the Starbucks... *4...* It's an elderly woman with laughably tan skin, the kind of woman who might glamorously describe herself as sun bird while everyone else sees her as a wrinkled leather handbag with nothing but a bucket of quarters to her name... *3...* She's followed by a skinny guy with a goatee and a gaudy, bloodstained Tommy Bahama Hawaiian shirt, and then an overweight security guard missing one eye and most of his lower jaw...

2.

The elevator beeps out a tone and the doors slide open, and I drag Vee inside and slap my palm randomly at the buttons. The doors remain open, and the infected are just a dozen steps away.

We're not gonna make it.

I punch the door close button with both hands, and as the security guard breaks to the front of the group and passes the final row of slot machines Vee drops the book to the ground, then slides her knife from its sheath. I can feel a scream begin to bubble at the back of my throat, and I fumble for the gun tucked in the waist of my pants, but find it missing. I grab the heavy book from the floor, lift it over my shoulder and prepare to bring it down hard on the head of the first bastard to reach us.

Vee turns to me as the security guard reaches out for the door, and everything falls into slow motion as a smile flickers on her lips.

"*Don't fuck up,*" she whispers, her voice almost drowned out by the roars of the infected.

And then she jumps forward.

"*No!*" I barely recognize the ferocity of my own voice as Vee leaps from the elevator and launches herself knife first into the security guard. I take a step forward to help just as the doors finally slide closed, and by the time I turn to find the door open button the elevator is already moving. The last thing I saw as the doors closed was Vee falling to the ground with her knife buried in the neck of the security guard, and the wrinkled, tan old woman throwing her scrawny body down towards her.

In the tight, claustrophobic space of the elevator I let out a guttural roar and slide down the wall until I slump to the ground. I feel tears prick at my eyes and a sob works its way up my throat. I bury my head in my hands as the elevator lets out a beep with each passing floor, and I barely notice when we finally come to a halt and the doors slide open.

For a moment I wonder if I should press the button to return to the second floor. I reach out for the keypad and my finger hovers above the button, but then I remember what's in my pocket. I reach down and take out the plastic Petri dish, and through my tears I stare at the little black dots peppering the agar jelly trapped within.

This is why she jumped out. *This* is what she was protecting. She didn't leap from the elevator to save me, but to save *this*. This little plastic tub that holds the secret to saving everyone still living on the planet.

Don't fuck up.

I take a deep breath and pull myself together. The doors of the elevator begin to close, but I reach out with a leg to break the sensor beam. The doors slide open once more, and I grab the book and lift myself from the ground.

I wipe my eyes and step from the elevator, finding myself on one of the balconies that run around the interior of the hotel looking down on the atrium below. I set down the book on the lip of the wall and begin to flip through, searching the handwritten entries until I find the block of people I'm looking for.

Dr. Simon Monroe, MD, MPH... Room 412

Dr. Saanvi Kapoor, MD, MPH... Room 412

Dinh Nguyen, PhD... Room 413

Dr. Karen Wyatt, MD, MHCDS... Room 413

Besides their names is a scrawled, handwritten notation:

CDC staff. Useful skills?

I look back at the elevator and see that I'm

on the fifth floor, so I step back inside just as the doors begin to close and hit the button for four. I turn just as the doors close once more, and in the final moments before the doors seal closed I see movement on the opposite side of the hotel. I see figures running along the balcony.

A chill runs through me as the elevator begins to move, and moments later comes to a stop at the floor below. I grip the book tight and get ready to swing at whatever might be waiting outside, but the doors open to an empty corridor.

I step out and read the sign hanging above the door, then turn right for rooms 401-419. From this angle I can no longer see the fifth floor balcony clearly but I can hear the sounds of the infected both above and below. I know they've found their way up to the higher floors, and I feel my pace speed up until I reach room 412.

I knock quietly on the door and hold my breath as I hear movement inside. Shuffling feet approach, and after a few moments of fiddling the door cracks open a few inches and I see a small, owlish Asian woman looking up at me through oversized glasses.

"H-Hello?" she says, looking me up and down with alarm. I look down at myself and for the first time notice that my hands are red with blood from the elevator keypad. My forehead is still bloody from the crack I took from the soldiers at the airport, and I'm still dressed in the same stinking, dirty fatigues I've been wearing since escaping Newark Airport days ago. I must look like some dangerous monster to this little old woman who thinks she's living in safety.

"Are you the CDC guys?" I demand, jamming my foot in the door as she tries to push it closed on me.

The woman answers in a small, scared voice. "Ummm... yes, that's us."

I push the door open forcefully and nudge my way past her into the room, kicking the door closed behind me. "Find something to barricade that door," I order, looking back at the terrified woman.

Ahead of me a man and two women sit on the double bed, a messy pile of playing cards between them. "What the hell is this?" the man demands, standing and drawing himself to his full, haughty height.

"Dr. Monroe?" The man nods. "I'm Tom Freeman, and I need your help to save the world."

The doctor tosses his playing cards to the bed and reaches for the glasses hanging around his neck. "Young man, I must insist that you–"

"*Shut up.*" I point a bloodied finger in his direction, and his face turns white. "There are infected outside. They're coming for us, and I'm carrying what might be the only sample of a vaccine that still exists. I need your help to make more of it."

The skinny, middle-aged woman sitting on the bed – Dr. Wyatt, I presume – speaks up with a sharp, clipped English accent. "Vaccine? You have a vaccine? Let me see!" Her fear is suddenly gone, replaced with curiosity, and as I pull the Petri dish from my pocket she rushes across the room to take it from me.

I pull the tattered notebook from my jacket and hand it over to her. "You'll find all the notes in here. I've been reading about it. It's some kind of beta glucose anti-fungal vaccine."

Dr. Wyatt glances up from the notebook to correct me. "You probably mean Beta-glucan." She turns back to Dr. Monroe. "Good Lord, that was the answer?" She turns back and continues to flip through the pages. "It's... it's just a modified *Candida* strain. My God, it's so *simple!* Saanvi, look at the structure. We were so close!" She looks up at me as if she forgot I was there and waves her hand dismissively. "We were working on something similar ourselves, but we were following a completely different path. Look, Simon, we were searching for increased complexity but we should have been going back to basics. All we need to do is disrupt the cell wall and the spores won't be able to take hold! It's so bloody elegant it's untrue!"

I let the technical talk wash over me as I pace back to the door and wedge a flimsy chair under the handle. I can't be sure, but at the edge of my hearing I'd swear I could hear snarling and groaning noises growing ever closer. In the distance I hear what sounds like a scream.

I turn back to the room. "Doctors, listen to me. On the other side of that door there are hundreds of infected. We need to get out of here right now. We need to get back to your lab."

The doctors look fearfully at the door. "And how the hell do you propose we get out?" asks Dr Monroe, his hands shaking as he brings his glasses up to his face.

I look around the room and try to think of it like a puzzle. I know we'll never get out through the lobby. I almost died just getting up here, and now the infected know there are people here there isn't a chance I'll get past them with four passengers in tow. It occurs to me that there must be a fire escape, but when I move over to the window and look outside I remember that this is a pyramid. All the fire escapes must be internal, and that means we'd need to head out to the corridor to find one.

And then a crazy, desperate idea hits me.

"Wait here," I order, walking back to the door. With more hesitation than I'd like I pull the chair away from the door and carefully pull it open, peering out slowly into the corridor in case there's something waiting on the other side. It's empty, thank God, but I can now see infected running freely on several levels on the opposite side of the hotel. It's only a matter of time before they reach us.

I step out the door, and almost immediately I find what I was praying for. A red steel case with a glass cover is mounted to the wall beside the room, and in it sits a coiled fire hose.

With my elbow I break the glass seal that hides the door lock, and moments later I'm tugging the hose by its heavy steel nozzle back into the room. I walk back towards the window, pulling as I go until I finally reach the end and the hose pulls taut. Dr. Monroe begins to protest, but I silence him with a raised finger and tug the radio from my pocket. "Warren, do you read?"

Nothing but silence for a moment, but then his voice comes through loud and clear. "I read you, buddy. Did you guys find us a doc?"

"Yeah, four of them. Listen, where are you? We need a pickup at the main entrance of the Luxor right now."

Warren sounds a little nervous when he comes back. "Well... yeah, I mean I can be back there in a couple of minutes, but you know you're in a sketchy neighborhood, right? Looks like our plan to draw these fuckers away didn't really work out like we hoped it would. I've lost a couple of guys, and we just seem to be making the infected mad as hell."

"Never mind that, just be at the sphinx in two minutes, and keep the damned engine running."

"Will do. Stay safe, kid. Out."

I drop the radio back in my pocket and look back towards the doctors. "OK, time to go guys."

"What in the hell do you plan to do with that?" Monroe asks, pointing to the hose, no doubt already knowing the answer.

I ignore him and look for a window latch, but it seems these windows weren't designed to be opened. The steel nozzle solves the problem easily, and I grab the duvet from the double bed and use it to knock away the shards of glass clinging to the frame. "We have to go down the side," I say, matter of factly.

Dr. Monroe stares back at me open mouthed, and when he shakes his head and starts to protest I lose my cool. "Too many of my friends have died trying to get this vaccine to you, doctor. One of them sacrificed herself just downstairs, and if you don't come with me her death will have been for nothing. Now, are you coming, or do I have to fucking throw you out the window?"

Dr. Wyatt is the first to make a move. She takes the Petri dish and notebook from Dr. Nguyen and passes them back to me before looking out the window. "Come on Simon, this is no time to be a wet lettuce. Like the young man says, it seems to be our only option."

I smile at the woman and start to lower the hose down the side of the building, watching the nozzle bounce ever more quickly against the windowpanes as I feed more weight over the frame. By the time it jolts to a stop the nozzle is almost at the ground, maybe five yards from the manicured gardens at the base of the pyramid. "OK, we're ready. Dr. Wyatt, would you like to go first?"

The doctor looks terrified, but she covers well with what looks to me like the famous British stiff upper lip. She steels herself against the fear, grabs hold of the hose and slowly climbs over the edge of the window frame, planting the soles of her sensible flat shoes against the glass to hold herself steady. "Just lower yourself down slowly, there's no hurry," I assure her.

I turn back to the room and look to the three remaining doctors. "Who's next?"

Blank faces all around. Nobody makes a move, and I'm about to speak up when a sound from outside the door sends a chill down my spine. A scream erupts from the corridor, and it sounds like it's just a few doors away from us.

"*Now!*" I whisper, beckoning them to the window. "We have to go *now!*"

Still nobody moves. It's as if all three are frozen to the spot, and it's only when they hear a noise from directly outside the room that they reanimate. A shape flits by the door. I hold my breath and pray whatever it was continues on its way, but moments later it appears in the doorway again.

It's a young man, a kid who looks barely out of his teens. His white button down shirt is streaked with blood and there's a chunk of flesh missing from his throat. The wound bubbles as he lets out a roar, and before the doctors can react he runs into the room and collides with the hose pulled taut at waist height.

From out the window I hear Dr Wyatt scream, but I don't have time to worry about it. Without another thought I grab hold of the hose and throw myself out the window, landing with painful force on the glass. For a terrifying moment I lose my grip and begin to slide down the side of the building, only to flail out wildly and grab hold of the hose just as I was about to slide out of reach. I slide to a stop and take a firm grip, then begin to lower myself inch by careful inch down the glass.

A scream emerges from the broken window above me, and I look up and cling tight to the hose as someone comes leaping from the building. It's Dr. Nguyen, the owlish Asian doctor. She falls backwards against the glass and begins to slide down the building headfirst, too far from the hose the grab hold. As she reaches me I stretch out as far as I can and try to stop her fall, but she's just a couple of inches too far away from me. She sails past, screaming, and I look away. I don't want to see what happens to her when she hits the ground after sliding four floors down.

The hose jerks in my grip and once more I look up and see one of the doctors, but this time it's not someone trying to escape. It's Dr Monroe, his glasses shattered on his face and blood pouring from an open wound beneath his hairline. He looks down at me with a blank, vacant gaze, and then slowly he bears his teeth and begins to snarl.

Monroe climbs clumsily from the window, his aged body unsuited to the task even before, but now he lacks the coordination to move with any finesse. He topples over by the waist and ends up pointing down, his arms reaching out for me, and slowly he begins to slide, his momentum slowed by virtue of him lying on top of the hose.

I can see he'll reach me before I reach the ground, there's no question, and I know I won't be able to fight him off while clinging to the rope. I'll have no way to keep away from him, and I can already picture us falling to the ground clinging together, his teeth edging ever closer to my flesh.

I let go of the hose.

Right away I feel my speed pick up. I awkwardly turn onto my side, and beneath me I can see I still have two floors left to travel. I'm maybe twenty yards from the ground, and just ten beneath me I can see Dr. Wyatt struggling to edge her way down.

"Let go!" I yell, but she doesn't seem to hear me or even notice I'm there. She's staring right at the glass, terrified to look anywhere else.

There's nothing for it. I roll to the side to move my body a little to the right, and when I pull level with Dr. Wyatt I grab hold of her arm. I feel myself jerk to a sudden halt, and then as Wyatt loses her grip on the hose we both begin to pick up speed again.

Now we're just ten yards from the ground,

and I flip onto my ass and take a firm grip of Wyatt, pushing her aside so I don't land on top of her. The last floor passes in a blur, and with a painful roll I feel myself hit the ground and tumble on the thankfully soft, cushioned lawn surrounding the building. Wyatt tumbles gracelessly to the ground beside me, landing hard but seemingly uninjured.

I don't have time to think. Almost on autopilot I drag myself from the floor and lift Wyatt up by the elbow. Above me I see Dr. Monroe tumbling wildly down the side of the building, and to my side I see the battered body of Dr. Nguyen, twisted and broken. She landed face first on a tiled walkway, and I can see there's no point checking to see if she survived. "*Let's go!*" I yell into Wyatt's ear, loud enough to pull her back from shock and spur her into action.

The doctor breaks into a run, her eyes wide with fear, and I guide her by the arm in the direction of the tacky sphinx looming over the main entrance of the casino. I turn to look over my shoulder and see that Monroe landed softly enough that he can still stand, and despite what looks like a broken arm he lifts himself from the ground and sets after us at an off kilter jog. There's no chance the old man will catch up with us, but I'm terrified that the snarling groan escaping his throat will draw others near. I don't have so much as a stick to beat away an attacker, and if we're overwhelmed now we're finished.

The sphinx is just twenty yards ahead now, and as we leave the lawn and run onto the road leading to the drop off point by the entrance my heart leaps into my throat. The Jeep is nowhere to be seen, but in the darkness beneath the sphinx half a dozen infected stand staring at the twinkling blue lights attached to the ceiling at the entrance. Doctor Wyatt lets out a startled scream, and as one the infected look up and notice us.

"*Come on!*" I yell, dragging her by the arm through a row of palm trees lining the side of the road. She stumbles for a moment on the grass, barely keeping her feet, and by the time she starts running again the quickest of the infected is just a few steps behind us.

I run blindly, not thinking about where we're going but just concentrating on escaping. Ahead of us a chain link fence rises from the ground to separate the road from the sprawling parking lot out front, and I realize we're penned in, trapped between the casino and the fence, with nowhere to run but the narrow road leading back to the main street. I turn on my heel and run parallel to the fence, but even as I break into a sprint I can see there's no way out. Ahead of us another dozen infected are running in our direction, all of them attracted by the wails coming from the half dozen behind us.

I can hear the breath of the man behind us. He's quick. I could outrun him alone, but Dr. Wyatt has no chance. She can only manage a brisk jog at best, and I know that in just a few moments I'll feel her pulled from my grip as the man behind us finally comes within reaching distance.

I barely feel it when the toe of Dr. Wyatt's shoe lands on my heel. As I lift my leg I begin to stumble, and I feel myself fall to the side as my foot buckles at the ankle. I still have a tight grip of the doctor's arm, and as I fall she begins to tumble alongside me, rolling to the ground as the man behind us finally catches up. I land painfully on my side and roll, and looming above me I see the man silhouetted against the bright sun, reaching out with both hands ready to lunge down at us.

This is it, I think. *This is how it's going to end.*

I squeeze my eyes closed and try to curl into a ball, bracing for the pain and hoping against hope that I'll be lucky enough to go quickly. I hope he'll just kill me right away. I don't want to come back as one of those things.

Dr. Wyatt lets out a piercing scream right in my ear, deafening me to the rest of the world, and I clamp my hands over my ears as I wait for the teeth to puncture my skin, but after a few seconds nothing comes.

I open my eyes and look up, confused. The infected man is still standing above me, but as I look up at him he makes no move to attack. He just stands there, looking down at us without interest, and it's not until he slowly teeters forward and falls on top of me that I see why.

Warren sits in the driver's seat of the Jeep, back in the direction of the casino entrance. Behind him lie the flattened bodies of the other five infected, and he flashes me a grin as he brings his pistol up to his lips and blows the smoke from the barrel.

Fucking showboat.

I push the body to the side and lift myself to my feet, dragging the insensible doctor up like a sack of potatoes. She's unharmed but struck mute with the shock, and as Warren pulls up beside us and kicks open the door I push her in with some force before hopping in the back seat.

"You fucking took long enough!" is all I can manage to say.

I see the cogs turn in Warren's mind as he comes up with a snappy retort, but as he opens his mouth to speak another thought occurs to him. He doesn't have to ask the question. He just looks at the empty seat in the Jeep, and I shake my head.

"Was it quick?" he asks in a quiet voice.

I can't bring myself to tell him the truth. I can't admit that I didn't see her die, and that she might have been infected. I know she swore from the beginning that she'd never allow that to happen. "Let's talk about it later," I reply, averting my eyes. "We need to get out of here."

Warren stares off into space for a moment, lost in his own thoughts, before the real world finally creeps back in around the edges and he realizes we're far from safe. A dozen infected are still barreling towards us down the street, and the open top Jeep will do nothing to protect us if they catch up. He grabs the gear stick and angrily shifts into reverse before slamming his foot on the gas, screaming backwards and tugging the wheel sharply to send us into a wild J-turn before roaring beneath the sphinx and back towards the Strip.

Behind us the small crowd of infected howl angrily as we speed away, denying them their prize.

•🜚•

:::28:::

DR. WYATT STARES at the notebook, working her way quickly through the chicken scratch handwriting and crudely drawn diagrams. Now she has the book all her fear seems to be gone, as if she's able to withdraw from the world and pretend she's not a part of it any more. It must be nice to be able to hide in a book, but I'm all too conscious of the danger around us.

The casinos and hotels lining the Strip are under siege. There aren't all that many infected around – maybe just a few hundred out on the streets – but they're congregating around the doorways of the casinos. We know the Luxor has already been overwhelmed, and the scattered bodies around the entrance to the Excalibur tell me the refugees there didn't fare any better, but the Tropicana and MGM Grand seem to be holding up. Maybe our warning as we drove past bought them enough time to barricade the doors, but we know they won't last forever. The infected own the city now. Unless the refugees can find some way to fight back they'll all be lost, but right now that's not our concern. Right now we need to save everyone else.

"Doctor, can you show us the quickest way back to your lab? We need to get there right now."

Dr. Wyatt doesn't respond until I shake her shoulder, and as I pull her attention from the notebook she jumps with fright, as if she forgot we were even there. "Sorry, I missed what you said."

"Which way is you lab, doctor? We need to head over there right away."

Wyatt points back in the direction of the airport. "Well it's about twenty miles to the south east, dear boy, but I'm afraid you'll find nothing of any use there." Her tone makes it sound as if she thinks it's silly that I'd even ask.

"What do you mean?"

She closes the notebook and turns in her seat to face me. "Well we lost power, poppet. Your damned fool engineers blew out all the local transformers while they were tinkering over at the dam. We kept soldiering on with the generators for a week or so, but we had to move to the city when the diesel ran dry."

"So let's just find some more," I reply,

surprised the idea didn't occur to her.

Doctor Wyatt chuckles. "Well I suppose we could, but first we'd have to immunize ourselves against... oh, let's see... anthrax, ricin, tularemia and legionella. Oh, and a nasty strain of avian flu, but I don't suppose we'd have to worry about the sniffles once our internal organs began to liquefy." She sees my confused look and continues. "The cold storage has been breached, dear boy. I'm afraid our lab was an old and not particularly well funded facility, if I'm being perfectly honest, so we didn't have all the fancy bells and whistles you'll find at the CDC in Atlanta. Our cold storage unit was really little more than a meat locker, and when we lost power we lost everything. Refrigeration, door locks, positive pressure seals, air filtration, contamination sensors... the lot. It's all gone, love." She shakes her head and looks out at the road ahead. "No, we wouldn't be able to go back in there without isolation suits for *years*, I'd imagine."

I slump back in my seat and watch the spectacle at the side of the road. To my left I see the fountains out front of the Bellagio, and as we pass they burst spectacularly into life. The central circular column of water erupts high into the air, but it looks like only around half the jets are working. As I watch more and more of them begin to fire, and as each new shaft of water explodes heavenward it carries with it a writhing body. It's only when we pass a row of scrubby hedges blocking our view that I see why.

Dozens of infected have been drawn in by the movement of the fountains and the glowing lights beneath the water, and as each jet fires they throw themselves dumbly at the movement, attacking them like a cat chasing the red dot cast by a laser pointer. As each one falls blindly into the path of a jet they're thrown into the air by the water, and as soon as they come splashing back down into the pool they climb to their feet and do it all over again.

I just can't believe humanity is going to be destroyed by these fucking morons. These mindless creatures, hypnotized by flashing lights and confused by jets of water. Aliens I could understand. If some technologically superior alien species arrived to blast us from the face of the planet at least we'd go out like men, swinging to the last against an opponent we could never hope to outmatch. It'd be an honorable loss, something we could at least be proud of as we fought valiantly through our final days.

But *this?* What a fucking embarrassment. Losing to these idiots is just humiliating. They're just mean, dumb, violent versions of us, and we've been taken out like a bunch of pussies. How did it happen? Three hundred million guns in the country, not to mention our tanks, fighter planes and fucking drones. We should have brushed this attack aside before lunch on the first day, but we were caught asleep at the wheel. Too fat. Too lazy. Too slow. Too enthralled by the latest shitty reality show and the new seasonal coffee at fucking Starbucks to get off our asses and fight back when we had the chance. We allowed ourselves to sleep through the apocalypse, and now we're doomed to watch the end of the human race. We'll have to watch as these dumb fucks lay down and die before their bodies swell and distend, erupting in a cloud of spores that will shroud the earth until the last of us falls.

How God damn disappointing.

I turn away from the infected, more disgusted with myself than I am with them. I made it all this way and I still can't get the job done. If only someone else had–

"Huh." Dr. Wyatt interrupts my self-pitying train of thought.

"What is it?" Warren asks, keeping his eyes on the road ahead.

She stays silent for a moment, running her finger down a page of the notebook. "Well I don't want to get you too excited, but if I'm reading this correctly we may not need the lab after all." She turns to face me. "Thomas, please may I see the Petri dish for a moment?"

I reach into my pocket and slide it out, remarkably still intact after everything we've been through. Dr. Wyatt takes it carefully from me and holds it up to the light, studying the black dots held within the agar jelly.

"Hmmm. Looks like there's more than enough to get started." She grabs the notebook and studies a passage. "I'm afraid I've been coming at this from the wrong angle once again. I've been thinking the solution must be complex, but I think it might be really very simple indeed." She turns back to me and gives me a toothy grin. "Tell me, Thomas, are you a fan of craft beer?"

I shake my head. "Not really, I'm a Scotch drinker. Why?"

Dr, Wyatt taps Warren on the shoulder. "Take a right here please, poppet." She turns back to me. "Well, we're about to save the world from a micro brewery." She smiles and turns her attention back to the notebook. "It looks like those annoying hipsters might have been good for something after all."

•⸙•

:::29:::

THE JEEP DRAWS to a stop outside a small, cramped bar squeezed into a small space between a rundown low rent casino called the Red Rock and a branch of McDonalds that looked like its decor hadn't been updated since Ray Kroc opened the doors. Above the door a small sign reads *The Pilgrim's Rest* in a bullshit Olde English font, and as soon as I get a look through the window I know it's the kind of bar I'd never patronize in a million years.

Dr Wyatt notices my expression as we climb of out the Jeep. "Yes, it's an overpriced dive popular with navel gazing self-obsessed hipster wankers, I know," she says, a hint of a smile on her lips, "but the barman was the only bloke in town who knew how to properly pour a pint of Guinness. It was my one guilty pleasure." She leads the way, pushing open the door and leading us into a bar that seemed almost entirely full of furniture that was cobbled together from reclaimed wood and self-satisfaction. "Anyway, we're not here to drink. Come on."

She leads us through the bar and down the corridor to the bathrooms, beyond which a heavy door blocks our way. "Could one of you strapping gentlemen kindly break this lock?"

I look around the walls until I see a fire extinguisher mounted in the corner, and with a few sharp cracks the handle of the door breaks off and loosens the lock just enough that Warren can force open the door. It swings open to reveal what looks like a miniature Soviet version of Willy Wonka's chocolate factory. Copper vats line the far wall of the large room, and against the wall to the left rests a long table covered in all manner of bizarre equipment.

"They brew wheat beer in-house. Awful stuff. I tried it just to be polite, but I'm afraid they have a tendency to overdo it on the hops and it ends up tasting like cheap coffee. Still, mustn't grumble. At least they left us with everything we need."

"And what's that?" I ask. "What are we planning to do?"

The doctor strides over to the long table and roots around beneath it until she finds a cardboard box full of white plastic jars. "Aha, there it is." She pulls one out and tosses it over to me. "We're going to channel the great Alexander Fleming, my dear boy. We're going to grow our own vaccine."

I look down at the plastic jar in my hand. *Malt extract agar, 1kg.* I unscrew the cap, and within I find a light brown powder. "What do you want me to do with this?"

"I want you to... ummm... Warren, is it? Lovely. Warren, please pass me that steel pot." She turns back to me. "I want you to find some distilled water – they should have plenty around here somewhere – and empty two parts water to one part agar into this pot. Chop chop, don't dilly dally."

I scan the room until my gaze lands on a pallet of CVS brand gallon jugs. *Sodium free distilled water.* "Got it." I grab one of the heavy bottles with both hands and swing it across the room between my legs.

"Good boy, now get pouring." Dr Wyatt carefully pops the lid of the Petri dish as I awkwardly lift the enormous bottle to the pot, spilling half of it before I manage to find the target. "Careful, lad. Now, I'm afraid this first batch will be a little rough and ready. We're not exactly working in ideal sterile conditions, but I think we'll be able to cobble through with what we have. Let's show a bit of Blitz spirit, what?"

I look up at her with a frown. "Huh?"

"Never mind. OK, that's quite enough water. Now comes the agar." She pops the cap and pours the powder into the water. "Right," she says, turning back to the Petri dish, "now for the secret ingredient." She grabs a knife from the table and carefully cuts away one of the tiny black dots from the agar in the dish, then drops it in the pot. "*Ta-da!*" she exclaims with a smile, as if she's just done a magic trick. "Now, be a good lad and lift it onto the hob." She taps the electric stove at the end of the table.

I lift the heavy pot from the floor up to the burner, and Dr. Wyatt places the lid on top and clamps it down with the kind of clasps you find on a Mason jar. "Now," she says, turning a knob on the stove, "all we need to do is apply a little heat and let the magic happen."

"What exactly did we just do?" Warren asks.

Dr. Wyatt grins. "We just did science, my boy, and we might have saved what's left of humanity along with it." She grabs the Petri dish from the table. "Take a close look at this agar. See the little black spots? They're vaccine colonies. They're... oh, how to explain it in layman's terms?" She ponders the problem for a moment.

"OK, imagine the colonies as an Oreo. The biscuit layers are made from something called

Beta-glucan. That's... ummm, well, this particular type is a glucose polysaccharide that naturally occurs in the cell walls of certain types of fungus, including *Candida albicans* – that's the nasty stuff that causes thrush when it gets out of control – and *Cordyceps bangkokii*." She sees the blank expressions shared by me and Warren. "Doesn't matter, you don't need to understand it. Anyway, that's the biscuit layer. The cream layer is made up of *Cordyceps* cells. They're still alive, but they're perfectly harmless when they're bound to the Beta-glucan. Now, when you introduce this stuff into your bloodstream it multiplies just like the *Cordyceps* itself, but instead of melting your brain to mush and turning you into an unpleasant bitey sort of chap it just sits there, perfectly peacefully." She turns back to the Petri dish and cuts out another tiny black spot.

"Now, here's the important bit. When a live *Cordyceps* spore gets into your system it'll try to latch onto your blood cells and use them as energy to multiply, but when you have the vaccine coursing through your veins... well, it'll find it has a pretty tricky job of it. Your white blood cells, you see, will recognize the *Cordyceps* from the get go, and they'll... oh, it's all very tricky technical stuff, but they'll essentially break down the cell walls of the fungus. They simply won't allow it to replicate fast enough to colonize the body. You might find yourself with a nasty yeast infection, but you won't become fully infected."

I still have no idea what she's talking about, but she seems confident. I nod to the pot warming on the stove. "So we're cooking up a batch of vaccine right now?"

Dr. Wyatt nods as she drops a tiny black colony of vaccine into a cup of distilled water and begins to stir it in. "That's right. The heat will speed up the growth. It's basically the same process by which they grow their own brewer's yeast here. We've dumped in a little agar – that's the growth medium – along with distilled water as a carrier for the vaccine, and then we've seeded the solution with a sample of the vaccine itself, which will replicate using the agar for fuel." She grins. "It's so simple. The most advanced fungal pathogen we've ever seen in the history of the planet, and we can cure it using pretty much the same technology Alexander Fleming would have used to produce penicillin. Marvelous. Just bloody marvelous." Her grin stretches from ear to ear.

I take the radio from my belt and click the transmit button with a victorious smile. "Calling anyone who can read me. I'm happy to report that we're cooking up a fresh batch of the finest vaccine down at..." I lower the radio. "What's this place called again?"

"The Pilgrim's Rest," Dr. Wyatt answers, pulling a packet of syringes from her pocket.

"... Down at the Pilgrim's Rest on East Harmon Avenue. If anyone's reading this we'd love a little backup, and in return we'll shoot you up with the good stuff. Out." I lower the radio.

Warren grins with relief. "OK, I'm gonna go check out the street and make sure we're not about to get rushed by a thousand hungry fuckers."

Dr Wyatt grabs him by the arm as he starts to turn for the door. "Wait a minute. I'm afraid I'm going to need you for just a little while longer." Her smile fades. "See, we need to test this vaccine before we start distributing it. Everything looks good on paper, but the proof is in the pudding. I'll need to inject myself, and if it doesn't go well..." She looks down at Warren's holstered gun. "Well, you'll need to deal with what happens next." She pulls one of the syringes from its wrapper. "Thank God for diabetes, otherwise I'd have to stab myself with a sharpened pen."

She lowers the syringe to the cup and draws out some of the solution, then tips it up and taps the air bubbles from the reservoir. "Well, wish me luck."

"*No!*" The word leaves my mouth without passing through my mind first, and Dr. Wyatt freezes with the needle just an inch from her skin. "No, stop," I say, snatching it from her. "Doc, you're our only hope. If this doesn't work out we'll need someone who knows how to find the solution. We can't risk losing you. But me... I'm not important. I'll be the guinea pig."

The doctor shakes her head forcefully. "No, I can't allow that. You saved my life. If it wasn't for you I'd already be one of those things. I can't ask you to take the risk."

Before she can say another word I slide the needle beneath the skin of my forearm and press the plunger. "You're not asking. I'm volunteering." I pull the needle out and watch as a bead of blood blooms from my arm. "Warren? Get ready."

Warren pulls his gun from its holster and nervously holds it, pointing at the ground.

15 seconds.

"I've never seen it take more than a minute for them to turn," I say, balling my hands into fists so tight I can feel my fingernails break the skin. I know I'm probably imagining it, but I'd swear I can feel the vaccine course through my veins.

30 seconds.

Warren takes a tighter grip on the gun. I can see him study me for signs of infection. He stares nervously at my hands, waiting for me to lash out.

45 seconds.

I can feel my heart racing in my chest, and it feels as if there's a hand gripping my neck, squeezing my airways. My breath comes in short, panting bursts. I feel a tear roll unbidden down my cheek and I wonder if this, right now, will be the last real thought I ever have. I wonder if these are my dying moments. I squeeze my eyes closed and try to stretch these last seconds as far as possible, to be aware of every breath, and every beat of my heart; just to be aware, for what could be the last time, of being *human.*

60 seconds.

•፣•

:::30:::

THE COLORED LIGHTS flash from the slot machines on the casino floor of the Luxor. A video poker game boasts that the pot is up to $37,500, and from somewhere unseen a defective machine spits out quarters onto the bloodstained carpet.

Down in the basement levels, in a deserted security control room hidden away somewhere amongst the labyrinthine corridors, a hundred monitors play live images from around the casino. Up on the guest levels can be seen the infected, sprinting along the corridors hunting for the refugees barricaded in their rooms. One guest suddenly makes a run for it, choosing exactly the wrong moment to leave her room and dash for the elevators, running right into an infected running the other way. They struggle together for a moment, and then the monitor records the two toppling over the edge of the balcony, falling silently in high definition to the atrium floor far below.

The monitors covering the casino floor show nothing but the endless repeating of patterns and colors from the gaming machines. Lights flash and buzzers sound, watched by no one. The monitors flicker through their programmed routine, displaying one part of the floor for fifteen seconds before switching to another. In all of them the images are still.

Except one.

At an escalator close to the north entrance of the casino a figure appears. It's a woman, dressed in military fatigues and drenched with blood from head to toe. In her hand she carries a long knife, and before the monitor cycles to the next camera it catches her wiping the blade on her jacket and slipping it back in it sheath strapped to her belt.

The camera switches, catching the bottom of the escalator where a body lies. This one is also dressed in fatigues, but only a few scraps remain. The body has been torn apart. In the grainy image it twitches, uselessly flailing its arms and legs, or at least what's left of them.

The woman limps into frame, carefully sidestepping the twitching body. For a moment she pauses, staring down at the wretch, before pulling out her knife once more and slipping it into an eye socket. The movement stops.

She pauses for a while, resting against the wall. She looks as if she's exhausted the last of her strength, but as she slumps closer to the floor something distracts her. She looks down in surprise at something attached to her belt, and moments later pulls her radio to her ear, listening in rapt attention.

A smile cracks her lips.

She clips the radio back to her belt, and pulls herself up to her full height with renewed energy.

She starts to run.

•▼•

:::31:::

"AM I SPEAKING right now?" My voice emerges from my throat in a dry croak.

"Yeah, buddy, you're speaking," Warren replies softly.

"And I'm not trying to kill anyone?"

"Not unless you're trying to do it with your body odor, no."

I slowly open my eyes. Warren slides his gun back into its holster, and Dr. Wyatt grins excitedly as she looks at me. "Well," she says pulling down my lower eyelids and leaning in close, "it didn't kill you or infect you, love. I'd say that's a pretty good sign."

"I'm calling that a solid win, doc," I reply, feeling my muscles relax for the first time in minutes. I look down at my hands, noting the small cuts in my palms where I dug my fingernails in. "It's a weird feeling to know I've got the fungus flowing through my veins right now. Kinda scary, actually."

The doctor waves her hand dismissively. "It's no different from getting any other vaccine, really. I'm old enough to remember being vaccinated against smallpox, and that was some scary stuff, let me tell you." She pats me on the cheek and smiles. "What doesn't kill you only makes you stronger."

Warren takes another syringe from Dr. Wyatt's pack and fills it from the cup, injecting himself with all the confidence of a lifelong junkie. "If this kills me and leaves you alive, Tom, I'll be seriously pissed off. Doc, your turn."

The doctor lets Warren jab her without so much as flinching, or even turning away from her examination of me. "I hope we're not stuck here forever," she says, glancing over at Warren. "That was my last clean needle, and my insulin doesn't work if I drink it."

"Don't worry, we'll get you out of here as soon as we can," Warren replies. He sets down the syringe and wanders through to the main bar as Dr. Wyatt pokes and prods at me, checking the injection site for any kind of reaction. She eventually lets out a curt harrumph, which I take as a particularly British way to say 'OK, I'm satisfied you're not going to die,' and she turns back to the pot warming on the stove.

I'm rolling down the sleeve of my jacket when Warren returns from the bar, and as soon as I see his face I know something is wrong.

"Doc? How long does that stuff need to stay on the stove?" I can tell he's trying to keep his voice casual to avoid alarming her.

The doctor ponders the question for a moment. "Hmmmm. Well, I'd say half an hour at this temperature should be enough to kick start the growth, but if you're asking when we'll be able to start administering it I'd say a day or two at 90 degrees would give us a decent batch."

He looks back through the circular window in the door, stepping from one foot to the other. "And what'd happen if we took it off the stove now? Would it be ruined?"

"Oh no, not at all. The vaccine would just replicate a lot slower, but you can't spoil it."

Warren sighs with relief. "OK, here's what I want you to do. Pack up all the gear you'll need as quickly as you can." He turns to me, widening his eyes and nodding his head back towards the door. "Tom, can you grab the pot and turn off the stove?"

I grab a dish towel from the edge of the table and lift the warm pot by its handles, struggling for a moment under the weight. "Where do you want me to take it?"

Warren peers out the window again. "OK, we're all gonna step *quietly* through the door and take the first door on the right. That's the staircase. You good, Tom? OK, Dr. Wyatt, I don't want to alarm you, but I need you to know that we're not safe here any more. Do you understand?"

The doctor nods stiffly, her face draining of color "They found us?"

"Yeah," Warren sighs. "The front of the building is blocked and I can't seem to find any kind of fire escape, so we're gonna head for the roof, OK?" He pulls out his gun. "Ready? Real quiet now."

The doctor and I line up behind Warren, and after a deep breath he slowly pushes open the door, taking care not to let it hit the wall outside, then turns back and holds a finger to his lips. It isn't necessary. Even from back here we can hear the infected outside, and as soon as we step out into the hallway we can see them. Through the plate glass windows about two dozen of them mill around the Jeep, seemingly confused and docile.

When we're halfway down the hallway I suddenly realize why they're here. From the front seat of the Jeep comes a static crackle. Warren stops in his tracks as he realizes it's his mistake that drew them here. He left his radio out in the car.

Dr. Wyatt goes on ahead, tiptoeing down the hallway towards the doorway to the staircase. I adjust my grip on the heavy pot in my arms then step forward to reach for the handle, but the doctor beats me to it. She reaches out and turns the handle, but as the door swings open she loses her grip on the spatula in her hand and it falls to the ground. We all freeze, watching it as it tumbles, but we know there's nothing we can do to reach it in time. As it hits the ground with a clatter I close my eyes and grit my teeth.

Out front the infected snap their heads up from the Jeep and face us, and for a moment it seems they haven't seen us. It looks like they're staring at their own reflections in the plate glass window, but then one of them steps to the side and gets a clear view of us through the open front door.

We don't wait to see what happens next. Warren shoves the doctor through the door and chases close after her, waiting for me to lumber through with the pot before he slams it closed behind him. We're suddenly plunged into pitch darkness, and Warren blindly searches the door with his hands for some kind of latch but comes up wanting.

"*Go!*" he hisses. "*Get her to the roof!*"

Something slams against the door as I begin to climb the staircase in the darkness. As my eyes adjust I can see nothing but the faint outline of the stairs, and a little further up the vague shape of Dr. Wyatt, her breath ragged with sobbing panicked gulps as she reaches out ahead of her. I see her stop suddenly, and beyond her sobs I hear the click of a door handle.

The stairway is suddenly lit by sunlight from above. Dr. Wyatt steps through and holds the door wide open, allowing Warren to finally see what he's doing.

"There's no fucking lock here!" he yells, twisting towards me as he braces himself against the door. By his waist I can see the handle turn downwards, and the door bursts halfway open before he manages to push it closed with his shoulder. "Find the roof access, *now!*"

I set the pot down on the floor and look around at the new floor. I'm in an office of sorts, cramped and sparsely furnished, with every available surface covered in old craft beer magazines. A little further back is a small bathroom, and beyond that a flight of steps ending in a wooden hatch.

I push past the doctor and leap up the stairs, thanking God when the hatch pops open as I push against it. I poke my head up and see it leads to a flat, tar-coated roof.

"Doc, get up here," I order, climbing through the hatch and out onto the roof. I turn back and reach down, taking the doctor's hand and pulling her out into the sunlight. "Wait for us up here, OK? I gotta go get the vaccine and fetch Warren."

Wyatt nods and turns to scan the roof, and as I begin to climb down into the hatch she stops me. "Wait! Tom, look at this," she says, pointing out to the west.

"What is it?" I ask impatiently. Down below I can hear Warren struggling to hold the door.

"I... well, I think it might be rescue." The doctor smiles broadly and gazes out over the rooftops, and I climb back up and look in the same direction.

About a block to the west an image appears through the heat haze, and then another, and another. Vehicles. In the lead of the convoy an open top Jeep clears the way, a rifleman perched on top of the rear seat scanning the street, and behind it two canvas topped M939 trucks follow, trundling slowly towards us. As they approach the Jeep veers off and takes up position on the opposite side of the street, while one of the trucks rides right up against the wall of the building as Dr. Wyatt excitedly waves her arms back and forth. It stops with a sigh, and moments later I hear a voice that sends me rushing to the edge of the roof.

"This is the second time I've had to save your sorry ass today, Tom." I look over the edge, and I can't quite believe what I'm seeing. Slowly, carefully and with what looks like great pain Vee pulls herself from the cab of the truck and climbs up to the taut canvas roof. Her clothes are torn and she's covered in so much blood it's hard to tell her from the infected, but there's no mistaking her smile.

"Come on, climb down." Over the sound of the engine she hears the angry snarls of the infected inside. "I'm guessing the stairs aren't an option right now."

I hold up my hand. "Wait there, I gotta get Warren." I turn back to the hatch, so excited I'm almost skipping across the roof, and lower myself through. I take the steps two at a time and run through the office, skidding at the top of the stairs.

"Warren, we're saved! Get your ass up here quick. There's a hatch to the roof on your right at the top of the stairs. I'm taking the vaccine up, OK?"

Warren turns and nods, clearly struggling to hold the door. "Any way to lock the hatch?"

"No idea," I reply. "But it doesn't matter, there's someone up here you're gonna be very happy to see."

He lets out a panicked gasp. "This door's about to give!" Almost as soon as he gets out the words one of the flimsy door panels begins to break, and an arm reaches through almost far enough to grab Warren by the hair. "Get the fuck up there!" he yells, "and be ready to close the hatch behind me. *Go!*"

I grab the pot of vaccine and hurry back to the steps, hefting it up one step at a time until I can lift it over the lip of the roof. I climb after it, dragging it aside before poking my head back through the hatch. "OK, Warren, I'm ready!"

The next sound I hear is of cracking wood, and something that sounds like the door slamming into the wall. There's the sound of shuffling feet and panting, and moments later Warren appears through the door, scans around wildly and makes a dash for the steps as soon as he spots me. The first of the infected arrive just a few steps behind him, exploding into the room at high speed, rebounding off the far wall before turning and laying in pursuit.

Warren reaches the steps and bounds up them two at a time, and I reach down to lift him through the hatch. His hands clasp around my forearms and I pull with all my strength, but it feels as if he weighs a few hundred pounds. I can't pull him closer, and it's only when I look down that I see why.

One of the infected has managed to get a grip on his foot. He tries to shake off his boot and slip free but the laces are tied too tight. He kicks out with his other foot and scores a direct hit to the face of his attacker, but it's not enough to loosen his grip.

"My gun!" he screams, twisting and kicking out wildly at the air. "*Get my fucking gun!*"

I let go of one of his arms and let him grab the lip of the hatch for purchase, and I lean through and reach down to his belt holster as more infected reach the steps. Warren kicks out at them and manages a lucky hit, sending two tumbling to the ground, but his other foot is still caught and the man holding it pulls close enough to bite down on Warren's boot.

With a final stretch I pull the gun from the holster, and without taking the time to aim I squeeze the trigger in the general direction of the head. Before I'm even aware of the report in my ears the man falls to his knees, and Warren desperately scrambles up the steps and flips himself out onto the roof.

I pull myself back through and swing the hatch down, sitting on it to weigh it down while I search for some way to lock it. "Warren, give me your belt, quick!"

He doesn't respond. "*Warren!*" I yell again,

but still nothing. I lean back and reach for my own belt, careful not to lean my weight too far off the hatch, and yank it from my waist. With a quick movement I slip the leather strap through the padlock loops and pull it taut, knotting it as best I can before finally standing from the hatch. The wood shakes in its frame, but it looks like it'll hold long enough to get to the truck.

"For the love of God, Warren, what the fuck are you..."

My voice fades away when I look towards him. He's sitting on the tar, staring at his ankle with his trouser leg pulled up his calf and his sock pulled down.

Just above the lip of his boot is a pink half moon of teeth marks pressed into the pale skin. As we both watch a few beads of blood begin to form at the wound.

"Never takes more than 60 seconds, right?" He asks, looking up at me with fear in his eyes. He sighs. "Fuck. You know what to do if..." His voice trails off, and he nods to the gun in my hand.

I don't say anything. There's nothing *to* say. It's all down to the vaccine now, and hope. Hope that the thing we've fought to bring across the country actually works. Hope that this hasn't all been for nothing. Hope that this hasn't all been just a cruel joke.

Warren closes his eyes and drops his head to his chest, his lips moving as he mumbles a prayer. Moments later Dr. Wyatt steps to his side and falls to her knees, taking his hand tight and joining him.

I'm not religious. I've never really *believed*. I grew up with the firm belief that it was all nonsense, and I only went to church on the holidays to keep my parents happy, but right now I realize it's true that there really are no atheists in foxholes. I grip the gun tight in my hand, close my eyes tight and whisper a prayer. A prayer for Warren. For Bishop. For Lewis, and for Kate. For everyone who's been taken by this senseless cruelty.

I feel a tear roll down my cheek. I don't want to lose another friend. I don't want to have to look into his eyes as I pull the trigger. *Please*, God. *Please* don't make me do that again. I just want this all to stop. No more death. No more killing. *Please*.

I feel a hand on my arm, and I open my eyes to find Vee clutching at me, her eyes questioning and fearful. I nod towards Warren, and she understands. She clutches me tight and joins me in prayer. The infected hammering against the hatch are all but forgotten. Only one thing matters now.

I whisper amen, and I open my eyes as I

realize a minute must have passed by now. As I look up the clouds above us break. The sun shines down on us. Warren looks up at us, his eyes red with tears.

He smiles.

"I'm still here."

.▾.

EPILOGUE

THE SPORE CLOUDS shimmer in the air, likes motes of dust caught in a shaft of sunlight. For four days now the sky has been thick with them, an endless stream carried on the wind and blanketing the ground wherever they fall. In a way they're almost beautiful, now we know they can't hurt us.

We tell the kids the spores are fairy dust. Wherever they fall there will be no more monsters. No need to tell them the truth. Their young eyes have already seen far too much of the darkness. The truth can take a number.

It's been two weeks since Dr. Wyatt cooked up the first batch of vaccine, and it all snowballed from there. Dozens of the survivors volunteered to help make more, and then hundreds. After the first week all the gas pumps in the city ran dry when the final cars departed, carrying with them batches of vaccine and as many syringes as we could scavenge from the local hospitals. They left for LA, San Francisco, Reno. A few left to the north for Portland and Seattle. Warren and Vee left together last week, heading south east for Abilene where we learned of a refugee camp harboring a million survivors from all around Texas. I don't know for sure, but I saw a few looks pass between them in that last week before they left. I get the feeling there's a reason they wanted to travel together.

We're still finding infected in the wild here and there. The Strip is quarantined and the hotels still need to be cleared floor by floor, but in the grand scheme of things Vegas came through well. We lost tens of thousands. Nobody knows exactly how many, but out of two million it could have been much worse.

All around me in the air traffic control tower voices ring out over the radios, directing air traffic to all four runways. Vera, the matronly chief controller, brusquely shoves me aside as she runs to deal with a Qantas pilot demanding the fuel tankers serve him before the Air France 737 waiting to depart.

We're still learning of what happened to the rest of the world, picking up fragments as the flights arrive to collect their vaccine samples, but nobody sticks around long enough for a real talk. The spore clouds have already begun to head west, drifting out over the Pacific towards Asia. We may be safe here in Vegas but it's yet to be seen if they can get the vaccine out quickly enough, especially with governments fallen and survivors scattered. It may be a long time before we can finally declare the world safe, but for now, at least, we can breathe easy.

I set down my coffee and leave the control room, heading down the dimly lit staircase until I emerge into the sun at the ground floor. Stacks of supplies sit unguarded by the tower, gifts from foreign visitors to thank us for donating our vaccine. I pull open the plastic covering of a pallet of Coke bottles and help myself to one, popping the cap and downing the warm, sickly sweet liquid in a few gulps. I feel a little guilty that the refugees outside the airport are still on emergency rations, but fuck it. I've earned a Coke.

We still don't know where *Cordyceps* came from. We don't know who seeded the infection in New York and D.C., and we don't know who spread it throughout the rest of the world. Was it the Sons of the Father, the shadowy religious sect who warned us this was coming? Who knows? Since their warning they've remained silent, if they ever really existed at all. They – whoever they are – may be out there right now working on other, yet more horrific ways to punish us for our sins, but we have enough to worry about for now without fearing the future.

I look out to the terminal, where a small All Nippon Airways twin prop plane waits to taxi out to the runway, and beyond it to the rising sun. I reach into my pocket and pull out a pack of Lucky Strike – we ran out of Marlboros a week ago – and fumble through my pockets looking for a lighter. My hand closes on something unfamiliar, and I tug out a creased, crumpled sheet of paper.

Dear Jack,

As I write this I don't know where you are. I don't even know for sure if you're still alive, but my heart tells me that you and your mom are safe and sound. Mom was always much smarter than me, as I'm sure she'll remind you often when you're old enough to ask her, and I know she has what it takes to keep you safe.

My eyes scan down the page, and it dawns on me that this came from Private Rhodes' notebook. It must have slipped out from the elastic band before I handed everything over to Dr. Wyatt.

I read on.

I want to tell you, Jack, that I've been given a chance to redeem myself. A very brave young lady has given me something that could help save us all. I have a long way to travel and the road ahead is dangerous, but I'll do my best to make it. I'll try to make you proud, son.

I miss you both so much.

Forever your loving father,

Lewis Rhodes

I feel tears well in my eyes as I carefully fold the paper and return it to my pocket. They're not tears of sadness, but of... *joy*, I guess. Joy that there are many more like Rhodes out there among the survivors.

I've seen the worst of humanity. I've seen people so poisoned by hate they'd try to destroy us all. Men so obsessed with power that they'd enslave the weak, and others so cowardly they'd follow orders no matter where they led.

And then there are people like Rhodes. Like Warren, and Vee, who found themselves on the wrong side of good and evil and made the choice to fight for good, whatever the cost. People like Bishop, who risked his life to save a stranger. Like Jack Benson, a scared kid who stood and fought when everyone else ran. They didn't have to be good, but when they were faced with a fork in the road they made the right choice.

Maybe they'll lose in the end. Maybe we all will, eventually. Maybe one day evil will win out, and we'll let stupidity and greed and hate and fear get the best of us. Maybe one day the sun will set, and when it rises the next day they'll be no one left to fight on the side of good.

Maybe one day.

But not today.

THE END